WHAT IT MEANS TO BE FOUND

What It Means To Be Found

WHAT IT MEANS: BOOK 3

Andrea Andersen

Contents

Content Notes

This story has been read by sensitivity readers. Meaning, though the author is neither deaf nor hard of hearing, persons who are hard of hearing, wear hearing aids, and use American Sign Language have read this story and provided feedback on its authenticity, as well as what verbiage to use regarding D/HH culture.

There are discussions in this story between characters that might be upsetting to some readers. Though there are no on-page, real-time descriptions of sexual assault, Eloise's character does a lot of self-reflecting and re-evaluating of past sexual experiences and starts to critically think about what true forms of consent should look like beyond just a verbal agreement. Noting that Eloise's internal monologue might be difficult for some, discussions about communication and consent during sexual encounters will always be important, and therefore, worth writing in some cases. All on-page and real-time sexual activity is between consenting *and* enthusiastic adults.

The hope is that this story discusses these topics with the respect and care that they deserve.

Trigger Warning:

This book contains sensitive subjects, such as:

Foul Language
Explicit Sex (between consenting and enthusiastic adults)
Cannabis Use
Alcohol Consumption
Injuries From a Car Accident (referenced, in the past)
Death of a Family Member (referenced, in the past)
Stalking and/or Harassment
Discussions About Consent

*To those who haven't found their place or people
in this world, you will.*

Prologue

LOGAN

The first moment I met Eloise Bane would haunt me.

This was for several reasons.

The first, which made my stomach churn every time I remembered it, was because I was blatantly rude to her when we first met. I knew I was being rude, and I knew I was attempting to scare her away, and unfortunately, I had been successful. She had left in tears, which instantly made me re-evaluate my emotional maturity and all of my life choices.

Let me back up.

I had never been a social butterfly. I wasn't that outgoing growing up, and ever since my accident, it had gotten significantly worse. I could go into all the details, but the reality was that an eighteen-year-old boy losing both his mother and little sister, and being left with an alcoholic father was enough of a reason for anyone to withdraw into themselves. It wouldn't be until the NHL got sick of my overly aggressive shit on the ice and forced me into therapy that I realized how textbook my behavior really was.

While I would always attribute the sport of hockey to

helping me process all the anger and bitterness that had developed and erupted to the surface my first year of college, I had known it wouldn't end up being enough long term. I was able to join my college's hockey team my first year, a special treatment since I had missed tryouts. Apparently, some other guy on the team had injured himself during the first week, ending any chance he had of continuing any sort of physical sport. So when the coach saw one of his players practicing drills on his own time, with a kid who learned quickly and seemed to enjoy the sport enough to keep helping his roommate practice, I think he just jumped on the opportunity that was available.

The college team was a massive clusterfuck.

I joined, and I officially became a hockey douche. One of those guys who made the sport his entire personality. I dated only when I felt I absolutely needed to, usually a handful of times a year. Other than focusing on my sports management degree, all I did was play hockey.

After college, I got drafted by the NHL. I was offered a mediocre deal to play for a mediocre team, and I took it because, well, what else was I supposed to do, I had nothing else to live for. My father was flittering in and out of my life, always asking for money, and seemingly drunker as time marched on. Hockey grounded me. It allowed me to feel like I had a purpose or a goal of some sort, something to keep me going. It was also an excellent excuse to beat the shit out of anyone who said the wrong thing to me on the ice.

After a few years of developing a reputation as someone who was violent and aggressive on the ice, and after slapping a number of fines on me, the NHL eventually didn't give me a choice and forced me to attend therapy to help with my obvious anger issues.

It was encouraging. Therapy taught me that I wasn't an abnormality. A lost cause. It taught me that being an extreme introvert was something that I could address and improve going forward.

That I wasn't something to be fixed, but someone to be understood better.

And I tried.

I pushed myself in little ways. Even though being part of an NHL team allowed me to get unrestricted access to top-tier facilities to help me stay on top of training and practice during the off-season, I decided to take my therapist's advice and branch out.

Nestled in between the cities of Tustin and Irvine, California, was a small hole-in-the-wall gym that didn't intimidate me. There was no chance in hell that I was ever going to attend a mainstream gym—a gym that had thousands of locations across the states and far too many people. No, if I was going to push myself to get out of a rut, and expand my social circles to hopefully develop better people skills, it was going to be at a small mom-and-pop place where people bothered to learn each other's names and my membership money would actually go somewhere.

The problem was, though, that simply attending a public gym wasn't enough.

To no one's surprise, my face didn't exactly welcome friendly people to come up and say hi, and the thought of their pitying expressions when they realized I couldn't speak meant that I sure as hell wasn't going to go out of my way to communicate with anyone beyond a head nod in passing. And so even though I had been publicly attending this gym for about two years, I still hadn't made any lasting relationships from the change.

That was something that my therapist really pushed me to do. She didn't even want me to find a best friend, necessarily. Just someone that I could maybe meet up with intentionally at the gym, for the bare minimum. At this point, my big plan to expand my routine by attending a gym not provided by the NHL, had become just another rut I clung to for familiarity.

It was hard. I was already frequently drained by playing on a team with over a dozen loud, social, and handsy men. Finding the energy to socialize beyond that was taxing. But not impossible.

Then entered Courtney Henderson, an extremely extroverted woman who approached me with no hesitation one random day. I was so shocked to see someone willingly walking towards me, that I almost missed the terrifying resemblance she had to my little sister, Anna, before she passed away.

In my panic, I even tried to scare Courtney off. I signed something quick and blunt, which usually worked because others assumed I was deaf and didn't think they could communicate with me.

Nope, not Courtney.

She signed right back at me, and I accepted the fate the universe dealt me. As if it was sick and tired of me not making any progress in my private social life, and it threw her my way.

Thankfully, becoming friends with Courtney Henderson was relatively easy. We met up at least once a week, if not a few times a week, at this random gym on the edge of Tustin and we chatted about our day. Well, Courtney chatted about her day. I listened and kept my cards held close. She didn't push me that hard, the most she'd ever do was say hi to someone in passing and then raise her eyebrows at me expectantly to follow suit. Since I had almost no use of my vocal cords, those people would get a head nod or a wave of my hand.

It was good enough for her.

She originally signed to me, even though she knew that I could hear her just fine. I eventually learned that she lived with two women who had hearing loss and that she had picked up American Sign Language incredibly well in order to meet them halfway.

I eventually encouraged her to just speak to me. This threw her off at first since my primary form of outward communication was still ASL, but she shrugged her shoulders and went along with it. She only signed to me if it was a private conversation of some sort.

I liked the idea of others seeing Courtney speak to me vocally, and so did my therapist. Mostly because they suggested that other people could see her vocalize to me, and that it could make them more comfortable about approaching me, too.

Honestly, hearing her voice rambling on about whatever, it made me feel a little less alone and isolated from society.

After a year or so of meeting up with Courtney at the gym, I finally opened up to her regarding certain details about my life, per my therapist's suggestion. I finally told her about my accident, which explained my damaged voice and the visible scars on my skin. I shared that I had a little sister, who passed away in that same accident, and that Courtney reminded me of her.

The problem was that exposing that history of mine suddenly made me feel bare. I wasn't used to it, and I immediately hated it. That also happened to be the day Eloise Bane showed up at the gym, openly admitting that she had followed Courtney there for some reason. I had heard of

Eloise before. Courtney had mentioned all her friends to me multiple times. I could keep up with the names and relationships easily enough, but I wasn't prepared for the *reality* of meeting Eloise.

It was all too much for my introverted antisocial brain to handle. My heart was racing in my chest and I was sweating from the vulnerability (and maybe the workout) I had just experienced with Courtney, and suddenly I was sitting in front of this woman who looked like she was made specifically from my fantasies.

We had just met, and I was overwhelmed by her direct attention. I clammed up. When that didn't divert her attention from me, I signed to her because that was literally all I could do to communicate with the woman.

Courtney scolded me because ASL is a blunt language and I was also a rude person, which made my words sound very off-putting. Picking up on my annoyed energy, Eloise ran off quickly after that. I remember that her cheeks flushed underneath her freckles and that her clear blue eyes were lined red.

Courtney, being Courtney, told me that I needed to apologize. I agreed because even though I was an asshole, I also knew when I was wrong.

Every single interaction I had with Eloise Bane from that moment on was a fumble. That woman could hold a grudge like no other, and apparently, she wasn't used to being so easily dismissed. It made trying to regain favor with her incredibly difficult, especially when I was consistently surrounded by all of her friends, already nervous about hanging out with so many people outside of work—who also didn't know what I did for a living.

No one asked, so I never offered the information.

Courtney and Josh only learned of my profession because

they had randomly attended one of my hockey games and saw me playing on the ice.

Anyway, I digress.

I tried to compliment Eloise's (very) beautiful singing voice the next time I saw her, and somehow, she interpreted that as an insult. Another time we all got together, I tried to joke around with her like everyone else in the group does, but I ended up getting a slice of pie smashed on my chest. Later, we all carpooled together to see Courtney's fiancé sing, and Eloise took one look at my truck before she started insinuating that I had a small dick.

For the record, I don't.

Dick size doesn't matter, everyone knows that.

But, just so we're clear, mine isn't.

I know about a dozen hockey players who can vouch for me.

Moving on.

Then there was Courtney and Josh's engagement party, where I was struggling the entire night to not stare at Eloise in her beautiful dress with her beautiful face and smile (when she wasn't glaring at me), and I desperately tried to throw down a white flag. But Eloise Bane was stubborn. Therefore, it was still a rough conversation. The interaction included me, desperately trying to communicate without my voice and strictly ASL, and Eloise, trying to understand my signs even though she was still a beginner and could only catch a word here or there.

Then I kissed her hand.

Don't ask me why I did that, because to this day I have no idea. I was desperate and panicking that I would lose the one close friend that I had made outside of the NHL because *her* friend continued to hate me.

What I wasn't expecting, however, was Eloise's reaction to getting her hand kissed. It was quick, and if I hadn't locked in on every single expression that flickered across her face when I pressed my lips to her knuckles, I would have missed the glimmer in her eyes.

I would be lying if I said I didn't hope that the look in her gaze was arousal.

Regardless, the moment ended, and we pretended like nothing happened. It wasn't the first time I had seen Eloise look at me in a way that made my chest heat, but I had a feeling it would be the last. Which was a shame because Eloise was exactly my type. I, unfortunately, wasn't hers. And that was okay.

I had moved on.

Until Courtney informed me that she would be attending my hockey game one night. Courtney and Josh were both dramatic people and loved surprises, and no one else in the group knew that I played on the local Anaheim Ducks hockey team. I had been casually hanging out with this group for over a year now, and it was time to open up another side of me to them. Because, as my therapist helpfully pointed out in our sessions, friends know what friends do for work. It was, in fact, weird for me to keep it so close to my chest for this long.

This was how I ended up sitting on the bench in the locker room with my teammates and listening to our coach talk about the game, the plays, and everything we needed to prepare for as we went against the Blackhawks that night. The Ducks weren't the best team in the NHL, and with it being near the end of the season, I was ready for the break.

However, I was sure I looked eager to get out there and play my heart out from the way my leg was bouncing nervously. Only, I knew that wasn't the case. I knew my nerves had absolutely nothing to do with playing a sport I had been playing almost every single day of my life since I turned nineteen. No, instead my nerves were all over the place because it had been literal months since I had seen the small woman who reminded me of an angry pixie. And the next time Eloise saw me after all that time, she would see me doing the thing I did best. The thing that helped me channel my anger towards life before therapy and friendship ever became part of it. The sport that became my safe place in college. The sport that allowed me to build a life of my own and also allowed me to isolate as much as I possibly could before I decided to reevaluate some things.

Hockey would always have a special place in my heart, and every nerve-ending I had felt like it was on the brink of short-circuiting at the thought of Eloise Bane watching me play it.

I just didn't allow myself to think too hard about why that was.

1

ELOISE

"I don't understand why women want to look like that." My mother scrunched her nose at the picture I was showing her, making disappointment flood my stomach at her words. I shouldn't have been surprised by her comment, and yet, here I was. I guess because I had been putting in the work the last few years to become a better version of myself, I forgot that my mother simply, well, hadn't.

"What's wrong with how she looks?" I dropped my smile, something that felt a little unnatural to me still, as I pulled my phone back to look at the image of Courtney Henderson that I was showing her. Courtney had just posted a picture of herself on her social media page, a page that had significantly more followers since she and Joshua Madey, the lead singer of the most popular punk rock band in the world, got engaged.

"What man wants their woman to look so muscular? She's losing her natural femininity by doing that to herself." My mother sipped her tea as she explained, eyeballing the newspaper in front of her. That's right, a real newspaper. Not an article on her phone or e-reader. My mother literally still read the newspaper.

I silently scolded myself for even bothering with her.

I had simply seen my friend post a picture of herself at the gym and wanted to share it. She was wearing black exercise shorts and a sports bra, and was posing in the mirror for a selfie, her body turned so you could see her profile, and flexing her now-defined four-pack abs. She had been exercising more intentionally for almost two years now, and I was proud of her for reaching her goals to become stronger. She still looked feminine to me. Her ass was tight and lifted, and her breasts were still bigger than mine.

I didn't bother explaining to my mother that one of the most sought-after men, by women everywhere, was engaged to her. That the man who held the gaze of most women in the world had his sights set on Courtney and had every intention of locking her down.

"You're assuming that her goal is to get the attention of men."

"You're right," she glanced up at me with a small smile, making me blink in surprise at her quick agreement, "She clearly isn't. She probably just likes attention from likes and comments." My mother shook her head once, as if her assumptions about Courtney weren't ridiculous and that she was one hundred percent right in her interpretations.

As if exercising simply to hit your own goals was silly.

As if not giving a damn about what other men thought of your body was equally ridiculous.

This was yet another domino to fall for me, and many had fallen over the past couple of years.

I had been living at home with my parents in their beach-side home in Dana Point, California. I moved back in with them after my ex-boyfriend, Adam Hall, dumped me. I was in denial about the breakup at first because we seemed like the perfect match on paper. Our families were close. We had grown up together. A part of me had even beamed at the fact that the cute red-headed boy who was a grade ahead of me in high school ended up falling for me as an adult. It was the dream every teenager had whenever their high school crush didn't reciprocate during their high school years.

We dated for about a year.

Then Adam had a serious bout with depression, which resulted in him tanking his Olympic surfing career, breaking up with me, and starting a new job working with special needs children as a Physical Therapist.

Both of our mothers had come to me to help me try to win him back, which I was all about. My ego was hit by our breakup. I had become too comfortable with our relation-ship, even though it had been pretty surface-level now that I looked back on it. I was able to figure that out quickly once Adam started dating one of his co-workers, Beck Scott. She was a speech therapist at the same early intervention clinic he worked at.

They fell in love and had been together for the last couple of years. Beck had even moved into Adam's condo recently. They were clearly *it* for each other, and I still felt like an ass-hole every now and then for trying to win Adam back when the reality was, I didn't actually like him for him. I just liked the idea of us together.

I was growing, though. I knew I had a lot of work to do on myself, and that was mostly thanks to Courtney, Beck, and Taylor. I had seen their friendship during a company retreat that I had helped organize a few years ago (you know, back when I was trying to win Adam back but he was clearly head over heels for Beck and I was blind to it), and I realized that their bond was so special and unique. Their friendships with each other were so comfortable and achingly honest.

I wanted that.

I may have not so discreetly weaseled myself into their little social circle, blatantly ignoring how awkward it must have been for Adam to have his ex-girlfriend become part of his friend group at work.

I even went as far as to start working at the same early intervention clinic as all of them, even though my parents didn't understand why I felt the need to get a job like that. I wanted a nine-to-five. I wanted to work consistently and build up my own income so that I didn't need to rely on my parents or their trust fund for the entirety of my life.

This brunch with my mother was making me happier about that choice, as she said way too much in the few words that she had spoken to me since seeing that picture of Courtney.

"Well, anyways," I cleared my throat, determination only making the fear I felt slightly dissipate, "I wanted to let you know that I am moving out."

My mother set her tea mug down and looked at me with raised blonde eyebrows. We looked so much alike, my mother and me. I was always referred to as her "Mini-Me" by her and her friends. We both had light blonde hair that only became paler during the summertime, clear blue eyes, and small frames. The only difference was that I had a slight smattering of freckles over my nose, and she didn't.

Last year I chopped my hair shorter and kept it that way. It hovered just above my shoulders, and I loved how little maintenance it took to take care of now. My mother hated it, frowning when she first saw the spontaneous cut. She had never let me cut my hair too short as a child, saying that it was too pretty to destroy like that.

I realized last year that I was a grown-ass woman in her late twenties and that I could do whatever the fuck I wanted.

That wasn't the only alteration I had made to my appearance. I also had three beautiful tattoos. One under my breast along my left ribcage, one on my right hip that went down my thigh halfway, and one on my right forearm. They were all bouquets of flowers. Was it a basic white girl design? Yes, but I loved flowers. I had also discovered that I weirdly loved getting tattoos, and I loved having visual art on my body. They didn't have any special meanings, I simply thought they were pretty and found a woman tattoo artist I had felt comfortable with to design them.

My mother also hated that, stating that I would need a foundation to cover up my tattoos whenever I attended formal fundraising events that she and the Halls put on. I agreed, knowing I would find an excuse to simply never attend those events. It has worked out so far.

"Why?" my mother asked, a slight downturn to her lips

WHAT IT MEANS TO BE FOUND | 15

making me pull out of my thoughts. "Is something wrong with your space?"

"No," I shook my head as I stalled by sipping my own tea, "I just think it's time for me to, well, no longer live with my parents again. I appreciate you guys helping me out so much." I smiled. My fake smile, the smile that Beck had once told me made her convinced that butterflies would shoot right out of my ass the first time we met. That memory still made me giggle sometimes.

"Oh, I guess you have a point," she nodded. "Where do you want to go? We have the condo in Laguna Beach being rented right now, but based on the lease they signed we could have them out within a month or two." My mother lifted a shoulder as if uprooting a family renting from them was absolutely nothing. As if housing in Orange County wasn't a massive clusterfuck right now, and that family would probably struggle to find somewhere to live on such short notice.

"No, no," I wanted to shut that thought down immediately. I would rather die than live on a property my parents owned again, "I already found a room." I smiled at some of the other members who were also having brunch in the country club dining room, waving a little bit as I avoided my mother's gaze.

"I'm sorry, a room?" she asked, disgust blanketing her tone.

I nodded. "Yes, it's affordable. And I already know the other two women who live there." This was also something I was going out of my way to pretend wasn't awkward. I was moving in with Beck's grandmother, Susan. That's right, I was moving into my ex-boyfriend's, current girlfriend's, old bedroom. Her grandmother was around seventy-six years old now and liked the idea of having roommates around just in case. Courtney was already renting the room right across the hallway from mine.

We had been helping Beck move her boxes over to Adam's condo when they mentioned that they hadn't found someone to take over Beck's room yet. It wasn't an urgent need since the mortgage was already being split two ways between Courtney and Susan. That was when I had mentioned in passing that I might be interested in staying there, and to my surprise, everyone jumped at the idea.

I had movers loading my things from my parents' house and taking it over to the townhome at this very moment while my father was at the office and my mother was here at brunch with me. They couldn't stop me, and it would already be done by the time we were finished here.

"Honey," my mother gave me a disbelieving look, "You know you don't need to live in such confinement. Your father and I are happy to help cover things if your little job can't afford a more functional space."

I tried not to be offended by her condescending tone, mostly because I knew that my mother truly didn't mean to belittle me this way. My "little job" was just that to her. It didn't make sense in her mind for me to work forty hours a week when she and my dad were capable of providing everything that I needed so that I could be comfortable.

I just didn't want to be comfortable anymore.

"Hey, girl, hey!" I heard Lucy's voice call from the side. Though her voice now sounded like nails on a chalkboard in my mind, I was grateful for the interruption. I turned away from my mother and smiled at my old friend.

Old, because I hardly hung out with her and the others at the country club anymore.

I stood from my chair and wrapped my arms around her in a hug that she happily returned.

"Hey, you!" I grinned, trying my best not to make it a grimace. Lucy used to be my best friend. Used to be, because I had realized way too late in life that best friends don't consistently bail on you, they don't say mean things about you behind your back, and they don't try to go after your ex-boyfriend once it was obvious you two weren't going to get back together.

"I haven't seen you in forever!" Lucy smiled, sitting down in an empty chair at my mother's table. She was wearing a swimsuit cover-up, clearly getting ready to tan by the pool.

"Oh, there's Barbara. I'll be back in a moment." My mother stood from her chair and gave me a quick kiss on the head before she hurried off to one of her old friends. I felt my shoulders visibly relax with her absence, which really said a lot.

"I know, it's been a while," I smiled at Lucy. She was beautiful. Tanned skin, bright red hair, bright green eyes, and lips that she had just recently gotten filler in.

"So, what's new? How are you?" she asked, leaning her arms on the table as if she was going to settle in. I knew better. It took all of one second for her to lean back and hold her palms out to me. "Oh! Did you hear about Connor?" Of course. She didn't actually care about what I had been up to. In a way I was grateful, it made distancing myself from her that much easier.

However, the mention of that man's name made my gut sour again.

In the last five minutes of speaking with my mother, and now this conversation with Lucy, I had gotten a blatant reminder as to why I avoided coming back to the country club.

"No, what happened?" I asked, widening my eyes with fake curiosity for Lucy's benefit.

"He and Michelle hooked up last weekend." Lucy's plump lips turned downwards with her eye roll. "Lucky bitch."

I held my calm façade in place, glad she still didn't know about my mistake with Connor.

Connor James was a friend of my father's. He was single, in his late-forties, and had a young daughter named Stella. She had Down Syndrome and was the absolute cutest toddler. He was blonde-haired, blue-eyed, tan, and literally a carbon copy of every other man in South Orange County. To be fair, he really was good-looking for his age. And that is the one thing I kept telling myself so that I didn't spiral about how gross my decision was last year.

I had been upset with my father. He had belittled me again, unintentionally. I couldn't even remember what he had said or done specifically, only that I was feeling very spiteful and petty.

Connor and the other men from the country club had come over to my father's den for poker night.

During a break in the game where the men smoked cigars on the back deck that overlooked the ocean, I bumped into Connor in the hallway. Connor had let his gaze travel over my body, letting me know he definitely liked what he saw. That was all it took, really. To know that I could give my dad this one massive middle finger even if he never knew what happened. So, I flirted with Connor. He, obviously, flirted back. I hadn't done anything more than slightly graze my fingers along his forearm in passing, and that was it. The next day, I got a call from him asking what I was up to that night. If I was interested in seeing some paintings that he had just purchased from the Laguna Beach Art Fair.

I wasn't an idiot.

He wanted to get laid.

I was disappointed with where I was in life, and disappointed in my father, and wanted to make self-destructive choices.

So, I went over to Connor's house.

Other girls my age at the country club ogled Connor James often. They called him a silver fox based on the white hair that just barely started to dust above his ears. Other girls would go out of their way to hook up with Connor like it was a game to them, or an item to check off their to-do list.

I leaned into the game a little farther than I should have.

One thing that I learned immediately, was that if *that* was how he was intimate with his ex-wife the entirety of their marriage, she should have left him a lot sooner.

No foreplay took place.

Kissing was not his strong suit, let alone kissing with his tongue.

I was lost thinking about my to-do list at work the next morning as Connor was thrusting inside me, hitting nothing of significance, but panting as if he was sprinting.

I also had to remind him to use a condom multiple times.

As if he assumed I would be totally cool with him going forward with this hookup completely bare.

Needless to say, he came and I didn't.

He didn't even ask if I did, that's how much of a shit stain he was.

He had rolled off of me and promptly passed out in his bed, and I wasted no time in getting the hell out of there. I immediately regretted my decision to sleep with an older man out of spite. That was one of the many other dominoes to fall, I realized later on. I wasn't fit for the culture in my mother's world anymore. The world I was raised in was full of privilege and of wanting to sleep with conventionally attractive men, simply because the opportunity arose and I had nothing better to do. A world where my mother felt completely comfortable judging other women's bodies and making demeaning comments as if men's approval was what all women should strive for.

I was done.

Connor, however, wasn't. He had reached out to me multiple times after that. He left me voicemails (like the older man he was) and texted me asking for another round. I ghosted him, because obviously. A few months after that mistake, I saw him at a club in LA with my friends and told them why I was avoiding a random man at the club.

They had laughed with me, reminding me that I didn't need to explain why I slept with a man and regretted it. They told me that his daughter, Stella, used to be a client of theirs at the early intervention clinic before I started and that Connor had been ballsy enough to ask Beck out at her place of work.

They also called him Daddy James, which was both disgusting and hilarious.

"How is Michelle?" I asked, trying to blink away the gross image of my one night with him.

"She said she was sore the next morning." Lucy winked at me. "Ugh, I knew he would be a beast in the sack."

I wanted to roll my eyes but refrained. I had no doubt Michelle was sore, because so was I. Not because it was good sex, but because he sucked at foreplay and getting a woman ready for penetrative sex. Michelle cared a lot about image and what other people thought of her, though, so I wasn't surprised that she would simply lie about how good Daddy James was in bed.

"Wow, that's wild." I didn't know what else to say that wasn't a lie. "How are you, Luce?" I knew this question would get her going for a while. She started monologuing about her newest yoga class, and how I *needed* to go with her sometime. She also mentioned a few casual hookups she had, that I barely paid attention to. My mother had eventually come back to the table and was nodding animatedly at Lucy's tales of what she had been up to the last few months.

In short, absolutely nothing.

She was a trust fund kid, like me. Except she loved it. To be fair, I used to as well. Having the kind of money our families did was awesome. We could do whatever we wanted with very little repercussions. I got it, I had just outgrown it.

I didn't want to be comfortable anymore.

"...you have to come!" Lucy said, reaching out to grab my

arm. My polite smile was in place, an attempt to hide the fact that I wasn't listening to her the last few minutes.

"Pardon?"

"Tonight! Michelle's party!" Lucy grinned, showing freshly whitened teeth. I shrugged.

"I'm sorry, I already have plans." I pulled my phone out to check the time. The moving company had recently sent me a text message with a thumbs up emoji, indicating that all my belongings had been properly moved. I was free to go to my new home now.

"What are you doing tonight?" my mother asked, eyeballing my phone that I pocketed as I made my way to stand.

"My friends have tickets to the Ducks' game in Anaheim. I promised I would go." I leaned forward to kiss my mother on the head and waved my fingers at Lucy. "You'll have to tell me all the dirty details of what happens tonight."

"Oh, I will." Lucy wiggled her eyebrows at me while my mother just giggled at us. I waved goodbye to them both as I started speed walking for the country club exit. I wasn't positive my mother even remembered our conversation before our friends distracted us, so I wasn't sure how she would react when she eventually came home this afternoon and her only daughter would be nowhere to be found and her bedroom was completely empty, minus the large four-post bed frame that simply wouldn't fit in my new bedroom.

I left the club and rushed into my car, accidentally slamming the door behind me as I landed in the driver's seat. The exhale I made was loud and dramatic, which was another physical reminder of how important it was for me to distance myself from this part of my life.

I was improving, and I wanted to keep improving.

I didn't want to be the kind of woman my mother was; the woman who looked at a picture of another woman at her physical peak and turned up her nose at it. The woman who loved gossip and sleeping with men simply for the status of it, like Lucy.

I wanted to be like Courtney and Beck. Maybe even a little bit like Taylor, unapologetically true to themselves.

I wanted to be comfortable in my own skin, while surrounded by people who allowed me to be. Friends who cheered and admired my new tattoos and welcomed me into the townhome with open arms. Who welcomed me into their workplace with the occasional coffee left on my administration desk in the morning. Who bent over backward to not make things weird since my ex-boyfriend was dating Beck, someone I now considered to be one of my good friends.

People who, and I cannot stress this enough, introduced me to the wonderful world of romance novels and happily shared smutty recommendations with me.

I have read more in the last year than I have read in the entirety of my life. I also learned so much more about what kind of woman I want to be after reading hundreds of romance novels. I want to be strong, independent, loving, and safe. Who knew romance novels would make me realize what kind of partner I deserved? Not just a man to fill the role as husband, or spouse. I want a partner, what Beck and Adam have with each other. What Courtney and Josh have with each other. Someone I don't exactly need, but someone I specifically want. Who also wants me in return.

I want someone who will be my cheerleader.

That didn't mean I needed to settle for anyone, like what I was unintentionally doing with Adam when we were dating. Sure, the sex between us was good. I got off more with Adam than with any other man I had dated, but that was it. There wasn't a lot of emotional connection between us. We didn't even like watching the same kinds of TV shows and movies. He loved reading science fiction and fantasy, and I didn't. Come to think of it, I was genuinely surprised that we lasted a whole year.

I was just about to pull out of the parking space when my phone buzzed in my pocket.

Court: Is everyone set to meet at the townhouse tonight before the game? I'm eating at old-person dinner time with Susan before we leave.

Beck: Adam and I will be there for dinner, too.

Taylor: Yup, I'll be there after.

Josh: I can have my driver take us since the car can fit us all in one vehicle.

Adam: I guess I can ride in your gas-guzzler this time.

Josh: Adam is officially uninvited to the carpool.

Adam: Oh no, I guess I'll have to drive in my environmentally friendly vehicle instead.

Court: If your driver had an electric car available, I know you'd take that instead J-shua.

Taylor: Lo, are you coming?

I smiled. I loved my nickname; it was so cute and simple. It felt like me. I replied immediately, warmth filling my chest at simply being remembered.

Me: I'll be there after the old-person dinner.

Taylor: Is Logan sitting with us?

My stomach soured. Fuck that guy.

Court: Nope.

Thank fuck he couldn't join us for whatever reason. I pocketed my phone and pulled out of the driveway. How someone as loveable and friendly as Courtney was able to befriend an asshat like Logan St. James was beyond me. I had only a handful of interactions with the man, and they all sucked. He seemed to charm literally everyone else in the group, all except for me. Just looking at him filled me with anger.

I was glad he wouldn't be coming tonight. After this morning with my mother and Lucy, I wanted time to let loose and relax with my friends. Without Logan's silent glares and frowns and various looks of disapproval for simply existing.

No, tonight I would treat myself to an alcoholic beverage.

Maybe some stale stadium popcorn.

I would pretend to understand or care about what was happening during the hockey game. I would laugh and joke around with my friend's company, not caring what I looked like or how I sounded. I would simply exist and find peace in that.

2

ELOISE

Hockey wasn't that cool of a sport.

I can see why a lot of hockey romance novels lean more toward straight-up erotica instead of a novel with a plot revolving around the sport of hockey. I would be lying if I said I didn't immediately get bored as soon as we found our seats. I even pulled out my phone and was mindlessly scrolling through social media when the teams finally hit the ice.

"It's not as cold as I expected it to be." I heard Beck speak as she unwrapped a scarf from around her neck. Like me, she hadn't been to a hockey game before. In fact, I was pretty sure Courtney, Josh, and Taylor were the only ones who had actually gone to a professional game.

"Yeah, all the warm bodies in the seats help with the temperature control," Courtney replied, reaching over her fiancé's lap to squeeze my thigh as I sat on his other side. I lifted my gaze from my phone and smiled at her.

"Are you okay?" she asked, her dark eyes boring into mine.

Her fiancé, Josh, looked over at me and gave me a friendly smile at her question.

"Yup! Sorry." I shoved my hands, phone included, into my pockets, realizing I probably shouldn't be zoning out. "So, when does it start?"

"A couple of minutes, they're all warming up right now," Josh replied as his dark gaze went to the ice.

"Thanks again for getting us these seats." Adam leaned forward from where he was sitting with Beck and Taylor directly behind Courtney, Josh, and me. "These probably aren't cheap."

Josh shrugged, money not being a huge issue for him. "It's more exciting this close to the rink, maybe they'll get in a fight right in front of us."

I laughed at the celebrity next to me. I hadn't thought too much about it until Adam said something, but having seats directly in the front row probably was a special thing to acknowledge. It showed how privileged my life had been, because any sort of sport I had gone to see with my parents always ended up with us in the front row, if not the first few rows. We even sat courtside during a Lakers game during my childhood one time.

I'm pretty sure I was on my phone during the entirety of that game, too.

"Maybe we'll even get blood on us!" I smiled and wiggled my eyebrows at Courtney's fiancé, earning a laugh and a fist bump from him. I quickly admired the various tattoos on his knuckles and fingers before he pulled his hand back.

"Oh, I almost forgot!" Courtney jumped up and pulled out something from her bulging fanny pack. The ice rink didn't actually allow large bags or purses inside. Instead, we put all our credit cards and IDs into Courtney and Beck's matching camo fanny packs. Courtney's was much fuller for some reason, which is why Beck carried almost everyone's cards. Once Courtney pulled out a hockey jersey, I realized why hers was so big. How she managed to stuff that massive jersey in there, I'd never know.

"Whose jersey is that?" Taylor asked, leaning forward to get a read on the name. Their dark blue eyes widened before they turned their baseball cap around in surprise. "Wait, as in?"

"Yup!" Courtney interrupted them, a giggle erupting from her mouth as Taylor's dark brown eyebrows shot up. They then looked over Courtney's head and narrowed their eyes as they scanned the ice.

"Well, as I live and breathe!" Taylor exclaimed with a hand to their chest, a fake Southern accent masking their voice.

I laughed, raising an eyebrow at Josh who just tugged on his lip ring with his teeth as he smiled.

"What is it?" Adam asked, eyeballing Taylor.

"Check out the name on Courtney's jersey." Taylor elbowed Adam, making the red-head narrow his eyes as he obeyed to Taylor's command. Because of where I was sitting, I still couldn't read it.

"What's it say?" I asked, leaning back behind Josh to get a better look. I still couldn't see, because Courtney was sitting perfectly in her seat to where I couldn't see her back. Beck just shrugged at me as well.

"Wait…" Adam's lips pulled into a confused frown as he mirrored Taylor's earlier facial expression, narrowing his eyes as he searched for something on the ice. I followed his gaze, seeing nothing but a bunch of men in matching jerseys twirling on the ice with their sticks.

Okay, they weren't twirling, but still.

Beck didn't know what the big deal was either, but I noticed when she caught Courtney's gaze, and Courtney finger spelled something to her. Josh had adjusted in his seat, blocking off the visual I had of Courtney's hand before I could see what she had just spelled out, but I saw Beck's hazel eyes widen before a big smile erupted over her face.

"Whoa, really?" She then glued her eyes to the rink in front of us. I refused to ask again, it was embarrassing to be left out of something and to be ignored multiple times when asked for clarification. I figured if it was actually that cool, I would learn about whatever the big deal was anyway.

"Does he know we're here?" I heard Adam ask behind me. I frowned a little. *Was he talking about Logan? Was that guy joining us later? I thought he couldn't come, based on the texts.*

"Yup!" was Courtney's cheery reply. A few players skated past us and Courtney and Josh both stood up to bang on the plexiglass and cheer, making me startle in my seat. I eyeballed them and a confused but nervous laugh escaped me as I looked over my shoulder, only to see the other three members of our group cheering and clapping too.

Okay.

Courtney and Josh were settling back in their seats, their hands waving with big smiles on their faces as they stared at the rink. I had just turned my head to try to see who they were specifically cheering for when a large body dressed in black filled my vision, just about to collide with me.

I yelped, hiding my face in my hands seconds after his body and hockey stick hit the plexiglass a foot away from me.

I parted my fingers enough for my eye to see what the fuck that was about, only to come face-to-face with a smirking Logan St. James. He eyeballed my terrified reaction before winking at the group and skating off toward the center of the rink. I could tell it was him based on his dark eyes, bordered with thick dark eyelashes and brows, and light pink scars marring the side of his face under his hockey mask. He had just popped his mouthguard back in before taking off, and sure enough, the back of his jersey had his name and number.

St. James. Number 29

Great.

The asshole was a player, and we were all here in support of him, apparently.

Maybe I should have stayed back and gone to that stupid party with Michelle and Lucy instead.

"That's so cool! How did I not know this about him?" Beck asked, her voice full of surprise. I tried to smile, but it clearly wavered. I eventually gave up and rubbed at my cheeks instead, an excuse in case anyone was wondering why I wasn't smiling at the big guy on the ice.

It wasn't really a secret to anybody that Logan and I didn't get along.

I had smashed pie on his chest in front of Courtney and Josh, after all.

"Because he specifically asked me not to tell anybody for months," Courtney replied.

"We only figured it out when Court and I went to the hockey game with the guys, remember?" Josh leaned back to chat with our friends behind us, his comment making Taylor and Beck's eyes widen.

"What the hell? That was years ago."

"That was a little over one year ago, but sure," Courtney replied to Taylor, taking a drink from her soda can.

"Still, that's such a long time. How did you keep that to yourself? How did none of us google him and figure this out ourselves?" Beck asked, her lips quirking to the side as if the concept really did confuse her. I just laughed at all their shock and awe, not willing to add anything to the conversation as long as Logan was concerned.

A few moments passed. The puck was dropped and the game started, grown men scattered everywhere as everyone chased the puck and swatted their little sticks. It took everything in me not to pull out my phone again, because the game seemed even less interesting to me now.

"What do you think?" Josh elbowed me in the arm, making me look up at him. The guy was tall, even when sitting in a seat.

"About what?" I smiled up at him.

"Logan," Josh nodded towards the ice as he replied, "He's a beast out there."

I narrowed my eyes at Josh before I followed his gaze, spotting number twenty-nine way too easily. Logan wasn't as tall as Josh, but he was right up there around six-three or so. He towered over most of the other players, and he was fast. I eyeballed him as he shoved a guy from the visiting team away so that he could swat at the puck, easily passing it to one of his teammates.

"Yeah. Full beast mode," I agreed, my tone only sounding a little deadpan to my own ears. Josh's chuckle let me know I didn't fool him.

"Wow, you really hate the guy," he replied, pinching my arm once. I ignored the pinch and folded my arms across my chest, crossing my legs as well. It was a defensive pose.

"Hate is a strong word to describe my feelings towards him," I lied, "I just...don't really care about hockey."

"I don't either." Josh leaned back, winking at me before he said, "But I like watching the men play."

I narrowed my eyes. Josh was bisexual and, unfortunately, there was one fact about Logan that everyone in our group universally accepted.

Logan St. James was hot.

I accepted it, even though I refused to acknowledge it.

He was unfairly good-looking. He had those sharp facial features that belonged on magazine covers. I would know, having been on some myself for my temporary gig as an underwear model for size-inclusive underwear. He had those high cheekbones and thick tendons on his neck that made women's mouths go dry. His jawline was so sharp he could probably cut stone with it. He was extremely physically fit, with toned muscles everywhere. Which, now that I knew he was a professional athlete, made a little more sense as to why he was so fit. His dark curly hair, which he usually kept a little too long, was what did me in the first time I saw him.

As I said, he was hot. So much so that sometimes, rarely, Josh would even get flustered if Logan stared at him too long or happened to wink in his direction. Because of this, there was now a rule that stated that Logan could not use his crazy good looks to manipulate his opponents into flirtatious stupors, in an attempt to win charades or whatever party game we were in the middle of.

I only knew about this from the grapevine, because whenever our friends mentioned that Logan was attending a group hang, I usually ended up finding an excuse not to go that time.

"Ah, have you been reading some of Courtney's hockey romances?" I asked Josh, in an attempt to divert the subject away from the guy who took one look at me and decided that I wasn't worth his time. And has embarrassed me every chance he's had since.

"I am unapologetically hooked." Josh shook his head. "We started reading this nonfiction book a few weeks back that has wonderful reviews and ratings, and the whole time I kept asking Court, 'When are they gonna bang?'"

That made a laugh erupt out of me, because holy shit, Josh was perfect.

"I totally get that!" I agreed. "If there isn't a happily ever after, I am not interested!"

"I don't even need the happily ever after," Josh shrugged, "Just a few chapters of vividly descriptive fucking."

"What are you talking about?" Beck asked, her head leaning in between Josh and me.

"Hockey romances," Josh replied.

"Oh," Beck nodded once, her face taking in a dreamy look as she stared out on the ice. "Those are nice. Has Court shared her alien erotica with either of you yet?"

"What?" I turned in my seat to face Beck. "Alien erotica?" That did not sound fun to read.

"She has!" Josh turned a little to face Beck as well. "It started off as a joke. Like, I genuinely was not interested in the book at all. But that writer got me hooked on the story! And the way he greeted her the first time—"

"Oh, I know!" Beck gasped, gripping Josh's shoulder in comradery.

"I'm sorry," I interrupted the two of them, "Alien erotica? Aliens? Little green men?"

"I'm telling you," Josh rested one of his hands on my shoulders then, while Beck's still rested one his, as if he was initiating me into the alien erotica consumers club, "It sounds terrible. But it'll catch you by surprise."

I laughed again at that, shrugging. "Send me the title, and I'll add it to my list."

"Oh, you better add it near the top. It's..." Beck kissed the tips of her fingers as if she was a chef giving a stamp of approval over a meal. "It's wonderful. Ten out of ten."

I didn't believe her, but I appreciated her and Josh's enthusiasm.

Everyone erupted into cheers then. Josh had even stood up from his seat to whistle his celebration, making Beck pull her hearing aids out of her ears until all the excessive whistling died down.

The Ducks must have just scored a goal. I stayed sitting in my seat as I clapped, scanning the ice as if I had been watching the game this entire time instead of learning about my friends' enthusiasm for alien erotica.

One of the players on the opposing team (something I only

knew because they wore white jerseys) cursed, and punched his hockey stick down on the ice, glaring at our little group who was now loudly chanting variations of "twenty-nine!"

I guess Logan was the one who scored that goal everyone cheered for.

Whoop-de-doo.

I clapped and put on my polite smile, going out of my way to avoid eye contact as Logan skated by our group and lifted his hockey stick up in a hello. I was too busy ignoring Logan entirely, which was why I had noticed the opposing team's player, number eighteen, watching the whole interaction with anger.

What a child.

The game went on, alien erotica taking a back seat in the conversation as everyone chatted about how well Logan was doing. What position he was playing. Why he was put in the time-out box.

It took all of my willpower to avoid rolling my eyes when Logan had stolen the puck from the opposite team and started speeding down the ice. Nobody was in his way as he pulled his stick back and scored through. Another goal, another stadium erupting with cheers at his success.

God, he was probably going to be so annoying about this.

As everyone else was standing up and cheering, I noticed number eighteen glaring at Logan's cheering squad (us, it was us) once again. I met his gaze and lifted an eyebrow.

He responded by giving me the finger, with his glove and everything.

It was so absurd, I started laughing.

Not only that, but when the others noticed me laughing

all I could do was point at number eighteen on the opposing team and choke out bits and pieces of, "He flipped us off." Which made the others laugh too.

Did number eighteen like that? No, no he did not. He flipped us all off again, making us all laugh even harder.

Seriously. What a child.

The players were circling around the ice, getting ready for the next play, when Logan noticed us as well and cocked his head to the side at all our laughter. Courtney sat forward in her seat, her hands moving rapidly, and as soon as she lifted her middle finger, I realized that she was telling him what we were all laughing about.

I couldn't see Logan's facial expression that far away through his hockey mask, but by the way his head dropped and his shoulder shook a couple of times, I figured he must have been laughing too.

…I mildly wondered what his laugh would sound like, considering I hadn't ever heard it before and his voice box wasn't in the best shape.

The play started again, fans cheered, and hockey players skittered around each other all over the rink. Lots of stick slapping took place. Lots of shoves and body checks happened as well. Another of Logan's teammates had gotten the puck and had started skating away from our end of the rink where the goal was, and I found myself scooting closer and closer to the edge of my seat. Suddenly, they lost the puck. The other team sped towards it at an alarming rate, successfully stealing it from the Ducks. I found myself clutching the armrest of the chair in angst, before realizing I was actually into the game.

Suddenly, everyone was over on our end of the rink as

the opposing team shot and scored a goal. Number eighteen was the one who made the shot, and he decided to do a quick lap right past our group, spreading his fingers and licking his tongue in between them as he eyeballed Courtney and me on his pass.

"Eww," I grumbled.

"What the fuck?" Courtney gasped, clapping a hand over her mouth in surprise. Josh's face turned to stone as he glared at the player, who gave him a gross smile before he turned to skate away.

However, Logan body-slammed him up against the boards in front of us, halting his attempt.

They were fighting less than a foot away—they probably would have pummeled right into us had the rink wall and plexiglass not been there. By the way their fists were flying and their bodies were cracking against the plexiglass, I was surprised it stayed intact at all.

"Oh my god!" I gasped and stood up, not sure what my plan was because it wasn't like I was able to do anything about the fight. Josh and Courtney stood up too, except Courtney was pulling Josh back because he was cussing at number eighteen for the gesture that he made toward us.

Logan looked furious.

Their helmets and gloves had flown off at some point, and the look on Logan's face was pure rage. His dark eyes were somehow narrow while still being able to view the whites of them. His teeth clenched as he blocked one fist from number eighteen and quickly returned the gesture by planting his fist in his opponent's jaw. He was heaving his breath, the muscles in his neck straining as he fought the other player.

"Logan!" I cried, banging my fists on the glass. Logan had a busted lip, but number eighteen looked worse. Eventually, one more fist to the face and number eighteen had collapsed to the ground, making Logan finally let up on the brawl. The refs' whistles screeched as other players finally swarmed the two and put distance between them. Logan was already skating away, ignoring the refs calling towards him as he went towards the time-out box.

"That's at least a five-minute penalty, if not more," Josh grumbled, frowning at number eighteen as he stood up and shook off his teammate's assistance. It looked like number eighteen was also headed for the time-out box.

"Oh my god," I was still standing at the plexiglass, remembering to use my legs and step back into my seat as I folded my fingers over each other. "Can Logan get kicked off the team for that?"

"What? No. It's just a fight," Josh explained, his lips twitching a little bit.

"What do you mean, it's just a fight?" I asked. The others seemed interested in this conversation as well, if the way that they leaned forward in their seats meant anything.

"Fighting is allowed in hockey," Courtney explained, "It's how players solve issues between themselves."

I just blinked at her. "Are you messing with me?"

Courtney and Josh both laughed at my reaction. "Nope."

"They can hurt themselves! Logan's lip was bleeding!" I gestured vaguely to the side where I knew Logan was sitting in time-out. I even glanced over at him, just to make sure I hadn't imagined the whole thing. His helmet was off as he glared at the timer at the bottom of the Jumbo-Tron, mindlessly wiping at his lip which was only bleeding a little bit now. His curly dark hair was wet with sweat as he brushed a few curls off of his forehead to glare properly at the screen holding him hostage.

"Yeah, that's why the fight has to end as soon as there is blood, or a player hits the ice." Josh continued the conversation as if this sport was sane.

"Okay," I could feel the sarcasm dripping from my voice, "What happens when there are both? Logan's lip was bleeding, but he kept throwing punches until that guy hit the ice."

"I have no idea," Josh shrugged, "Again, I don't actually care about the sport that much. I only know the gist."

"Oh my god," I pinched the bridge of my nose, "This sport is so toxic."

"I mean," Courtney shrugged, "You're not wrong."

"That was crazy to witness," Beck mumbled from behind me. I nodded with her, agreeing.

"...Anyone else get kind of turned on by the fight?" Taylor asked, finally joining the conversation. Josh raised his hand and pointed directly at himself, and then at Courtney, who nodded her confirmation.

"You all are nuts!" I gasped, a hysterical giggle escaping my lips.

"Oh please, like you didn't feel anything watching Logan beat the shit out of some punk for your honor." Courtney leaned forward to give me a disbelieving look across Josh's lap.

"What are you talking about?" I widened my eyes at her. She was the biggest feminist I knew. I couldn't handle the fact that *she* of all people was genuinely turned on by a guy going out of his way to harm another person.

"Logan saw number eighteen do that gross thing with his hand, and he didn't hesitate to step in. I'm not saying fighting was the way to go, but watching Logan react that instinctively to defend his friends was kind of hot," Courtney explained. Taylor started snapping their fingers in agreement with her. I rolled my eyes hard, glaring at all of them as I still couldn't believe my ears.

"I'm just going to say it," Josh held both of his palms up, "Logan also looked hot while he was punching that other guy in the face. You can acknowledge the toxic masculinity that comes with that statement, I understand. But I said what I said."

I glanced behind me to see Adam pinching his nose, silent laughter shaking his shoulders as he tugged Beck close to his side, her quiet giggles mirroring his as she gazed lovingly at him. Taylor snapped their fingers again, this time agreeing with Josh before saying, "Preach."

"You're nuts. There was nothing hot about that." I argued.

"You sure?" Josh asked, giving Courtney a look I couldn't interpret before he leaned closer to my seat and lowering his voice. "Did you see his face during the fight?"

I frowned at his question, glancing over at Logan once more before answering the rock star, "Yes."

"So you saw how his jaw clenched?" Josh asked, his voice a tone I didn't quite understand. All I knew was that I had to strain to focus on his words with the noise of the stadium around us. I was still staring at Logan, who hadn't bothered glancing over at us the entire time he was sitting in time-out.

"Yeah," I replied, not sure what Josh was getting at.

"How focused and determined he was? How his breath exhaled through his nose with each punch of his fist? The tendons in his neck flexing each time." Josh paused his questioning, waiting for my answer. I simply nodded my head, my eyes studying Logan as he frowned at the timer once more before putting his helmet back on his head. "You can't picture that look on him in any other position?"

I blushed. Hard.

I wasn't quite sure if Josh was saying what I thought he was saying, but I didn't really have time to question it further, because he kept speaking. "Picture his jaw clenched, his breath fanning your neck"—Oh dear god—"His arms caging you in, his breathing sharp like he's focused and determined on something else."

My heartbeat was unstable, I was sweating under my clothes. Logan had just stood up from his bench and kicked the door from the time-out box open a second after the timer showed that he was allowed back on the ice.

"Picture him exerting that much energy purely for your benefit," Josh mumbled against my ear, right when Logan turned his head to glance over at us. He was skating by our section, which was the only reason I could see his dark brow loosen a little bit after he scanned our group and made eye contact with me. I don't know what my facial expression was, but I knew it wasn't normal based on Logan's reaction to it.

I gasped and quickly punched Josh in the arm before Logan turned away and focused on the game.

"What the hell is wrong with you?" I grumbled at Josh, who was laughing right along with Courtney.

"I'm simply calling you on your holier-than-thou bullshit, Lo." Josh chuckled. Beck had reached forward and patted me on the shoulder, her silent way of apologizing for our friends embarrassing me. I squeezed her hand back and faced forward, trying not to smile from being so easily bamboozled by Josh.

Thankfully, the rest of the game went by without additional fights. I had managed to pay attention to some of the plays, but it happened so fast and players swapped positions off and on the ice so quickly that it was sometimes difficult to keep up.

Afterward, Josh was caught by a few fans who had recognized him, so we lingered a little bit so that he could do his celebrity rock star thing. Even Courtney got asked for an autograph or two, and she literally was only famous for being engaged to him.

Well, and for signing at his concert that one time, but that was a while back.

When Courtney and Josh asked if we should go to the bar with the team to celebrate their win, I was thankful that Beck and Adam were the ones to speak up and say that they were tired and wanted to call it a night.

That way, I didn't have to be the loser who asked to skip out on the bar where I knew Logan would be. I wasn't in the mood to be judged or teased by him again, especially after he had intentionally startled me by slamming against the plexiglass before the game started.

***

I had just gotten into bed, my bedroom mostly put together already from the moving company earlier in the day when my phone buzzed with a text.

Josh: Here's the title by the way.

With that message, he sent along an image of the cover of the alien erotica series he and Beck were hyping up earlier. I laugh-reacted to the image and tossed my phone on the bed while I showered and got changed.

I wasn't exactly sleepy yet, but I kept picturing that image that Josh had painted so well with his words during the game.

Logan caging me in.

Neck tendons flexing, etc.

So I decided to download the first book since it was free on my e-reader app. Generally, the fact that it was free wasn't a great sign. But I said I would give it a shot, and I was curious to see what Josh and Beck were so excited about.

3

ELOISE

I don't know what happened.

I blinked and rubbed my eyes, wondering how I got here.

It was like I was sucked into a black hole.

I checked the time on my phone, which flashed four a.m. on the screen.

Thank goodness it was Saturday, and that I didn't have to wake up for work soon. I could sleep in as much as I wanted with little to no repercussions.

I only had a couple of chapters left. I was ninety percent of the way through the book, and I had made it this far, so I figured I might as well see it through.

How did I get so absorbed in this story? Well, what little story there is. I had a glass of wine that I kept topping off with a bottle I had resting on my nightstand as I read the alien erotica, and even though I was definitely buzzed from drinking nothing but wine the last five hours, I was still aware enough to want to keep reading.

The woman and the alien man had done the deed half a

dozen times already, and I was still desperate to see the story through.

Did the author find a way to put crack into her stories? Why was I so invested? Why was I willingly choosing to ignore most of the features the author used to describe the alien man. Horns? Pass. Tail? Pass. The skin texture she kept describing every second she could? Ick.

Everything else? Smash.

I'd smash this alien so hard.

I opened my phone to send a voice memo to my friends, the brightness from my phone screen made my eyes squint and blurred my vision before I found the group chat they had been messaging on earlier while I was reading.

Adam: Logan, you alright man?

Court: Yeah, it looked like you had a busted lip after.

Josh: Need me to ice it better for ya, big guy? (;

Logan: I'm flattered, but the swelling has already gone down.

Beck: Are you in trouble for the fight?

Blah. Who gave a shit. I didn't participate in the group chat but instead went to tap on either Josh or Beck's contact information. I was too tired and lazy to make extra taps on the screen that would result in a smaller group chat with the two of them, and I figured I would tell them both in detail my experience with their recommendation at some point. I just wanted to treat them to some live reactions I had thus far. Because my fingers felt a little tingly from the excess wine, I decided to go with a voice message.

"First of all," I started, hearing my own smile and tipsiness in my voice, "The communication barrier? Hot. The pro-tectiveness? Hot. I get it now. Holy hell. I am so blown away by all of this." I sent that first, figuring that was a good place to start. I read a couple more sentences before the alien made another grand gesture for his lady friend, making my lady parts warm and my heart melt.

I held my phone up again as I started another voice message. "The things I would let him do to me. I'm so glad I charged my vibrator recently. Hot. *Damn!*" I laughed a little before I cut off the message and sent that one too. I knew I was intoxicated, and I knew that Beck or Josh would absolutely roast me for staying up late and getting tipsy and reading alien erotica, but they created this monster, so it was fine.

I read a few more lines, my heart rate picking up yet again when it looked like the couple was about to do the deed another fucking time in their little cave. This story had very little plot, but I didn't care. It was enough plot to justify all the sex for me.

I picked up my phone again for one last voice message. "I'm ruined. I can't come back from this. Am I into grunting, pushy men with communication barriers now? I'm feeling the feminism leave my body little by little." I sent that one too, giggling to myself before I finally put my phone down and continued the story.

How the author could balance the line between feminism and possessive instincts was fascinating. I understood that this was clearly fiction and that in reality, I would probably punch a guy in the face who acted like this. However, books were meant to be enjoyed. And I sure as hell was enjoying the shit out of this.

An hour and a half later, I finally finished. I plugged in my e-reader and phone on my nightstand before I simply crawled under the covers and passed out. I had filthy dreams of alien men with weird skin and phenomenal genitalia designed specifically for the female orgasm, for seven hours.

***

My phone buzzing woke me up. Not the sunlight peeping through my blinds. I was a little hungover, but not enough to where I couldn't slap my hand around and find my buzzing phone. My head was just a little sore, so I stayed lying down as I squinted my eyes at the screen.

Beck was calling me.

I also noticed that it was about twelve thirty, I needed to get up and say hello to Susan and thank her again for letting me move in.

"Beck, how did this happen?" I answered the FaceTime call, snuggling a little more under the covers until they were tucked close to my chin. She was sitting on Adam's black leather couch, clearly having been awake for a few hours at this point on her Saturday. She gave me a confused look, making me giggle like a crazy person.

"How did what happen?" Beck asked. I pulled my face free from the covers a little bit more so that she could see my lips move. Beck was hard of hearing, and even though her hearing aids happened to pull a lot of weight for her ears, it was still best for her to see the lips of whoever was speaking to her just in case.

"This!" I reached over and grabbed my e-reader, pulling up

the cover image of the book I had burned through last night. Beck squinted at her phone screen and then her face lit up.

"Oh my god, you read it already?" Beck asked, giggles escaping her. Adam walked behind the couch in the background, stopping to plant a peck on the crown of her head before he continued past.

"Yes! Did you not get my voice messages last night?" I asked. Beck's brow furrowed and she shook her head.

"Huh, I must have just sent them to Josh," I shrugged. "I'm so invested. I'm going to download the other books today."

"I knew you'd love it," Beck smiled, "I was just calling to see if you need help unpacking anything today. I know you hired movers, but I figured you still had stuff to unpack."

"Beck," I sighed, pretending to sound irritated with her. "Why are you the sweetest?"

She rolled her eyes at me in response, I crossed my eyes back at her.

"Sorry for breathing," Beck spoke, a smile on her lips.

"I'm fine actually, but I'm down to hang out today if you want to come say hi to Susan."

"I was going to stop by anyway, just to see if she needed any errands run." Beck really was the sweetest. Last I heard, she had no contact with her parents. As a result, she poured all her love and energy into the only other family member she was friendly with, her grandmother. Who was now my roommate. Which reminded me, I really needed to wake up and get my day started. How rude was I to move in and then sleep in past noon?

"Cool, I'll see you soon, then," I saluted her, she saluted me back, and we hung up the call. I rubbed the sleep out of my eyes and slowly sat up in bed, aware of the minor ache in my head as I changed positions. Eventually, I put on sweatpants and a tank top before heading downstairs in search of ibuprofen. I clearly had too much wine last night.

I had just made it downstairs when I was greeted by my other roommate, Courtney, who I thought was staying the night at Josh's last night.

"Hey! Did you sleep here last night?" I asked, finger-combing my hair out of my face as I stepped out of her way so she could ascend the stairs.

"What? No. Josh and I just got here." Courtney gave me a funny look and trotted upstairs to her bedroom. I shrugged and walked over to the kitchen, where Josh and Susan were sitting at the kitchen table with two mugs of tea.

"Morning, sleepyhead." Susan greeted me with a very pointed look at her cell phone, checking the time with raised eyebrows.

"I know, I'm so sorry. I usually don't do this." I smiled sheepishly as I made my way over to the coffee maker.

"You just woke up?" Josh asked, disbelief on his expression as he sipped his tea.

"Yeah, I stayed up all night finishing the book you recommended," I replied, getting a clean mug from the cupboard, and putting it under the drip of the coffee maker.

"What? Really?" I lifted my eyebrows at Josh's surprised tone.

"Didn't you listen to my voice messages?" I asked him, an embarrassed blush heating my cheeks.

"You sent me voice messages?" Josh asked, leaning to his side so he could pull his phone out of his pocket to check. I nodded and waited patiently while he pulled them up. I was preparing for what I sounded like on the recordings since I was still a little foggy on what exactly I said. I tried to remember, but I only remembered feeling silly and horny. Hopefully, Courtney wouldn't be weirded out by the messages I sent her fiancé at four a.m.

"I don't have any voice messages from you." Josh frowned a little, his thumb swiping as he scrolled through his screen.

"Really? Beck didn't have any either. I thought I sent them to one of you." I frowned too, pulling my own phone out of my sweatpants to double-check.

"Maybe you sent them to someone else?" Susan suggested, slurping loudly from her mug as soon as she saw Courtney come back down the stairs.

"Ugh, Susan, if you want me to move out, just say so." Courtney came over and took Susan's empty tea mug from her hands and promptly set it in the sink so that the older woman would cease her loud slurping. I giggled before glancing back down at my phone.

Huh, the most recent message thread I had was unread messages from the group chat.

Directly underneath that was Logan.

Why did I have a message thread with Logan? We never texted each other—

"Oh no," I mumbled, my heart sinking into my gut as I tapped on the conversation with Logan to see three voice messages from me, "Oh, no, no, no."

"What?" Courtney asked, walking over to stand by me and look over my shoulder.

"I sent them to Logan by accident," I wheezed. God, this was so embarrassing. Now Logan was going to know I read alien erotica at four a.m. like a crazy person. "He's going to tease me so bad for reading this."

"What did the voice messages say?" Josh asked, his eyes bouncing between his fiancée and me.

"I can't remember, but I know I was tipsy and now he has yet another reason to make fun of me." I pinched the bridge of my nose in irritation with myself.

"Play them. If you were tipsy, you probably just didn't make sense. Which would explain why he hasn't responded to them yet." Courtney shrugged with a nod of her chin towards my phone. I tapped on the first recording I sent him.

"First of all, the communication barrier? Hot. The protectiveness? Hot. Holy hell. I am so blown away by all of this."

Oh dear god.

The kitchen was silent.

"Um," Josh nodded, his eyes wide as he tried to make it not weird, "That's fine, what was the next one?"

My blood was running colder than normal, so I tapped on the second message.

"The things I would let him do to me. I'm so glad I charged my vibrator recently. Hot. Damn!"

Oh fuck. I tapped on the last one while everyone sat in silence absorbing that message.

"I'm ruined. I can't come back from this. Am I into grunting, pushy men with communication barriers now? I'm feeling the feminism leave my body little by little."

Fuck. I knew that this was worse, but my sleepy brain

couldn't quite fathom why yet. All I knew was that my heart was racing and I wanted to hide in a hole for the rest of my life. I slowly slid down the cupboards until I was sitting on the kitchen floor, my own eyes wide as I stared at the message thread with Logan.

I assumed my face conveyed the horror I felt.

"Oh my god!" Josh started laughing, and soon Courtney and Susan joined him. I didn't care. They could laugh as much as they wanted, but that didn't change how mortified I was, "This is my favorite day!" Josh cried as he covered his eyes with one of his hands.

"Screw you all, this is humiliating!" I flipped the room off, my eyes still glued to my phone. It was like if I stared at it long enough, it would magically disappear and cease to exist.

Nope. The voice messages still sat there on my screen.

"Logan thinks you want him now," Courtney giggled, sliding down next to me on the floor. "This is amazing."

"What?" I was blinking rapidly at her, my mind racing with her words. "Why would he think that?"

"Because!" Courtney pointed directly at my phone with a grin she couldn't hide, "You're talking about how hot you are for quiet, grunting men with communication barriers. Getting into fights and defending your honor. Why *wouldn't* he think that, after getting into a fight during the game just last night? No man would listen to that and assume you were talking about erotica."

"It's true," Josh was still laughing as he spoke, his face buried in both of his hands as his elbows rested on the kitchen table. "If I was Logan, I would one hundred percent assume you were into me. Regardless of how buzzed you sound in those recordings."

No, no, no.

This was horrible.

Logan and I had gotten into it in the past due to my inability to understand ASL as well as everyone else in the group. In fact, I had specifically smushed pie all over him because he had teased me for the inappropriate signs I accidentally used.

Logan was going to think I was making a pass at him.

Oh fuck, oh fuck, oh fuck.

Just then, I glanced at my phone and saw three dots start to bounce at the bottom of the message thread. *Oh shit, he was responding!*

"Fuck!" I cried, fumbling my phone out of my hands. Courtney was trying to control her laughter as she retrieved my phone from the kitchen floor and held it up. I could see that his message had come through, but not what it said until she grinned like the Cheshire cat and turned the phone to show me after reading it herself.

Logan: We should probably talk.

"I told you!" Courtney pulled my phone away from me and clutched it to her chest, pointing a finger at me as she jumped off of the kitchen floor and cackled. She then hopped over to Josh and Susan to show them the message, making them both laugh some more.

"Help! Help!" I started flapping my hands like a bird, unable to make a movement with my body that made sense. Anxiety was taking over my muscles.

"With what?" Courtney asked, setting the phone down on

the table before she plopped herself down on Josh's lap. He wrapped both of his arms around her waist before resting his forehead against her shoulder, his own shoulders still shaking with silent laughter.

"How do I explain this?!" I cried, rubbing my palms on my cheeks in stress. Josh lifted his head from Courtney's shoulder to smirk at me.

"You say, 'Don't worry, Logan, I wasn't talking about you. I was talking about this big hunky alien in my book that I masturbated to last night.'" I sarcastically laughed at Josh's summary of the situation, pulling open a kitchen drawer next to me, and wadding a hand towel into a ball before chucking it at him.

He dodged the ball easily. To be fair, it was a bad throw.

"I can't say that! Then he'll know I read alien erotica!" I explained with angst.

"So?" Courtney lifted a shoulder, her smile becoming a little more confused.

"So, I don't want him to tease me for what I read!" Courtney shook her head at my explanation as if she was struggling to come up with another solution to the problem.

"Well, you could always pretend you're into him and just allow him to let you down easy." Courtney quirked her lips to the side. "Actually, that's not a bad idea. If you pretend you want to sleep with him and he turns you down, he probably won't make fun of you for anything anymore. He'd be too embarrassed to be anything other than cordial with you."

"Hold up." Josh kept his arms around Courtney, but leaned back to get a better look at her. "What makes you think Logan wants to turn her down?"

"He responded with, 'We should probably talk,' which never means a good talk." Courtney lifted her eyebrows at Josh as if her explanation was obvious.

"You don't know that. You're assuming a lot, love." Josh nipped once at Courtney's ear, making her shoulders scrunch and playfully shove him away.

"You're telling me you would respond with 'we should probably talk' if you were all for what you heard in those voice memos from Lo?" Courtney countered, staring her fiancé down. It was his turn to quirk his lips to the side.

"Courtney," Josh's voice dropped, "If you had sent me those voice memos when we were unofficially dating, I would have called you immediately to initiate some sort of phone sex with you."

"And that," she tapped her fiancé on the nose with her index finger, "Is exactly my point."

Josh frowned at this.

So did I.

Was I into Logan? No. I mean, he was physically attractive, but that didn't mean I wanted to give him a ride of any sort. Even though the mental image Josh had painted for me may have lingered in my mind. Perhaps that mental image was why I started reading the alien erotica in the first place last night, just so I'd stop fantasizing about a panting Logan above me.

I was a warm-blooded woman after all.

However, why the fuck *wouldn't* Logan be into me? I was a good-looking woman. I was a fucking underwear model at one point, goddammit.

...Probably for the same mysterious reason he was so rude to you when you first met, my mind answered for me. I frowned a little.

Courtney's idea made a huge dent in my pride, but she had a point. Which was more embarrassing, getting turned down by Logan, or Logan knowing about my alien erotica and using that as ammunition to tease me for however long he wanted?

"Or," I responded, coming to a standing position, and retrieving my coffee mug before it cooled off too fast, "I could just ignore him and the messages and pretend none of this happened."

"That's the more childish way to go about this, yes," Susan spoke up with a nod of her head. I nibbled on my bottom lip and shrugged.

"I'll figure something out, but for now I'm ignoring this whole thing. I can't handle acknowledging this." I took my phone back from where Courtney rested it on the kitchen table, turned on the lock screen, and shoved it in my sweatpants pocket.

"You do you, Lo." Josh encouraged me with a pump of his fist. Courtney just smiled at her fiancé before planting a loud smack of a kiss on his cheek. Soon, they were making googly eyes at each other, and I took that as my cue to retreat back to my new room to finish unpacking.

I was spiraling.

Do I want Logan to make fun of me for my reading material? Or feel pity for me because he has to turn me down? It was a lose-lose situation for me. I hated that I was torn between these two options. For now, I was hoping that maybe he wouldn't think too much about the messages and would probably move on from the whole thing as well.

Maybe, if I was super lucky, we could both move forward and pretend that I never sent those voice messages in the first place. I leaned into this fantasy of mine as I organized my new closet, determined to get rid of the butterflies wreaking havoc in my stomach through tried-and-true denial.

4

LOGAN

I stood there, staring at my reflection in my bathroom mirror. My toothbrush hung loosely in my mouth as I listened to the last of Eloise's voice memos. My hand halted mid-brush at the sound of Eloise's giggly, intoxicated voice.

I was stunned.

I wasn't sure what to expect when I woke up this morning with three unheard voice messages from Eloise, sent directly to me and nobody else, but it sure wasn't this. I had seen the notification on my phone, thought it was weird, and took a shower without listening. Once I was awake enough after my shower and started brushing my teeth, I finally listened to them. Which brought me to this moment, staring at myself blankly in the mirror.

Was she talking about me?

Did she mean to send these *to* me?

The time stamp said she sent these around four a.m., just four hours ago. Which was an odd time to masturbate to someone and send them voice memos about it. But I knew very little about Eloise at this point, so maybe this wasn't that unusual for her.

"*The communication barrier? Hot.*"

I had never been told that my inability to vocalize was hot, but I guess everyone had their kinks.

"*The protectiveness? Hot.*"

She must have been talking about when I went after Monet, number eighteen, during the game last night. Courtney had signed to me during the game that he flipped them off for cheering me on, after stealing the puck from him. What I didn't expect, however, was for him to retaliate by making crude gestures to my friends. I didn't think twice, really. I dropped my gloves and swung.

He was labeled as the instigator since everyone could see his tongue swiping between his parted fingers as he made very specific and direct eye contact with the group. Even Josh looked a little pissed off, and that guy never got mad.

We each got five minutes in the penalty box as a result of our fight, but it was worth it. He was a young kid, barely in his twenties, and clearly had a chip on his shoulder. I had no problem putting him in his place.

I played Eloise's next message again because I still couldn't believe what I was listening to.

"*The things I would let him do to me. I'm so glad I charged my vibrator recently. Hot. Damn!*" the fact that she left me hanging after that message felt almost painful.

What? I thought. *What would you let "him" do to you, specifically? Leave no detail out, please, and thank you.* The mental image I was immediately able to create of Eloise pleasuring herself with a vibrator was alarming. Had I thought about her before? Yes. I hadn't in a while, though. The last time I had thought that Eloise may be into me was almost a year ago after she smashed a plate of pie against my chest, and we were both in the bathroom cleaning up.

She had stormed off, probably to cry. Unfortunately, that wasn't the first time I had unintentionally made her do so. I had gotten most of the pie off of my shirt in the kitchen sink and had found my way to the bathroom to try to rinse the stain out. Eloise was in there when I walked in, both of her hands bracing either edge of the bathroom sink as her head turned sharply to see who was interrupting her privacy.

I had stood frozen in the doorway, my chest wrenched at the red and water rimming her eyes as she glared at me.

Then she had looked down at my shirt and sniffed, stepping away to make room for me to move in front of the sink. I had been surprised she didn't push me out of the bathroom, so I stiffly followed her instructions and turned on the tap. I had used my fingers to try to rub the stain out, which made Eloise roll her clear blue eyes at me in irritation before she had grabbed my shirt and taken over rinsing the stain out.

I was just surprised she wasn't punching me at that point, so I stood there like an idiot and let her take over the task of washing my shirt.

After getting as much of the stain out as she could, she had pulled a towel off of the rack of Josh's first-floor bathroom and tried to dry off my shirt as much as possible, her knuckles grazing the bare skin of my abdomen as she held my shirt with one hand and the dry towel with the other.

I thought about that touch too often.

I also thought about how she felt me up a few seconds later. Satisfied with how she was able to dry off my shirt enough, she then tugged the hem of it down. She brushed her hands over the front of my shirt in an attempt to straighten it and remove any unnecessary wrinkles.

Her fingertips pressed firmly against my chest and abdomen, and I held my breath as her eyes widened a little after the first pass of her hands.

Then she made a second pass, a third. That one felt more deliberate and exploratory. She brushed her fingers down my torso slower as her eyelids drooped the slightest bit, feeling the ridges of my muscles underneath the shirt.

Holy shit, I thought, *she's feeling me up.*

My cock twitched in response, not understanding that we had absolutely no chance in hell with this woman.

Something made her snap out of it, pulling her hands back quickly and shooting me one last glare with her eyes before she slid past me and stormed out of the bathroom. I waited only a few seconds before following her out, brushing the moment off as nothing.

Have I gotten off to the thought of Eloise enjoying what she felt? Yes. More times than I'd like to admit. At first, I told myself it was because I was a guy, and that I was doomed to think dirty thoughts about a woman who enjoyed the feel of my body under her hands. I, later on, accepted that my gender had absolutely nothing to do with it and realized that I was simply attracted to Eloise.

Who wouldn't be? She was a beautiful woman.

She was smaller and thinner than other women I usually

preferred to hook up with. However, her smaller curves still caught my eye regularly. Especially the night of Courtney and Josh's engagement party. The dress she wore was a light pink-colored thing that hid nothing about her body. I was an asshole that eyeballed her as much as I could when she wasn't looking.

She wore this dress that exposed every line and curve of her body, smiling at the guests with what felt like the brightness of the sun. Her shoulder-length blonde hair was perfectly styled down. I was a guy, and I knew that "natural makeup" looks existed, but I would have bet all my money that because I could see her freckles, she wasn't wearing makeup and her skin was naturally flawless. I knew my attraction to Eloise was unreciprocated, so I let the sleeping dog lie. If I had to control my thoughts around her, that was my own problem and I could deal with it. I could be mature about one-sided attraction and move on.

And for a while, I had.

But...these voice memos from her were insinuating that she wasn't exactly as indifferent to me as I thought.

I played the last one, just to make myself suffer a little more. "*I'm ruined. I can't come back from this. Am I into grunting, pushy men with communication barriers now?*" That was a great question, Eloise. One I'd like an answer to as soon as possible.

I had the feeling she didn't mean to send these to me. She kept speaking about me as if I was in the third person, and she was clearly a little drunk. But why else would she accidentally send these to me if I wasn't already on her mind?

Or was I just trying to make this into something I was clearly hopeful for?

I spiraled about the messages for a few hours. I decided not to respond right away and instead went for a jog to ponder the situation. I was already planning on going to the gym with Courtney tomorrow evening before her work week started, and the off-season was starting for me, so I didn't need to overdo it.

I thought about Eloise for the entirety of the run. I had music playing in my earbuds, an attempt for a small distraction from the curveball she had thrown at me early this morning.

What if she meant what she said?

What if my suspicion was right and she was talking about me? That she thought about me when she was alone with herself at night.

What if…she didn't exactly want to be *alone* as she thought about me at night?

The thought of those blue eyes looking at me with anything other than anger or irritation made my heart race irregularly in my chest, and I had to pause and catch my breath, my hands going to my waist as I breathed through my nose and out my mouth.

My phone buzzed against my bicep, where it was securely strapped to my arm for my run. I silenced the call; it was just my annoying agent. He probably had more sponsorship ideas for me, but I was too busy thinking about Eloise Bane to focus on anything work-related during the beginning of the off-season.

Eloise, and her full, light pink lips. And how they would feel.

Eloise, and her cropped light blonde hair that looked delicately soft to the touch.

Eloise and her tattoos that I only knew about because Courtney had mentioned them, but wouldn't hate to see for myself.

Fuck, I wanted Eloise.

Finally, I gathered some bravery before I decided to head home and typed a message back to her. Nodding my head once, I took off, trying not to think too hard about other various forms of exercise I would be willing to try out with Eloise if she was truly open to it.

5

ELOISE

"Still nothing?" Courtney asked as we walked towards the gym doors.

"Nope. Not a word." I smiled at my friend, glad to see that my tried-and-true denial approach to the Logan clusterfuck seemed to be working so far.

Courtney rolled her eyes. "I'm still going to find a way to leave you two alone together, in case he wants to take the opportunity to talk to you one-on-one." I rolled my eyes back at her.

"I doubt he will. Neither of us has said anything since yesterday. I doubt he'd want to turn me down when I randomly show up at the gym with you." I had decided to go with Courtney to the gym and face Logan simply because my mother pissed me off again. She had told me about the yoga class that Lucy had mentioned before and wanted me to go. Actually, she didn't even ask if I wanted to go. She just raved about it, sent me the details, and nothing else. As if she expected me to attend.

Not a mention about me moving out.

I was still mad about her rude comments regarding Courtney and thought that a fun way to give my mother the finger would be to gain some muscle mass myself.

So here I was.

Ready for Courtney to teach me her ways, which were really ways that she had learned from Logan.

I was still completely humiliated by the thought of facing him again, but if I was going to pretend that none of my mess-ups had happened, I needed to be okay with being in his presence. That's what I told myself, anyway.

…And maybe a teeny-tiny part of me wanted to experience what it would be like to be rejected by Logan St. James. I was curious if he would be an asshole about it, which seemed likely to me. Or, if he would try to pull some sort of "It's not you, it's me" cliché.

Courtney shouldered the door open and scanned her pass at the front desk, smiling at the kid working there. The guy did an obvious perusal of Courtney, and I made direct eye contact with him until she passed, letting him know I saw him.

The tips of his ears turned a little red, and then he cleared his throat and turned back to his computer screen.

"So, what are you going to do today?" I asked her.

"It's arms and shoulders day, I think," Courtney replied, her dark eyes scanning the gym until she spotted whom she was looking for and sauntered on. It was a smaller gym, and only a handful of people were there exercising. Courtney and I were the only women at the moment.

"Hey!" Courtney walked ahead of me and waved, and

I stepped to the side to confirm who I suspected she was talking to.

Logan was just racking the bar he was lifting and then sat up on his bench. He gave a quick head nod in Courtney's direction before he hesitated the slightest bit when his eyes slid over and noticed me. It was a subtle movement, but I caught it. I also saw how quickly he dismissed my appearance and bent down to grab a towel to wipe all over his face and neck. He was already working up a sweat.

Then I noticed the number of circle-weight things on either end of his bar, and I realized that that checked out.

"Getting a head start?" Courtney asked as she reached her fist out for him to bump. He returned the gesture with a nod. No smile, just a nod. That was the Logan way. The only time his facial expressions really changed from his bored ones, was when he was signing because facial expressions were integrated with ASL.

"Lo decided to join us today," Courtney threw a thumb over her shoulder to address me, clearly having missed his hesitation when he noticed me earlier, "So we gotta show her the ropes."

"Show me the ropes?" I asked, setting my purse down as I pretended to check my phone. I had no notifications; I just didn't want to make eye contact with Logan. I felt like my racing heart and the heat I suddenly felt in my cheeks was embarrassing enough. Though I could blame the temperature it was inside the gym.

"How many pull-ups can you do?" Courtney asked as she walked around towards the head of Logan's bench and nodded for him to continue his set. He also avoided looking at me as he leaned back and gripped the bar with his hands. Watching him pull the bar down towards his chest and push it away distracted me for a moment before I remembered to respond to Courtney's question.

"I don't know, a couple?" I asked, watching how Logan's legs flexed even though his feet stayed flat on the ground on either side of the bench. He was wearing some type of black compression shorts that fell to his mid-thigh, showing off the many muscles in his legs. He then wore shorter, looser shorts over the top of them. I assumed they were for modesty, because there was no way his compression shorts underneath concealed anything.

"We like to do sets of ten, if possible," Courtney spoke, barely distracting me from ogling Logan's body as he breathed through his nose with every push of the bar, "So we can show you how to use the little rubber band things to help get familiar with the movement of a pull-up."

I wasn't a huge fan of how she just assumed I couldn't do a single pull-up, but I also wasn't going to correct her because I truly didn't know what my arm strength was. I wasn't used to exercising with weights, push-ups, and pull-ups ever. My exercises were usually yoga, aerobics…and occasional bedroom gymnastics.

"Sounds good," I said, my eyes trailing higher on Logan's body, where it reclined on the bench. He wore a black men's tank top that hugged his pecs, showing the muscles flexing as he finished off his set. I was eyeballing his biceps and forearms as he racked the bar again, and when he sat up his dark eyes met mine briefly.

Briefly, because I broke our eye contact and glanced down at my phone. Clearing my throat for literally no reason.

God, he was so nice to look at.

I tossed the phone in my bag as Courtney and Logan made their way a few feet over from the bench Logan had claimed. They approached what looked like the world's most boring jungle gym. Various bars leveled at different heights as Courtney skipped over to one of the tallest ones, jumped up, and started swiftly doing a couple of pull-ups. Logan shook his head at her, tugged on her ponytail in jest, and bent down to retrieve what must have been the rubber band things Courtney mentioned earlier.

"Have you used these before?" Courtney asked after hopping down gracefully and pointing at the bands in Logan's hands. He walked over to me, and it took every muscle in my neck and face not to glance up and meet his eyes as he handed me one. I took it without question, even though I shook my head to respond to Courtney.

"You use this to help pull yourself up," Courtney explained as she tugged my band out of my hands and started securing it on one of the medium-level height monkey bars.

"Oh, so my feet rest on it?" I asked, starting to piece together what she was doing. I had been to gyms before, so I had seen other people do pull-ups like this.

"Exactly—" Suddenly, the band snapped in half as Courtney secured it to the pole. It cracked loudly, making both of us flinch. Courtney blinked at the broken band once before shrugging and tossing it aside.

"These are pretty old," Courtney explained, "I'll give it to the guy at the front when we're done."

"Okay."

Logan waved his hand, catching Courtney's peripheral vision, and started signing to her. His hands moved quickly, and my basic understanding of ASL couldn't keep up with him. Ugh. Irritation started to fill me again.

Courtney nodded at him and didn't say anything.

Okay, I guessed whatever he said was private, then.

"Okay, this one should work. There's only one left, so let's leave that for someone else." Courtney wiggled her eyebrows at Logan and me. "Plus, I can finally do pull-ups without the assistance."

Logan's lips tipped up the smallest bit at her before he shook his head and motioned for the two of us to claim our spots. He, of course, went for the highest monkey bar on the other side of Courtney.

I took the one with the rubber band, grabbing the monkey bar with my hands before I stepped onto it. I bounced on it a little, checking to see if it would snap in half like the first one. Nope. I then started to pull myself up, surprised at how fast I was able to do that.

"I'm not sure I need this," I spoke after a few pulls, "This feels too easy."

"The first couple reps should feel easy," Courtney explained. "It's when you get to the last half of them that you should feel some strain in your muscles."

"Oh." I nodded, continuing with the pull-up.

"Wait, Lo, what are you doing?" Courtney asked, a giggle escaping her lips as she eyeballed my hands on the bar.

"A pull-up?" I asked, eyeballing my own hands now because I didn't trust myself.

"Why are your hands like that?" Courtney smiled a little as she lifted a blonde eyebrow at me.

"Like what?"

"Backwards."

"This is backward?"

"Well, no, it's just significantly harder to do a pull-up that way."

"Hmm, well maybe I'm just great at pull-ups."

"Really? Do one like that without the rubber band."

I crossed my eyes at Courtney, making her laugh as I hopped down and untied the rubber band. I felt eyes on me and allowed myself one single quick glance at Logan as he stopped his pull-ups to watch me bend down and remove the assistance.

I then reached up on my tip toes and grabbed the bar like I had before, the back of my hands facing me as I tried to lift myself up.

My body stayed put.

Holy hell I was heavy.

"Give me a moment, I just gotta warm up first," I grunted, relaxing my muscles, and shaking my hands out. Courtney laughed.

"Of course." Her voice was dripping with sarcasm.

I closed my eyes and tried again, my toes still not leaving the ground as a grumble escaped my throat at my failure.

"I thought you were great at pull-ups?" Courtney asked. I kept my eyes closed but smiled, shaking my head at her. Suddenly, I felt a warm presence behind me right when I relaxed and the heels of my feet touched the ground again.

Two large, rough hands grabbed my wrists. My eyes flew

open to see Logan standing directly behind me, his hands twisting my wrists around so that I was holding the bar like Courtney was. The back of my hands facing away from me.

He eyeballed me in the mirror we were doing pull-ups in front of.

We never stood this close to each other before.

Well, with the exception of Courtney and Josh's engagement party.

However, this was the first time I truly got a visual representation of our size differences. He was both taller and wider than me. I was stunned. I knew I wasn't the largest woman in the world, but I felt like a child compared to him. His chin would brush against the top of my head if he leaned forward instead of to the side of me. His tanned skin was a large contrast to see against my paler complexion. The blush on my face and neck that resulted from his close proximity completely gave me away.

I was affected by how close he was, which was only slightly humiliating considering he was already convinced that I wanted to ride his dick.

His dark eyes scanned my face for only a couple of seconds before the jut of his chin told me to try again. So I did. This time, my body lifted off the ground just a little bit more. My toes only left the ground for a second before my arms shook and I landed on the ground again.

"Fuck me," I breathed, surprised at how little strength my arms had. I felt Logan stiffen behind me, his dark eyebrows inching up the slightest bit based on what I saw in the reflection of the mirror before he jutted his chin forward for me to try again.

"Bossy," I grumbled, squeezing my eyes shut as I inhaled and pulled.

Large warm hands wrapping themselves around my waist startled me. It wasn't a firm grip, it felt more like Logan's hands ghosted across my skin as he gently helped me get some more air under my feet with this pull.

"There ya go!" I heard Courtney cheer as I finally completed one single pull-up.

I ignored her and went for another one, Logan's hands staying in place on my bare skin as he helped guide my movements. I was only wearing a black sports bra and exercise shorts because even though I planned to get sweaty and gross this afternoon, I also wanted to look cute. I loved matching sets, and this one showed my ribcage tattoo as well as the tattoo I had on my hip, the top and bottom of the flowers on my skin playing peekaboo out of my bike shorts. I opened my eyes again, wanting to see how I looked exercising like a fucking badass. I could feel every muscle in my forearms, biceps, and shoulders working.

As soon as I lifted myself again, my arms folding as my chin made it over the bar, I noticed Logan's eyes drop from the back of my head to what was almost eye level with him.

My ass.

I gasped, and accidentally let go of the bar to my surprise.

"Whoa!" Courtney called as I fell, Logan's grip on my waist tightened enough to hold me up until I regained my footing on the ground, "Are you okay?"

"Yup!" I replied a little too loudly, stepping out of Logan's hands and shaking my arms out as if I didn't just catch him staring at my ass. "I think my arms just gave out. I must be more out of shape than I expected." My voice was only a little shaky, but thankfully I could excuse that with the pull-ups I had just done.

"You did great, Lo!" Courtney finished her last set and dropped to the ground, picking up her water bottle and shaking it to find it empty. She frowned before she looked behind her to where a water fountain was on the far wall near the bathrooms.

"How is your water bottle already empty? We just got here." I asked her, skepticism on my face. Courtney shrugged.

"I must have forgotten to fill it before we left," she glanced between Logan and me, "I'm going to go pee and then fill it up. Be right back." She then turned on her heel and took off, her blonde ponytail swishing with her movement. I widened my eyes in panic at her retreating form, because I didn't want to be left alone with Logan. I was still recovering from how warm his hands were on me. How my heart jumped up into my throat when I felt his gaze move to my ass.

I didn't want to be rejected by him now when my body was still physically recovering from that experience.

I turned away from him and pulled my phone out of my bag. I had zero notifications, but I unlocked the screen anyway and pulled up my email as if I had something to read. I could feel his eyes on me, and I thought I could literally feel my heart slowly climbing up into my throat.

"Did you do your set?" I asked, a little louder than normal. I gave up on pretending to read emails. I was feeling weirdly jittery about having to deal with being rejected by Logan, even though I didn't even intentionally hit on him in the first place.

I glanced up to see Logan nod, his eyes slightly narrowed as he eyeballed the phone I had just tossed back into my bag.

Fuck, I was acting so weird.

"Okay…" I rocked back on my heels, my arms crossing over my chest as if to protect myself from his gaze. "What's next?" Logan blinked at me once before he nodded toward some weights behind me. I smiled and nodded too, walking over to the rack to find the smallest ones.

"What do we do?" I asked, lifting two fives in each of my hands. Logan stared at me before he lifted his hands, signing something too quick for me to catch and pointing his thumb over his shoulder where Courtney ran off to.

"What was that?" I asked, dropping my hands to my sides that still gripped the weights. Logan redid Courtney's name sign for me a little slower, and then fingerspelled, *FOMO*.

"Oh, yeah she would want us to properly wait for her," I agreed, twisting my wrists in and out a little bit more as I continued to avoid eye contact with Logan. I nibbled on my bottom lip, looking everywhere but at him. I understood that it was kind of a dick move because he couldn't speak up to get my attention. He required people to look at him in order to communicate, but I was also a huge chicken.

Finally, Logan stepped into my line of sight. I blinked up at him while he frowned at the weights in my hands and reached towards the rack to get a set of tens. He then held them out to me, telling me to size up my weights.

"I thought we established I had no arm strength?" I asked, even as I put the fives back and took the tens from his hands. Before I could pull my arm all the way back, Logan's hand gripped my wrist and he held my arm up a little higher. I had to gulp what felt like my heart back down my throat before I realized he was just using his grip to look at my newest tattoo.

Is it hot in here?

"If you're judging me for another basic bouquet of flowers, Taylor already beat you to it." I piped up, feeling defensive as he inspected my latest artwork as if it needed his stamp of approval. Logan's dark gaze flicked over to mine as his lips twitched at the corners, and I felt my cheeks heat again.

He noticed, his eyes barely bouncing between either side of my nose.

My body was such a traitor. Didn't it know we didn't like him? That he was mean to us for literally no reason?

I was screwed. There was no chance I could act normal around him now.

I was torn between begging him to reject my solicitations from my voice messages already or turning on my heel and running away. I had already run away from him once in this gym, the first time we met. So I wasn't ready to do that again. It would be just as embarrassing.

6

LOGAN

I had no idea how to act around Eloise.

What was the social construct for this situation?

I had responded to her voice memos, saying that we should talk. She never responded to that, so I assumed that meant that she didn't want to. However, she showed up here at the gym, knowing that I would be here with Courtney. Did that mean that she wanted to talk? Was I misreading her signals? Did she understand how difficult it was for me to communicate with someone who wasn't competent in ASL?

She definitely checked me out, that much was obvious when I finished my reps on the bench press and caught her eyes. Eloise had a similar look on her face during the game once I left the penalty box. A look that almost took me out of the zone based on how easy to read she was.

She liked what she saw.

What threw me off was how she quickly punched Josh in the arm after we made eye contact, but I had to focus, so I hadn't let myself think too much about the horny eyes she had blatantly given me during my game. But then I saw her horny eyes again tonight, catching her staring at me as I pressed what I assumed to be over twice her body weight.

She was attracted to me, that much I was sure of. What I couldn't quite figure out was if she wanted me to *do* something about it. I assumed that if she really liked what she saw she would make the first move. Considering the communication barrier we had that, possibly, she had a kink about.

I was still holding Eloise's wrist, warring with myself about how to approach this subject with her. Her breathing was shallow, her cheeks were flushed, and her pupils would expand if I stared at her directly for too long.

Suddenly, she tugged her wrist out of my grip and blurted, "I read alien erotica."

I stared at her, my mouth parting at the sudden confession. That was...unexpected. Her face immediately turned tomato red, angering the freckles that dotted her nose.

Okay, I signed, feeling the confusion take over my facial features.

"I-I don't know why I told you that." Eloise closed her eyes as she set her weights on the ground, before covering her face with both of her palms. She was clearly embarrassed. Was she shaking? "I'm so sorry. Could you just," she waved her hands at me, expecting me to cough something up I guess, "Get on with it already?"

What? I asked. I couldn't keep up with the conversation we were having.

"Just say whatever you were going to say to let me know you aren't interested," Eloise rushed out on an exhale, scraping a hand down her flushed face again as her eyes avoided me. Let her down? So, those voice memos *were* about me? *She is, in fact, interested in me?*

"You know what," Eloise waved a hand in between the both of us, "It's okay, you don't actually need to tell me. I already know. Don't worry about it." She nodded as she placed both of her hands on her hips, taking a deep breath through her nose and exhaling through her mouth as she lifted her head to stare at the ceiling.

Know what? I asked, but she wasn't looking at me. She didn't see my signing. My heart was racing, she had both confirmed my suspicions and assumed that I wasn't interested in seconds.

I was interested.

I was *very* interested.

Did Eloise seem a little high-strung? Yes, but I was willing to look past that. Maybe it was because I hadn't had sex in literal years. Maybe it was because Eloise was hot as sin. Whatever the reason was, I wanted to take this opportunity by the reins if it was available.

But I couldn't fucking do that if she wouldn't *look* at me.

I wouldn't be able to get a word in with her even if I did vocalize.

I felt my frown take over before I thought better of it, stepping forward and wrapping one of my hands on the side of her face. Fingers behind her ear and my thumb on the line of her jaw, I forced her to lower her gaze from the ceiling and look at me. Her clear blue eyes widened in shock at the physical contact, and part of me scolded myself for touching her again without clear and obvious permission, but I was running out of options.

I held her gaze, relaxing my frown so that I wouldn't scare her.

Courtney had already told me multiple times about how harsh my resting bitch face was.

I had already used it unintentionally on Eloise multiple times, I wasn't about to fuck up another social interaction between us again.

I quickly let go of her face, now that I had her attention, and signed *Stop.* Her lips slammed shut at the word. I still had no idea how much ASL she really knew, but she managed to know basic core words at this point. How was I going to explain this to her in a way she would understand?

"You losers ready?" Courtney spoke up from behind me, making me clench my jaw at her timing. Like fuck was I going to try to explain myself to Eloise with Courtney nearby. I frowned, making Eloise's eyes narrow a little in reaction. I gave up, stepping away from Eloise before I bent down to pick up her weights, handing them back to her.

Eloise took them again without a word.

"Tens? Wow, you're really pushing yourself today, Lo." Courtney winked at Eloise before grabbing her own weights.

I tried not to look too irritated because it wasn't anyone's fault really.

Except for maybe Eloise, for planting the idea of sex in my head, and then immediately shutting it down before I could even give her a proper response.

Fuck, I didn't realize how badly I wanted her until we

had to suffer through the rest of the workout with Courtney unintentionally third-wheeling us.

Oh really, moron? I thought, *The number of times you jerked off in the shower simply because she brushed her hands over your stomach didn't clue you in?*

I was pathetic.

Eventually, we wrapped up our workout at the gym. We cooled off on the treadmills, me at a light jog whereas the girls strolled leisurely and held a conversation the entire fifteen minutes we were there. Then, we went over to the black mats near the front of the gym and stretched.

I was stretching forward, touching my toes with my hands when I glanced up and saw Eloise dislocate her hips mid-conversation.

Alright, she didn't really dislocate her hips. I just couldn't fathom stretching the way she was. She had leaned forward, pressing her palms flat in front of her as she tucked one of her legs high up, almost against her stomach. Her other leg was fully stretched out behind her. She then planted her hips down, over her tucked leg, and folded forward. She crossed her arms over each other and everything, continuing to chat with Courtney about who-the-fuck-knows-what as she became a human pretzel.

I was frozen mid-stretch, ignoring the pull in my hamstrings as I stared at her profile as she did this. The stretch did interesting things to her ass, which looked fantastic in those little bike shorts she was wearing.

Snapping fingers in my vision interrupted my thoughts, making me blink a couple of times and glare at Courtney.

"Were you paying attention to what we were saying?" Courtney asked, giving me a look that let me know she would for sure be roasting me for staring at Eloise's ass later. It wasn't even the first time I had stared at her ass tonight but, as far as I knew, it was the first time I had been busted for it.

What? I asked as I sat back up. I leaned back on my hands on the mats as I pretended to care about whatever Courtney had to say.

"Beach day, next weekend. You in?"

Was Eloise going to be there? Would she be wearing even less clothing than she was now?

Yes, I replied without really thinking too much more about it. I glanced over to the small woman who plagued my thoughts. She gave me a small, nervous smile in return. *Holy fucking shit, did Eloise just smile at me?* I was positive that was the first time that had happened since the first time we met and I was a grade-A prick to her.

A win is a win.

I followed the women out of the gym. The sun was setting, painting the sky in pinks and oranges. The glare from the sunset lit up Eloise's blonde hair, which helped me keep my gaze on the back of her head as I saw them safely to their car. I waved as Courtney and Eloise pulled out of the parking lot and I walked a few feet over to my truck, replaying every moment tonight with Eloise.

To my knowledge, I hadn't accidentally done anything to offend her.

And to top it all off, she gave me a small smile at the end of the night.

Hope sparked in my chest, and a little bit of excitement as well. I couldn't remember the last time I had pursued a woman, because frankly, I hadn't really needed to since I joined the NHL after college. There was always someone available, most of the time looking for something easy with no strings attached like I was.

Would Eloise want strings attached?

The thought made me pause as I reached for the handle of my truck. If anyone saw me, they would probably think I had forgotten how to open a car door. Shaking my head once and stepping up into my vehicle, I thought about that question a little more before deciding that it was a little too early to think about it. First, I needed to find a way to confirm that Eloise did, in fact, want to sleep with me. If she wasn't even interested in sex, then the thought of a relationship with her was wasted energy. One step at a time.

***

Sometimes, more often than I'd like, I wanted to strangle my agent.

This was one of those times.

Connor James stood back behind the cameras in grey slacks and a perfectly pressed button-up shirt, staring down at his phone. His dark blonde brows furrowed at whatever he was reading. Not paying attention at all to the fuckery he was putting me through today.

Connor was also the agent of two other players on my team. Apparently, the Ducks' social media manager decided that we needed to spend more time online during the off-season to hype everybody up. Overall, we didn't play well last year, and I guess by the end our ticket sales had proven that. When the social media manager, whose name escaped me, told Connor what she had in mind, he wasted no time agreeing.

Even though I hated this type of shit.

So here I was, taking my turn to pose wearing far too little hockey gear. Earlier today we filmed some shots at the rink where we all lip-synced to a popular trending sound on the internet. I was only included in about two seconds of the clip, and I had no idea why we were lip-syncing to a pop song, but I was contractually obliged to put up with a certain level of bullshit.

Was this considered pornographic? I asked myself. How else would you describe me wearing nothing but hockey pants and skates, posing in front of a white background with a freshly oiled and bare chest?

"Holy shit," I heard our team social media manager breathe, and I turned to give her an annoyed look as she stared at me. "If anything, this content will definitely get more women to support the team."

"You think?" Connor asked, the way his eyes trailed up and down the social media manager's body made me want to roll my eyes.

"Oh yeah." She ignored Connor's perusal and met my gaze, a smirk tugging at her lips at my clearly annoyed expression. "If I wasn't head over heels for my wife, I would definitely follow his account, specifically." She smiled at me before glancing down at her iPad and tapping away on something. At the mention of a spouse, Connor noticeably took a half step away from her side.

God, the guy was the worst.

But he was all I had. He was the one who was willing to work with me after my previous agent quit. Connor stepped in during that clusterfuck, when my previous team was desperate to trade me because I was an aggressive asshole on the ice. Connor kept what was left of my career afloat, so I couldn't just ditch him. No other agents, or even teams, have shown interest in me in the last few years, even after I had attended therapy and improved my overall performance.

"Can you look over there?" the photographer asked, making me turn my face to his. When our eyes met, he gulped and quickly hid behind the camera.

"Logan," John Larsen, number thirty-one, called out right when the photographer snapped a photo. I was pretty sure I turned towards his voice too quickly because I heard the photographer grumble as soon as the flash went off. "Tug your pants down a little more."

I furrowed my brows at him.

I glanced at the photographer, Connor, and the social media manager. They all gave me expectant looks.

Marketing.

I obliged, tugging them indecently low, earning a whistle from John. I lifted my middle finger at him in response.

"Sex sells, buddy." John laughed. The photographer snapped a few more images and waved for the next player to take my place. I could feel every muscle in my body relax as I stepped off-set toward John.

You okay? John signed. John's husband was completely deaf, which resulted in his ability to communicate with me via ASL. I was grateful because when I joined the team, he was a ringleader in getting the coaches to learn a few short-hand phrases that would help me be able to communicate on the ice since I couldn't shout like everyone else.

I lifted a shoulder and responded, *Just don't like being paraded around like a show dog.*

"Yeah, I'm sure your paycheck will help you get over it," John replied. I flipped him off again before signing, *asshole.* I quickly tugged a shirt on, hating the feeling of the sticky oil against the fabric.

"Hockey romances are really having their moment," John shrugged, "Having read a few myself, I understand Angie's angle here." John was always upbeat and good-natured, never irritated about anything. He was my opposite and sometimes reminded me of a guy version of Courtney.

I remembered Courtney telling me about hockey romances a while ago because she was introducing Josh to her love of reading romance novels, and for a while that was literally all they would talk about. I had gotten good at disassociating whenever the topic came up because I hadn't read a romance novel once in my life and didn't really plan to.

I remembered Eloise's random declaration a few nights ago, *I read alien erotica.* The thought brought a smile to my face. It was so out of left field, and for some reason seeing her so embarrassed about it was almost endearing.

...Did Eloise read hockey romance novels? Or was she specifically into aliens?

Perhaps the social media manager (Angie, apparently) was going to be more helpful to me than I thought.

"All right, that's it for today!" Angie clapped her hands after calling the group. Half the guys started clapping and cheering, too, as if we had all actually done something instead of lip sync pop songs and stand around half naked for the sake of sales.

"Hey, can I ask you guys something?" Connor had walked up to John and me right when we had each grabbed our bags to leave for the day.

"Sure, what's up?" John replied. Connor thumbed away at his phone for a second longer before pocketing it and making eye contact with the two of us.

"If I had an opportunity for you guys to work with kids, would you be interested in that?" I hesitated, but John shrugged.

"Depends, what is it?"

"My daughter, Stella, used to go to this early intervention clinic"—Connor's words were ringing a bell in my head for some reason—"It's basically a place where kids with Down Syndrome and other conditions go for help. Anyway, if I set something up where you guys got involved, would that be something you're into?"

"Yeah, I don't mind kids," John smiled, glancing over at me, and waited for my answer. I faced Connor and shrugged before a nod, confirming that I was okay with that.

Working with kids seemed better than stripping for the camera.

"It would be a good PR move, obviously," Connor lowered his voice, as if discussing PR strategies was secretive, "And it's not like we don't need positive PR."

Over recent years, many men in the NHL were getting

expelled because of women speaking out about their sexual harassment. Recently, a number of claims have come up across the country. This was also happening with almost every male-dominated sport, ever. Based on what I had personally heard men say in the confines of the locker room over the entirety of my life, I wasn't shocked that women were coming forward. Men in this field tended to have fragile egos, and women were almost always the victims of that.

So, in a roundabout way, I guess hockey really did need a bit of rebranding.

Was taking some pictures with kids for our social media accounts going to be the rebrand it really needed? No. But whatever.

I had also personally heard Connor say, "It's not *all* men" whenever NHL allegations had come up in conversation, so I didn't really bother to ask for his opinion on anything beyond our professional relationship. Courtney had explained it to me perfectly a few years ago. If you were a man who knew that he had never pressured a woman, you simply wouldn't feel offended or threatened when women say blanket statements like, "men are trash." You would be confident enough deep down to know that you did not fall into that category, but also be able to recognize that men are still ninety-nine percent of the perpetrators in sexual assault cases.

I hadn't thought about the issue too much before that conversation, but that made a lot of sense to me. It stuck.

"Plus," John spoke up, pulling me from my thoughts, "It would give me a way to show Alonzo what a wonderful parent I'd be." John wiggled his blonde eyebrows at me and pulled his shoulder-length hair back into a bun. The guy had baby fever the last few years, and his husband was more hesitant (or realistic, however you wanted to look at it) about having children.

"Oh, yeah," Connor smiled, as if he cared, "Anyways, I'll reach out to you guys when I have more details." John nodded and waved before taking off. I had intended to leave as well, but my phone buzzed and I halted my step to pull it out.

Courtney: Why are hockey terms so filthy?

Me: What do you mean?

Courtney: Gong show? Bender? Crease? Poke-check? Third man in?

Me: Lay off the smut.

Courtney: No. But also, gong show. Gong. Show.

"Do you date at all?" Connor's voice made me glance up from my phone, confusion was evident on my face based on the sheepish smile that showed off his freshly whitened teeth. "I'm not hitting on you. I'm into women. I was just curious." He eyeballed my phone as it buzzed again in my hand.

Courtney: I have successfully convinced Eloise that it is legitimately called the time-out box.

Courtney: I'm not correcting her. That's what it's called now.

Me: Classic.

"You probably don't have any issue with women," Connor's voice reminded me that he was still here for some reason, so I gave him a bored look. "I get it. I can pull a bit myself, though, there is this one girl who has pretty much given me the cold shoulder." His brows furrowed a little, his eyes distant as he thought about the, I assumed, intelligent woman who blew him off.

I shrugged; *It happens.* I signed. Connor didn't know ASL, so he pretended to know what I said and just continued talking.

"We hooked up a while back. It was great, and then she just stopped responding to me. I tried not to worry about it, because it's not like I don't have other options." It took everything in my power to not roll my eyes at him. He had shown me some pictures of women he had slept with, and they all looked half his age. It wasn't something to brag about, in my mind.

It just made me wonder why he couldn't seem to date a woman his own age.

"But I just ran into one of her friends recently, and now I can't get her out of my head," Connor sighed, crossing his arms as he stared at a point on the wall over my shoulder, "I don't know. Should I try again?"

I shook my head, and then signed, *No* for good measure. Connor shrugged.

"Yeah, you're probably right," Connor patted me on the shoulder, as if he and I were anything other than business associates and said goodbye as he walked over to speak with another one of his clients.

Courtney: You're still coming on Saturday?

Ah, yes, the beach day. I was one hundred percent going to be there.

Me: I'm planning on it.

Courtney: Great. Could you do me a favor and wear a shirt? I don't want to give my fiancé a stroke by being in a bikini and having him struggle between ogling me and ogling you.

I smirked as I walked through the facility doors that led to the parking lot, tapping away a reply as I made it to my car again. At first, it was weird to joke about Josh's crush on my physique so openly, but that was how Courtney was. It was also how Josh was, and after a few jokes and seeing those two together, I knew that there was no chance in hell that Josh was actually interested in me when he had Courtney. The confidence and security they had with each other in their relationship was admirable.

Me: If Josh can't control his thoughts when he sees too much of my skin, that's his problem.

Words I had heard Courtney use in reference to other men ogling her at the gym.

Courtney: You know what? Fair.

Courtney: Want to carpool?

And be at someone else's mercy in case I get bored and want to bail? No.

Me: I have some things to do beforehand, I'll meet you guys there.

Me: Who is going?

Courtney: Everyone, minus the band. So be nice to Eloise.

Me: I was perfectly nice to her last time.

Courtney: Yeah, perfectly nice as you stared directly at her ass.

Courtney: You're lucky that I caught you and she didn't.

I frowned. I didn't respond to that text until I had driven all the way home from the rink. I currently lived on the outskirts of Irvine, bordering Tustin where the gym that Courtney and I attended was. I lived in a small one-bedroom apartment and had for years. Most of the other guys on the team felt like they needed to blow their paycheck on luxury living, but I wasn't one of them. I liked simplicity. I didn't need much, and I liked the comfort of having spare funds in case of emergencies.

Courtney's text still bounced around in my brain. What would have happened if Eloise caught me staring at her ass?

Me: You're right. She probably would have dumped her water bottle on me or something.

I figured just admitting that I was an ass-starer would be the easiest route to go with Courtney.

Courtney: Probably.

I frowned again. Would Eloise react that way? Or would she be pleased to know that I appreciated her body like that? Would she tease me, wearing those little shorts more often whenever we were together with our friends?

I was getting ahead of myself. I still wasn't sure where I stood with Eloise. I felt so unstable like one wrong move could send me plummeting down a black hole of nothing but hate and frustration from her. More pies squished to my chest, more insults to my genitalia.

I didn't want that.

I generally didn't care if people liked me or not. Such was life. You win some, you lose some. Even if I had let my little crush on her grow a little larger than was appropriate lately, I would settle for her simply not hating me anymore. She didn't need to like me like I was starting to like her.

Because, let's be honest, a grown man didn't think about a grown woman as much as I thought about Eloise unless he was very romantically interested in her. It was bad. I was constantly thinking about her in my spare time, especially late at night when I was plagued with dirty thoughts and made-up scenarios about what the two of us would be like together physically.

The last time I had masturbated this much I was a teenage boy.

I needed to do something about this, to get out of this weird limbo I felt like I was in with her. Attending the beach day, and successfully having another outing that didn't result in Eloise glaring daggers at me, seemed like a good start.

7

ELOISE

"Thanks for getting us in, Lo." Courtney squeezed my bicep as she trudged to where everyone else had found a spot to set up. Three Arch was a private gated community in Laguna Beach, with its own beachfront. It was smaller, cleaner, and ideal when you wanted to spend the day at the beach with your friends, if one of them was a popular, noticeable celebrity.

Half of my parents' friends lived here. It took one single call to get my name on the entry list.

"No problem," I smiled. I was a little relieved because Logan hadn't driven with us. Courtney told me to put his name on the list anyway and to let the guy at the gate know that he would use ASL to spell his name, but I figured the chance of him actually showing up was slim. He was known to bail and didn't hang out with us nearly as often as the rest of us got together.

Plus, I wasn't thrilled about Logan seeing me in my bikini.

…Okay, that was only a little bit of a lie.

I was still a little unsettled by the last time we were together. Where he had blatantly stared at my ass as I did pull-ups, but also didn't deny that he wanted to turn down my accidental advances on him.

Beck and Adam, the two paler people in the group, had set up their towels and umbrellas. I had brought one as well, but I actually looked forward to getting some sun on my skin.

"I'm sitting with the albinos." Taylor had pulled their sunglasses down off of their hat and slid them on their face. They were wearing a cutoff shirt with dark blue board shorts that matched their eyes.

"Do you need sunscreen on your scalp?" I asked them as I laid my towel down a little bit away. Taylor had a faded haircut, with fun geometrical designs shaved into the back of their head.

"Huh, actually that's not a bad idea." They then handed me a bottle of spray-on sunscreen and turned around. I stood on my toes a little bit as I sprayed and rubbed my finger along the designs, making sure every inch of the exposed skin in their hair was covered. "Thanks, girl."

"My turn." I handed them the bottle and pulled my shorts down before ripping off my t-shirt. I dropped my clothes on my towel and held my arms out to the side for Taylor to spray me.

Taylor blinked, their eyes scanning my body for a moment before clearing their throat. "Damn," they mumbled as they started on my arms.

"Are you okay?" I asked.

"Yeah," Taylor rubbed the sunscreen onto my arm before

spraying my other one, "Sometimes I just forget when my friends are really attractive."

I blinked, a warm blush covering my cheeks. "Oh."

Taylor glanced at me, their dark blue eyes a little narrow against the sun. "I'm not hitting on you, Lo," they reassured me with a low chuckle of their own, "I'm not ready for monogamy."

I gave them a quizzical look before they sprayed my chest and rubbed the sunscreen on there as well. "Wait, how do you know that I am? Maybe I'm not ready to settle down either."

"I promise you that you are," Taylor smiled as they sprayed my stomach and hips. I got to work rubbing that part in as they knelt down and sprayed my legs, rubbing the lotion in well afterward. "Plus, I'm not your type."

I frowned a little, considering that they were the last person I would expect to assume someone's sexuality. "How do you know what my type is?" I asked, planting my hands on my hips at my question.

Taylor stood tall and glanced at something over my shoulder, reaching their arm out and handing the bottle to someone as they spoke, "Hey, can you finish covering her back? I want to get in the water."

I saw Beck and Adam a few feet in front of us lounging on their towels, so I assumed Courtney had approached Taylor and me. I felt a presence step closer to me at the same time that a large, tanned, masculine hand reached over my shoulder and grabbed the spray bottle. My whole body stiffened at the realization of who was here. I would analyze how I knew that was Logan's hand later, but for now, I struggled to not panic at the thought of Logan's hands rubbing sunscreen all over my body.

"That," Taylor lifted a finger and gestured to the entirety of my face and neck, which were perfectly flushed, "Is how I know." Then they winked and jogged off towards the waves.

I swallowed a lump in my throat before I glanced over my shoulder to see the large man standing behind me, his hand with the sunscreen lifted, with his eyebrows raised in question. I gave him my back and looked down, allowing him enough skin to coat my neck and shoulders well. Then the spray dragged down my back.

Then it stopped.

I glanced behind myself again, getting caught by the way the sun made Logan's dark curly hair have some red in it before I asked, "Can you get my legs too?"

Logan's nod was stiff, but his dark eyes lowered towards my legs as I watched him spray me over my shoulder. I was wearing my thong bikini. A peach-colored thing that I liked wearing when I wanted to expose as much of my skin as possible, in hopes of having minimal tan lines.

Logan's jaw was clenched as he stared at my thighs and sprayed down towards my ankles.

"Can you—" I stopped, realizing that wasn't his job. "Actually..." I ended up just holding my hand out for the sunscreen. He handed me the bottle silently, and I twisted around and tried to spray my ass cheeks.

I sprayed them enough and used my hands to rub them in. "Thanks," I smiled up at him, but he was already looking away and setting his stuff down. He wore light gray board shorts and a white t-shirt that contrasted with his golden skin well.

Alright, then.

"Do you need some?" I asked, eyeballing him. Logan paused before standing to his full height again to look at me. I wasn't sure what he was thinking. His lips were in a hard line and it looked like there was a muscle popping in his cheeks, as if he was clenching his jaw.

I frowned, "You can just say no, you don't need to act all offended at the thought of needing sunscreen."

Logan's lips parted a little as he blinked, his dark brows furrowed as he lifted his hands, *I am not.* I frowned at this too, so he moved his hands again, *Yes, please.* And then he ripped his shirt off and stepped towards me, his arms hanging slightly away from his body as he looked over my head towards Adam and Beck.

It was glorious.

Logan must have had one hell of a dietitian and work-out regimen because his shirtless torso almost looked unreal. He had the body that fitness models dreamed of. Flawless skin, and a light smattering of dark hair on his chest. Sharp, defined pecs and abs and those little side ab things I had only seen on men who were photoshopped. He even had that sharp V low on his hips, guiding a light dusting of dark hair that led from his belly button to below his swim shorts. I was stupefied for a second or two before I remembered to start spraying him. The only flaw on the image was a couple of thick pink, jagged scars that cut across one of his pecs. It was the same type of scarring that trailed up the side of his face and neck. *Okay. So he did want sunscreen. Why did he look all annoyed at my question, then?*

I started spraying his shoulders, making him tip his chin up so that the spray wouldn't go into his mouth, I started rubbing it into his skin afterward as well. He didn't bother doing that to me, but I was trying to be a bigger person.

Okay, fine. I also really wanted to rub my hands all over his body. I wasn't one to look a gift horse in the mouth.

"I was just confused about the look you were giving me," I mumbled as I rubbed it in on his arm and shoulder, barely glancing at Logan as I rubbed the sunscreen into his arm. He was watching me. "I feel like whenever I try to talk to you, you look at me like I'm some sort of alien."

I sprayed his other shoulder and arm, rubbing it in. He shook a little, letting me know he was restraining laughter. So I paused my ministrations and glanced up at him.

Damn, he was tall.

Logan's lips were pressed a little tightly together, and the corner of his lips turned up just enough to let me know he was trying to hold it in. I narrowed my eyes at him as his hands lifted.

Your book. Logan signed. I cocked my head to the side, confused.

"What do you mean?" I asked. I kept my hand on his pec, mostly because it was a nice dense pec, but I played it off like I was distracted by our conversation and forgot my hand was still on him. He wasn't shrugging out of my touch or anything.

A-L-I-E-N P-O-R-N, Logan finger spelled for me, *I look at you like the porn you read?*

I pressed my lips together as my eyes widened, my cheeks heating from embarrassment. Fuck, was he really already teasing me? I knew blurting that out at the gym would come back to bite me in the ass. I knew that explaining to him that I read alien erotica would be worse than him thinking I had a crush on him. At least at the time, he was polite to me. Courtney was right when she suggested that if he thought I liked him he would be nicer. He didn't roast me as much at the gym.

Now, though, he was back to teasing me again. And it still felt condescending.

"No," I replied with a defiant raise of my chin, lowering my voice as I lifted the sunscreen to spray the rest of his chest. "Because in the porn that I read, the men look at the women they're interested in as if they'll starve without her," I explained, aggressively rubbing the sunscreen across Logan's abs. "They look like they're using every muscle in their body to keep from grabbing her and taking her, right then and there." I knelt down, ignoring how Logan stepped away from me one pace as I sloppily sprayed his legs and bare feet. "They don't look at women as you look at me; like you're disgusted."

I stood up and motioned for Logan to turn around, staring pointedly in between his pecs. God, they were massive.

Logan ignored me and lifted his hands, *You – me.*

"Huh?" I asked, not understanding all the words he used.

Logan signed again, stepping forward and lowering his head closer to mine as he mouthed, *You are blind.*

"How?" I rolled my eyes and walked around him, spraying his back and shoulders. I was lazy and knew that I would miss spots, but I didn't care. Why I was even continuing to coat him in sunscreen at this point was a mystery to me.

"Do I get to rub my hands all over him next?" Josh's voice interrupted our conversation, and Logan's jaw clenched again before we both turned to the side to see Courtney and Josh approaching us. They were both wet from their waists down, having already dipped into the ocean.

"Are you arguing again?" Courtney placed her fisted hands on her hips, frowning at Logan and me.

"Yeah," I replied, slapping the bottle of sunscreen against Logan's chest, and walking towards the ocean, "But we're done." I wanted to get away from him, because I wasn't going to look at Logan the rest of the day. I had gotten my fill. Honestly, minus the conversation, rubbing sunscreen on him would be enough to fuel my spank bank for the time being. I knew that was shitty of me, but I accepted that.

I had dipped into the ocean, going completely under, and wetting my hair in an attempt to cool myself off. I only stayed in there for a few minutes, hanging out with Taylor who was in the water with their cutoff shirt on and everything. After we started splashing each other so much that I was coughing up salty ocean water, we finally called a truce and trudged back to the group.

Adam and Beck were making out on their towels under their umbrellas.

Josh and Courtney were on the other side of Logan's towel, chatting with him.

Taylor had just gently crawled on top of Adam and Beck

in a silly attempt to remind them that they weren't alone and had made Beck gasp loudly from the shock of a wet body pressing against her. I had accepted that I would sit by myself on my towel next to Logan.

I pulled on my sunglasses, grabbed my phone, and laid back in the sun.

I was reading a historical romance on my e-reader app, immediately lost in the story of corsets and sexism and swooning and exposed ankles, when I noticed it had gotten suddenly quieter around me. Unsure of how much time had passed, I glanced around to see that Beck, Adam, and Taylor were gone, back in the ocean on surfboards that Adam had brought. Beck and Taylor couldn't stand up on the board to save their lives, and Adam was laughing at their failed attempts.

Courtney and Josh were closer to the waves where the sand was wet, clearly digging some sort of hole and occasionally tossing dirt on each other.

I glanced to my side, and Logan was right there, reclined on his back a foot away from me with a baseball cap resting over his face, and his hands tucked behind his head. He had dark tufts of hair in his armpits, and his biceps popped with the position he lay in.

I allowed myself time to ogle Logan.

He was unfairly good-looking.

Suddenly, his arm shifted and he lifted the cap from his face. His dark eyes were on me as I quickly turned my attention back to my phone. Movement from his hands caught my vision and I turned to glance at him, breaking my ignoring Logan rule I had set for the day.

Are you mad at me? Logan asked.

I let out a loud, dramatic, annoyed sigh.

"No," I replied, only lying a little bit, "I'm just not bothering with you anymore."

What do you mean? He asked. I didn't know all the signs in that sentence, but Logan had clearly mouthed the words to his question for my benefit, helping me understand him.

"It means," I inhaled again and set my phone down, sitting up to face him as I spoke, "That I'm not letting you get to me anymore." I needed to do this a long time ago, but no better time than the present. "I'm not going to let you mock or bully me for things that don't matter. So what if I read alien porn? It's probably better than whatever horseshit you watch on Pornhub."

Logan frowned before he sat up to face me back, his hands going to work as he mouthed his sentence for me, *I don't try to be mean to you, Eloise.*

Seeing him use my name sign made my heart thump hard in my chest, and I went out of my way to ignore it.

"That doesn't make me feel better, Logan." My voice sounded small even to my own ears, but it was true. I knew I was sensitive; I thought it came with the whole people-pleasing part of my personality that I had been working hard to deconstruct the last few years. So the fact that he supposedly, unintentionally hurt my feelings was more embarrassing than anything.

Logan scrubbed a hand down his face, clearly struggling. Part of me felt bad for not being better at ASL. I didn't truly try to start learning until after I had started working at the clinic with everyone, because a lot of the kids relied on ASL as well. I picked up core words easily enough, but shorthand and filler words, and sentence structure were all things that I was still struggling with.

I was trying, though. Just last night I felt the need to restart a free online course.

We both sat there, silently watching all our friends either attempt to surf or dig a massive hole in the sand. They were much too far away to hear us, the sound of the ocean draining any chance of my voice carrying over. Logan had taken a deep breath before facing me again, waving his hand in my peripheral to get me to turn and look at him.

I'm sorry, Logan signed and mouthed, *I want to do better.*

I lifted a shoulder because he had already told me the same thing at the engagement party a few weeks ago.

I'm serious, Logan tried again, narrowing his eyes as he shifted closer to me, *I don't want to hurt your feelings. Or embarrass you.*

I lifted an eyebrow at him, my expression flat.

Okay, Logan's lips twitched a little before he continued to sign and mouth his words to me, *I don't want to embarrass you* too *much.* I rolled my eyes and tried to turn away from him before he reached forward and wrapped one of his large hands around my thigh. I was immediately reminded of our size difference from the gesture. His thumb brushed against the inside of my leg and his pinky wrapped around the other side, his fingertips pressing a little into my skin.

It made my nervous system take off, which is probably why I blurted out this next sentence while I stared at the way his hand firmly gripped my thigh, "Are you just trying to be nice because of the messages I sent you?"

Logan's hand flexed on my leg at my words, before he gently removed his hand and signed again, *No.*

"You sure? Because you were much nicer to me at the gym. The nicest you'd ever been, actually." I felt the corners of my lips turn down a little bit. "I don't know if I really want your pity."

I don't pity you, Logan signed and mouthed for me, *I—*

"We need you!" I heard Josh gasping from a few feet away, making me turn my head before Logan could finish the rest of his sentence. Josh was jogging closer to us and stopped a few feet away before he braced his hands on his knees and let his head fall, catching his breath.

"What?" I asked, smirking at how exhausted he looked.

"We didn't bring shovels, so we need more hands," Josh explained, "For the hole."

"Why are you digging a hole?" I asked, looking behind Josh to see Taylor and Courtney's thighs deep into the hole as they scooped handfuls of sand out.

"Because we're at the beach? It's what you do. You in?" Josh lifted his head and eyeballed Logan and me, his dark brown eyes narrowing a little bit.

I feigned an annoyed sigh and started to stand up from my place on the towel, "I guess I can help."

Josh smiled and lifted both of his fists in the air before pointing at Logan, "You, too!" I didn't bother to turn around to see if Logan was following us. I just knew that he was, based on who Josh must have been chatting with. I was mildly grateful for the interruption from Josh because I felt anxiety rise in me the more Logan and I attempted to iron out the wrinkles in our acquaintance. I'd like to get to the point where he and I would consider each other friends, but I wondered if I really wanted to settle for a pity friendship from Logan.

I knew that I would have settled for that a few years ago, but I didn't think I wanted a pity friendship now. I had been working on myself. I wanted to become someone who didn't rely on the acceptance of others to feel valued as a person. If Logan wanted to actually be my friend because he respected me to some degree, or simply didn't hate me, then sure. I would befriend him like everyone else.

A pity friendship? Because he thought I had an unrequited crush? Nah. Hard pass.

8

LOGAN

There was no excuse, I sucked.

That beach trip with Eloise was really what made me come to this conclusion. I guess it had started when I'd walked down the wooden steps to the beach, happy that it really was so empty and quiet like Courtney had said. However, when I approached the group and saw Eloise strip down into her little bikini set, I had felt all moisture leave my mouth and every one of my brain cells die.

Taylor was lathering her up in sunscreen, chatting about something I hadn't bothered to try to pay attention to because I was too busy struggling to not stare at her bare ass cheeks. I had walked over to the umbrellas they were standing by, waving at Courtney and Josh who were walking hand in hand in the waves, and nodding at Taylor as I met their eyes and approached.

And then Taylor had told me to finish spraying down Eloise.

I was able to without getting too hard. Hard enough for

others to notice, at least. I'd had to think about some pretty horrible and disgusting things to keep my dick focused, but it worked. I hadn't dared rub the sunscreen into her skin, though. I knew I would be made if I laid a single hand on her. My eyes couldn't stop flicking all over her exposed skin, the flower tattoos on her hip and thigh, and the one that I had now finally seen the entirety of on her ribs, curving with the shape of her breast. Plus, I wanted to talk to her about whatever was hovering in between us before I laid a finger on her. Before I assumed that she truly, truly wanted me to touch her like that. I did not want any mixed signals or misunderstandings between us if there was a reality where I *could* touch her like that.

That day changed me because now I physically ached for Eloise.

Prophecy fulfilled; I still managed to upset her again. Thankfully she didn't shove a dessert in my chest or assume the size of my penis, instead, she just seemed resigned. Which felt oddly worse than her usual anger and glares. I didn't want her to feel like she had to give up, and her comment about me being nice to her simply out of pity didn't sit right with me either. But then the universe decided to give me the middle finger by allowing someone else to interrupt yet another fucking conversation between the small woman and me.

"Thoughts?" Josh asked, making me blink to clear my vision and focus on the task at hand. We were all at a swanky high-end suit store somewhere in LA. It was exclusive, required reservations months in advance, and catered to celebrities like Joshua Madey. The rest of the band was here too, Tom and Kyle, inseparable as Kyle gave Tom multiple ties and squares to try out. The bassist silently accepted all the accessories that I had the feeling he would never wear if Kyle wasn't his partner.

Garrett was there too, sitting in between Adam and Taylor as all our heads lifted to attention at the sight of Josh in his new suit combination.

This was one of two fittings, we all still needed to get our measurements taken.

"No," Taylor shook their head, eyeballing Josh up and down before pulling their phone out again, "That tone will wash Courtney out when you stand next to her. You either need to go lighter or darker if you like that color."

Josh frowned as he held his arms out and circled once, taking in his appearance from all angles thanks to the multiple mirrors that surrounded him.

"I wouldn't have even thought about that," Josh shrugged and stepped back into the dressing room as he tugged off the suit coat, "Thanks, T."

"Yup."

"Are you bringing anyone to the wedding?" Garrett, Carbon Cut's lead guitarist, asked Taylor. He elbowed them with a dramatic wiggle of his black eyebrows. He recently let his hair grow out a bit, concealing the tattoos he had on the sides of his head.

"Not sure, it's kind of hard to secure a casual date when the wedding is a year from now," Taylor smiled. "Are you?"

Garrett responded by punching Taylor in the thigh, who just cackled at the response.

"Believe it or not, Kate is still with me, you asshole." Garrett chuckled at the ribbing he was used to from everyone.

"It's true," Kyle piped up from his position over the table of pocket squares, his bright blue hair sticking out on all sides, "She's even kissing him in front of us now."

"I almost couldn't believe it," Tom added, holding up a pocket square for Kyle to eyeball next to a tie, "I didn't know they actually kissed until a few weeks ago."

"Shut the fuck up," Garrett smirked, flipping off his drummer and bassist.

"She likes her privacy, then?" Adam asked, crossing one ankle over his knee as he leaned his head back against the wall that the bench that they were all sitting on was up against. I was in a chair off to the side, listening like always.

"Mostly she just didn't want to show a lot of PDA in front of the other guys on the off chance that we didn't work out," Garrett shrugged, "Which made sense to me. If we broke up, it would be easier to go back to our business relationship without the habit of kissing each other goodbye on set, you know?"

"I understand that." Adam nodded as he scratched a spot on his head, messing up his dark red locks, "Beck and I are strictly professional at work as well."

Taylor snorted, "Yeah, okay."

Adam rolled his eyes at Taylor's remark, "You only saw us one time, T."

"It was enough." Taylor sat forward to address the rest of us, "I had walked into Beck's office and was surprised when I hit something on the other side of her door, so I peeked around it and saw Beck literally jumping off of Adam."

The guys chuckled at Taylor's retelling, making Adam blush enough to conceal some of the freckles that dotted his face.

Eloise's freckles on her nose did similar things when she blushed.

Fuck, now I was thinking about all the fun ways that I could make her blush.

But first I had to fucking talk to her.

"Are you bringing anyone to the wedding, Logan?" Josh had joined the conversation again, stepping out of the changing room for one second before glancing at himself in the mirror and aggressively shaking his head. He went back into the changing room without another word.

That was the right call. He was not the kind of guy who could pull off an all-white suit.

No, I replied.

"Why not? I'm sure you have options." Taylor asked, eyeballing my arms that were crossed over my chest. I stared at them until they met my eyes again, and then they just winked at me before glancing down at their phone. No shame for checking me out.

"Do you want to bring anyone?" Kyle asked, his eyes still glued to all the accessories. Tom shook his head before he rubbed a free hand through his short military-style cut.

"Leave him alone," Tom warned his boyfriend. Kyle stuck his tongue out at Tom in response.

I shrugged at that, rubbing the back of my neck as I thought about it.

I hadn't needed a formal date for anything in a very long

time, and the thought of finding someone to fill that role stressed me out.

Eloise's glacial blue eyes and pink lips came to mind, and I shoved the thought away before I got lost in my fantasies again.

"I think you should go with Eloise," Adam chimed in , his eyes glued to his phone as if his words didn't shock me to my core. Adam was Eloise's ex, and that comment from him felt very weird.

Taylor leaned forward to give Adam a confused look. "She hates him."

Adam shrugged. "She's just intimidated by him."

All the guys turned to look at me, waiting for me to add something to the conversation. I frowned. Adam was the only one proficient enough in ASL, and Taylor only knew the dirty words and slang. This conversation was already stressing me out.

Eloise doesn't want to be my date, I confirmed, mouthing my words clearly for everyone else's benefit.

"I've been trying to get Courtney to set the two of you up since before she and I got together," Josh piped in, stepping in front of the mirror as he stared at himself in a dark navy suit. His sentence made my shoulders tense and my jaw clench because that was news to me.

"Oh, I like that one," Taylor added. I felt my shoulders relax because the conversation would easily move on now. We all agreed that the one Josh was currently wearing would be the suit for the big day and that we all wanted to match. So we each had to stand up on the platform while the seamstress squatted around each of us and took her sweet time getting our measurements. We would have to come back later and try all the suits on to confirm the fit.

The band finished getting their measurements, and Taylor was taking their turn standing up for the seamstress, when the conversation came right back to haunt me.

"So why did you try to set up Logan and Eloise?" Taylor asked, their arms fully extended away from their bodies.

"Oh," Josh blinked, remembering what he had brought up earlier, "Because they would be cute together." Everyone turned to stare at me, making embarrassment course through my veins. I shifted uncomfortably in my seat before Adam nodded his head almost as if he was approving the pairing.

"You'd be good for her," Adam added, leveling me with his stare. I tugged the collar away from my shirt, suddenly feeling like I was suffocating. Everyone was waiting for me to say something, so I fumbled my next signs with my hands due to randomly being under the spotlight.

Eloise would disagree with you, I signed and mouthed.

"Probably," Adam replied, a small smile on his face, "But I'm sure you could convince her."

I furrowed my brows a little bit at his words, *I should not have to convince a woman to be my date to a wedding.*

"You're right," Adam nodded once in agreement with me, "But I don't think you realize how very little convincing you would actually need to do. You like her, yeah?"

What the fuck? Was I that fucking obvious? Since when were Eloise and I so openly discussed like this? Heat from embarrassment crawled up my neck, I rubbed my hand on the back of my scalp as I frowned and tried to find a way out of this conversation.

"She sure as shit likes his body." Taylor nodded at the seamstress before stepping down off the stool and switching places with Adam.

I blinked at Taylor's words.

Eloise does *like me.*

"Is that a blush that I see?" Josh lifted a tattooed finger towards my face as if he was about to poke my cheek, and I smacked his hand away in irritation. He laughed before he continued speaking, "I mean, she did send you some spicy voice memos."

I lifted my eyebrows at Josh, unsure how he knew that. "Yeah, I know about it." He confirmed with a wink, "I was there the morning after when she was pacing around the kitchen and freaking out about what she had done after having a little too much wine."

If she was drunk, then she probably didn't mean it. I replied.

"That's not how alcohol works," Garrett added, after watching my mouth that formed the words my hands signaled. "It lowers your inhibitions; it doesn't magically make you develop an attraction towards people."

I felt my frown melt away at his words, pondering them.

He had a point.

I kept going back and forth regarding hypothetical reasons to explain Eloise and her behavior towards me after I received those voice memos, but every time I tried to broach the subject with her, it got derailed. Did I want something intimate with Eloise? Obviously. I just didn't know what to do about it. How to talk to her without someone fucking interrupting us, or her misinterpreting my words.

Eventually, through signing, and Adam having to vocalize a good chunk of my communication to the rest of the guys and Taylor, I briefly explained my predicament with Eloise. As soon as Adam had confirmed that I was interested in Eloise like *that*, Josh shot both fists up into the air in celebration, pumping them a couple of times before settling back in his seat.

"So, talk to her. Tell her how you feel." Josh encouraged.

"It sounds like you two just need space to communicate without everyone else around. One-on-one." Tom added, standing straighter after Kyle rested a top hat on his head.

Easier said than done, I explained, adrenaline pumping in my veins at the knowledge everyone in this room had of me now, *We have a communication barrier.*

"Hot," Josh smirked, clearly referring to the voice memos that Eloise sent me. I wasn't sure what to think of that.

"You have a phone, yes?" Garrett asked, his gaze landing on where the rectangle stuck out in my pocket, "Use it."

I frowned; *I don't know if I can text her unannounced yet.*

"I think you can." Josh encouraged, his teeth playing with his lip ring as he eyeballed my phone in my pocket as well.

"You won't know unless you try!" Kyle sang as he pulled the top hat off of Tom and stood up on his toes for a kiss. Tom obliged before turning to face me with his words of encouragement.

"Just text her. Start small. The worst she could do is say

she isn't into you like that, which really seems unlikely after what everyone else has said."

I stared at the couple on the far side of the room, at how comfortable Kyle and Tom were reaching for each other. How Kyle could wander over to the cufflinks and Tom would follow him without a word and wrap his arms around his partner's shoulders, planting a quiet kiss on Kyle's head while Kyle just smiled and leaned into the contact, content as he browsed men's accessories.

I felt an ache in my chest and reached my hand up to rub it a little before I thought about the sensation too much.

"Just text her," Adam encouraged from his new spot on the seamstress' stool. "Worst case scenario, you still don't have a date for the wedding. Best case scenario…" he let his sentence trail off and shrugged, standing taller at the seamstress's silent wave of her hand for him to do so.

The conversation shifted again, which I was only a little grateful for. Part of me wanted to blurt out a number of questions to the group, along the lines of "What do I say?" and "What should I start with?" or even "Do people just text 'hey' anymore?" I felt out of my league, I hadn't texted a woman specifically to have a conversation with her in years.

I decided that I would do it, though.

I couldn't remember the last time I had openly spoken with another group of masculine people about a woman I was interested in. I think the last time I truly did so was back in high school before my accident. Damaged vocal cords made life significantly more difficult when it came to establishing relationships, especially for someone like me who was already introverted. In college, very little communication needed to take place for a woman to want to have sex with me. The same goes for all the hookups I had after signing with the NHL.

I thought about it some more as I took my turn to get measured, noticing how the seamstress's cheeks blushed as she ran the measuring tape up my leg, across my chest, and around my arms.

I knew I was attractive to some degree.

Courtney and Josh went out of their way to remind me of that every fucking day.

…Was that something I could use to my advantage when it came to Eloise?

9

Weeks had passed since I had both seen or spoken to Logan St. James.

Not going to lie, it was kind of a relief. Thankfully our schedules hadn't synced up, because I was busy helping my boss, Pat, organize a few events for the early intervention clinic, and I was usually too tired and burnt out at the end of the day to do too much with my friends.

I had a lot going on.

My mother was constantly calling and trying to get me to hang out with her and her friends again. I had limited myself to two brunches over the last month and a half, which seemed reasonable to me. She was clearly upset about the distance I had quickly put between us since moving out, but she was a prideful woman and went out of her way to avoid letting me know that she was struggling with all of it.

I was okay with that.

Which was huge, considering it was me. I was raised by my parents to smile politely, never stir the pot, and never say no. It was wildly unhealthy, but that was the world they lived in. They were both raised the same way as kids, so it checked out. I, however, was breaking the generational curse. Saying no was okay, and I didn't always have to smile and bend over backward to avoid hurting the feelings of others at the expense of my own comfort and peace.

Eloise Bane was a new woman, and I liked this version of myself much better.

"Lo?" I heard Pat ask from behind me. I swiveled in my chair at the front desk and smiled at the older woman and her use of my new nickname.

"Yes?" I replied as I saved my work on the schedule and gave her my full attention.

"I have a meeting in the next half hour, and I was hoping you would join me for it and take notes," Pat explained as she set her bag down. She had just returned from lunch.

"Sure, what's the meeting for?" I reached across my desk and grabbed one of the notebooks I had for such occasions. Pat was a great leader, but detailed organization was not her strong suit.

That's where I came in.

"Were you here when Mr. James and his daughter Stella were clients?" Pat asked, sitting at her desk and staring at her computer screen. I froze, my thumb pressing on my pen to click it open before I wrote today's date on the paper.

"Um. No," I replied. I knew that Daddy James had been a client here because Beck and Courtney had told me so when I ran into him last year at a random club in LA. Apparently, he had the balls to ask Beck out at her place of work, in the middle of her workday. They knew that I had regretfully slept with him and made sure I didn't bump into him again the rest of the night. I had avoided his random texts and calls throughout the last year, simply ignoring them. When I knew my dad was hosting another poker night, I went out of my way to be out of the house and do literally anything else with my time. I hadn't actually seen him face-to-face since the night we spent together.

"Oh, well he reached out and wanted to see if I would be interested in an opportunity he had," Pat shrugged, "I thought I would hear him out."

I gulped, anxiety taking over my stiff movements.

"Alright," what was I going to tell Pat? Can I please not be in the same building when he shows up? I may or may not have slept with him in some attempt at self-sabotage and I didn't want to face the consequences of my actions? I nodded and turned back towards my computer screen, tapping my fingers on the desk as I mentally braced myself for seeing him in the next half hour.

It wasn't like he would bring up what we did once he realized I worked here, and that I would be taking notes during this meeting. He wasn't a total idiot, I figured.

I rattled off a text to Courtney, letting her know I would be panicking the rest of the day depending on how the upcoming meeting with Daddy James went. Minutes later, Courtney wandered up to the front desk that I was sitting at and rested her elbows on the surface, placing her chin in her fists.

"How are you doing?" she asked, raising her eyebrows at me expectantly.

"Alright." I smiled nervously, letting her know with my

eyes that I didn't want Pat to know why I would be weird. Courtney nodded subtly, but then came around the desk and pulled up a spare chair, playing with a rainbow pop-it toy that we sold to a couple of kids who benefitted from fidget toys.

"Did Rosie's mom cancel again?" Pat asked Courtney. Courtney nodded; eyes focused on the popper.

"I could use the break anyway, so I thought I'd hang out with you guys before whatever meeting is on the calendar today." Courtney casually replied. I really appreciated her. She was a true, supportive friend. My other friends I had growing up would never bend over backward like this to stay with me to make sure I was doing okay. Courtney didn't even need to be specifically asked to do this for me, instead she just saw that I was in some sort of distress from my text message and came right in. She didn't question the fact that her presence would be appreciated when Daddy James walked through those doors.

The next half hour went by smoothly, Courtney making Pat and I laugh as she spun around in her chair like a bored child before the glass doors to the clinic opened and a bell chimed. I held my breath before I glanced up, bracing myself for over-whitened teeth and orange-tinted skin, when my heart jumped out of my chest at the sight before me.

"Whoa, what are you doing here?" Courtney asked, leaning forward on the desk, and holding a fist out for Logan to bump.

That's right, Logan St. James had just walked through the front doors of the clinic. He looked just as surprised to see Courtney and me here but quickly recovered as he fist-bumped Courtney. He had two other large men with him, who were glancing around the clinic curiously.

Logan's hands started working, and Courtney's eyes widened as she flicked her eyes toward me.

"You're here for the meeting with Pat?" Courtney vocalized his words for Pat and me. Pat stood up from her seat and walked around the front desk to properly shake hands with Logan and the other two men I hadn't met before.

"Do you work with Connor James?" Pat asked after she introduced herself.

Logan nodded his confirmation.

Oh dear god. My stomach sank into my gut.

This was the worst.

The absolute worst.

Not only was I going to be nervous taking notes in a meeting with Connor, but Logan had to fucking be here too? How did he even work with Daddy James?

"Oh, I didn't know Dad—Connor was your agent." Courtney's voice sounded through the slight ringing in my ears. I was gripping my notebook so tightly that the knuckles in my fingers ached, and I quickly dropped the notebook to flex some blood flow back into them.

Fuck me.

Logan had noticed my hand fidgeting, his dark eyebrows raising a little bit as he took me in before signing again. I was too focused on the reality I had to face as soon as the last man I had slept with came through that door.

"Yeah, she started last year!" Courtney's voice started again. I blinked to clear my almost tunnel vision before I willed myself to focus on the conversation happening in front of me. Pat was chatting with the other two men who entered the facility with Logan, while he and Courtney were leaning on the front desk a few inches from me and staring at me.

I gave a wobbly smile to them both, inhaling a little more loudly than what was appropriate before I spoke, "Yup! I'll be taking notes in the meeting." I smiled, holding up my notebook again as if I needed to provide evidence for that statement.

Logan's dark eyes glanced at the notebook and then back at me, before narrowing the slightest bit. He was suspicious. I didn't blame him. Courtney signed something to Logan, making his brows lower as he took in her words.

The door chimed, and I felt my whole body stiffen.

"You guys beat me here, I see," Daddy James's voice sounded. Logan's large body was blocking my view of the door, and I had accidentally locked eyes with him as I struggled to will my body to function normally. Logan's lips pulled down, and his eyes took me in as he slid closer to me and mouthed the words, *You, okay?*

I nodded stiffly, giving him a tight smile as Pat started gesturing for everyone to follow her to the conference room.

I went out of my way to walk behind the group, ignoring the questioning glances that Logan was giving me.

Daddy James didn't notice my presence until I had closed the conference room door, and he turned toward the sound. He didn't even seem shocked to see me, his smile came a little too easily and quickly. He went out of his way to shake my hand specifically before I had a chance to escape to my chair opposite him at the table. I felt my stomach churn, my heart galloping in my chest as I had to deal with the fact that this man had seen me naked, and clearly wanted a repeat experience, if the way he let his eyes dance all over my body was any indication.

I let the duty of taking notes during the meeting become a hyper-fixation simply to get through this experience. I kept my eyes down as I wrote more detailed notes than I ever had for any meeting.

The gist of it was, Daddy James wanted Logan and a couple of other players from the Ducks to have an opportunity to sponsor events with the clinic. During the off-season was a good time to work on PR and social media, and Daddy James wanted to do something that meant a lot to him and his daughter.

I could feel his eyes on me throughout the entirety of the meeting, and it made me want to peel the skin off of my body.

It lasted about forty-five minutes before Pat called it, letting the guys know that we had other meetings to attend. We didn't, but based on Pat's response throughout the meeting I had a feeling she really wasn't interested in whatever idea Daddy James had.

Thank fuck. I couldn't deal with Daddy James coming back to my place of work regularly.

We all stood up, and Pat and I shook hands with all the men and gestured for them to leave the conference room first. Daddy James lingered when he took my hand one final time, his fingertips brushing against the palm of my hand in a way that made my skin crawl.

"I'll see you around, Eloise," he mumbled low enough for

my ears only. I gave him a tight smile and fleeting glance before dropping my hand and clutching my notebook to my chest, clearly in a defensive posture.

I hated this.

I felt so gross whenever he looked at me.

Like he knew I wanted to forget about what we did, but he had no intention of letting me do so. Maybe I was just panicking. It wasn't like he was maliciously seeking me out that much anymore. The last text he sent me had been months ago, this was just a horrible coincidence. Logan didn't even know that Courtney and I would be there when he walked in.

Speaking of, in an attempt to keep myself from catching Daddy James's eyes and unintentionally leading him on, I let my eyes land on the least threatening option in the room: Logan was already staring at me, a confused and concerned look on his face as he took me in. He had his hands in his pockets as he turned and left the conference room, Pat following closely behind him.

I exhaled a breath of relief and ended up shutting the door behind Pat, allowing myself some privacy as I worked on my breathing in the safety of isolation. I even sat back down in a chair and did some breathing exercises I had seen Beck and Courtney teach overwhelmed kids that they were working with here.

A soft knock sounded, and Courtney and Pat were back in the conference room with me.

"Are you alright?" Pat asked, concern etching her features as Courtney took the chair next to me and started rubbing my back.

"I'm fine," I lied, "I just. I don't feel comfortable around

Da—I mean, Mr. James." I realized during the meeting that I needed to tell Pat enough for her to know where I stood. Why I had acted so closed off and quiet instead of my usual friendly bubbly work persona.

"Oh," Pat blinked, "Thank you for telling me…but, did something happen that I should know about?" She had pulled up a chair at the table as well. "I wasn't super inclined to let him use the clinic as a publicity stunt for his athletes, but now that I know you aren't comfortable working with him, I'll definitely be emailing Connor to let him know that we aren't interested."

"Thank you." I felt my lip wobble as a tear escaped my eye, relief washing over me at Pat's words. I wouldn't have to see him again here. I wouldn't have to email or correspond with him, or anything like that.

"Lo," Courtney's calm voice made me look at her. "Did something happen?"

"What do you mean?" I asked, having a feeling, but feigning ignorance just in case.

Pat leaned forward, exchanging a look with Courtney before they both focused on me and Courtney continued, "Between you and him. I know you mentioned that you hooked up before"—I glanced at Pat, embarrassed that my boss now knew why I was uncomfy around a former client's parent, but her expression held no judgment—"But was that…it?"

I shook my head, "We just hooked up one time. And yeah, it wasn't great." I huffed a laugh that didn't sound too funny to me.

Pat gave Courtney another look, before asking me, "Did he hurt you?"

I widened my eyes, "What? No." I shook my head again for good measure. "I mean, I didn't enjoy it. But he didn't force himself or anything. I consented." I thought back to the night for a moment, remembering just how immediately turned off I felt after I realized how much I didn't enjoy his touch. But I'd already made it that far, and he clearly had no intention of stopping, so I figured I would just rip off the band-aid and then leave as soon as possible afterward.

"Okay," Courtney's brows furrowed a little, "But he has reached out to you, right? Do you think his behavior is feeling dangerous?"

I could feel myself frown at her question, "No, no he isn't dangerous." Maybe just kind of a creep, and clearly clueless, but not dangerous. I thought for a moment, determined to ease their worries, "He's just, I don't know, annoying. He isn't taking the hint."

"Is he stalking you?" Pat asked. I felt my cheeks burn with humiliation. Dear god, how terrified did I look? I must have looked like a mess if this was where their line of questioning was leading. I quickly gave them a smile that was still on *this* side of wobbly before I reached out and touched Courtney's hand.

"No, no," I shook my head, "I am positive it was just a bad coincidence today. I didn't tell him I worked here. We know one of the players, and he was even surprised to see us here."

Pat and Courtney glanced at each other again before Pat nodded once and stood up from her chair.

"Thank you, though," I didn't want to brush off Pat's concern. I smiled at her and took a deep breath before continuing, "I appreciate you checking in. I'm sorry I got a little spooked."

"You're welcome, and don't apologize." Pat reached forward to squeeze my arm before standing again, "Take all the time you need in here. If you need to go home, just let me know. I'm sorry I even took the meeting with him in the first place, Eloise."

"Don't be. Please, don't be." I waved her apology away, wiping away the second stray tear of relief that fell down my cheek. "I wanted to be brave about it. I didn't realize how anxious I would be until now."

"Of course, no problem at all." Pat squeezed my arm once more and left, leaving Courtney and me in the room.

My phone buzzed in my pocket, and because I was thankful for a distraction, I pulled it out to immediately see who was reaching out.

My heart skipped when I read Logan's name in the text message.

Logan: Are you all right?

A nervous giggle fueled by the remaining adrenaline in my veins escaped my lips at his message, allowing Courtney to lean over my shoulder to read it. She rested her head on my shoulder as I typed back a reply to him.

Me: I'm fine. I just wasn't expecting Daddy James to show up at my work today.

Logan: Fuck. I was worried it was because *I* showed up at your work today.

Logan: I was ready to apologize for ruining your day and everything.

Me: I mean, you brought him. So you can still apologize if you want.

Logan: I'm sorry for bringing Connor. I had no idea that my agent was the "Daddy James" Courtney had told me about.

Courtney giggled, "Look at you two, texting each other without insulting each other." I smiled at her encouragement, pinching her thigh a little in response to her teasing. She slapped my hand away and lifted her head off of my shoulder to rest her elbows on the table.

"I know." I let my brows furrow. "I don't think I have ever texted him casually like this...did you tell Logan why I was so uncomfortable around Connor?"

"No," Courtney replied. "When you were sitting there stunned at the front desk, I just told him that you weren't looking forward to seeing Daddy James. I never said why. I don't think I would have had time to, anyway."

I nodded.

Taylor had already told me before that I didn't need to justify why I had chosen to sleep with Connor, and that I was allowed to make that decision for myself and regret it afterward. However, part of me didn't want Logan to know the details of why I had been so uncomfortable around him simply due to pride and embarrassment.

Another part of me weirdly *wanted* him to know, for reasons I couldn't quite explain yet.

"Want to watch *Persuasion* tonight?" Courtney asked, rubbing my arm and providing the comfort I didn't need to ask for. I nodded my head and pocketed my phone, letting the conversation naturally end with the sometimes kind, large man.

10

ELOISE

My phone buzzed again as soon as the movie started. Susan was settled in one of her ugly accent chairs, me in the other, while Courtney and Josh were cuddled on the couch. It was Friday night, and we were too tired from our weeks to go out and do anything fun or exciting.

Logan: Was that not a good enough apology?

I blinked, confused. Then I realized I hadn't ever responded to his apology earlier today. I quirked my lips to the side and flicked my gaze up at the TV, pondering how to best respond. I liked that we weren't at each other's throats and that we were texting as if we were actually friends.

My heart was starting to pick up its pace for an entirely different form of anticipation as I settled deeper into the ugly accent chair, bundled in a throw blanket, and tapped my response back to him.

Me: It was a solid 6/10, not bad.

I was holding my breath as I waited for his response, hoping that my little text didn't come off as snobby or truly irritated. The teasing hadn't ever worked out for us in the past, but a certain type of consensual teasing clearly needed to happen.

Logan: A 6/10 is basically a D, which could be argued as a bad grade.

Me: It's not an F, though.

Logan: What kind of apology would earn me an A?

Me: You were one of those high-strung A+ students in school, weren't you?

Logan: I wasn't high-strung. I just earned perfect grades.

I smirked a little, happy with the tone of the conversation. What was he up to right now? It was late at night, and Susan would be in bed if we weren't formally having a movie night together. Was Logan out with the guys from his team? Was he home alone, watching some sports channel as he texted me?

Did he *want* to text me?

Me: A handwritten letter goes a long way, I think.

Logan: Like, with a pen and paper? Do you have any idea how much would have to go into me acquiring a pen and paper to simply write a letter?

Me: How badly do you want that A?

I bit my bottom lip after I sent that text, my pulse picking up a little bit as the movie in front of me was completely forgotten. I had been reading an absurd amount of romance novels the last few weeks, so I had that to blame for the fact that our conversation discussing giving grades seemed like the lead into an innuendo.

I had already told Logan I would let "him" do "things" to me in the voice memos that still haunted me with embarrassment at random times in my day, and we had recovered from that to some degree. Therefore, I didn't let myself spiral too much about this.

Logan: Hypothetically, if I didn't have supplies to write a letter at my apartment, what other options would I have to earn that A?

I popped my lip out from between my teeth.

Was this flirty?

Was Logan flirting with me?

Did he want me to say something flirty back?

I pressed my phone against my chest, my brain struggling to come up with something that balanced the line between flirty and friendly. Or should I take a leap and lean flirtier? This felt flirty. It had to be flirty. No grown man texted a grown woman this kind of question in total innocence.

Holy shit. Logan was probably flirting with me.

I didn't want to think too hard about the excitement I felt at the thought.

Me: Well, unfortunately for you I'm not interested in signed hockey merch or anything.

Logan: That would have made things a little easier on my end.

Me: I'm open to ideas if you have any.

There, the ball was thrown into his court. Or the puck into his rink? The point was, I had thrown the option back to him. I wanted to see if he would get flirty again, or if I was going crazy and misreading the tone of this conversation.

Logan: I have a few, but I'm not sure you would be interested in them.

Me: Oh?

Oh? Good job Eloise. I rattled off something else in an attempt to sound less lame.

Me: Feel free to share with the class.

That…didn't make me sound less lame. But it was better than a one-word response.

Logan: Are you alone?

I blinked, my mind racing with hypotheticals as to why Logan would ask that question right now.

Me: I'm in the living room watching TV with Susan, Court, and Josh. But they don't know who I am texting.

I glanced over my shoulder to see Josh fast asleep in Courtney's lap as she combed her fingers through his hair. Her eyes were glued to the TV. Susan's as well.

Me: Actually, I don't think that they even know I'm texting someone.

Me: Why?

Logan: Because what I had in mind is probably best kept private, just between us.

Holy fucking shit. Was he thinking what I thought he was thinking? Was this conversation flirtier than I anticipated? Dare I say, becoming spicy?

Me: Like a secret handshake?

Logan: No, not like that.

Logan: First, I need to know something.

Logan: Were you serious when you sent me those voice messages?

I felt my heart jump up into my throat. Holy shit, he was bringing that up? I thought we were supposed to be talking about ways he could apologize to me. What did those have to do with this?

Oh.

Me: When you say serious, what do you mean?

Because I was a lame, lame person who didn't know how to properly text a grown man to save my life.

Logan: Do you want me?

My face and neck flushed at the words he had intentionally typed out. I felt a little odd having this conversation over text message, but then I remembered who I was talking to, and realized that being able to write down our messages instead of blurting out words without thought was probably for the best. I gnawed at my bottom lip again, struggling to decide whether to lie or tell the truth. Or come up with an odd gray area between the two.

Me: In the spirit of being honest, I didn't mean to send those voice memos to you.

Logan: I figured.

Me: But.

Me: To answer your question.

I was such an ass. I hesitated for a few minutes before typing out the rest of my response. I closed my eyes and focused on controlling my body's physical reaction to the experience of telling Logan this version of the truth. How vulnerable I would be, and how I knew there was a possibility that I would be turned down yet again. Rejected. But I was okay with that. I was Eloise Bane 2.0, the Eloise who didn't mold herself to make others comfortable around her. I was the Eloise who laid it all out there and let people take it or leave it, in love with myself first.

Me: I do want you, even though I feel like I shouldn't.

I pressed send before I could talk myself out of it. I swore I felt my heart stop at the sight of the little "delivered" message underneath my text, letting me know he for sure saw it by now. I watched the three longest minutes of my life tick by on the clock on my phone before I saw those three little dots appear at the bottom of the screen, letting me know that he was replying to my confession.

Logan: Well.

Logan: That makes the ideas that I had in mind for ways to apologize to you significantly more fun, then.

Air rushed out of my lungs.

Was he…? Was he talking about sex? With me? He had to have been talking about sex. Was Logan saying that he wanted to have sex with me? Apologize to me with orgasms that I didn't have to give myself? The thought made a swarm of butterflies take off in my stomach.

Me: Feel free to describe your ideas in vivid detail.

Wow, bold much, Eloise? I was grinning to myself, re-reading his last message over and over and over again as I eagerly, anxiously waited for his reply.

Logan: I would if you weren't sitting in a room with other people right now.

I frowned, not taking the time to second guess my actions before I sat up from my chair and abruptly announced that I was tired and going to bed. Susan simply lifted her mug up to me in farewell whereas Courtney asked if I was okay before I waved her question off and sprinted upstairs. I jogged to my bedroom, quickly shut the door, and locked it (I had heard many stories of Courtney and Beck almost walking in on each other at inopportune times), and got underneath the covers of my bed, and responded to him.

Me: What if I told you I was alone in my room, hiding under my blankets?

Logan: I would like the sound of that, but I would probably want proof.

I smiled, the dirty dog.

I glanced down at my tank top and sleep shorts set, wondering how I could make it look more appealing. I ended up tugging my tank lower, adjusting my breasts in the built-in camisole bra thing so that they looked nice and plump. I also lifted the bottom a little and tried to make it fall naturally on my stomach, showing off my belly button, and tugged the legs of my sleep shorts up a little more to show off my flower tattoo as well as more thigh. I then quickly lifted my phone, bit my lip the tiniest bit, and snapped a picture. I glanced at the image, glad to see some of my face cut off so that only my nose and mouth showed. I was propped up on the elbow of my other arm, which helped my body look a little curvier than it was in reality.

Though Logan had seen me in a skimpy little bikini, so he already knew what I looked like.

I sent the picture to him anyway, adrenaline pumping in my veins from the excitement of what I was doing with him.

I couldn't remember the last time I had sent a flirty selfie to a guy.

His response came in quickly.

Logan: Fuck, Eloise.

Me: Your turn.

I grinned and smiled even wider when a picture message came in from him.

Logan was also in his bed, making heat flood in my lower belly at the image he had taken just for me. Logan was shirtless, his covers pulled low on his waist so that the band of his boxer shorts was peeking out the top. His head was cut off, but the jagged scar on his pec proved that it really was him. He was all golden skin and sharp muscle definition, with a light dusting of dark hair on his chest. His large hand rested low on his abdomen, just an inch or two away from the band of his boxers.

A second image came in.

I tapped on it with greedy fingers.

His hand was lower, the tips of his fingers tucked just underneath his boxers.

I gasped, my hand naturally falling towards my lower belly where excitement was burning throughout my skin.

Me: Would your apology include letting me touch you?

Me: I think it's only fair, after all.

Logan: I think it would make more sense if my apology included me touching you.

Logan: You wouldn't have to lift a finger.

Holy mother of god.

Me: Oh, of course. If you must. But I would probably get distracted if you were shirtless like that in front of me.

Me: I don't think I could resist touching you back.

Logan: I would distract you well enough.

I believed him. I reached underneath my bed and opened my DIY box, finding my favorite hot pink vibrator.

Feeling bold, I decided to take another picture of myself holding the toy. Then I decided to tug my sleep shorts down just enough to press the tip of it just where I was planning on using it, over the fabric of my panties. I took a second picture.

I sent the images before I could talk myself out of it.

Logan: You're killing me, sweetheart.

My heart thumped at the term of endearment, but I also chastised myself and reminded myself that this was spicy time, not lovey-romantic time.

Me: Where is your hand now, Logan?

I turned on the toy, teasing myself with it over my panties as my cheeks flushed and I anxiously waited for his reply.

Instead of a message, my phone started buzzing with an incoming FaceTime call.

Oh god, oh god, oh god, I thought as I hesitated. Texting felt safe, like there was a barrier between us as we teased each other. For some reason, a FaceTime call where we could both see each other in real time felt a little too real.

Don't be a chicken shit, Eloise. I chastised myself before I answered.

My toy was still buzzing in my other hand under my shorts, so I set my phone down next to me propped up against some spare throw pillows I set up before I settled back in my bed and took in the image on Logan's screen. He was holding his phone with one hand, his handsome face and shoulders taking up the image as he stared at me with a very hooded and flushed expression.

His other arm was moving off-screen, and I zeroed in on the movement.

"Let me see," I panted, focusing on working myself over with my toy while also enjoying the once-in-a-lifetime opportunity I had with Logan right now. "Let me see what you're doing."

Logan made a gasping sort of moan that sounded strained, due to his damaged voice. He glanced down at himself before he met my eyes through the phone again. An aroused challenge in his heavy gaze as he lowered the phone down to show his hand hiding underneath his black boxers.

Holy fucking shit. I was watching Logan masturbate. To me. He was looking at me and touching himself from it.

Suddenly, the image became fuzzy as he fixed something on his shorts and pulled the screen back.

He had pulled himself out of his boxers, gripping himself as he pumped roughly.

"Oh, my god." I gasped, my eyes widening at what I was

seeing. I knew Logan had large hands; I had felt them on my thigh weeks ago at the beach. What I was startled by was the proportion of...himself in his hand as he, well, worked himself.

Suddenly, the phone screen showed his face and neck again, and he nodded to me expectantly.

Your turn, his nod seemed to tell me. I bit my lip and squeezed my eyes closed as I tilted the camera angle down a little so that he could see where my hand disappeared underneath my shorts. I then pulled the toy out and pulled my panties away from me so that I could use the toy directly over my clit.

A string started tightening in my core at an alarming rate.

"Do you like this?" I asked him, glancing at the screen to see him nodding his head once. It was like he struggled between keeping his eyes open to watch me, or close them and focus on the feeling he was experiencing. "Do you wish you were here, making me feel like this?" I continued, feeling heat course through my veins at his nod of agreement, his arm moving a little faster at the sound of my question.

"I wish—" My orgasm was rising in me at an alarming rate, and it made words halt in my mouth for a moment before I powered through. "I wish you were the one touching me." I gasped the last sentence out before it bulldozed through me. I felt my arm stiffen as it held the toy perfectly over my clit, causing waves and waves of ecstasy to pulse through my core and wash over my limbs. My abs were painfully tight as my high lasted and lasted, putting on a show for Logan.

I heard a pained, low grunt from my phone and opened

my eyes to see Logan throwing his head back on the pillows on his bed, the veins in his neck bulging as he clenched his jaw and showed off his teeth. His eyes were squeezed shut as his teeth parted and he seemed to gasp through his release. His body jolted a little bit as I imagined what his hand looked like right now.

Finally, the last of my orgasm pulsed through me, and I quickly turned off my toy and tossed it away as I collapsed on my side. My breathing was labored after putting on that show for him.

Logan was still there, eyes closed as he lay on his pillows and caught his breath. His chest heaving.

Reality came crashing back down all around me.

Did I just...? Oh god, I did.

Without thinking about it, I quickly grabbed my phone and ended the FaceTime call. I was feeling embarrassed, and slightly scared from what I had just done. As seconds passed in silence, I knew I rationally shouldn't feel embarrassed at all. What I had done was totally normal, and we were two consenting adults. Also, and probably more importantly...I thoroughly enjoyed it.

Logan was clearly just as into it as I was, and we both rode the wave until the end goal was met.

But what do we do now?

When we see each other again, do we go about our day as if we hadn't jerked it to each other over FaceTime?

I lay in the darkness, my muscles slowly relaxing as my body came down from its incredible orgasm, when my phone buzzed with a message from Logan.

Before I could feel even more embarrassed, I opened the message from him.

Logan: Next time, I want to be there to hear those sweet little noises you make.

Logan: I want to feel that pretty blush on your skin.

My mouth dropped open, *holy mother of hell.*

He wasn't done.

Was he not embarrassed like I was? Of course not, he clearly wasn't spiraling about what we had just done. Fuck me. *Be brave, Eloise. He's offering hands-on orgasms, are you really going to say no to that?*

Me: Deal.

11

LOGAN

How do you start a conversation with another person after you both masturbated together over a FaceTime call?

What was the proper procedure?

Socially, what was the expected next move?

I was completely out of my element, feeling like I was driving blind when it came to Eloise. The number of times I stared at the pictures she had sent me the following nights were alarming. I ended up deleting the images after a week, thinking that she probably wouldn't feel comfortable knowing that I kept them for my own personal spank bank. I hated to do it because I was starting to become obsessed with her bedtime look, but it had to be done. I needed to keep a small shred of self-respect.

Two weeks had passed, and I had been too much of a wuss to text her again.

Two weeks had passed, and she hadn't texted me either.

Was that just because I hadn't texted her first? I texted her first last time, though I wasn't expecting to escalate the conversation to where it went. I figured it was her turn to text me first, right?

Was I overthinking this?

Courtney dropped her weights on the ground, making a loud crash echo throughout the gym, and successfully snapped me out of my thoughts.

I was startled, stepping forward too late to help her with her deadlift and realizing she was already bending down to grab her water bottle.

"You're in another world today," Courtney commented, looking me up and down like she was suspicious.

Sorry, I apologized, scrubbing a hand down my face.

The advice I received from Josh and the others was helpful in one sense. Through the powers of texting, as if we were teenagers, I had managed to communicate to Eloise that I wanted her. She was clearly receptive. This was good to know, even though I still had dozens of questions floating around in my mind.

Did she want me to take her on a date?

Did she want to keep it casual?

Did she change her mind, and she doesn't want to hook up with me anymore?

I frowned at that question. I knew she had the right to change her mind, but I couldn't help but feel like I was punched in the stomach at the thought. Oddly enough, jerking off to risqué pictures of her wasn't enough for me.

I wanted more.

How *much* more was yet to be determined.

"Hey," Courtney snapped her fingers in my face, making me focus back on her again, "Were you even listening?"

I shook my head in the negative.

Sorry, Court, I'm too busy obsessing about Eloise Bane to listen to you talk about your wedding plans again.

"I was talking about Daddy James emailing Pat again," Courtney repeated, making me frown. Why was he trying so hard to work with Courtney's clinic? It was odd how excited he was about the discussion that was clearly an utter failure. I was staring at Eloise the entirety of the meeting, feeling the waves of unease come off her, but even I was socially aware enough to know that Courtney's boss was not interested in partnering with us at all.

Why? I asked.

"I don't know, I thought you might," Courtney shrugged. I shook my head in the negative again. "That guy always gave me the ick, but he seemed worse than usual when he showed up."

I frowned, *How?*

Courtney frowned, capping her water bottle before she explained, "Call it a woman's intuition? I don't know, the way he stared at Eloise made me pretty uncomfortable. And Eloise's reaction to him didn't ease my concerns."

I halted whatever step I was making toward my bag and looked at Courtney pointedly.

Was Connor...into Eloise like that?

She was over a decade younger than him, or close to it.

...Which was just his type, if I remember correctly.

"Eloise was very obviously uncomfortable around him.

Anyone could have picked up on that, but he didn't seem to care at all." I replayed the visit in my mind after Courtney's words sank in. Eloise was very noticeably, pointedly uncomfortable the whole time. Courtney had explained that she wasn't looking forward to Connor coming but didn't explain why. Now that I thought about it, Eloise stiffened more whenever Connor reached out to shake her hand. He smiled at her and made very direct eye contact even though she avoided looking at him for too long.

What the fuck?

You're right, I told Courtney, *Now that I remember, he seemed happy to see Eloise.*

"Ugh," Courtney sighed, picking up her bag and leading the way to the mats we stretched on, "I hope she's not the reason he wants to come back to the clinic."

The thought made me sick to my stomach. Connor was annoying and sometimes acted like a douche, but I never expected him to be predatory. I didn't think he was dumb enough to be predatory like that, but maybe he was socially unaware enough to not see how he was acting. Who knew?

Want me to talk to him? I asked Courtney. She quickly shook her head.

"No, as long as Pat keeps telling him we're not interested, he shouldn't have a reason to come back. Eloise has avoided him for this long, anyway."

I halted, staring at Courtney until she noticed and looked my way. *Why does she need to avoid Connor?*

Courtney frowned a little, "...Oh, sometimes I forget that you weren't there in LA when she told everyone."

I shook my head, *Did he hurt her*? Anger was starting to simmer in my veins. I had no idea how Eloise and Connor became acquainted, but it didn't matter. She was avoiding him, and that was enough of a red flag.

It also provided me with a little bit of relief that she "got the ick" from him just like Courtney did.

Courtney's lips frowned again as she stared at me. "According to Eloise, no, he didn't hurt her. They just hooked up a while back."

That didn't make me feel better.

Which really proved how much of an asshole I was. Whoever Eloise decided to spend time with was none of my business, but I couldn't help the sour feeling in my stomach at the thought of Connor having an opportunity to be intimate with her like that. Did he realize how lucky he was? That he should really be kicking himself for blowing such an opportunity to the point where she wanted to avoid him completely?

Oh, I replied, plopping down on the mats next to Courtney. I specifically refused to acknowledge her, even though I could feel her staring at me. She let us sit in silence for a few seconds before breaking it.

"All that she really says about it is that it was terrible," Courtney added. I gave her a look, unsure of what the look was, but she must have interpreted it as interest because she kept speaking. "She said that she was busy thinking about work the next day as it was happening." Courtney shrugged. "All I know is that I have had bad sex before, but even then, I have never felt the need to mentally remove myself from the situation and disassociate. Eloise says she consented, but...no woman has that type of reaction to a man unless she is scared of him...that, or perhaps she's truly just embarrassed and completely regrets it."

Did she regret what happened between us a couple of weeks ago?

I nodded, not sure how to respond to that. Eloise's history with my agent was still none of my business, but I hated the situation that Courtney was describing. I couldn't imagine being intimate with a woman and having her completely check out on me. It would be easy to notice, I figured. I would feel wildly uncomfortable if I was having sex with a woman, and she just...laid there. Staring off into space, thinking about work the next day.

"Apparently she hasn't hooked up with a guy since, because it was so unenjoyable," Courtney spoke up again as she stretched her arm across her chest. Then after a few moments of silence, her expression flickered and she raised her eyebrows at me playfully, "...You know where the clit is, right?"

I smirked and glanced up at Courtney, *Yes.*

"You are *positive* women haven't faked it with you before?" Courtney asked again, raising a blonde eyebrow as if it was important for me to know that that was an option.

I have had women fake it with me when I was young and uneducated. It was humiliating. It wasn't like high school sex education focused on how to help a woman reach orgasm, all it really taught me was that condoms were non-negotiable and where a man was supposed to put it. Since then, the female orgasm was something I had researched thoroughly, and accomplished throughout my twenties. Any asshole who had access to the internet had no excuse for being unable to help a woman reach orgasm.

Women have faked it with me, I admitted, *and I have learned the error of my ways. No woman has faked it with me since.*

I'd like to think I could tell the difference. Any woman could sound like she was having an orgasm. She could even make it feel like she was having an orgasm, but I learned to look for other things that were significantly more difficult to fake.

The flush that coated Eloise's skin, for example.

I felt honored to know what she looked like when she climaxed.

Now, I just needed to figure out if I could get the opportunity again.

"Good," Courtney nodded. "Nothing is worse than being vulnerable with a man, showing the most private parts of yourself to him, and then not getting over that edge." I nodded in agreement. That wasn't a problem men generally had when they had sex with women, which resulted in women having to fake orgasms with them just to get it over with.

However, I did not want to somehow get into bed with Eloise, only for her to hate my touch and get lost in her thoughts to disassociate the experience. I didn't think I could stomach continuing touching her if she ever reacted like that underneath me.

…I decided that it would be worth it to look up additional educational videos online tonight, just to refresh my knowledge should the opportunity arise to see Eloise at her most vulnerable.

"Anyways, want to come?" I wasn't listening to Courtney again, so I turned to give her a look that let her know that.

"Where is your head tonight?" Courtney shook her head once at me. "We're going over to Adam and Beck's tomorrow. Susan won't be there, because it'll be too late, but they wanted to have game night since Josh has a break from recording."

I nodded, *Yeah. Send me their address.*

Courtney nodded, "I will. Now I just need to convince Eloise to go."

She doesn't want to? I asked. Was she avoiding me again?

"She's been kind of down the last couple of weeks. Her parents are being really annoying I guess, and it's draining her." Courtney had volunteered a lot of information about Eloise tonight, and part of me was suspicious at how freely her mouth flowed, but I didn't want to stop her. I wanted any and all offered information about Eloise.

Sounds like she could use a night out, I offered with a shrug. With me, specifically. Preferably with nobody else around. In bed. Mine or hers. Maybe a bed wasn't even necessary. Maybe she needed a night out on a couch, on a countertop, or against a wall? Who's to say, really?

I glanced over at Courtney, who gave me a suspicious smile in return.

"Yeah, it does."

12

ELOISE

"I think I needed this," I winced as I spoke, still feeling the residual burn in my throat from the shot Courtney and I had just taken. We showed up at Adam and Beck's condo a few minutes ago with Josh and Taylor, who immediately encouraged us to take shots with them. The rest of the band wasn't going to come, so it was just the seven of us.

Seven, because according to Courtney, Logan would be showing up tonight.

I was both excited and terrified to see him.

We hadn't spoken since the night we texted.

Part of me felt like I needed to be the one to break the ice, but I was too nervous to. I didn't initiate the conversation that led us to climaxing over the phone together, and I had no idea how to initiate a conversation with the large man afterward. I hadn't ever done anything like that before.

Plus, my mom was up my ass lately, taking up all my time.

She needed my help with everything. Redecorating her house, helping the Halls (Adam's parents) with their garden parties, and of course brunches at the golf course. I had even run into Daddy James one time at my parents' house, and my mother was still upset with me about how I rudely left without any notice.

…Perhaps I *was* just being rude.

It wasn't like he was stalking me, like Courtney and Pat had suggested at work. He had been friends with my father for years before I ever slept with him, and I only worked at the early intervention clinic after his daughter had been a client there. It really seemed like a coincidence, and it wasn't uncommon for men to not get the hint. He wasn't angry or demanding my attention. Hell, he didn't even hurt or abuse me the night we spent together. He just…didn't really care about how I was feeling. It was gross how self-absorbed he was when it came to simple sex, honestly.

But what could I tell my mother? *Sorry, Mom, but I banged Dad's golf buddy last year and now that guy makes me uncomfortable and I hate being around him.*

No thanks.

I had felt so drained from my full-time job, putting in just enough effort with my relationship with my mother so that she would get off my back about moving out, that I had crashed early almost every night. I had very little time to brainstorm how to converse with him again.

So I took tonight as an opportunity.

Nobody, to my knowledge, knew what Logan and I did together. This would be the first time we had seen each other since then. How he acted would give me an idea of how to move forward from this weird limbo I felt trapped in.

The front door opened, and Taylor lifted their hand in greeting as they approached the entryway. I decided I needed to play it cool, so I rinsed out the used shot glasses in the sink while everyone greeted Logan loudly.

It wouldn't be unusual to anyone for me to ignore him for a little bit.

"We're doing shots!" I heard Courtney declare behind me in the kitchen. "Hey, Lo, can you pour one for him? Try not to spit in it or anything." I giggled a little at her comment. Of course, she thought I still hated him. Would we have to pretend like we hated each other? ...Did I still hate him? I didn't think so.

That sounded like fun.

I rinsed out the last shot glass, and reached for a towel to dry it off, before turning to finally take him in.

He *was* large. Wider than Josh and taller than Adam. I felt my breath catch in my throat as I absorbed his presence. Logan had one hip propped against Adam's large kitchen island, his arms crossed as his gray t-shirt struggled to hold its seams together. His dark curly hair looked a little damp as if he had showered right before he came over. His black jeans stretched over his thighs as he crossed one foot over the other. His dark eyes were already on me, making their way up from whatever he was staring at before I turned around.

Oh god, was he staring at my ass?

Did I just catch Logan staring at my ass again?

I felt my lips twitch, fighting a smile at the thought.

"I promise I won't spit in it," I made my voice sound disappointed as I replied to Courtney's request. "Here." I handed the glass to him, and he silently accepted it as he reached for the bottle of vodka that we had left out for him.

His fingers brushed across mine, unnecessary but purposeful.

My heart skipped a beat at the touch.

I weirdly loved it.

"What are we playing first?" Beck asked, rubbing her hands together as if she was a competitive person. She wasn't. She was just happy to have everyone over.

"Pictionary?" Courtney offered. All of us agreed, and after Logan took his shot and we all wrote down random prompts on slips of paper, the games began.

The night played out smoothly. Logan and I caught each other's gaze on occasion, but each time we did I felt my cheeks heat from remembering that night. I couldn't think too much about the presence of our current company, so I quickly broke contact. It was obvious he was thinking about it as much as I was if the heat in his eyes indicated anything.

Or maybe I was just desperate to get laid.

I was sitting on the edge of the couch, on the leather chaise since I wasn't part of the two couples who occupied the majority of Adam's couch. Taylor was standing in front of Adam's TV, frustrated with us for not understanding their scribbles on the large notepad as the timer ran out. Logan was sitting on the floor in front of the couch, thumbing something on his phone when the timer was ticking off its last seconds.

"You all suck!" Taylor cried, angrily scribbling nonsense over their picture when it was clear none of us were going to guess what they drew.

"Time!" Courtney called, making Taylor collapse on the ground, face-down in irritation. I was laughing, wiping tears from my eyes as I felt my phone vibrate in my pocket. While everyone laughed at Taylor's failure and started asking them to explain their drawing, I pulled it out to check the notification.

Logan had texted me. I felt my cheeks warm again, seeing his name at the top of my screen, and held my phone a little closer to my body before glancing around the room. I didn't want everyone else to see that I was reading a text from him for some reason.

"What the hell is that?" Beck asked, waving her hand towards Taylor's drawing.

"It's a penis! It's just a plain ol' penis! *How* did you not get that?"

"Why did you draw it like *that*?" Courtney cackled.

"Are we supposed to be staring down the barrel of it?" Josh asked, pushing his black-framed glasses higher on his nose and squinting at the drawing. Everyone was distracted, so I tapped on the notification without meeting Logan's gaze.

Logan: Please tell me I am not the only one suffering tonight.

I felt the corner of my mouth lift as I typed out my reply.

Me: Suffering how? I'm having a wonderful time.

I rested my phone in my lap and glanced around the room again, giggling at Taylor's disbelief in everyone else. I then let my gaze fall on Logan, who was staring down at his phone which he also held close to his chest to conceal his messages.

Logan: If I didn't see you smile before you sent that,

I would be more worried that you weren't thinking about our call as much as I was.

He went there. Just like that. In front of everyone, he was bringing up the last time I gave myself an orgasm. In front of him. Kind of. I tugged the collar of my shirt away from my chest as if I was fanning myself from the laughter everyone else was recovering from. Courtney took her place up front, and Taylor took the empty seat next to Josh.

She drew a prompt on a piece of paper and quickly got to work on her drawing.

Me: Are you distracted? Can't focus on the games tonight?

I pressed my lips together as I rested my phone on my lap and stared at Courtney's drawing, calling out a random answer I knew would be wrong to look like I was properly participating in the game until I felt my phone vibrate again.

Logan: I have been distracted for a while, Eloise.

My heart thumped in my chest, and before I could think better of it, I glanced to the side to where Logan was still sitting on the floor, his eyes on me for a second before he tore his gaze away and stared up at where Courtney was hopping up and down as she drew.

Holy hell, my lady parts loved reading that message from him.

Me: If only our friends weren't around.

Logan: Really? What would you do if they weren't?

I felt my heart take off in my ribs, pressing my lips against each other in anticipation. Were we doing this? In front of everyone?

Then a throw pillow hit me in the face. I pulled my attention away from my phone as Courtney continued to whack me with the pillow for not paying attention to her drawing and letting us fail. I laughed, pocketed my phone, and surrendered my attention to the game. When I stood up to draw, I may have added a little sway in my step. I may have popped my booty a little more than necessary when I bent down to grab a prompt from the bowl.

I could feel the heat of Logan's gaze on me the entire time, and the adrenaline coursing through my veins was thriving on it.

Eventually, we got bored with Pictionary, so then we started playing Uno around the kitchen island. It got a little aggressive when we played with Courtney and Beck's house rules and everyone kept stacking draw-fours on each other. Taylor may have thrown their deck down in rage before grabbing the bottle of vodka and taking a direct swig from it to help them cope with the size of their hand doubling.

It was a fun night. Nobody seemed suspicious of the fact that Logan and I were sitting as far away from each other as possible, and hardly glancing at each other when people were paying attention. It felt normal for us, and I was having fun with my friends.

Suddenly, everyone wanted to watch a movie. It was pretty late, and as soon as the two couples in the group snuggled up on the couch and got cozy, Taylor announced that they just matched with a person on their dating app and had better things to do. Everyone let them leave without much complaint.

That left Logan and me.

Beck had collected a number of blankets and pillows for Logan to lay on the ground, which he happily did with his head propped up against the foot of the couch. Courtney and Josh had scooted over to make room for me on the chaise lounge I was sitting on earlier for Pictionary.

We were flipping through Beck and Adam's movie collection on the TV screen debating options when Logan sparked a familiar rage in me.

"What about this one?" Courtney asked about a newer romantic comedy that I hadn't seen before but was excited to fill the screen, the trailer for it already playing in the background before anyone pressed play.

Logan had rolled his eyes.

"Excuse me?" Courtney had also seen his eye roll. "Do you have a problem with this movie?"

Logan turned and gave Courtney a raised eyebrow, an expression on his face that indicated he didn't have to explain his reasoning to dismiss the movie.

"I could probably do a romcom tonight," Josh said, wrapping a tattooed arm around Courtney, and tugging her back into his side. It was a fruitless effort—once Courtney got started, it was difficult to stop her.

"No, no, please," Courtney smirked at the hockey player in the room, a challenge in her eyes. "Enlighten us with why this movie deserved an eye roll."

Logan lifted his hands to sign, and I found myself studying them more. I was still in the middle of completing one of my online ASL programs whenever I had time at night, but not as much as I was hoping to have done by now (thanks, Mom), so I was very curious to see if I could pick up anything with the speed in which Logan signed.

He had been using ASL as his preferred form of communication since he was in college, according to Courtney.

"First of all, how dare you," Courtney challenged. "I think you're the only one in this room who thinks the movie is fluff."

And at that, even though I didn't understand Logan's hands, Courtney had made his opinion perfectly clear.

The spark of rage I felt started to burn.

"Fluff? Are you kidding me?" I sat up on my seat, facing Logan entirely. "What makes it fluff? What would you like to see to make it not fluff?" Logan faced me, his dark eyes narrowed a little as he took in my confrontational body language and lifted his hands to sign. Beck vocalized for him because his hands were moving quickly.

Nothing actually happens in these movies, Logan explained, *Where is the action? Adventure? Movies where the love story is the main event, are too predictable.*

It was my turn to roll my eyes at him, because *men.* "So, what you're saying is, movies where good things happen to women and women are treated with respect by their romantic partners are too boring for you?"

Logan's eyes widened a little at my words, his hands quickly coming up to deny my claim, *No, that's not what I'm saying.* Courtney had settled back against Josh, a smirk on her lips as she watched Logan and I go back and forth.

"That *is* what you're saying, though!" I lifted my hands in the air, adrenaline coursing in my veins at the familiar irritation I felt for this man. "You just said 'nothing happens' in these movies. What you really mean is, you need there to be some sort of violence or betrayal or action-adventure in order to be interested in the story. Because a story entirely based on emotional vulnerability and everlasting love of women is not enough!"

That's not just my opinion, Logan signed as Beck vocalized for him, *That's the opinion of the Oscars, IMDb, Rotten Tomatoes, and every other movie rating service.*

"Which are run entirely by, say it with me—" I lifted my hands in the air again as if I was a conductor at an orchestra as our friends spoke with me, "—Men."

Logan raised his eyebrows as he glanced at Josh and Adam, who had spoken with the ladies in the room.

"She's right, man," Adam shrugged, making Beck shift against his side. "If women were given the same amount of power that men had in Hollywood, romantic comedies would get higher ratings and appreciation. Romance is the most popular genre of movies and books because of how many women consume them, and yet, they get the lowest ratings because men control the system."

Logan pursed his lips, a thoughtful nod on his head as he took in Adam's explanation, *I guess I can see your point.*

I saw red. "The fuck?"

Courtney and Josh laughed at my reaction, probably assuming what I was going to say next.

I didn't need anyone's vocalization to understand Logan's next sign of, *What?*

"Do you not understand what just happened?" I stood,

making Josh cackle and hide his face in Courtney's shoulder at my animation. "You were literally just arguing with me, but then Adam—a *man*—chimed in and stood up for my argument, and *then* you started to 'see *his* point.'"

Beck and Adam were both trying their best to hide amused smiles, whereas Courtney and Josh were both openly laughing without shame at the situation.

Logan narrowed his eyes at me as he sat up, even though I was standing taller than him, his body language still held a bit of dominance as he met my gaze and started signing. No one was vocalizing, so he tapped Courtney's leg to get her attention so that she could vocalize for him.

That's not what happened, Logan argued, *Adam just happened to make a clearer argument than you.*

I gaped at him, making Josh snort at my expression.

"Logan, you're digging yourself a hole, buddy," Josh chuckled.

"You know what?" I shook my head in frustration as I growled in irritation and turned to leave the living room, heading towards the doorway where our shoes and bags were laying around. Maybe it was because Logan and I had always struggled to get along, or maybe it was because he was choosing to be ignorantly misogynistic. Or maybe I was tired and sensitive because of everything going on in my life.

Or…maybe I was sensitive because he and I shared something personal over FaceTime, and he had willingly dug his heels in for the sake of arguing with me in front of our friends.

"Lo, are you leaving?" Courtney giggled, but I could hear the concern in her tone.

"Yeah, I'm going home."

I turned around to face the group as I shoved one sneaker on my foot, standing on the other foot awkwardly as I used my index finger to pull the heel over and step into it.

Logan looked concerned, a deep pinch in his brow as he stared at me and made his way to stand up, looking like he was going to come after me. Courtney had stuck her leg out to halt his progress, making him look down at her in confusion.

"Nah, let her go. You fucked up again, so let her be angry." Courtney shook her head at Logan, like he was just a silly boy. A little sibling she took pity on.

"Are you calling an Uber?" Beck asked, sitting up from Adam's side.

"Yes, I'll text you all when I'm home safe." Because a woman traveling alone was never a safe time, because the world hated women. As Logan had just weirdly proved.

I waved goodbye, glad that my friends were willing to let me leave in a huff.

My phone buzzed in my pocket, but I was too angry to look at it. I only pulled it out when I needed to confirm that the car driving towards me was my ride, and thankfully the woman driving the vehicle was able to read body language and didn't try to make chit-chat with me.

Finally, I made it home. Susan was already asleep, and I found myself kicking my shoes off disorderly and running upstairs to my room. Then, after setting my bag down and taking in my surroundings, I realized I didn't want to go to bed angry or irritated. So, instead, I snuck across the hall to borrow a couple of copies of some romance novels of Courtney's that I was interested in reading.

Tiptoeing back to my room, I closed the door and locked it, then snuggled under the covers.

***

An hour later I checked the time, and it was about ten o'clock before I pulled my phone out to read my texts. I had managed to send off an "I'm home" text as I was kicking my shoes off, but I didn't bother reading the others.

I sighed when I saw the ones from Logan.

Logan: Hey, I'm so sorry.

Logan: I thought we were just teasing each other.

Logan: I didn't mean to undervalue your argument. That was a shit thing for me to do.

I rolled my eyes and tossed my phone on the bed.

I heard the front door downstairs open, and a couple sets of footsteps climb the stairs a few seconds before a gentle knock sounded at my door. The knob jiggled, but I had locked it, so Courtney's voice called out to me softly, "Lo? Are you good?"

"I'm good," I called back to her, "I'm just reading."

"Alright. Josh and I are going to bed."

"Goodnight."

"Night." Then I heard the sound of her bedroom door closing across the hall.

13

ELOISE

Twenty minutes later I heard a tap against my bedroom window, and I glanced quickly over to see if a bird had flown into it. It wasn't the first time it had happened in my life, but it would be the first time it happened in the townhome.

My phone buzzed again, another text from Logan.

Logan: Are you awake?

I frowned.

Me: Yes.

Logan: Can I come up?

My frown smoothed into a line.

Me: Are you here?

Logan: Yes. I threw a pebble at your window since you weren't responding.

I blinked at my phone before I set my bookmark in the paperback I was reading and slid out of bed to shuffle over to my window, pulling the curtains to the side to see Logan on the side of the house, staring up at me. He had a backpack slung on his shoulder as he stood by one of the trees scattered around this building of townhomes. He had a nervous smirk on his face that was barely lit up by a string of lights Susan had hung around the house. He even lifted his hand and gave me a tentative wave.

I grabbed my phone and typed a text while glaring down at him.

Me: Courtney and Josh are home and will hear the front door open.

The message was clear. I wasn't letting him in. I set my phone down on the desk and reached towards my dresser to pull my sleep shorts on since I was just in a tank and undies. The likelihood of Courtney and Josh being asleep already was low, and I didn't want to alert them to who was currently outside right now, so I curiously glanced out the window.

Logan was already standing in the tree, reaching up and wrapping his hands around the branches as he lifted his massive body higher and higher to reach my window.

"What the *fuck* are you doing?" I whisper-screeched after shoving my window open, shivering a little from the cool humid air I was letting into the room. Logan gave me a playful smirk as he lifted himself up on another branch, making him high enough to palm the screen over my window. With one gentle push, the screen popped out of my window. I made a startled noise as I struggled to catch it before it clanked on the floor.

I'm sorry, Logan signed immediately, his lips twitching a little as he stepped onto the small patch of roof underneath my window. This thirty-year-old man gripped the edge of the windowsill with both of his hands, his eyes meeting mine with question and apology. I set the screen down and gave him a disgruntled look of my own, letting the silence between us linger as I let him support himself on the roof.

I felt my face, which was pinched in irritation, start to loosen at the immediate apology. However, I wasn't wearing a bra (something the cool air made very apparent), and I didn't want to keep having this conversation with the window open and all the bugs flying inside.

"Come in," I nodded my head towards him, my voice a whisper as I stepped to the side for him to enter. He hung his head low, his body language clearly one of insecurity and nervousness as he lifted his leg and squeezed through the window. I tried not to focus on his firm grip on the window-sill, or how his shoulders and leg muscles flexed as he maneu-vered, something I had only ever seen in the movies.

After Logan made it inside, he stood tall and stared at me nervously. I walked over to my bedroom door to double-check that it was locked. I wanted to clear my head after getting a fill of his body when I was still annoyed with him. I turned around to see Logan raising an eyebrow at me, his eyes glancing at the doorknob pointedly.

"Courtney is known to let herself in without warning," I explained, keeping my voice quiet so she couldn't hear us. Logan nodded in understanding, his eyes doing a quick scan around my tidy room before he found my desk chair and plopped himself down.

"Please, make yourself at home," I mumbled sarcastically, sitting down on the edge of my bed, and crossing my arms over my body. Logan smirked at me before pulling his back-pack around so that he could unzip it, and he pulled out a shiny silver laptop. His eyes lifted to mine for a moment as he set the laptop on my desk.

His hands lifted to sign, but then he stopped and frowned, realizing no one was here to interpret for him.

"I'll never learn ASL if you don't keep signing to me," I grumbled, irritated that the language barrier was so difficult for us. Well, for me. Logan at least had his hearing, which made it easy for me to communicate my side of things. I hated that I was so far behind in the language compared to the others in our group, though.

Logan's dark eyes bore into mine, and I felt my heart flutter from the intensity of his dark gaze. After just a moment or two, Logan swallowed and nodded, but continued to sign.

I only caught a single word from his sentence, *watch*.

"Watch what?" I asked. Logan nodded, a nervous smile on his lips from my little understanding, and he lifted his laptop off the desk to flip it open and turn it on. He then stood up from his seat at the desk, walked around my side of the bed, and kicked off his shoes. I lifted an eyebrow, and my lips parted in surprise when Logan pulled the covers back to slide into where I was just lying as I read my book.

"What are you doing?" I asked, standing from my bed because his feet hit my butt underneath the covers. Logan bit his bottom lip and tapped on his laptop, before flipping it around so that I could see the screen.

He had pulled up the romantic comedy we were discussing earlier at Beck and Adam's condo.

I kept my arms crossed and leaned my weight onto one

hip, a look of disbelief on my face at how presumptuous he was being.

"Suddenly you're interested in the movie?"

Logan shook his head, so I rolled my eyes at him. He then snapped his fingers at me to regain my attention when I glanced away, and he started signing. He signed slower, mouthing his words for me clearly.

I want to watch with you, he said.

"Why?"

Logan frowned at me, then he turned the laptop back around and started typing away on it, a determined pinch in his brow as he studied the screen.

I stood there, hip popped, arms folded, waiting.

Eventually, he finished typing and sat up, reaching out for me with his hand. I stared at it for a moment, my heart racing at the thought of Logan's hands on me. It was something I had fantasized about quite often, especially after our last call. But we hadn't actually intentionally touched each other yet.

I met his eyes once more, a look in them that seemed both challenging and pleading at the same time. Eventually, I released an exaggerated sigh and placed my hand in his, letting him pull me towards him on the bed. He scooted over, giving me room to slide in next to him and to get my legs under the covers before he handed me his laptop. The notes app was open, and he had typed his response instead of trying to sign.

I fucked up earlier. At first, I thought we were just bickering, going back and forth. It was insensitive of me to brush off your arguments and feelings so quickly.

**I didn't mean to embarrass you or make you think that
I didn't care about your opinion.**

I do value your opinion.

Probably more than anyone else in that room.

I glanced up at him, his face turned down towards me as
his eyes bounced between me and the words he typed out.
Was he holding his breath? Our arms brushed against each
other as I gripped the laptop and adjusted my seat in my bed
to get more comfortable.

Ignoring the warmth seeping into my skin from the accidental arm brush, I started typing my response to him.

I'm sorry for getting so upset.

I think I can be a little sensitive sometimes.

Logan made a rumbling sound, his hand instinctively
coming up to rub at his neck over his scars before that hand
lifted and covered his mouth to hide a smile. He also looked
away from me, as if that would help hide the humor he found
in my response.

I raised both of my eyebrows at him, "Do you think that's
funny?"

Logan nodded behind his hand before his dark eyes landed
on me, his hand dropping to reveal the smallest upturn in
his lips.

"Okay, well, sorry for breathing," I felt my own lips
twitching at how obvious my sensitive feelings were before
I shrugged and handed the laptop back to Logan. He quickly
set the laptop down and reached a hand up to cup my jaw,
the contact making my breath catch.

Gently, so gently, Logan used his hand on me to ensure

my face was tilted towards his. Our eyes met in a clash that made my pulse start to race.

I'm sorry, Logan mouthed, *Forgive me?*

He looked so serious. He had apologized a number of times already, which was more than I had ever heard a man apologize for anything, ever. He showed up at my house late at night because I wouldn't respond to his texts. He patiently tried to communicate his words to me the best way he knew how.

"I forgive you." I smiled, the tug of my cheek pulling against his thumb that gently brushed back and forth across my skin, "…Almost."

His thumb halted, and Logan's dark eyebrows lowered a little in concern at my response. I swallowed a lump in my throat, and I could feel the heaviness of my eyelids start to drop as I found myself focusing on Logan's lips that were slightly turned down.

"What I mean is," I cleared my throat again, my tongue coming out to taste my own bottom lip before I met his gaze, "If you felt the need to make it up to me in other ways, I wouldn't object."

Yup.

I had just made a pass at Logan.

I had gone from mad and irritated at him, to wanting to get into his pants. Within minutes. Because I was a pathetic woman and had no self-respect, apparently.

Logan's eyes dipped to my lips as well, and my heart skipped a beat when his thumb moved to barely trace over my bottom one. A shuttered breath left my lungs, and his dark eyes lifted to meet mine.

Logan leaned down towards me, and I held my breath. He held eye contact with me as he came closer, waiting for me to either give permission or not. I held still, so still that he was a hair away from my lips. His face was blurry; it was so close.

I couldn't take it anymore.

I tilted my head up and pressed my lips against his.

My heart stopped.

…and then immediately took off again.

It was gentle, a get-to-know-you kiss. Logan's grip on my jaw kept me in place as he brushed his warm lips across mine. Nothing urgent, nothing heavy, but just enough for me to distinctively remind myself that I needed to keep breathing. A minute of gentle lip presses passed and, finally, he pulled away an inch or two to look at me.

We blinked at each other, and the fact that I could barely make out the difference between his pupils and his dark brown irises gave me just the tiniest bit of confidence to breathe my next request. "More."

He didn't need to be told twice.

Both of Logan's hands came to cup my face as his lips slammed against mine. I gasped against him, my arms sliding up to wrap around his neck and my fingers scraping until they tangled themselves in his dark curls.

I swore I felt Logan's lips pull back into a smile for the quickest second before he invaded my mouth with his tongue.

I groaned against it, the feel of his tongue sliding against mine in the slowest, most sexual passes made my skin heat.

I gripped fistfuls of his hair as I tried to get closer, and he responded by lowering his hands to grip my waist, before pulling me over to his lap.

I was now straddling Logan's lap.

Repeat, I was now *straddling Logan's lap.*

"Of course, you're an amazing kisser," I gasped against his mouth quickly to catch my breath. I was only able to get a couple of lungfuls of air before he took my lips with his again. His deep rumble against my chest sent a buzz of electricity through my core, and I found myself shifting in his lap on instinct.

His hands gripped my hips tight, before they skimmed down my thighs, then back up around towards my ass. Before his hands could get their fill, they stopped right when his fingertips pressed into the swell of muscle.

He pulled away from me, his eyes meeting mine in a question.

Oh, *this* was how he asked for consent.

"Yes." I shifted in his lap, an attempt at wiggling my butt enticingly.

Logan lifted a dark eyebrow, his face not convinced. I pictured him asking something like, *Are you sure?*

"Logan," I released my grip on his hair and pressed my forehead to his, my hands sliding down his muscular arms until my fingers laced over his, guiding his hands to grip my flesh, "Grab my ass. Grab whatever you want. If I'm not into it, I'll say so."

Logan released a staggered breath as he squeezed the globes of my muscles of his own accord, and while he was busy playing with my ass, I allowed my hands the opportunity to slowly smooth their way back up his arms. The number of divots and muscles and tendons he had in each was wildly impressive and made my own arms feel 2D in comparison. I stopped when my hand reached his bicep, and I stared at how much paler my hand looked over his tanned skin.

I then glanced up to meet his dark gaze, and a wildly bold sentence blurted out of my lips before I could stop it. "You look so good underneath me."

Logan blinked at me in surprise, and I felt all the blood on my face drain as horror and humiliation washed over me at my stupid ass statement.

"Oh my god, I'm so sorry!" I let go of his arms and covered my face with my hands. *Good god, Lo, how much erotica have you been reading?*

Logan kept one hand on my ass while the other slid up my back, hiking underneath my sleep tank, his lips tracing themselves near my ear.

Was I sweating?

I was such a dumbass.

I fell forward and hid my face and hands in his neck, mildly aware of the scars on his skin, and how the rough texture of them felt against the back of my hands.

"I'm so sorry, I'm so sorry," I repeated the apology several times. "I don't know why I said that. You're just so handsome, and I'm not usually this focused on looks, but I saw my hand on your arm, and I didn't mean—" Logan had released his grip on my ass to wrap his fingers around the back of my neck, pulling me out of his shoulder just enough for his lips to slam back on mine again.

I was still embarrassed and mortified, but his kisses were so drugging that my head started spinning, and I was forgetting why I was so embarrassed after a few gasping passes of his tongue.

Finally, he tugged my neck back so that he could look at me. His lips were swollen and wet from our kisses, and his eyes looked like he was drugged. They were heavy and dark, and the way he licked his lips as he caught my gaze, made my heart skip.

"I'm sorry—" Logan shook his head once, making me snap my mouth shut.

It's okay, Logan mouthed to me, he pulled his hand out from under the back of my tank as his lips quirked to the side, and then he blinked and I swore I could see a lightbulb light up in his head, *Actually, no.* Logan shook his head and lifted his hands in between us, slowly signing and mouthing his words to me, *If you're sorry, make it up to me.*

I blinked.

He was trying to make a game. A sexy, super thrilling game I had every intention of participating in. He wasn't scared off by my unsolicited dirty talk.

"Yes," I nodded, my hands gripping the hem of his shirt, "I should. Definitely. How would you like me to do that?"

Logan smirked, pressed his lips firmly against mine, and pulled back just enough to grip my waist and twist me down so that I was laying on my back next to where he was sitting. He slid down under the covers more, resting his weight on one arm as his body hovered over mine and his hand slid up the front of my shirt. I gasped and pressed my thighs together at the suddenly filthy images I had of Logan hovering over me like this.

Logan's hand paused, his fingertips barely brushing the bottom swells of my breasts, his eyes on mine as he waited for me to give him confirmation that this new position was okay. I grabbed his wrist and helped him continue his slide, his large palm covering almost the entirety of my breast.

"Just so we're clear," I gasped as his thumb brushed across the stiff peak of my nipple, "I'm totally down for a home run tonight if you are."

Logan paused and gave me a confused look, making me gulp as I used my grip on his hand to encourage him to keep going. "Meaning...I have no intention of stopping anything. I have condoms in my nightstand drawer."

If Logan's eyes were dark before, now they were black pits as he struggled to take a deep breath. His gaze bounced between my face, and where his hand was hiding underneath my tank top. I wasn't wearing a bra, so he could see how his ministrations affected me based on the show my untouched breast gave him through the cotton.

I arched my back and released Logan's wrist, using my hands to pull my tank top over my head and tossing it carelessly somewhere else in the room before I tucked my thumbs in the waistband of my sleep shorts, and started to pull them down. My legs were still under the covers, so Logan lifted them out of the way for me to toss my shorts to the side. He sat up just a little as I laid down on my back again, and he scraped a hand down his face as a deep rumbly sound came from his chest, his eyes closing as if he was struggling with restraint.

"Don't hold back on my account, please," I whispered, removing his hand from his face, and bringing it back to my stomach. He let me guide his rough, calloused hand again. I slowly slid it up my rib cage, barely over my other breast in the slowest pass that made me gasp. I didn't stop there, and I loved how Logan's eyes were purely focused on the path his hand traveled on my body as it made its way up towards my collarbone, slowly up my neck, and halting as I encouraged his fingers to gently squeeze the sides.

Logan lost control. He pulled his hand away, a movement that made me whimper from the loss of his touch, only to gasp in delight as Logan pulled on the back collar of his shirt and ripped it over his head.

He didn't give me a chance to admire him, instead, he launched toward me. His mouth immediately found mine for the briefest moment, his hands unable to find a place to settle on my skin. Shoulders, neck, chest, stomach, hips, chest, breasts, neck.

I immediately reached down to undo the button of his jeans between us, and he paused his exploration with his hands to settle them on the mattress on either side of my shoulders so that he could lift his hips and help me tug his jeans down. He then awkwardly kicked them off the rest of the way, letting them get lost underneath the covers of the bed.

"Holy shit," I gasped when my hand cupped him through his boxer briefs. And the longer my hand had to slide down to reach the tip of him, the more shocked my expression was. The dirty smile Logan gave me when I finally reached the end of him was mind-numbing. This was the hottest I had felt with another person in a very long time. I was so turned on by touching him and being trapped under his weight, that I was certain only a few perfectly placed grinds of his hips would set me off.

"I mean," I lifted a shoulder as my hand gripped him through his boxers and started making leisurely passes, "I'm willing to try if you are." I used my free hand to reach over and open up my side table, patting around chaotically until I found what I was looking for. A silver foil pinched in between my fingers, and I handed it to Logan.

He took it, then tossed it on the bed beside us.

"Um—?" I didn't finish that thought because Logan started sliding down my body. "Oh god, oh god." I dug the heels of my palms into my eyes at the feel of Logan's hands wrapping themselves around my thighs, his mouth leaving a trail of wet kisses on my skin as he passed between my breasts, my belly button, lower, lower, lower.

"Wait, shouldn't *I* be making it up to *you*?" I gasped, sitting up just enough to see the almost comical image of Logan almost completely hidden underneath my comforter, his head only peeking out enough to lift and make eye contact with me. He didn't stop his travels, instead, he kept his eyes locked on mine as he used his hands to skim over my skin, toying with the edge of my plain cotton underwear.

I gasped as his thumb barely brushed me, my breathing short and heavy and overall embarrassing.

I was hyper-focused on him, which was probably the only reason I was able to register Logan's nod of approval before he mouthed the words, *you are,* to me. I blinked, then gasped again when he roughly tugged my panties out of his way and lowered his head to devour me.

That was the only way to describe it.

I couldn't focus on what exactly his lips and tongue were doing to me, only that it made me feel dizzy, and I could feel the invisible string tightening inside of me at a shocking rate. I immediately fisted the sheets next to my hips, biting my bottom lip in an attempt to smother the embarrassing sounds I made so as not to alarm anyone else in the house.

Before I could inhale my next breath, I was coming.

My back arched off of the bed, and Logan's grip on my upper thighs kept me in place as he continued to eat me out. He never stopped what he was doing, not when I went silent as warm waves of heat unfurled from my core and spread through the entirety of my body, waves and waves of pure bliss coursing through all the way to my fingertips.

After an agonizing and euphoric amount of time, my body flattened on the bed again, and I was gasping for air.

Logan lifted his head from between my legs, his lips shining as his eyes sparkled. He kissed the juncture between my leg and hip, gently wiping his mouth off before he crawled back up toward me.

"I can't, I can't," Logan tilted his head to the side as he lifted his hand to brush some of my hair away from my face. I was sweaty, and the fine strands stuck to my forehead until his calloused fingers brushed them out of the way. He tilted his head as he looked down at me, amused but questioning. I inhaled another lungful of air, before gently exhaling through my nose. "How did you do that?"

Logan's shoulders shook with silent laughter as he bit his bottom lip, his dark eyes skimming all over my face as he lowered his head to my neck to leave more kisses against my skin.

"That was—wow—I've never come that fast," I breathed. Logan's teeth gently bit my collarbone, and I shivered from the contact. I patted around until I found the foil square he tossed aside and held it up to Logan's face once he was done making out with my neck and shoulders.

He gently bit the corner of the foil in between his teeth, firm enough for me to be able to rip the package open. I smirked as I pulled the condom out, tossed the wrapper aside, and snuck both of my hands down toward his boxers. Before I could do it, he quickly rolled to the side to shuck his shorts down his legs, leaving him completely bare whereas I still technically wore my panties.

"Here," I rolled the condom onto him, blinking at the massive erection as it bounced against my thigh. I then shimmied out of my underwear, leaving us both completely naked.

Before I could swing one leg over him, his rough hand grabbed my shoulder to keep me on my back, his body caging mine in a way I had specifically pictured in my DIY time.

"Why are you so hot?" I asked, my voice sounding a little too pathetic to my own ears as I traced my hands over his massive shoulders, and his hard chest. He was ripped. He was a professional athlete, and it showed. No tattoos of any kind on his skin, just the light pink scarring on the upper half of his body, neck, and face. I found myself gently tracing the largest scar up his pec before I looked up to see him studying me. His dark eyes were heavy, and his lush lips were only parted a hair.

"If you're not inside me in the next minute," I whispered, reaching down to guide him toward where I wanted him, "I will cry."

Logan smirked and shook his head, lowering himself on his elbows as he followed the movement of my hand to push forward.

Shit, this was going to take some effort.

"Go slow," I breathed as he started to push in. I gasped and held my breath before I watched him stiffen and halt his movement. I didn't want that. I shook my head at him and wrapped my arms around his shoulders, canting my hips to encourage him to continue.

"Actually," I gasped as he kept going, "Maybe you should rip the band-aid off." Logan's brow furrowed, and I barely noticed a hint of sweat starting to coat his brow. "Yeah, yeah I think you should just go for it."

He frowned a little and shook his head.

"Please," I whimpered, *whimpered*, something I never thought I would do in front of this man mere weeks ago, "I want it. I want you. Please give it to me." I canted my hips again, encouraging him to go deeper, and gasping at the stretch. It was unreal how full I felt, and yet I knew he wasn't all the way in yet.

Logan shifted one of his hands to cradle itself around the back of my neck, encouraging me to focus on his face instead of the pleasurable pain I felt from him.

"Yes," I spoke, "Yes. Please. Do it."

Logan lowered his head to capture my lips in a deep, open-mouthed kiss. As soon as I slid my tongue past his lips, he slammed his hips against mine.

I cried out. Thankfully, it was slightly smothered with his mouth over mine, but the shock of his invasion made my whole body stiffen around him. He didn't move, instead, he just continued to kiss me, kiss me, and kiss me. Languid, sensual kisses that made my brain feel foggy, that made warmth pool in my lower belly and relax my muscles that were desperately clenching around him.

It wasn't until Logan could feel the muscles in my body relax, loosening its death grip on him, that he separated our lips and let my head fall back enough to tell him, "Move."

He did. Slow, deep thrusts. They were designed to see how I would react; if I needed him to stop or slow down again. I tried to convey with my body language that I wanted him to keep going because I was feeling a delicious burn from it and I was almost desperate to see where this ended.

I hadn't been this stretched out and lubricated with penetrative sex in a very, very long time.

I didn't realize I had closed my eyes; I think that happened during the kisses, but I opened them to see Logan lift his head from where he had settled it in between my shoulder and neck to look at me.

"I'm sorry," I gasped against one of his thrusts, and Logan's brow pinched at my apology. He halted his last thrust, but I tried to meet his movements. "I was wrong."

His confusion didn't leave his face, but he listened to my body language and continued to move deep inside me. His confidence in his invasion of me slowly grew the more I encouraged him.

"You don't remember?" I asked, loving how he was so clearly confused and had no idea what I was talking about. Logan shook his head in the negative, his eyes rolling in the back of his head when he hit a spot just right inside of me that made me flutter once around him.

"I think it was last year," I was whispering now, his momentum speeding up a little. "I said, 'sorry about your penis'." At that, Logan's grin spread wide across his cheeks as he lowered his head onto my shoulder and huffed out some choked and strained laughter. I giggled with him as he paused his movement to regain his composure, rubbing his back and shoulder muscles with my hands.

"I was *so* wrong," I continued, "You weren't overcompensating for anything. In fact, I think you need a bigger truck."

Logan shook his head against my shoulder as he thrust hard, almost in some sort of retaliation for the teasing. I gasped, and he responded accordingly. Suddenly, he wasn't holding back anymore. He was more confident, or at least, more confident in what I could take. His thrust turned a little more aggressive, and my body loved it. It looked like he was losing control, his body responding on instinct as he fucked me into my mattress.

I finally released my grip on his shoulders as I planted my hands flat against my headboard above my head, my back arching the slightest bit. Logan shifted just enough to put his weight on one arm while his other hand gripped my waist tight, holding me in place as he continued to take me.

His breathing was short, labored, and made my body burn.

This newer angle he was hitting me with made my eyes widen. "Oh god, oh god." Logan made eye contact with me as he continued to hold the position, and continued to thrust at exactly the momentum and energy that suddenly made me religious. "Oh god. Fuck. Fuck-fuck-fuck."

He smirked as he eyeballed my chest, I was positive that my breasts were giving him a wonderful show as he impaled me like this.

"Shit!"

Fireworks erupted out of me. That was the only logical explanation for the type of orgasm I had. It was rising like slowly climbing to the top of the roller coaster, only instead of dropping on the other side of the tracks, the cart just blasted off into the atmosphere, grazing past the heat of the sun.

I felt it everywhere, in every muscle of my body.

I saw stars. I saw the heavens. I was pretty sure I saw some type of deity too, but all too soon I was falling from the high, gently gliding back down to earth as my muscles started to loosen one by one.

It wasn't until I had finally regained my senses (and vision) that I felt Logan's large body collapse on top of me, his arms wrapping themselves around me as he ground his hips one last time and pulsed erratically inside me.

"Oh, oh," I whimpered in his ear because somehow his orgasm was creating aftershocks for me. Smaller, delicious little flutters that made my eyes roll. I was gasping for air, partially because I had a massive man crushing me to his chest, but also because my body just got the workout of a lifetime.

And I didn't even have to lift a finger, just like he had said before.

Finally, Logan shifted as he slid out of me, making a disappointed sound erupt from the back of my throat before he rolled us so that he was now on his back and I was tucked into his side. His large arms were still around me as his face nuzzled in my hair. I wrapped my arms around his waist, swung my leg over one of his, and snuggled in.

Within seconds, I was asleep.

14

LOGAN

I'm not saying that sliding out of a sleeping Eloise's grip to dispose of a condom and get dressed was the hardest thing I've ever done, but it sure as hell wasn't easy either. She had passed out on me almost immediately, which made weird feelings stir within my chest. I hadn't ever had sex with a woman, only to then have her immediately fall asleep on me.

It was so intimate.

Also, a bit of an ego boost for me.

I quietly slipped my clothes back on, careful with my movements because Eloise was breathing deeply on her stomach, half her face smothered in her pillow now. Her freckles peeked through the blonde locks of hair that fanned around her face.

After straightening my clothing I stepped towards her, taking the opportunity to brush some of that hair off of her face. She looked so peaceful, her blush still lingering on her cheeks as if it was sticking around just for me. I traced my finger along the apple of her cheek, only pulling back when her mouth twitched and she made a soft noise.

I stood straight again, glancing around her bedroom to see if there was anything for me to use. Examining her desk, I saw a small notepad and a cup of pens. I gently ripped a blank page off the notepad, checking over my shoulder to ensure that she was still asleep, before plucking a pen out of the cup.

What do I say?

Thanks for the fuck?

It felt too crude, too casual for what I experienced with Eloise just now. Not that we were in a committed relationship or anything. The fact that she immediately fell asleep let me know that we wouldn't be defining whatever this was tonight.

I thought for a moment, before smiling to myself and scribbling something down.

For the record, you look beautiful underneath me, too.

There. That way she would know that I wasn't offended by her spontaneous dirty talk and that I wasn't leaving because I never wanted to talk to her again. Sure, it caught me off guard, but I was also excited to learn more about this woman.

She clearly had some sides to her that she didn't show others that often. Based on how embarrassed she was with her words, I had a feeling that she kept a lot of herself close to her chest.

…Kind of like I did.

Plus, her words were an obvious slip of the tongue. She immediately regretted saying how good I looked underneath her, which made me want to tease her for it. But I held back, instead trying to lean into her regret by telling her to make it up to me. Frankly, I had somehow found a way to offend her almost every time we were in the same room, so I figured I'd like that awkward moment to pass.

Plus, I wanted to see her again.

To no one's surprise.

I shouldered my backpack after leaving the note next to her on the bed, when my shoe nudged something on the floor, making me pause on my way out of the room to see what it was. It was a book, a well-used book by the looks of it.

I reached down to pick it up, intending to set it on her desk or something, when the cover art caught me by surprise.

It was clearly a romance novel.

Courtney had told me many times about how romance covers were starting to be more and more discreet. Instead of covers of half-naked models, a lot of them were brightly colored cartoons. Which was exactly what this was. I glanced over at Eloise, still sound asleep with my note next to her on the bed, then I glanced at the book in my hand, the bookmark of where she left off peeking out in the middle of it.

I knew I should put it back.

Instead, I found myself unzipping my backpack and shoving the novel inside before I could talk myself out of it, then quickly unlocking her bedroom door to hopefully sneak out through the front door.

I paused when I heard voices coming from Courtney's room, her bedroom light shining underneath the door.

"Don't you dare," Josh scolded.

"Don't you want to know who Eloise just had over?" Courtney whisper-hissed, sounding like she was close to the door.

"Yeah, but instead of ambushing the guy, we could just ask her about it in the morning," Josh chuckled, making Courtney grumble a disgruntled noise.

I stood frozen in the hallway, my heartbeat rapid in my chest as I wondered how to proceed.

I knew Eloise had been loud, but I didn't realize how thin the walls of the townhome were. Would she tell Courtney about us? …Would I? To my knowledge, nobody knew about our FaceTime call that I had thought about for the last couple of weeks. Would it be different now that she and I had actually, well, had sex?

"How did she even find someone so fast? Those dating apps really don't mess around." Courtney's voice got quieter as she retreated from her bedroom door and the squeak of a mattress let me know she settled in for the night.

I exhaled a harsh breath of relief, before continuing my quiet journey downstairs.

***

A week passed. I exercised, practiced on the ice, and ran. I was consumed with reliving that experience with Eloise in my mind. I kept replaying it over and over again.

I was addicted.

It wasn't until the following weekend when I was waiting for Courtney and Josh to show up at the gym that I realized how excited I was to see her again. We had texted only a few times, short flirty notes that ended after just a couple of messages back and forth. It never escalated to a repeat of the night we FaceTimed, and I was okay with that. Part of me wanted to wait until we could get together again, just the two of us.

I also read her romance novel.

Eloise had clearly highlighted her favorite parts, which weren't philosophical or educational. No, Eloise instead liked to highlight parts simply because she liked them. The highlighted lines were either cheesy pickup lines from the male love interest or dirty lines he would say during the many, many sex scenes the book had. Sometimes there were little drawings of a fireball or a panting face in the margins, letting me know exactly what her thoughts on the dialogue of the story were.

I had never gotten hard from reading a book before...but I did now.

I then googled the phenomenon and learned what book boners were. And thus, I suddenly wanted to learn more about the romance novels that Eloise read. It didn't take me long to find her social media accounts on the internet, but none of them showed what she liked to read. I did, however, see her comment on one of Courtney's posts. It was a picture of Courtney and Josh reading in bed together, with millions of likes and comments, but Eloise's comment is what caught my eye, "I saw your review for this one on Goodreads and immediately added it to my TBR!"

And just like that, I learned what Goodreads was and found Eloise's account. I was able to see all the books she read, what she rated them, and why.

So here I was, a week after I had snuck through Eloise's

window and four romance novels deep, thanks to her online recommendations.

I was sitting on my bench, taking a break from my reps to read a couple more paragraphs of the latest romance novel I was on. It was categorized as a hockey romance, which un-surprisingly, had very little to do with the sport itself and had more to do with the love story between the man and woman.

"Well, well, well." I heard Josh's voice before I saw them, smirking to myself as I quickly pocketed my phone and turned to face him. "If it isn't exactly who we came to see."

Josh was weird.

"Who started without us, again." Courtney made a show of glaring at me before she set her bag down and pulled her sticker-clad water bottle out.

That was when I spotted Eloise.

My heart thudded in my chest.

I struggled to remember what I was doing so that I could continue the movement and not be super obvious about what her presence did to me.

"Shocker." Eloise's lips twitched a little as we made eye contact, but she broke it first by bending to drop her bag next to Courtney's and digging around in it. There was no indica-tion in her body language that she was just as affected by my presence as I was by hers. While Josh and Courtney chatted about, well, something, I took a moment to take in Eloise.

She was wearing a black headband that kept most of her hair out of her face. Her light blue sports bra was the kind with only one strap over one shoulder—I wasn't an expert on sports bras, but I figured that wasn't one she could con-fidently wear while running. She wore the same little black shorts she had worn last time, showing off her dainty flower tattoos on her hip and thigh. The shorts did wonderful things to her ass, her ass that I couldn't keep my eyes off of *before* I knew how it felt in the palms of my hands.

I stared at the flowers on her hip, promising myself that I would take the time to trace them with my tongue should Eloise allow it.

Fuck me.

Eloise stood with her water bottle in hand, pausing only a moment when she realized I had been staring at her. Courtney and Josh were grabbing their weights to the side, so I took an opportunity to hold her gaze.

I wanted to see how she wanted to play this.

Eloise was a woman, and it was a universal truth that women talked to each other about who they hooked up with. Did she tell Courtney about what happened between us in her bedroom? I wouldn't be upset if she had. Maybe I would have been upset a few years ago, but after being friends with a raging feminist like Courtney, I now understood how important it was for women to discuss these types of things with each other.

Not just to gossip, but for their own safety.

Such as, to learn what a sexually healthy relationship was, versus not.

To know if the guy behaved inappropriately during the hookup.

Sometimes, though, it was just to gossip. Usually, women only gossiped if it was either a great experience or a hilariously bad one. I was fairly confident that our experience in her bedroom wasn't bad. I would argue that it was great, actually.

Still, I wanted to know if I needed to brace myself for any sort of interrogation from Courtney after hooking up with her friend whom she thought still hated me.

Eloise's skin flushed under my gaze, making a smile form on my lips that I quickly tried to hide with my hand as I rubbed it down my face.

"So, what are we doing today?" Eloise asked, her voice a little higher than normal as she tucked her hair behind her ears, even though she was already wearing a headband.

"Ass and legs," Courtney replied, adding weights to the squat rack I was previously using.

Josh was watching Courtney add the weights with an obvious look of admiration in his eyes. His fiancée was fit, and he clearly appreciated that.

"Cool, is this one available?" Eloise asked, pointing to the empty station next to Courtney and Josh. I nodded and followed her over to that one.

"I've never lifted like this before," Eloise spoke, pointedly going out of her way to avoid my gaze as I set the bar on the rack. "Can you show me how to form myself, Court?"

"Logan can," Courtney replied, getting into position underneath the bar as she wrapped her hands around it, "Josh is going to spot me here."

"Oh, okay." Eloise sounded nervous, which immediately set off alarm bells in my head. If Eloise didn't want me to help her, I wasn't going to force her. I had set some tens on either side of the bar before I paused and gave Eloise a questioning look. She stared at me with her wide blue eyes, her teeth gnawing on her bottom lip hesitantly as she contemplated while Courtney and Josh ignored us.

Are you okay? I asked Eloise, remembering to dramatically mouth my words for her so she could understand. Her eyes glanced between my hands and my lips, and she took a moment to inhale a deep breath before she nodded and surprised me.

I'm N-E-R-V-O-U-S, Eloise signed, slightly mouthing her words.

I blinked at her.

That was pretty good. It was clean, I didn't see an error with her fingerspelling at all.

She smirked at my expression.

Nervous, because of me? I asked, showing her the correct sign for the word.

She nodded.

I frowned, then took a step back away from the weights to give her space and reached for my water bottle that sat on the ground in between the two stations.

"Alright, show me how to do this, big guy." Eloise's voice sounded like it had an edge to it, like how she spoke to me before we hooked up. Before we both admitted that we wanted each other. I lifted an eyebrow, seeing that she was glancing at our friends next to us before she stood underneath the bar that I had racked and gave me a challenging look.

I took a sip from my water bottle, watching her.

Her gaze dropped to my throat as I swallowed, and the gulp she subtly made before she dropped her eyes to the ground made heat run in my veins.

Oh, maybe I did make her nervous, but in a good way.

Chin up, I told her, sauntering back over to her. Her cheeks flushed again, but barely. She was putting on a show as if my presence didn't affect her the same way her presence affected me.

This probably brought me more joy than it should have.

"You're crushing it, love," Josh encouraged as he stood behind Courtney, his hands hovering underneath the bar just in case her muscles gave out. His eyes could have had literal stars in them as he watched his fiancée squat.

Courtney grunted before racking the bar and standing to her full height, shaking out her arms and stretching her shoulders.

Back straight, I corrected Eloise with my hand on her spine, making her freeze as she made eye contact with me in the mirror. I mouthed the words to her again, and she nodded.

Fuck, her soft skin still felt amazing under my hands.

Eloise unracked the bar and started to slowly bend herself in half, barely bending her legs at all.

I quickly reached out from behind her and grabbed the bar, just enough to keep her from continuing the movement. It would be a dangerous thing for me to do if it was anyone else lifting (and if the weight wasn't light enough for me to catch with one hand) but my instincts took over. At Eloise's frustrated look, I shook my head at her and waited for her to rerack the weight.

I released the bar from my own hands and explained to her, *You need to activate your legs.* I then stood in front of her, showed her my profile, and demonstrated how her body should look squatting.

Eloise's eyes darkened a little as they glued themselves to my thighs, then my ass as I showed the angle the legs should bend.

"Oh, I get it," Eloise nodded. "I was focused on how heavy the bar was, I think." I nodded because it was a common mistake people made when they lifted for the first time.

"Want to lower your weights, Lo?" Courtney asked as she settled underneath her own bar again, bumping Josh's body with her ass playfully. He gently tapped it once before hovering his hands underneath her bar again.

"Actually, yeah I might." Eloise stood as if she was about to rerack them, but I beat her to it. I quickly removed the tens on either side and added fives. The bar itself was close to forty-five pounds , so it made sense that I was overzealous with giving her tens on either side to start.

"Alrighty," Eloise arched under the bar, tipping her chin up and checking her form thoroughly before giving me a look.

I stood in front of her, wondering what she was waiting for.

"Are you going to spot me?" Eloise asked, nodding her head for me to step behind her like Josh was doing for Courtney.

I could easily spot standing in front of her, but who was I to correct her? I smirked before walking around and hovering my own hands underneath the bar, careful not to touch any part of her body.

Eloise's form was almost perfect now. She paced herself and didn't try to complete the set as fast as possible. Her breathing was controlled, even though she was clearly struggling by the sixth squat.

After eight, she racked the bar and stood, her hands immediately going to her ass as she turned and gave us all a surprised expression.

"Holy shit, is my ass ripped yet?" She made a show of twisting around so she could see her own backside.

Josh and Courtney laughed, and I smiled.

"Right? You feel it immediately when you do it right." Courtney encouraged, swapping places with Josh. He had to set the bar higher up because the guy was tall.

"No kidding," Eloise nodded toward me. "Okay, your turn."

I shrugged and went to add more weights to the bar.

After the fourth set of forty, I could feel her eyes on me. I paused what I was doing and glanced over at the little woman standing tall with her arms crossed over her chest, a small frown on her face.

"Are you trying to rack more than my body weight?" Eloise grumbled.

"He's such a showoff sometimes." Courtney agreed.

I flipped them both off as I positioned myself under the bar. I was obviously stronger than both of them simply because I had been regularly exercising for the past decade of my life. Not my fault if they felt self-conscious about that.

"I got you," Eloise said as she waltzed behind me. I hesitated and gave her a look over my shoulders. "What?" she asked.

I straightened and turned around to rest my elbows on the bar, looking down at her, *You think you can catch me?* I barely mouthed that question to her as I signed it, but I wanted to see how much ASL she could communicate with and understand.

Eloise frowned, glancing over at Josh and Courtney for help, but they were distracted again. It had been a week since Eloise scolded me for not signing in front of her, which made me realize how much of an asshole I was to her the first time we met.

Simply because she couldn't understand ASL, and I had the emotional depth of a puddle.

However, she had clearly picked up on some things.

Yes, Eloise signed.

I felt the grin spread across my face before I could stop it, making her frown loosen a little as she took in my expression. I shrugged; *Just checking.* How much had she learned?

Have you been learning ASL? I asked, forgetting completely that it was my turn to squat. Eloise's cheeks turned pink again, was she embarrassed?

Yes, Eloise signed, glancing over at our friends who seemed to be in their own world; *I am in a class.*

I smiled fully at her then, making the corners of her lips turn up as well.

That's great, I then turned around and positioned myself under the squat rack. Why was she learning ASL now? When we first met, she hadn't taken a class for it or anything. Last I heard, she didn't know more than the core words they used at the early intervention clinic with kids. Beck and Susan relied on ASL half the time to communicate without their hearing aids, and Courtney was basically fluent, so did she just not want to be left out?

Was it to show me up for being an ass to her over a year ago?

I wouldn't blame her if it was.

Even if she was learning the language out of spite, I couldn't ignore the fact that I would directly benefit from Eloise learning my preferred form of communication. It would make things easier on my end, in general.

Maybe Eloise would understand how blunt of a language ASL was.

Maybe I wouldn't put my foot in my mouth as often around her.

…Maybe we could get to know each other better.

I finished my set, robotically reracking the weight before I stepped away to grab my sweat towel and water bottle. I wiped off the damp skin on my neck before turning back to glance at her.

Her eyes were hooded as she watched me, not bothering to hide her interest as her clear blue eyes took in their fill. Everywhere her eyes touched made heat break out over my skin. As if her gaze was physically caressing me. She was openly checking me out, still standing in the same place that she was as she spotted me.

I glanced over at Courtney and Josh, who were aware of the blatant ogling Eloise was doing. Josh wiggled his eyebrows suggestively, while Courtney gave me curious looks as her eyes bounced between Eloise and me.

I took another swig of my water bottle, tipping my head back to give Eloise a show of my neck, and wanted to pump my fists in pride when I saw her gaze go towards my throat again. She licked her lips and blinked as if she was coming out of a daze.

Weirdly, neither Courtney nor Josh mentioned anything about that awkward moment.

Well, awkward for them. It wasn't awkward for me. If Eloise liked what she saw, that meant that she'd probably want to get together again. Which was something I was very, very interested in.

15

ELOISE

I wanted to have sex with Logan again.

However, I was a huge chicken and didn't know how to bring it up again.

I thought he might have wanted to have sex with me, too, if the way he looked at me at the gym meant anything.

I thought for sure our hook up would be discovered right then and there. There was already a close call with Courtney and Josh the morning after Logan snuck through my window. I unintentionally winced as I sat down at the kitchen table, still half asleep. So the sound of Courtney throwing her head back and cackling startled me, before Josh blushed and tried to smother her laugh for my sake. She eventually calmed herself enough to ask me who I had over that night, and what we did that made me so sore.

I blushed right along with Josh, and then lied and said it was a random dating app match.

Courtney reached her fist out for me to bump, and congratulated me for getting back on the horse. And then Josh made a joke about how hung the horse must have been for me to waddle downstairs like that in a half-asleep daze.

And then I promptly changed the subject.

Because I definitely wanted to get back on *that* horse again, that was for damn sure.

I just had the self-confidence of a child. Every time I thought about sending Logan a direct text asking for another round, I panicked and deleted it. I had managed to send him a text after reading the note he left me, though. The note made me horribly embarrassed, but also laugh.

I realized at that moment that I wouldn't have granted him the same humor if the roles were reversed, and I wasn't into that kind of playful banter in bed. I really had a lot of pent-up bitter feelings toward the guy, and if I wanted to have sex with him again, I probably needed to work on that.

So I would text him memes from the movie we never got around to watching.

He would laugh-react to them or send memes from manly action-adventure movies.

There was one time when the texting seemed to swing into flirtatious territory, and I panicked again and didn't push the conversation.

And then I saw him at the gym.

If I thought Logan exercising was attractive before, it was nothing compared to seeing him exercise after having the distinct memory of what it was like to feel him inside of me. It was a crude thought, I know. However, it was truthful. Every grunt he made brought back memories, every muscle he flexed reminded me of how it flexed for other reasons.

Every exhale of breath reminded me of how his mouth felt against my skin.

I was embarrassed because he definitely picked up on my horny vibes during our workout. Thankfully, he didn't seem irritated by it. He actually seemed pretty receptive, which made me wonder if I could somehow proposition him into crawling into bed with me again before I left, if Courtney and Josh wandered away at all.

They never did.

I had no one-on-one time with Logan, and we ended up leaving without another word between us.

So later that night I sent him another selfie of me, scantily dressed in bed. I felt my heart pounding in anticipation when I immediately saw the three dots appear before they disappeared. Then they appeared again. Then disappeared.

Finally, leaving me on the edge of my seat, a message from him came through.

He sent a picture back.

It was a bathroom selfie, and he had a white towel wrapped around his waist. He had clearly just gotten out of the shower and took the opportunity to tease me back.

One thing led to another, and within a couple of minutes, we were FaceTiming again, gasping for air as we both teased each other through our phones. My heart was pounding, and I was rubbing a bit of perspiration off my forehead as I grabbed my phone and smiled at the big guy, who was already smiling back at me.

That smile was what I thought about every time I saw him in person.

Which was starting to become more and more frequent.

Josh was taking a few weeks off from recording and performing to spend time with Courtney. Which also meant that occasionally we all got together to hang out with them. Thank fuck, because I didn't want to keep any time available in my schedule for my mother to claim. She was becoming relentless. Clearly irritated with my moving out without her approval of where I was going, she was growing more and more irritated the more I blew her off.

I knew I needed to sit down and talk with her about all this eventually, but I wasn't in the right headspace. Instead, I wanted to hang out with my friends, and the guy I was hooking up with behind all their backs.

Who, currently, was driving all of us to Orange because there was a cute little brunch spot Courtney wanted to try. It wasn't the first time Logan and I had shared space since the gym. We had gotten good at pretending like nothing was going on between us. We still hadn't really spoken to each other about how we both silently agreed to not tell our friends about us, but I weirdly loved it. How Logan and I were on the same page about our situation. How our physical relationship was sensitive information considering how rocky our friendship started all that time ago.

I sat in the middle of the back seat of his truck, and I would occasionally catch his dark eyes on me in the rearview mirror before they would quickly flick away. My stomach would heat at the moment our eyes met, making my nerves hum with energy the more and more we hung out without talking to or touching each other.

We finally made it to brunch and, just like Courtney hoped, it was cute and the food was delicious. I couldn't tell you what we spoke about the entire time though. I couldn't tell you what Taylor, Beck, Adam, or Josh chatted about. I could, however, tell you that the restaurant's AC system needed to be fixed because every time I caught Logan's gaze across the table, my skin would heat to the point where I was genuinely worried that I would start sweating.

We had texted the last few weeks, trying to see when we could meet up again. This was a task that was surprisingly difficult given his training schedule that was starting to prepare for the new hockey season and the schedule I had with work. There was an end-of-summer party the clinic was throwing for the clients and their families, and that ended up being much more time-consuming than I realized.

All of this to say, if I didn't get to touch or kiss Logan again soon, I would probably explode from frustration.

Based on the heavy looks he kept giving me before promptly turning away and pretending to focus on the conversation around us, I had a feeling he was right there with me.

"Want to come with?" Beck asked me, making me blink out of my horny thoughts and focus.

"Pardon?" I asked.

"There is a cute little bookstore down the street, everyone else is going to get ice cream and browse the farmers' market. Do you want to come with me?" Beck asked. I grinned and nodded my head. I wanted to buy a few books of my own, instead of always borrowing Courtney's. I had recently lost one of her paperbacks, and no matter how thoroughly I ripped my bedroom apart to try to find it, I knew I needed to accept my fuck up and replace the book.

So I decided to pair off with Beck while everyone else agreed to meet back up at the farmers' market in an hour (because otherwise Beck and I would spend the rest of the day in the bookstore).

Adam had just kissed Beck goodbye when Logan followed us out of the restaurant and glanced between the two groups. Josh, Courtney, Taylor, and Adam already all had their backs to us as they headed in the direction of the farmers' market, and to our surprise, Logan had turned and followed Beck and me to the bookstore.

"Do you like to read, Logan?" Beck asked, smiling up at the large man. If she was surprised that he followed us to the bookstore, she didn't show it.

Logan lifted his hands, and I tried my hardest to watch his ASL carefully while also watching where I was walking on the sidewalk.

Not a lot, Logan signed—and I mentally cheered for how helpful those online ASL classes I had been taking were, *I like – find – books – I can.*

I didn't catch all the words he signed, but thankfully I could get the gist.

"What do you like to read?" I asked him vocally while also signing my question the best I could. Beck smiled brightly at my sentence in ASL but didn't make a big deal out of it. Logan's gaze smoothed a little bit at the movement of my hands before he started responding.

I didn't know the signs he used, though.

The pinch in my brow gave me away.

"Adam likes science fiction too," Beck spoke up, helping

me out, "You and he have probably read some of the same stuff."

I nodded along and, after a couple of minutes of listening to Beck and Logan chat about some science fiction book they read, we made it to the shop. I walked inside without hesitation, determined to find the romance section in hopes of replacing the book I lost. Thankfully, the romance section was large and in the back of the store. It was a cute little shop, with clean lines and feminine plants and art, clearly intending to target women.

I sighed a breath of relief when I found the book, pulled it off the shelf, and flipped through the pages before tucking it to my chest. Now that I had what I needed to replace, I decided to browse and see which copies I wanted to buy for myself.

"Anything good?" Beck asked, catching up with me. I glanced behind her to see Logan following behind, and I could feel the blush stain my cheeks as I stood in front of the smutty romances.

"Always," I replied, holding up the book I grabbed first. "I lost Courtney's copy of this, so I need to replace it."

Beck's eyes widened, "Oh no! That one is so good, too. That's nice of you to get her a new one."

"She hasn't asked for it back, so I don't know if she knows I lost it—" Logan's dark eyes staring pointedly at the book I held up made me pause my sentence for half a second "—But I still feel bad for losing it." His ears started to turn pink before he tore his gaze away and started to look around at all the spines we stood in front of.

Odd.

"I should just get my own copy of that too," Beck agreed, finding the book, and grabbing one for herself. She then pulled her phone out of her back pocket, which was buzzing with a call. After tapping on her phone, she held it in her hand and spoke without placing it near her ear.

"Hey, Gram," Beck spoke. It was so cool that she could Bluetooth her phone to her hearing aids like that. "What's up?" Soon, she was mindlessly wandering off as she spoke on the phone to her grandmother, and Logan and I were left alone.

This was the first time we had been alone since the night he snuck through my window. Since we kissed for the first time. Since we slept together.

The image of him on top of me and gripping my waist made heat scorch my veins. I didn't have time to try to mask it before Logan's dark eyes landed on me, as he pulled a random spine off the shelf. He gave the back of it a quick glance, before shelving it and looking at me again.

I swallowed, clutched Courtney's book to my chest, and promptly turned to face away from him to stare at the books. I wasn't reading any of the spines, but I was too embarrassed to try to talk to him when it was painfully obvious from my blush that I couldn't look at him without thinking about sex.

A couple of moments of silence passed, where I only felt his presence next to me but didn't look at him, and my phone buzzed in my pocket.

I pulled it out and glanced down, before seeing a text from Logan. I looked up at him because he was less than a foot away from me, only to see him pull a romance novel off the shelf and read the back of it. As if he didn't just send me a text to read.

I glanced back down at my phone.

Logan: I want to feel you underneath me again, Eloise.

I sucked in a sharp breath at the words, my face hot with what I was sure was a bright red blush. He still didn't look at me, as if he didn't just send me a very spicy text with our friend nearby.

I just stood there, reading the text again and again, trying way too hard to regulate my breathing.

Then my phone buzzed with a second text, making my heart thump in anticipation as I quickly tapped on his next message.

Logan: I want to hear the sounds you make when I'm inside you.

I gasped and squeezed Courtney's book in my other hand. I barely lifted my head to finally look at him when suddenly, Logan was crowding my space. I blinked as I backed away from him. My butt hit the corner of the bookshelves in the romance section, and I held my breath when Logan reached up behind me to pull another book off the shelf, making it look like he was genuinely interested in the spines and not trying to drive me insane with his presence. He took another step, our legs brushing against each other as he rested one of his large arms on the shelf beside me, while the other held the book for him to browse.

He caged me in with his arms.

Logan had trapped me in an arm cage, a move that was tried-and-true in any romance novel ever.

"Beck will be back any second," I whispered, inhaling Logan's deodorant or cologne or whatever it was, and struggling to remember that others were nearby.

Logan nodded his head once, putting the book back as if he wasn't the one who sent me those texts moments ago.

I couldn't help myself, I leaned into him.

He responded by pressing the fronts of our chests together, both of his arms holding the shelf on either side of my head as he leaned his nose down to brush against my hair. I felt his chest expand on an inhale, and we both just stood there for the longest seconds of my life. Completely wrapped up in each other's space.

"I want you, too," I whispered, leaning close enough to brush my nose against his shoulder, moving in towards his neck. I felt more than heard the noise that rumbled in his chest, and that made me reach one arm out to clutch the hem of his t-shirt against his abdomen.

One of his hands left the bookshelf to brush my hair behind my ear, a touch that scorched my skin. I leaned away enough to tilt my face up towards him, getting completely lost in his dark hooded eyes. His hand was now twirling a lock of my hair around his index finger.

"Kiss me?" I asked him, desperate for anything I could get away with now. At my whispered words, Logan's hand released my lock of hair and snaked itself behind my head, cupping the top of my neck to angle my lips for him to reach.

He simply pressed his warm lips against mine, unhurried, patient, and thorough.

I tried my best to be good, to let him kiss me how he wanted, but all too quickly I brushed my tongue against the seam of his lips.

At that, I felt his smile spread across his lips before he used his grip on the back of my head to pull me away, just enough for his dark eyes to meet mine.

"Please," I whispered, clearly desperate for him. Logan's smirk tipped up a notch at my plea, and as soon as he lowered his head toward mine again, we heard a startled gasp to our left.

Logan immediately dropped his hold on me and took a step back, whereas when I tried to take a step back, I bumped into bookshelves and knocked a couple of paperbacks over. I was blushing hard, trying not to panic at the sight of Beck standing to the side and staring at us both wide-eyed.

"Sorry!" Beck flapped her hands once before covering her eyes, then her mouth, then her cheeks, and then she spun in an awkward circle before she probably realized running away was silly and faced us again with her hands over her mouth.

Logan and I both dropped to the ground to pick up the books I had knocked over before he pulled the fallen books out of my grip and quickly stood to put them back. This made him awkwardly hover over me again, and I froze half-crouched until he straightened and gave me room to stand.

I was spiraling.

Beck had just seen us kissing each other. And why wouldn't she? That's what we got for trying to sneak some kisses in a bookstore we all went to together. But…I didn't want everyone to know about Logan and me yet. I was pretty sure the way he backed off of me indicated that he felt the same way.

What Logan and I were doing was very new, and probably still very fragile. It was mostly physical, and who knew if it would turn into anything more than that.

I didn't want to risk being part of this social circle, these friendships, if anything with Logan and I ended...well, badly. If we never went beyond this physical relationship we were exploring because we weren't actually compatible in that way. If everyone knew about us, clearly there would be outside pressure, and people would take sides if we broke up. I didn't want that. I wanted to figure things out between us before others got involved.

Logan and I both gave each other nervous looks before we faced Beck again.

Her hands were on her cheeks now.

"I'm so sorry, I didn't mean—"

"It's fine," I cut her off, "You did nothing wrong."

"I didn't realize that you two—" she cut herself off again, shaking her head. "Sorry, it's none of my business."

I bit my lip and looked up at Logan, who had shoved both of his hands in his pockets. He had a pinch between his eyebrows before his gaze slid over to mine, and then the lines in his head loosened the slightest bit.

"We, uh," I waved my hand around vaguely, "We, um..." I sighed and lowered my hand, wrapping both around Courtney's book I still miraculously held in my grip, "It's new."

Beck pinched her fingers and dragged them over the firm press of her lips, zipping them closed. I smiled and glanced up at Logan, who offered a tiny lift in the corner of his mouth and a nod.

Beck tucked her top lip into her teeth, a facial expression

that Courtney often referred to as her Troll Face, before pulling her phone out to check the time and saying, "We still have, like, thirty minutes before we need to meet up with everyone else."

I shrugged my shoulders, "Okay."

Beck glanced behind her and then turned back to an awkward Logan and me. "I hear there are some good books in the poetry section."

I lifted another shoulder, "I'm not really into poetry."

Beck gave me a blank stare, then said, "Let me try that again." She lifted a thumb over her shoulder and made pointed eye contact with the both of us. "We have thirty minutes before we are expected anywhere. The poetry section, the partially hidden section around the corner that offers a decent amount of privacy, might have some books you both are interested in."

I furrowed my brows for a moment before it clicked and I widened my eyes at her.

"Oh, we don't—" But my sentence was cut off, because Logan had gripped my free hand in his and started tugging me past Beck, who was smiling brightly at the both of us as the large man bolted for the poetry section she spoke of.

"Your secret is safe with me!" Beck called to us as she took our place in front of the romance novels to browse.

I was giggling as I was yanked around the corner. A light was out, which made the poetry section a little dimmer than the rest of the bookshop. It felt a little cozier. I almost forgot why we were back here until Logan found a small patch of wall in between two large shelving units of books to shove me against and slammed his lips on mine.

"Holy shit," I gasped into his mouth. Gone was the gentle and controlled pressing of his lips. Now we were frantic, pawing at each other as Courtney's book got ripped out of my hands and set on the shelf so that he could guide my fingers into his hair.

Interesting.

I gripped the roots of his hair, making a damaged gasping sound release from his chest and free itself against my lips.

"Do you like this?" I tugged on the roots of his hair again, and he closed his eyes in clear bliss as his lips twitched in a smile. "Good to know." I tugged him back to my lips with my grip, loving how both of his large hands felt confident enough to snake around my back and down my waist so that he could grab each of my ass cheeks.

He pulled me against his hips, making me choke on a whine as we devoured each other. I had never made out with anyone this aggressively in a public space before. Even in high school, I hadn't done the thing where you go to the movies but don't watch the movies because you're too busy sucking face. No, this was a first for me.

And I fucking loved it.

Maybe I just liked the thrill of an employee possibly finding us and telling us to leave. Maybe I was still feeding off of the adrenaline rush of getting caught by Beck. Regardless, I couldn't find myself thinking about the situation too critically because Logan's mouth was on my mouth and he tasted amazing. His hips dug into mine and I could feel his arousal through his jeans, making me lift my leg so that I could grind against him just where I needed him.

He used his grip on my ass to lift me enough to make it work, dragging me over himself in frenzied desperation.

Twenty-six minutes later, Logan and I made the walk of shame out of the poetry section to Beck, who said nothing. Her only acknowledgment about us making out in a public bookstore was a smile as she reached up to help us both tame our messed-up hair.

"There," Beck finally spoke after helping me finger comb my hair back into place. "Now you don't look like you just had sex on a bookshelf."

I gasped, blinking up at Logan who rubbed a hand over his mouth as he glanced down at me, a move that I was starting to realize covered his smile. He dragged his hand down his jaw, making the pink scars on his face stretch a moment before pulling his phone out and checking the time.

"We didn't have sex," I whispered to Beck's back as she led us out of the bookstore.

"It's none of my business what you two did." She smiled at me over her shoulder, making me look back at Logan for help. He simply lifted his eyes from where he was clearly staring at my ass as I walked in front of him, and grinned at me. Not remorseful at all about his blatant ogling.

I gave him a narrowed look before I turned forward and stood confidently, letting him know that he could stare all he wanted.

I just couldn't look Logan in the eye for the rest of the afternoon—otherwise I was sure the blush my body would create from one glance at him would give us away.

16

LOGAN

Hockey season was only a few weeks away, and part of me was both excited and bummed about it. I had played in the NHL for almost a decade at that point. Perhaps I was getting close to experiencing burnout. Not necessarily physical burnout, since I still felt like my body could keep up. But the sport didn't thrill me anymore. It wasn't at the front of my mind like it used to be, and part of me suspected that was because of a certain little blonde woman.

I had just gotten home from practicing with John and his husband on the ice at an Irvine rink the team sometimes used for extra sessions, when my phone buzzed and I yanked it out of my jeans.

I felt myself smile as I kicked my front door shut and opened the message.

Eloise: I need help with my homework.

I dropped my bag near the laundry units in my small one-bedroom apartment before walking towards the shower. I could easily shower at the facilities we trained at, but I hated it. Nothing made me feel as clean as I did after showering in my own home.

Me: For your ASL class?

Eloise: Yes. I need to give a presentation in a couple of days and I think I need a tutor to help me practice.

Eloise: Preferably one who can motivate me with kissable lips and dark, grabbable hair.

I grinned at my phone as I turned the shower on.

Me: Then Beck is probably your gal.

Eloise: *middle finger emoji*

I huffed a laugh at that, before I decided to pull back on the teasing.

Me: I'm hopping in the shower, but I'll be out by the time you get here.

I sent her my address and set my phone down before letting the scalding hot water hit my skin.

As soon as I stepped out of the shower and started toweling off my hair, I heard the doorbell ring. She was faster than I anticipated, so I quickly wrapped the towel around my waist before checking the peephole to ensure that it was, in fact, Eloise at my door and not some door-to-door salesman.

I opened the door and waved for her to come in, smiling, when her eyes trailed over my naked torso.

As I shut the door behind her, she quietly clapped her palms together before tucking her hands under her chin, her eyes on my stomach.

"Speeding through those yellow lights *really* paid off," Eloise murmured reverently as she ogled my body. I laughed, knowing the sound was off compared to someone who didn't have a damaged voice like mine, but also knowing that Eloise didn't care.

I gestured to her that my eyes were, in fact, up *here*.

"I know, I know," Eloise adjusted her bag on her shoulder and finally made direct eye contact with me, "But you're the perfect motivation for me to get this right."

And that is how we ended up on my bed. After Eloise watched me get dressed in sweatpants and a t-shirt, she opened her laptop to the written words of her presentation and told me to help her correct her signs.

Her ASL was good, but her class didn't cover every single nuance and sentence structure rule ASL had. It usually took numerous classes to really get comfortable signing anything on the spot. So that was where I came in, helping Eloise sign the words and sentences she didn't know, to help fill in the gaps of her presentation, without ruining the flow.

"Party," Eloise vocalized after I showed her the sign. "Huh. It's similar to 'play', which we use a lot at work." She bit her lip as she repeated the sign back to me. I nodded, shifting so that I had one ankle crossed over the other as I watched her sign through the next couple of sentences of her presentation again.

I had to give Eloise credit, when she was determined to learn something, she perfected it. Her signs were crisp, not the lazy movements that beginners usually displayed for the sake of running through an ASL sentence as quickly as possible.

"Good?" Eloise asked, also signing *good* to me.

I nodded and gave her a thumbs up.

She sighed a breath of relief as she stopped the recording her laptop was making. She wanted to record herself signing the sentences so she could watch them back later tonight as she practiced running through the entire presentation in one sitting.

"This is genuinely helpful, thank you so much," Eloise gave me a shy look before slumping against my headboard and setting her laptop to the side, "I need a break, though."

My pants immediately tightened, so I bent one leg up in a poor attempt to try to conceal my body's immediate excitement to her words. Something that was more difficult to do while wearing sweatpants. She turned her head towards me, her gaze trailing over my body as if looking for the evidence of my arousal, before she twisted in her seat to face me directly and meet my eyes.

"...Can I ask you a personal question?" Eloise's voice was softer, lower, and it made me want to lean in towards her space even more. I resisted, because I had a feeling her question wasn't going to be of the sexy variety, and I wanted to keep my hands to myself if that was the case.

I nodded at her.

"...What happened?" Eloise's eyes dropped, indicating that she was taking in my scars that were plainly visible on my face and neck.

I felt heat prick my skin at the spot she stared at, and my heart started to pick up pace again. The last time I had shared this with someone was also the first time I had met Eloise. I had been feeling too exposed for opening up to someone so deeply about my past, that I lashed out at Eloise and made us start out on the worst foot possible.

That being said, I was genuinely surprised Courtney hadn't divulged the details of my accident to everyone else in the group. No one had ever asked me about my scars, or why I preferred to sign instead of vocalizing.

I inhaled a breath in preparation, before signing to Eloise.

Her brow scrunched, so I signed again a little slower. Using this as another ASL lesson created a bit of a buffer for the emotional exposure I was about to endure with her.

"Car crash?" Eloise asked, her voice almost a whisper still. I nodded my confirmation at her. "When?"

I was eighteen, I replied.

Eloise's wide, clear eyes studied me for a moment. Silence hung between us, and my skin itched as she let us sit in the silence. I was determined to make it through this with Eloise, though. Part of me was even surprised to admit that I *wanted* to share this with her. That I wanted her to get to know me. Why that was, I was pretty sure I knew, but I didn't let myself go down that train of thought too far in the moment.

"I'm sorry," Eloise simply said.

I shrugged in response.

"Was that what damaged your voice?" Eloise asked again, though she sounded nervous to get the words out. She probably didn't know if this was pushing it or not, but I didn't want to scare her off.

I never wanted to scare Eloise off ever again.

I would answer whatever she asked of me.

The thought made me pause for half a second before I

remembered to actually respond to her question, *Yes.* Eloise was quiet again, so I decided to keep the conversation going. I pulled my phone out, turning on my phone screen which showed a picture of my little sister, Anna.

I handed the phone to Eloise to look at before she lifted her eyes at me in curiosity. That was the moment that I truly realized how weird it was for a thirty-year-old man to have a picture of a teenage girl on his lock screen.

My little sister, I signed to Eloise. I noticed her eyes widening a fraction, before I continued, *She died in the car crash.*

Eloise sucked in a breath, before staring at the picture again.

Silence became less suffocating, and calmer before Eloise spoke up, "She looks like Courtney."

I smirked, nodding my head, *Imagine my reaction when Courtney talked to me at the gym the first time. I thought I was being haunted.*

It took me mouthing my words at Eloise with my signs for her to understand before a soft giggle escaped her lips at my sentence.

"Damn, that's crazy," Eloise lifted the phone closer to her face as if she was studying every detail of Anna. The picture was her at a restaurant, with two straws up either of her nostrils as she smiled at the camera, her hands clasped calmly on the table as if nothing was sticking out of her face. I loved the picture because it let me constantly remember what Anna looked like, as well as what a total weirdo she was.

"I'm so sorry you lost her," Eloise handed the phone back to me after one last glance, "And I'm sorry you had to experience the damage and pain you clearly have." I shrugged again. It sucked, and I had lingering symptoms from the trauma of the event, but I was also making improvements day by day. "Were your parents, okay?"

Ah, she must have assumed the crash happened with my parents in the vehicle too.

I frowned a little before continuing. It took a lot of repetition and extra mouthing on my end, but after stumbling through the story a couple of times, Eloise eventually learned a little bit more about me.

That my mother passed away from breast cancer when I was twelve.

That my father was a deadbeat alcoholic, who barely reacted to the accident and death of his daughter beyond continually skipping town for greater stretches.

That I hadn't spoken to my father for about five years now, and that he could also be dead for all I knew.

Eloise's face was crumbled by the time the gist of my life was exposed to her, and I wanted to put her bright smiles back on her face without brushing what I experienced under the rug.

I'm okay now, I signed to her, *I am doing better.*

Eloise nodded before shifting closer to me. My heart skipped a beat before she opened her arms and wrapped them around my shoulders, her face hiding in the crook of my neck and pulling me tight against her. It was instinct to embrace her back just as tight, and I felt a piece of my core shutter at the comfort that Eloise was willingly offering me.

This little woman had once assaulted me with pie, and

now we were both sitting on my bed while she embraced me with no intention other than to provide comfort.

"Thank you for sharing that with me," Eloise mumbled into my neck. I just nodded, a movement she could probably feel, but I decided to take a deep breath and give her something I didn't share with anyone else.

"...You're welcome." I whispered. Eloise stiffened in my arms. My voice didn't sound good. It sounded downright scary, and it was almost inaudible to anyone who wasn't right up against my lips. The whisper was scratchy. I had people in college tell me it sounded like something you would hear in an empty room in a horror movie.

Vocalizing those words created a small burn where the nerve damage in my body had taken the brunt of it, but I've experienced that pain before and had anticipated it enough to muscle through it for the moment. I didn't share my voice with just anyone. Not even Courtney had heard me vocalize before.

Eloise was different.

I wanted her to know she was different.

Eloise pulled back while keeping her arms around my neck, her red rimmed eyes meeting mine before she quickly blinked away tears that were pooling there.

I reached a hand up to cup her cheek and shook my head, *I'm sorry*, I mouthed, *Did I scare you?*

"No. No." Eloise shook her head, her lips pulling up a little bit in a nervous smirk, "I'm...weirdly honored."

I smiled at her, thumbing away a stray tear that she couldn't quite blink away.

"But," Eloise swallowed, "Please don't do that if it hurts too much."

I hesitated before I continued leisurely brushing my thumb against her cheek, *Why?*

"...I will never ask you to use your voice, Logan." Eloise's fingers gently traced up the back of my neck, into the roots of my hair. Goosebumps erupted on my skin from her touch, "Again, I am *honored* to know what you sound like," Eloise smiled, "But your voice is yours. Hearing you speak was a privilege, and nothing more." Eloise brushed her nose against mine, and I felt something in my chest squeeze at the contact. "I was able to find the kind, gentle man beneath this moody exterior, regardless."

I grinned before pressing my lips against hers for no other reason than I simply couldn't hold back any longer. She met my kisses with enthusiasm, but it wasn't frantic like how we were in the bookstore. No, this moment was one I hadn't experienced before. It was vulnerable. It was emotional. The kisses we exchanged illustrated the trust we now had between each other, and nothing more.

It took a while for us to get here, to this limbo of a relationship where she and I still hadn't discussed what we were to each other beyond lover and tutor. While I tasted Eloise's lips as if I had all the time in the world, I realized how *worth it* the journey was. How much I could kick myself for fucking up so royally the first time we met, but that I was willing to do what it took to even find ourselves here, in this moment.

This feisty woman who covered herself in flower tattoos for no other reason than she liked flowers.

This brilliant woman who could hold a grudge for however long she deemed necessary.

This beautiful woman who could make me feel like the luckiest man alive for simply having the honor to share these quiet kisses with her in the comfort of my bed, and nothing more.

I let myself fully come to the realization then.

I truly wanted Eloise Bane.

17

LOGAN

"She's at home, she's not feeling well," Courtney shrugged, taking a sip from her martini as she smiled at Taylor trying to shoot their shot with a guy on the other end of the bar top. A few nights later we all found ourselves at a new bar in downtown Dana Point. The bar was owned by someone Taylor had casually dated a few years ago, and they stayed friends even when the romance in their relationship fizzled out. Taylor asked all of us to show up to opening night to help support the small business.

I had met up with everyone at the bar after an annoying meeting with John and Connor. The meeting went like every other meeting. Because the scandalous pictures of the team had taken off on the internet, and resulted in a huge surge in presale tickets to the upcoming seasons games, Connor wanted to lean further into the sexualizing of the players.

John was all for it. He was body positive and did not care if people ogled what he worked so hard for.

I realized that I also didn't care too much about showing off my body, but I loved telling Connor "no" much more.

Because fuck Connor.

I wasn't his biggest fan before I knew that he slept with Eloise, but for some stupid reason, he irritated me even more now. How dare he touch Eloise and make her react the way she did? How dare he just not care about her reaction at all? Any moron could pay attention and notice when a woman wasn't into something he was doing. To see her shut down and lose enthusiasm for sex. The more I thought about it, the more I realized that Connor going through with everything, even when Eloise clearly wasn't enjoying herself, aggravated me. It showed how little he cared about Eloise as a person. The fact that he was willing to see the night through even though her head was clearly somewhere else was disgusting.

Part of me was mature enough to understand that part of this was good old-fashioned jealousy. The thought of someone like Connor being with Eloise that way made me want to rage. To shield Eloise behind my body, never to have his eyes land on her again, and shout "mine" in his face.

I also remembered what I had learned from another one of Eloise's romance novels that I finished the previous night, how what I was experiencing was best described as "alphahole" behavior. Possessive, controlling, toxic. Eloise's review online played through my mind, "...*I'm going through an alphahole phase. If a real man had the audacity to act like this, I would dump his ass. But for some reason, in these books, it's hot as hell...*"

Eventually, I'd need to tell Eloise that I stole Courtney's book. Part of me thought Eloise might even appreciate the fact that I was reading a lot of her favorite books, as long as she was able to get past the part that I stole from her. Yeah, I'd need to tell her sooner than later.

…Just not yet.

I remembered to tune back into the conversation I was having with Courtney. She had just answered my question, after all. I felt my face pinch before I made myself relax the muscles as I expressed my curiosity, *Is Eloise okay?*

Courtney's brown eyes slid over to me, something in them that made me hold my breath until she responded, "She's on her period."

I nodded, my shoulders relaxing the slightest bit. I didn't even know that they were tense until she answered my question. Eloise was fine; women got their periods all the time. It wasn't like she was sick or anything.

"I actually feel awful for her," Beck spoke up from my other side, leaning around me to make eye contact with Courtney. "She looked miserable when we picked you up tonight."

I felt a frown form on my lips as I listened to Beck's words.

"Yeah," Courtney shrugged, "Yesterday she was pretty functional, but today she's either been in bed or on the couch." Wait, what? "I thought I heard her throw up this morning."

What the fuck? Because of her period? Were they sure that she didn't have the flu or something?

Are periods really that bad? I signed my question to the two women on either side of me, and they both exchanged a knowing look before Beck simply said, "Yes." And Courtney added, "They can be."

Is it normal to throw up because of periods? I asked again, my curiosity piqued.

"Yeah," Courtney set her elbow on the bar top before resting her cheek on her fist, "Do you know what a period is?"

I rolled my eyes, *Yes.*

"But do you understand the reality of it?" Courtney pressed, making Beck giggle on my other side. "Because you know what it is, and yet you seem surprised to know that there can be a certain level of pain involved."

I didn't say anything, I just stared at her, waiting for her to eventually elaborate. She did.

"The uterus is literally shedding its lining," I nodded because I understood that "The organ is ripping itself apart from the inside out, piece by piece, which—call me crazy—doesn't sound too pleasant on paper."

I frowned because no, no it did not.

"Everyone has different pain tolerances," Beck spoke up, making me glance to my other side to look at her. "Some women have high pain tolerances, and can function just fine on their period." Beck shrugged, "Other women's periods are actually just worse. More brutal. They lose more blood, and therefore, are in more pain. Plus, there are additional medical conditions that can make periods so much worse." Beck's brows scrunched in thought as she stared at her own martini, "I wonder if Eloise has something like that."

"I think that she has something," Courtney replied. "The amount of pads and tampons she goes through is alarming. No one can lose that much blood and be totally functional.

She's gotten lucky by having her heavy flow days occur over the weekend when she doesn't have to work."

I widened my eyes.

Eloise was constantly bleeding.

She was bleeding out, throwing up, and unable to move.

And my heart twisted at that knowledge. All of us were at the bar, having a good time while Eloise was trying to hold herself together.

Can she take medicine to help? I asked, not too worried about how I looked at the moment.

Beck smiled at me, "Tylenol and Ibuprofen help. But not always."

I shook my head, before Courtney spoke up with a sarcastic tone, "Classic."

I gave her a questioning look before she continued, "You're such a man sometimes, Logan." I frowned because, coming from Courtney, it probably wasn't a compliment.

"Why is Logan such a man?" Josh asked, approaching his fiancée from behind and looping an arm around her neck to pull her against his chest.

"He is just learning about the severity of periods."

Josh smiled and winked at me. "Give him a break," he chastised Courtney and kissed her head, "None of us guys know until a woman teaches us."

I gave Josh a small smile of appreciation because I did feel a little bit like an asshole just learning about all of this in my thirties, but he eased my guilt a little with his words.

"It's true," Beck patted my shoulder before crossing her arms on the bar top to speak to our friends, "As soon as we get our periods, girls are immediately told not to talk about it. And then we go to health class in, like, middle school or something, and the lecture on periods weirdly gaslights us into believing that we are being over dramatic about the pain and maintenance, simply because every single uterus owner experiences it and also doesn't talk about it. And then when we do talk about it as adults, realizing how stupid it is to not talk about something we experience every single month, men gaslight us again because no other woman in their life has spoken about it. So we must be 'overdramatic', right? We must be 'exaggerating our pain'."

"So then," Courtney chimed in, nodding along with every sentence Beck spoke, "That leaves women like Eloise in the state she's currently in." My gut churned at the image they were so clearly painting for me. "At home, curled up on the couch with a heating pad, all by herself. In so much pain that she can't even walk around. After she weirdly shoved all her friends out the door to go out and have fun tonight without her because she feels bad for feeling bad. She doesn't want to inconvenience other uterus owners with the pain that she feels when her uterus destroys itself as some shitty reward for not getting pregnant this month."

I stared into my mug of beer, only having taken a couple of sips from it as I thought about their words. It was such a horrible reality, and part of me felt guilty for never thinking twice about it. I didn't have a uterus. The most inconvenient thing I ever had to experience because of my genitalia were no reason or inappropriately timed boners.

It's not like I had to deal with a constant bleed from my dick every month.

I couldn't fathom being able to function well enough to play hockey if men had to experience what women did.

And they were right.

The moment Courtney and Beck started talking about Eloise's current state, my immediate thought was that they must be mistaken. *Eloise must be sick. No way would a period affect her that badly.* Thanks, patriarchy. Thanks, society, for training men like me to always excuse and dismiss women.

That sounds horrible, I finally signed in response to the vivid descriptions the women in my life gave me.

"It *is* horrible," Courtney twirled the toothpick of grapes in her glass thoughtfully.

"That just means men like Logan and I have to lead by example," said Josh. The rockstar rested his chin on top of Courtney's head, looking at me intently, "It's up to us to listen, to learn, and to correct our expectations and behaviors."

I blinked at him, suspicion clawing at me when he narrowed his eyes a little and winked at me again. He was clearly trying to tell me something subtly, and as far as I knew he hadn't told Courtney about my attraction toward Eloise.

He also didn't know that Eloise and I had slept together, but that was neither here nor there.

But his words made me consider myself. My entire existence.

Conversation continued around me, but I pulled out my phone and started researching the topic a bit more. Josh was right, I was given the information. Now it was up to me to decide how to act going forward.

18

ELOISE

"Can I get you anything?" Susan asked, tucking the throw blanket over my feet on the couch. I only took up about half of it because I was curled into a ball on my side. We had just spent the last hour and a half watching a movie, and I was already feeling guilty that she stayed up later than usual to fuss over me. She didn't normally like to stay up late, but she knew how much pain I was in today. And she didn't want me to feel alone while everyone else met up at the new bar Taylor wanted to check out.

"I'm good, thank you though," I smiled up at her, blatantly ignoring the sharp jab of pain I randomly felt in my butthole. It was the worst day, and I was just desperate for it to be over. It's one thing to feel cramps in my uterus, but why the fuck did my body feel the need to cramp so hard that I felt like I had sat on a knife? This was just ridiculous.

"Holler if you change your mind," Susan brushed some hair off of my forehead and grinned before she stood up and shuffled her way towards her bedroom. Right as she started crossing the entryway, there was a knock on the door.

We both looked at each other, confirming that neither of us was expecting anybody before she shifted over to the front door and peered through the peep pole. Susan chuckled, before opening the door wide enough to show me who was at our home at ten thirty at night.

Logan, in all his physically fit glory, stood on the doorstep.

He was supposed to be at the bar with everyone else, but instead, he was here. Holding a plastic bag from somewhere.

"To what do we owe the pleasure?" Susan asked, stepping aside, and inviting him in. I was frozen. I stayed curled up under my blanket and just gaped at him. Why was he here? Before Logan could sign anything, Susan tugged on the mouth of the plastic bag he held in one hand and peered inside. Logan then opened the bag all the way for her to see, and the grin that spread across her face was full of mischievousness.

"She's all yours," Susan nodded towards me, making Logan's dark eyes meet mine across the open concept space. I felt my heart flutter in my chest when he finally looked at me, and I felt myself shrinking into the couch and tugging the blanket tighter around my neck.

Logan shut the door behind him and kicked off his shoes, setting them to the side where our guests usually kept their shoes and nodded politely at Susan as she turned to continue her way to her bedroom. Logan strode into the living room, coming to sit directly next to my feet on the couch.

"What's up?" I asked him, his face searching mine in silence. He didn't lift his hands to sign anything, he just stared at me, at my curled-up form under a throw blanket. His gaze flicked to the ibuprofen bottle on the coffee table and rested a hand on my ankle over the blanket before lifting his bag with the other.

"What is that?" I asked, struggling to keep my body still from his touch. The ache in my abdomen made me both want to lean into his touch and pull away.

Logan removed his hand from me before he dug around in the bag to start pulling items out of it. He set everything on the coffee table gently, nothing but the sounds of the movie playing in the room as he showed off his loot.

Double-Stuf Oreos.

Orange Gatorade.

Cool Ranch Doritos.

Popcorn.

Midol.

Extra-Strength Tylenol.

And gummies.

My heart twisted in my chest, and it was a struggle to breathe evenly.

"You got me weed?" I asked, eyeballing the gummies. Logan shrugged, before taking my legs that were still tucked under the blanket and lifting them up so that he could slide underneath. I shifted so that I was no longer on my side, but instead on my back with my legs resting over his thighs.

Through the blanket, he gently started rubbing my legs, before pausing and pulling his phone out from his pocket. He thumbed away at it while I just stared at him. His hard profile, his scars on his skin, his curly brown hair that he tamed with some type of product. The cream-colored button-down shirt he wore with the sleeves rolled up to his elbows, the forearm porn I was witnessing as he typed away on his phone.

Maybe it was just because I was on my period and hormonal, but Logan looked mouthwatering tonight.

He then turned his phone to give to me, and I had to untuck one of my arms from the blanket to grab it. He had written on the notes app for me to read.

I looked online for some ideas on how to help you out. I took a guess on what snacks you liked based on what I remembered you eating whenever food has been around before, and apparently marijuana helps with period cramps. If it doesn't end up helping you with the pain, it'll at least help you sleep through it. The Gatorade is to help you stay hydrated.

I stared at him, his phone motionless in my hand.

He stared right back at me, his eyes clearly desperate to flick away and look at something else, but he didn't. Logan held my gaze, his dark eyes only glancing to his phone once before meeting mine again.

"You…" I felt my lip quiver, and I one hundred percent blamed my sudden rush of emotions on my period, "Courtney told you I was on my period?"

Logan frowned before nodding his head and continuing to rub his large hands on the muscles of my calves, before slowly resting over my feet—still through the blanket. His thumbs pressed into the arch of my foot in a painfully pleasant way as he held my gaze.

"And you came here? With all this?" I flicked my gaze to the stash on the coffee table. Logan swallowed once and nodded his head, his gaze finally lowering to his hands as they massaged my feet.

I sniffed, and he immediately lifted his head to look at me, *What's wrong?* He asked, signing and mouthing for me. I sniffed again, the heat of tears pricking my eyes as I struggled to get a handle on myself. My gut instinct was to comfort him, to let him know that I was fine. That this wasn't a big deal, that I dealt with this every month and will for the foreseeable future. But then I realized that I hadn't ever held back with Logan. I never cared about getting him to like me because I assumed he already didn't. However, even though I never went out of my way to please Logan in any way, he still liked me.

I didn't need to mold myself into anything to make him more comfortable.

Why the fuck would I start doing that now, just because we were exploring this relationship between us?

I experienced a bad cramp, my legs naturally twitching towards myself as I breathed through it. Logan's face looked pained, and he gently rubbed a hand over my thighs as his body arched over me.

"My stomach hurts and it really sucks. Can you give me a gummy?" I asked, my voice small. I didn't want to think too hard about why he chose to leave our friends at the bar and come to me instead. None of them knew we had sex, except for Beck. None of them knew we liked each other. But he still ditched them and went to the store and showed up here. Because he heard I was on my period.

Logan nodded and opened the package, pulling out a

watermelon-flavored sugary circular gummy. I took it from his hands and immediately started chewing.

"How much is in this?" I asked as I swallowed, wincing from the gross marijuana aftertaste it had. Logan lifted the package for me to read, his finger tapping on the product description.

10mg THC, 1mg CBD.

Nice.

"I'm a lightweight," I explained after he set the package down on the coffee table, "So I'm probably going to be loopy and sleepy soon." Logan nodded, reaching for the Gatorade, and unscrewing the lid before handing it to me.

I felt my lip wobble as I sniffled again, desperately fighting back the tears in my eyes as I witnessed him caring for me.

Logan frowned and set the Gatorade down after I took a few gulps and leaned over me to gently brush my short hair back out of my face.

"God dammit," I whispered. He must not be that comfortable. My legs were still over his, and he had to awkwardly reach over my body to stretch his arm far enough to touch my face, "You're killing me, Logan."

Logan's lips twitched, *In a good way?* He lifted his hands to sign and mouthed for me like he always did. He signed and mouthed his words clearly so I could understand him. Because I still wasn't fluent in his preferred language. He carried the brunt of the mental load when it came to communicating with me in a way that I could understand him.

And it wasn't even like we were officially dating or anything.

We were literally just sleeping together.

"I'm sorry," I felt a tear escape and quickly wiped it away, but it was too late, he saw it. Logan shook his head as a pained expression coated his features. He started digging his arms under my legs and back, scooting me more toward his body as I continued talking through my sniffles, "I promise I'm trying." I swallowed, unable to remove the lump in my throat. "I'm trying to learn for you. I don't want this whole thing to be one-sided."

Logan had successfully shifted me onto his lap, his large arms wrapping around my body so that I was entirely curled up against his chest, my head resting between his neck and shoulder, while he pressed his scarred cheek on the top of my head. His hands held me tight, and his body shifted ever so slightly from side to side as if he were rocking me.

I let a few silent tears fall as I embraced the physical comfort that he was giving me. I didn't want to think too hard about why Logan showed up tonight. Why he ditched our friends to bring me treats and cuddle with me on the couch. I knew I wasn't in a proper state of mind to process those questions, so instead I tried to relax in his hold. I closed my eyes and focused on his breathing and his heartbeat against my side as we sat in silence, nothing but the sounds of the TV playing in the dim light.

The silence was comforting. Or maybe it was being completely supported by a large warm body. Regardless, I didn't bother to pretend to watch the TV, I just sat in his lap as he gently shifted his torso back and forth, and after some time, I felt the gummy start to kick in.

I fucking *loved* marijuana.

My brain had the slightest tingle to it, like something fuzzy was rubbing against it, and it made my limbs and chest and everything else feel loose and soft.

"You're so nice," I found myself whispering into Logan's chest. "I know I'm probably feeling heavy now, but I'm taking advantage of your niceness." Logan's head lifted off of mine to peer down at me, a smirk touching his lips as he shifted me a little in his lap. We both settled again as he lifted his gaze to the TV.

"My stomach still hurts," I whispered, "But it's not unbearable."

I weirdly knew this about myself. That when I drank enough alcohol or consumed enough marijuana, it was like something opened inside of me. I could talk for days and not feel the shame or embarrassment from my words. It was a relaxed sort of confidence. I enjoyed it most of the time.

"If I wasn't super gross right now," I whispered towards his neck, tipping my nose up to inhale his masculine scent, "I'd totally try to take advantage of you and your niceness to make a move."

Logan's chest constricted against me a couple of times, and I glanced up to see a smirk playing on his lips. Like he was trying to hold in a laugh, his eyes stuck on the TV.

"Did you know that orgasms can help period cramps?" I asked, not sure if I was still whispering or just mouthing the words. It took a lot of effort to communicate my thoughts for some reason. Logan's dark eyes glanced down at me, and as he took a good hard look at my eyes, he gave me a reluctant smile and shook his head in the negative.

"It's true, so like...hypothetically speaking..." I lifted one of my hands to trace a finger across his collarbone, trying to be mildly seductive and teasing as I felt his chest expand at my touch. Quickly, before my finger could trail too far down his chest, one of his arms around me lifted so that he could stop the journey my finger was making.

I pouted, glancing up at him through my eyelashes. I could see that he was affected by my touch, and the evidence of that was slowly growing under my ass, so I was determined to try to make my point.

"Why are you so attractive all the time?" I whispered against his neck, brushing my lips back and forth across his skin. "It's unfair. I'm only human," I breathed while tasting one of his scars with my tongue.

Logan's breath shuttered, and his hand that was holding mine hostage released so that he could cup the back of my head and gently pull me away from him, a smile on his lips as he gently shook his head at me again.

I jutted my bottom lip out farther, loving how his eyes dropped to it as if it was an appealing look. "You don't want me right now?" I knew I was currently on the heaviest day of my period, but for some reason, I really thought I had a chance of getting into his pants tonight.

Logan closed his eyes and inhaled, before opening them and nodding his head.

"Is it because I'm...bleeding? Because I could use a toy instead, you wouldn't have to touch me—" Logan's hand came up and covered my mouth, his teeth digging into his bottom lip as he shook his head and retrieved his phone that he had set to the side. He still supported most of my weight with one arm while he thumbed a message on his phone with the other. After a few quiet moments, he handed me his phone again with the notes app open.

You are high.

I always want you, Eloise.

But only if you are sober.

I shifted a little on his lap, feeling his erection under my ass again, and smiled up at him. The look in his eyes immediately softened at my smile, and I felt my heart constrict in my chest.

"I always want you, too," I whispered, staring at his lovely mouth. The mouth that I knew for a fact could do delicious, wicked things. "I haven't wanted anyone else in a long time." I could feel his chest expand with his breathing, and I leaned into it more, "I don't know if I ever will…Sometimes that scares me."

Logan blinked, something flickering across his expression that I was definitely too high to understand. I wrapped one arm around his chest as I snuggled back in, determined to behave myself since he was. I loved that. I loved that Logan had high standards for consent and that I could feel so safe with him. I could literally say that I wanted to sleep with him, but he cared more about my state of mind than the words that I spoke. He wanted to make sure that I was aware enough to ask for that. This man, who I genuinely thought was an asshole for the first year of our acquaintance. Who now I felt closer to than anyone else. How the tables have turned.

"Stay with me?" I asked. I wasn't sure how the logistics of that would work, considering our friends didn't know about our secret relationship, and that he had done an excellent job of sneaking out before anyone (except for Beck and Susan) caught us. But all I knew was that I didn't want him to leave tonight. I wanted him here, with me, as close as physically possible.

Logan's grip around me tightened as if answering me with his hold.

I grinned and found the dryness in my eyes difficult to blink away. Eventually, I settled for closing them, since the air in the room seemed to be making the dryness worse.

The next time I opened my eyes, the morning sun was shining in through my closed curtains. I was in my soft, warm bed, and the faintest scent of Logan filled the air. I stretched and patted my hand to the side, hoping to find his large warm body, but felt the cool sheets instead.

I lifted my head, frowning, noticing that the covers were pulled back like someone had snuck out of that side of the bed. I blinked my eyes a few times more, rubbing the sleep out of them when I realized that Logan was in here, but he must have left early in the morning. I frowned a little at that.

I...didn't want him to leave.

I realized that it made the most sense. To sneak out before anyone else in the house woke up and realized he had stayed the night. With me. In my bed. We hadn't talked about anything beyond Beck accidentally finding out about us at the bookstore. And that we were new and taking things slow. But...I remembered how he took care of me last night. How he prioritized me last night, instead of being with our friends.

Maybe I read too many romance novels, but something in my gut told me that if a grown man actively chose to stay in with a woman on her period, that he liked her for far more than her body.

I mean, Logan was an asshole sometimes, but he wasn't *that* much of an asshole.

And the thought of him, maybe hinting through his actions, that he wanted more from our relationship made me smile as I snuggled into my covers once more.

19

ELOISE

I had made a lot of headway in my ASL in the last few weeks. As far as I knew, nobody else knew I was taking online classes because, well, I hadn't told anyone. Except Logan. But he never asked me about them. This was probably due to the fact that hockey season was back in full swing, and his schedule was significantly busier. This made sneaking around our friends to meet up with him much more difficult. Yet it also gave me more time to focus on the language I was determined to learn. I had a feeling Logan held himself back from asking me about my lessons when we met up, though. He was receptive to helping me with signs and sentence structure whenever I asked, usually after we hooked up at his place or mine.

I wanted to be braver, though.

The day Logan and I made out like teenagers in the bookstore in Orange, I had tossed a few signs around in front of Beck, who didn't make a big deal out of it but just smiled at me.

Today, however, I was stepping it up. I had given on-line presentations with my choppy sign language a number of times already, so I was sure that my friends could fill in the blanks for me or correct me if I signed anything wrong. It was time for me to show off what all I had learned the last few months though.

Courtney and I had baked for everyone tonight.

Nothing fancy, just some classic chocolate chip cookies.

Beck and Adam showed up first, then Taylor strutted into the townhome seconds before Josh ran inside and tackle-hugged his fiancée onto the couch. After we all rolled our eyes at how physically affectionate Josh and Courtney were with each other, everyone had snagged a couple of cookies for themselves and were settled in various places around the kitchen.

It was then that, finally, Logan showed up.

God, Logan was so handsome.

He had cut his hair recently, making his dark curls look a little tamer compared to the haphazard mess they usually were. They were a little damp, as if he had just showered. Which made sense if he was coming straight from practice.

He smiled politely at Susan who, after embracing him in a one-arm hug, shuffled down the hallway toward her bedroom for the night.

Logan toed off his sneakers, making his way towards the dining area, fist bumping Adam and Taylor in greeting and saluting Courtney and her fiancé, before landing those dark eyes on me.

I gave him a nervous grin, trying my best to keep my body from blushing under his gaze. Based on the way his eyes heated as he rubbed the side of his neck with the scars, I had a feeling he was onto me.

Oh well.

I swallowed once, trying to play it cool while everyone else chatted around us.

I leaned a hip against the counter, my body language the air of confidence, as I lifted a chocolate chip cookie with one hand and signed to Logan with the other.

I gently pointed at him directly before signing my question, *Are you hungry?*

Logan's eyebrows went up, every muscle in his body stiff as he watched me sign. I thought I noticed a faint, very faint pink color tinge his cheeks and ears.

I cocked my head to the side in confusion and signed to him again, *You hungry?* I even held the cookie a little more in front of me, refusing to believe that he didn't understand what I was asking him.

"Oh my god," I heard Taylor snicker before clapping their hand over their mouth.

"What?" Beck asked, following their gaze to look at me.

"Lo…" Taylor asked after lowering their hand from their mouth, "What are you signing right now?"

I frowned, my cheeks heating from embarrassment but not entirely understanding why.

I froze, looking back at Logan again, who had one arm crossed against his large chest while the other came up to smother a smile he was clearly trying to hide.

I glanced back at Taylor before it clicked in my brain.

Oh my god.

It was happening again.

I pressed my lips together, the heat in my face making me want to fan my shirt away from my body before I decided to feign innocence.

Because I was signing wrong.

I wasn't asking Logan if he was *hungry*, by making a grip shape with my hand and stroking it down my throat to sternum once. I was asking Logan if he was *horny*, by making a grip shape with my hand and stroking it down my throat to sternum multiple times.

Everyone in this room remembered pie-maggedon, as Courtney so lovingly dubbed the event. The day I tried to be nice to Logan and offer him a *slice* of pie, but because I had little to no understanding of American Sign Language, I offered him *vagina* instead.

...An offer he later cashed in on, happily.

Multiple times.

Anyways.

I had grown since that day that felt so long ago. I wasn't embarrassed or intimidated by him anymore. I didn't feel humiliated any time anyone in the group poked fun at me, because we all poked fun at each other. That was the comfort of it all. We could tease and play and forgive and no one ever held a grudge. This was a safe space. So, I made direct eye contact with Logan again, trying to hide the humor from my expression by masking it with confusion and innocence. I widened my eyes and signed.

Are you horny?

Logan exhaled, huffing his form of laughter as he dropped his hand and shook his head at me.

Josh and Courtney cackled, while Beck peeked at us between her fingers that were covering her face in second-hand embarrassment. Adam just watched the two of us with amusement.

I frowned at Logan, *You're* not *horny*? I signed, offering him the cookie in my hand once again as if I was still clueless as to what my mess up was.

Logan shook his head again and stepped towards me, his large body towering over mine and reminding some very specific parts of me how much I liked that. How I wasn't intimidated by him anymore. Now, I was just excited.

Logan grabbed my hand that I was signing with and guided the movement correctly, *hungry.* He even mouthed the word for me so I would understand.

Before he could do more, I nodded my head at him, repeating the incorrect sign.

"Right, hungry." *Horny.*

Logan shook his head again, his bottom lip bitten in between his teeth while the others laughed, Taylor even wiped tears from their eyes at the comedy of this moment. History repeating itself. Logan's grip on my hand tightened, halting my repetitive sign. I could see that Logan was struggling. He wanted to tease me so badly, but the last time he did, I shoved a plate of pie in his chest.

We had a lot of animosity between us then.

We didn't now, but he clearly didn't know where my boundary with teasing was in front of everyone.

It was so, so sweet.

I *almost* felt bad for faking my confusion.

"Someone tell her," Josh chuckled, wrapping an arm around Courtney's shoulders and smothering his laughter in her hair.

"Um, Lo—" Beck started, but snapped her mouth shut when I suddenly stepped into Logan's space. I was so close to him that I had to arch my neck to look up. I had to keep one of my hips against the countertop to make room for one of my feet to stand in between his, but he didn't retreat.

Logan did drop his grip on my hand though, and his eyes became the slightest bit hooded at my sudden nearness.

"Did I sign something wrong?" I asked, widening my eyes in false distress as I took a small bite out of the cookie, splitting a large chocolate chunk with my teeth. I made what I would best describe as puppy-dog eyes at Logan as I chewed, but his eyes bounced between my gaze and my mouth.

Everyone else in the room quieted as they watched us.

I took my thumb and brushed the rest of the gooey chocolate chip from my cookie, before lifting my thumb near my mouth. "...Are you sure you're not?" I asked, my voice low and sultry, which took little effort on my part to accomplish. Logan always made me feel sexy, he brought out the wild woman in me.

I halted before the tip of my tongue came out and tasted the melted chocolate on my thumb, loving how Logan's eyes watched me intently before I lifted my thumb towards his parted lips.

"...Are you hungry, Logan?" I hardly recognized myself.

This was the flirtiest I had ever been with him in front of this group. But I didn't care. Logan was staring at my thumb like it pained him, and I could see his hand balled into a tight fist as it rested on the counter next to us.

I stretched up on my tiptoes, resting my arm against his chest to keep my thumb near his lips as I leaned in close to him and whispered, "Or are you…something else?"

Logan blinked and his eyes landed on mine, and I could see the switch flip in his brain as he realized I was teasing him.

I faintly remembered hearing Taylor mumble something along the lines of, "Fuck me" as they watched me playfully seduce Logan, but those words didn't receive acknowledgement because as soon as I knew that Logan was on to me, I smeared the chocolate from my thumb onto his face.

He stiffened, and the others gasped in surprise as I fell back on my heels and backed away a couple steps. My smile was uncontrollable, and I set the bitten gooey cookie down on the countertop as I gauged his response at my playful prank.

Logan was flushed, and his chest heaved as he lifted a hand to wipe the chocolate from his cheek.

Courtney was laughing. "She totally played you, Logan."

I bit my lip, feeling a little trapped because Logan's large body was blocking the only exit out of the kitchen.

Logan smirked at me, sucking the chocolate off of his fingers before taking a step back and reaching behind himself to open the refrigerator.

I narrowed my eyes at him.

"What are you—?" The question died on Josh's lips because Logan quickly pulled out a bottle of chocolate syrup before closing the refrigerator door. His dark eyes leveled with mine as he flipped the lid of the bottle open.

"Don't you dare." I held up a finger towards him in warning, but I was giggling from the high of playing with him like this. Especially in front of everyone. Logan's eyes searched mine for a little bit, clearly trying to read me.

I sunk my bottom teeth into my lip, my eyes clearly trying to find an escape route around him.

Logan just smiled, before charging me.

I squealed loud, and without shame, before quickly ducking around his side and sprinting out of the kitchen.

"Oh no!" Beck gasped at the same time Josh shouted, "Get her, Logan!"

I made it to the living room, jumping over the couch and turning around quickly to see Logan pausing on the other side of the furniture, his chocolate syrup bottle still in hand.

I faked going left, and his body followed my movements too quickly to be fooled.

He stayed put, stalking towards me.

"Run, Lo! Run!" Courtney encouraged with a flap of her hand.

I grinned at Logan before officially going right, towards the hallway and staircase.

He was hot on my heels, and my heart was racing with the thrill of being chased by him. The adrenaline rush was one I hadn't experienced before, and I fucking *loved* it.

I almost went down the hallway, before deciding not to bother Susan and sprinting up the staircase instead.

Logan almost lost his footing when I changed directions

so quickly, but he recovered enough to grab the banister and propel his body up after mine. Even though I was sprinting up the stairs, I was laughing. I was laughing almost hysterically as my body struggled to outrun the current professional athlete.

I went for my bedroom, knowing that there was a lock on the door before I realized that in half a second Logan would catch me no matter what.

However, I could fight back if I went to the bathroom.

So I did.

Logan barged in after me, a victorious grin on his face as he cornered me in the small space. His presence took up the entirety of the bathroom as I backed away with my hands out in defense, as if I was taming a wild animal instead of the man that I was developing big feelings for.

He shook his head once, letting me accept my fate as he slowly advanced on me enough to make me step back into the tub.

Right when our friend's faces appeared in the bathroom doorway, laughing, and cheering for me to escape, I switched on the water and detached the showerhead, aiming it at his chest.

Logan spluttered for half a second before jumping into the tub with me and squirting an alarming amount of chocolate syrup all over my hair and face.

"No!" Courtney's arms fell to her sides, her shoulders slumping in disappointment even though her smile lit up her face at the sight of Logan and I struggling against each other in the shower.

254 | ANDREA ANDERSEN

I had one hand on his wrist that was squirting syrup all over me.

He had one hand on my wrist that was spraying water all over his chest and face.

Within a handful of exhilarating seconds, Logan and I were both a mess.

Taylor started clapping, nodding their head as if they were a mediator calling a tie between a fight. "Well done, you two. Well done."

I laughed again as Logan finally yanked the showerhead from my grip and dropped the chocolate syrup to turn off the water, his dark eyes flared in amusement as he slumped against the tile.

I had chocolate syrup all over my hair, dripping off the sides of my face and neck. Probably a good amount of it went down my shirt. My leggings and feet were also soaked from the shower water.

But I had so much fun just then.

Logan and I were just grinning at each other as we took a few moments to catch our breath before Beck started to enter the bathroom with a stack of towels that she set on the countertop.

"Here, you two should get cleaned up," Beck smiled at us, in on a secret that only she knew about.

I thanked her, and laughed when Josh said, "Hold on, Court. I think some chocolate got on you. You should probably step into the shower, too."

Courtney playfully slapped Josh's chest in return, turning to leave down the hallway, "Are you sure you don't just want to take advantage of the fact that I'm wearing a white t-shirt right now?"

Josh didn't need any more encouragement. With a low, masculine grunt, he hauled Courtney into the bathroom, almost knocking Beck over before she supported her fall by grabbing onto the doorway.

I laughed as Josh and Courtney's bodies slammed into the shower wall in between Logan and I, happily handing Josh the shower head so that he could completely drench Courtney's body as she spluttered and swatted and cackled at her fiancé's ridiculousness.

The four of us eventually got cleaned up, and even took time to soak up all the water and rinse out all the chocolate syrup that got pooled at the bottom of the tub. I was just so giddy the rest of the night. Even with wet hair and a flushed face and comfy pajamas that I changed into, I felt like I had a place in the world.

Like I belonged and was supported.

I thought back to months ago, about how I brutally ripped myself out of my mother's clutches by moving out as quickly and efficiently as possible. I didn't realize how much my soul craved independence from her. From both of my parents. For the first time in my adult life, I felt like I fit.

Like these people saw me for me.

Even Logan, who currently sat on the floor in front of my spot on the couch, was able to make me feel both cherished and appreciated. Even though I had changed a lot since the first time we met.

I stared at the back of his head, admiring how much curlier his hair became after getting drenched in the shower fight, and noted how far I had come as a person. How we both had seen the worst in the other, but still managed to find the softer spots as well.

The part of Logan that had him rubbing my feet when my cramps were bad, or the part of me that originally started to learn his language out of spite, but now I fully intended to learn because I wanted to talk to him. To communicate with him in the way that he felt most comfortable. To show him my appreciation in such a way.

For no other reason than because I wanted him.

20

LOGAN

A couple more weeks passed with Eloise and I sneaking around our friends.

Multiple nights a week, she and I would find time to get together. We even went out on dates, not that either one of us formally called them that. Instead, we would make it casual. One of us would ask if the other had dinner yet before meeting up at either my place, or her place if everyone else was out of the house.

We would go out, go home, argue over which movie to turn on (we found ourselves alternating between her beloved romcoms or my preferred action movies), have amazing sex, and fall asleep tangled up with each other.

Some mornings I would sneak out of her room early enough to not get caught by Courtney or Susan. Other mornings she would sneak out of my bed early enough to make it back to her house without drawing too much suspicion. I respected that this was where we were at.

But I also hated it.

Every time I thought about broaching the subject into becoming something more, something real, the words wouldn't make themselves present. I chickened out.

Now, though, after a quick shower and dressing in a casual suit after our first home game of the season, I realized that my time with Eloise would become much more limited. I walked out of the locker rooms and headed towards the space where everyone would be waiting to congratulate me on the game. However, I was busy thinking about how I would be traveling a lot more for the next few months. Half of my time would be on the road, playing across the country. Training would take more of my day, which would naturally cut into our time together.

I was pondering about the reality of asking Eloise to become my official, known-to-everybody-else girlfriend, when I glanced up and felt irritation spike in my veins.

It took me a while to be able to name the burning inside of me at the sight of Eloise and Connor talking.

Even though Eloise was clearly uncomfortable.

But Connor didn't seem to care as he kept stepping into her space. She would immediately step back, her eyes flicking around as bodies swarmed the area outside of the locker rooms. The area where friends, families, and sometimes reporters waited to meet with players.

John had followed me out, taking his husband's hand as they left. I found my group of friends next. It was easy to do since Josh was the easiest to spot, even with his baseball cap underneath the hood of his sweatshirt. He also wore sunglasses, which no one questioned for some reason, even when we were indoors.

However, Josh and Courtney were not paying attention because they were talking to a large cluster of fans who recognized them, separating themselves from the rest of the group, including Eloise and Connor. She was shorter than Connor and refused to meet his gaze for more than half a second at a time. And still, he just kept talking, stepping closer and closer until they were near the wall.

Beck and Adam were somehow separated from Eloise as well, on the other side of the fandom, but I could see Adam looking over the crowd and tugging his girlfriend's hand, trying to make it over to where Eloise was clearly needing help. Taylor, who was on the other side of Josh and Courtney, staying back, saw Adam's struggle and followed his gaze to where Eloise was cornered. They cracked their neck once before grabbing Courtney's shoulder and gesturing with their chin to what was happening.

Eloise clearly required assistance, and none of our friends were able to immediately help her out.

I was disturbed by the sight of my agent so infatuated with her. A number of things clicked in my brain seeing the two of them. The woman Connor had spoken to me about who had ghosted him, the awkward meeting at Eloise's clinic, and everyone's general reaction to his presence.

Holy shit…Eloise was the woman Connor wanted to try hooking up with again.

Absolutely the fuck not, the words repeated themselves in my head over and over. I thought I saw someone start to approach me, but I ignored them when my feet started moving again.

Eloise had already made it perfectly clear that she had no desire to sleep with, or even talk to Connor again. But he didn't care. He just ignored her obvious dismissal and had been for months at this point. That knowledge infuriated me even more.

I marched toward her, my hockey bag bumping into some other players that I passed, but I couldn't find it within myself to apologize to anyone.

Eloise's eyes found mine, and I wasn't sure what expression my face was making, but when I saw her shift and start to walk toward me, I felt my chest expand. She flicked her eyes at Connor, clearly saying something dismissive to him, but he halted her obvious attempt at a retreat with a quick hand placed on the wall behind her, essentially locking her in.

At that, Courtney's eyes widened in clear alarm as she followed Taylor and Adam, leaving her fiancé to his fans, in an attempt to get to Eloise's side.

But they were too late because I was already there.

"I'm just saying," Connor's voice was low, and part of me wanted to hurl when I realized he was trying to sound seductive, "It's not like—"

"Nice game, Logan!" Eloise's voice was high and riddled with nerves, and it made certain instincts prick up inside me. I had reached my hand up to grab Connor's arm holding her hostage, but at the mention of my name, he had quickly dropped his arm and turned a surprised expression towards me.

Now my hand hovered in the air for half a second, and I was going to drop it again, but Eloise instead took my lifted hand as an opportunity to embrace me in a tight hug.

I froze, my eyes meeting Courtney's wide ones, and Adam's lifted eyebrow once he and Beck finally made it over.

I blinked my surprise away and wrapped my lifted arm tight around Eloise, successfully making it look like I had also been going in for the hug the entire time.

Connor's eyes bounced between me and Eloise, clearly trying to assess the situation.

I wanted to flip him off behind Eloise's back, but I refrained.

"You two know each other?" Connor asked, his hands gently fisting themselves in the pockets of his slacks as Eloise released her arms from around my neck. I wanted to hurt him. Possessiveness overpowered me. I knew it was stupid, and that Eloise and I were both trying to keep our extra-curricular activities private, but I didn't care at that moment.

This was the only reason that could explain why I kept my hand on Eloise. It had wrapped around her lower back during the hug, and even though she released me and stood on her feet, I kept my hand firm on her waist, my fingertips gently digging in enough to keep her from stepping too far away from me.

Courtney clocked my grip with surprised interest, while still mostly behind Connor's shoulder. Her eyes met mine for a brief moment before she spoke up, making Connor turn to look at her, and to force him to take a step back to expand the circle of conversation.

A step farther away from Eloise.

"What a gong show that game was!" Courtney smiled.

I gave her an unimpressed look because there were no

excess fights or problems during the game. She clearly just pulled a random hockey term out of her ass.

"Uh," Connor looked just as confused before he decidedly ignored Courtney and refocused on Eloise, his gaze doing a double take on my hand still holding her waist. "Are you all going to the bar?"

There was a bar right next to the rink in Anaheim that the players were known to visit after home games. It was large and had both an indoor and outdoor seating area, making it an obvious choice to celebrate wins with the fans. Connor's invite wasn't a polite one, and maybe I was paranoid because he was clearly interested in the woman that I was seeing, but it held a note of dismissiveness. Of challenge. Like he was trying to find an excuse to lose this group that had suddenly surrounded and ruined his chances of talking to Eloise.

"Of course!" Beck spoke up, interlacing her fingers with Adam's hand. Josh had finished with his fans, but stayed back behind Taylor, studying the odd exchange with a cool mask while Taylor crossed their arms and let their gaze trail around the room. "Eloise and Logan promised to do shots with me." Beck winked, making Courtney's lips part in a conspiratorial smile as she noticed the sudden stiffness in Connor's pose.

Eloise was also a stiff board next to me, but with one gentle tug on her waist, she stepped closer into my space, almost leaning into me. The message was clear, and Beck had helped out by speaking about us as a pair, that Eloise was unavailable.

Connor's blonde brow pinched. He nodded, and pasted a fake smile on his lips, "I'll see you all over there then." He lifted a hand and gave Eloise a longing look as he turned to retreat, making her turn her head away from him and to-wards me. One glance down at her bright red face made me realize that she was trembling.

I rubbed my thumb against her waist, a poor attempt to soothe her while anger with my agent still thrummed within me.

Once Connor disappeared into the crowd, Courtney whirled on the two of us. "Nice move, Logan," she smiled at me before looping her arm through Eloise's and successfully tugging her out of my grip, "It felt a little caveman-ey, but Connor is clearly the kind of guy who doesn't back off unless another man is involved."

Irritation burned my throat, my hand clenching into a fist from the loss of Eloise's body. Beck eyed me nervously. Courtney pulled a clearly stressed-out Eloise towards the doors, leaning down and murmuring to her. Taylor had rushed over to Eloise's other side, leaning in close as well. I could tell by the hunch in their shoulders, and how Josh rested a hand on Courtney's back as well, that our friends were discretely trying to check in with Eloise. To see how she was feeling.

While our friends were consoling the woman that I desperately wanted to soothe myself, Beck fell into step beside me.

We all paused in a small, quieter corner of the facility be-fore leaving out the doors. Others passed us, waving goodbye to players, or laughing, or getting ready to meet up at the bar with everyone, but our little group huddled close to Eloise.

"Lo," Taylor asked, grasping Eloise's fingers, and squeez-ing. Eloise's eyes were wide, and she kept blinking as if she was trying to focus them. At the sound of Taylor saying her name, she quickly snapped her head in their direction.

"Yeah?" She asked, releasing Taylor's fingers, and rubbing her hands on her cheeks.

"Are you okay?" Taylor mumbled, keeping the conversation low enough so others passing by couldn't possibly hear.

"Y-yeah. I'm fine. Just annoyed." Eloise shook her head once and rubbed her head, meeting the gaze of everyone circled around her before a wobbly smile touched her lips.

"Are you sure?" Courtney laid an arm around Eloise's shoulders, squeezing her close before she asked, "Because it's okay if you're not. He was being very forward and ignoring your discomfort about it."

"I know," Eloise shrugged. "He's just being a creep. Can't take a hint. Yada, yada." Eloise smiled at Courtney and patted her hand on the arm that was draped across her shoulders.

"I have to ask," Beck said, "Did something happen between you two? The night you…"

Eloise's face went tomato red, and I felt a lead weight in my stomach when her embarrassed expression turned to meet my gaze. I had no idea what expression I was making, but it took every bit of effort to smooth the muscles in my face to something comforting, a relaxed facial expression to let her know that she had absolutely nothing to be embarrassed about. Especially in front of me.

"No, nothing bad happened," Eloise lifted a shoulder, gently shrugging Courtney's arm off of her. "He was just a bad lay, and can't take the hint." Eloise's gaze met mine again, almost as if there was a challenge in them.

I had no idea how to react to that, so I just held her eyes and tried to silently convey that I was here for her.

She blew out a large breath, and then clapped her hands together. "I'd love to have a drink, though. Are we still going to the bar?"

Everyone exchanged not so subtle looks with each other, trying to see if that was the right call. When Eloise clapped her hands again to encourage us to get a move on, we all agreed to follow the team there. Courtney held her fiancé's hand, who had been a silent support at our sides this entire time, and wrapped her free arm around Eloise's shoulders before leading her towards the exit of the facility.

Taylor followed behind them.

Beck and Adam fell into step beside me.

"Sorry if I crossed a line," Beck whispered, careful to keep her words low so others wouldn't hear. Then, she switched over to ASL, *I saw you grab Eloise and thought I would lean into it to make DJ go away.*

Daddy James. Her and Courtney's disgusting nickname for my agent.

I lifted a shoulder and glanced up, catching Eloise peeking back at me before she pressed her lips in a firm line and faced forward again.

I lifted my hands to sign back to Beck, *No one else knows about me and Eloise?*

I specifically stared at Adam, who was walking on the other side of Beck and clearly saw my question. His expression didn't change, and he acted like nothing interesting was being discussed as he reached forward to hold the door open for Beck and me to walk through.

No, Beck responded, glancing at her boyfriend, *but I think Adam does now.*

"I suspected," was her boyfriend's low reply.

I didn't care.

I was getting tired of it. It had been months since Eloise and I started sneaking around our friends like this. I was reaching the point where I couldn't quite remember why it was still a secret. We had agreed to be monogamous and there had been moments between us that were clearly more than just sex. I had thought Eloise and I were starting to grow closer, maybe even heading toward a relationship outside of sex.

But we hadn't talked about it.

So I wasn't too upset about Beck stepping in and making it sound like Eloise and I were a couple. In my mind, we pretty much were outside of the fact that we hadn't discussed it and made it official. Courtney, however, clearly thought it was all a display for Connor's benefit.

I wasn't sure how Eloise felt about that whole inter-action, but by the way her legs stiffly walked to the car that Josh's driver had waiting for everyone, I didn't think she was doing well.

I made it over to my own truck, waving goodbye to Beck and Adam as they followed the rest of the group. Once I was seated in the driver's seat, I pulled my phone out and sent a text to Eloise.

Me: You okay?

I waited in my seat. We had turned on our 'read receipts'

for each other, and when I saw that she had read the text a few seconds later, I waited while those three little dots appeared.

Eloise: I'm fine.

Eloise: Thanks for stepping in.

I released a breath of relief because a small part of me was worried that I had overstepped. I didn't want Eloise to think that she couldn't handle herself, but I also didn't think she *needed* to handle things by herself. I waited in my truck for a while after that. I wanted time to critically think about this situation I was in with Eloise. A year ago, I never would have dreamed that she would even look at me with anything other than disgust.

I was a lucky man.

But was I lucky enough to push for more?

I hadn't had a serious relationship for the entirety of my adult life, and as a grown man in his thirties, that was more humiliating than I had originally considered. Eloise had dated, both casually and seriously. Would she even be open to giving me a shot? Or did she only want to be casual with me?

A small voice reminded me that Eloise was taking ASL classes online. That she had gone out of her way to learn my primary form of communication. The night I helped her during her period, she even hinted that she was learning *for* me. She was also stoned during that conversation, so I wasn't about to hold anything she said under the influence of marijuana against her. Sure, Beck and Susan and some others used ASL too, but Eloise didn't even tell me that she had an interest in seriously learning the language until after we had slept together.

She wanted to learn.

Eloise was constantly frustrated when she didn't understand my signs, and was more than willing to ask me questions about the language for her classes.

I thought about this as I drove to the bar. I thought about what it would look like if Eloise did decide to make things official. To define the relationship, or "DTR" as Courtney liked to call it.

I heard loud singing as I stepped out of the truck, but I didn't pay too much attention to it as I loitered just outside the bar, not seeing the bar itself, but only seeing Eloise's face.

Her face when she was stoned and curled up in my arms.

Her face when she blushed for me in the bookstore.

Her face when she laughed with me under the bedsheets.

I wanted to talk to Eloise. I *wanted* her. I never thought I would be at a point where I could both admit that to myself and also consider the reality of that being on the table. Maybe it wasn't, but I wouldn't know until I asked her.

Stepping into the bar, the blast of noise made me blink once to refocus on my surroundings. To the far left side, Beck and Adam were chatting with John and his husband, Alonzo. The four of them were clearly deep in their own conversation, and I saw Beck and Alonzo signing animatedly back and forth to each other.

Eloise's voice sounded across the bar, and my attention was immediately upon her.

Josh and Eloise were on the small karaoke stage near the back.

The memory of Eloise and Josh's band manager, Kate, singing karaoke in the living room of the townhome a year or so prior came to mind. Eloise's voice was just as beautiful now as it was then, even though she was laughing throughout the performance.

The two of them were singing "Love Story" by Taylor Swift.

And my team was whistling and shouting and encouraging them, also singing along to the words.

Within seconds, the entire bar filled with mostly men, were all singing along with Eloise and Josh, (who still donned his hat and sunglasses), to the corniest pop song of all time. Bodies of athletes were both jumping and moshing to the beat, making everyone else seated at the bar stools and tables laugh with joy and amusement at the scene.

I found myself grinning too, and didn't shrug off my teammates as they pulled me into the mosh pit.

This is what Eloise Bane did.

She was sunshine, and filled the room with such whenever she chose to.

Josh eventually looped a long arm around her shoulders, both of them laughing and singing the words to the song as Eloise's clear blue eyes met mine in the crowd, and my pulse skipped in my veins when she started pointedly singing the words to me.

There were dozens of guys around me, shoving each other, and dancing, and head banging to the pop music, but I locked my eyes with hers. I let her serenade me in a bar full of people.

I was laughing, the broken sound drowned out by shouting male voices and karaoke music, when I glanced to the side and met the irritated scowl of my agent.

Connor James sat at the bar top, watching the team cheer on Eloise as she sang with the disguised rock star, though I was positive that most of the people in the bar knew who Josh was. Connor quickly turned away from me when my eyes met his, but that didn't stop me from catching the glare he had made. The frown on his face, and the pinched brow on his forehead.

Connor had just realized, at this moment, that he wasn't going to get with Eloise again, and for some reason, something in my gut was warning me that this didn't bode well.

Perhaps it might be time for me to start sending feelers out for a new agent.

21

ELOISE

"I was so surprised to see that conversation turn out the way it did," Taylor commented from their spot on the floor as they laced their hiking shoes on.

I wrinkled my nose as I remembered the awkward inter-action I had witnessed between Beck, a woman who was hard of hearing and communicated with ASL when needed, and John's husband, Alonzo, a deaf man with no hearing aids, who solely relied on ASL for communication. At first, I thought that he would like Beck when they met at the bar after the hockey game, because I assumed it would be easier to hold a conversation with someone who could communi-cate the same as him.

So to hear that John's husband was bold enough to tell Beck to her face that she wasn't actually considered deaf, resulting in nothing more than an uncomfortable smile from her, made me very confused.

The fact that Alonzo was bold enough to essentially shut her down, and that Beck was able to take his words in stride and not be too ruffled by his dismissive attitude, threw me as well.

Courtney, Susan, and Beck were all very straightforward women. They did not seem to fluff their words, and they focused more on getting the message across. Somehow, these women didn't upset each other. They never became offended when someone was blunt to the point of, what I was taught to consider, rudeness.

"It's just…" I shook my head once, "That didn't bother you? How dismissive Alonzo was? I mean, he immediately invalidated a large part of your identity. That's just so rude to me. And you just smiled and shrugged. How did that not bother you?"

Adam smirked down at Beck after my weird explanation, which made me feel a little self-conscious about my thoughts until Beck started speaking again, "Well, to be fair, a lot of the deaf community is considered rude no matter what they say."

I widened my eyes, "What? Really?"

"Yeah," Beck lifted a shoulder before snuggling into Adam's side on the couch some more, "ASL doesn't have fluff words to make people more comfortable. The culture of people who use the language to communicate is known to be straightforward. To the point. Blunt."

I blinked at Beck.

Even though I had been taking online lessons for a while now, I hadn't ever considered that.

"It catches a lot of hearing people off guard," Susan nodded. "A common example is when I'm talking to an old friend, and I inform them that someone we both knew died. I don't usually say 'passed away', I just say 'died'. Because in

ASL, a language I use fairly often in my own home, there is no interpretation for 'passed away'. We just say 'they died' even though it sounds harsh out loud."

I nodded at Susan as she sipped her tea in the ugly accent chair.

"Wow," I lifted a shoulder, "I mean, I guess that does make the communication...clearer."

"Isn't there an actual term for it?" Courtney asked from Josh's lap, both of them sitting in the other ugly accent chair.

Susan nodded, "Deaf Blunt is what I hear most often."

"I understand where you're coming from though, Lo," Beck spoke up again, waiting for me to turn to look at her before she continued, "I think you and I were raised fairly similarly. Except you didn't have the extra fun layer of religious trauma that I did." Beck smiled, and my heart ached for her upbringing. "I wasn't born into a deaf community. I wasn't taught ASL from birth. I taught it mostly to myself as a teen, and only regularly started using it as a college student to gain more confidence in my studies. And more so with Gram when she would reach out to me." Beck smiled at her grandmother, who smiled lovingly back, "So it was kind of a culture shock to go from a religious community, where women were quiet and polite and always considered the feelings of others before themselves, to Deaf Blunt. A community that required direct forms of communication for the sake of getting the message across correctly, regardless of how uncomfy the blunt words made others."

I nodded at her, curling my legs up towards myself as I thought about her words.

"And even then, I still don't really feel like I truly fit in with the deaf and hard-of-hearing community."

I lifted my brows at Beck, tilting my head in confusion. "What do you mean? You have hearing loss. You use ASL. Isn't that…enough?"

Beck shook her head right when Adam's arms tightened around her shoulders. "A lot of people, those who are usually completely deaf and solely rely on ASL for external communication, refer to me as 'hearing with hearing aids'."

The room was silent for a moment, considering Beck's words.

"But…you're not completely hearing. You have hearing loss," Taylor said, the same confusion I felt was evident in their tone.

"Sure, but I still have *some* hearing. The aids help me identify specific words, and I get by extremely well with lip reading. I can speak very clearly when I focus hard enough or have my aids to help me distinguish the sounds." Beck shrugged a shoulder. "I have had members of the deaf and hard-of-hearing community tell me that I don't exactly 'count'. That being said, it's important to remember that *they* have had to deal with a lot of trauma and discrimination due to their experiences with complete hearing loss."

"But so have you," Courtney argued, "You literally weren't given resources to accommodate your hearing loss as a child."

"Sure, but not everyone knows that. They just see me vocalizing with others and that I wear hearing aids and they assume things. Everyone assumes things, and it's normal for people to feel threatened by those who do not understand their experiences entirely. Hearing people look at me, see how 'well' I get by in a hearing society, and they use me as an excuse to minimize the trauma and discrimination that those with more severe hearing loss or deafness have." Beck shrugged again. "I'm not offended by their concerns. In a way, I actually agree, that 'hearing with hearing aids' is an accurate category for my experience with hearing loss, but I also agree that I am simply hard of hearing. I have pretty severe hearing loss and therefore am a branch of the deaf and hard-of-hearing community. But I also have my own community," Beck gestured vaguely around the room, making my heart squeeze, "So I don't feel excluded from some club because of Alonzo's words. I'm sure if I integrated myself more in a formal deaf environment that they would accept me with open arms and teach me more about how they view the world. But I'm also okay where I am. I have come a long way to even be here, and I do not take that for granted."

I contemplated Beck's words, surprised at how empathetic she was.

If I was Beck, and I was talking to a man who was deaf, who had the confidence to tell me upon our first meeting that I was not the same as him simply because my hearing loss wasn't as significant, I would have been offended.

I would have probably said something rude back.

But Beck wasn't me.

I remembered a few years ago, when I had organized a trip to Big Bear for employees at the clinic, before I even officially worked there myself. Beck, Adam, Taylor, and Courtney were all lounging on the patio furniture after a long day. Before I had sat down with them, Beck mispronounced the word "libido," vocalizing it as "libby-do" because she had never heard the word out loud, and only read it in books. Taylor and Courtney teased her mercilessly for her slip-up, and instead of being offended by their relentless teasing, Beck laughed with them. She was embarrassed, her face red with it, but she wasn't upset or disgruntled. She even went as far as to tease herself for her slip-up.

It was admirable.

I...haven't always been like that.

I thought about how Logan and I started out. How I was so desperate to be liked by everyone here, that the first time Logan dismissed me, I immediately broke down. Later on, I toughened up a little bit, but I still let his teasing upset me to the point of smashing pie on him.

It was silly because I realized at that moment, when the conversation naturally drifted onto other things, that I didn't need to get so worked up anymore. Everyone in this room accepted and welcomed me with open arms. Adam was the only one who was hesitant about my friendship with these people, as he had every right to be. But now even he wasn't bothered by my intrusion anymore.

I stood up from my spot as the conversation shifted to something else and everyone finished putting their shoes on. We were all going for a small hike at Crystal Cove, and then meeting up back here to eat dinner. Logan would also be meeting us here after his practice.

If anyone else noticed that I was quieter today during the hike, no one said anything. Instead, I stayed near the back of the group on the trail, almost forgetting Josh's security detail lingering behind us, as we all took in the ocean views and landscapes. Inhaling that salty sea air was something I had always loved growing up here, and while everyone else joked around on the hike and laughed and chatted, I let myself get lost in my own thoughts.

Beck's conversation was still sticking with me. How she was able to validate Alonzo's truth, without worrying about jeopardizing the validity of her own.

Something that had bothered me the last few days, ever since that incident with Connor at Logan's hockey game, was everyone asking me if anything more happened. I knew what they were asking me without saying it explicitly. Based on my reaction to certain situations with Connor, my friends were concerned that I was unsafe, or taken advantage of, the one night we spent together.

However, I had consented. Hell, I even initiated. If I hadn't blatantly shown him my interest at my parents' house that one night, we probably wouldn't have hooked up at all. So, no, I didn't think that the experience I had with Connor was as concerning as my friends' questions would imply. He didn't take advantage of me. I was sober, and completely aware of my actions. I never told Connor no.

Then, naturally, I thought about the most recent night I wasn't sober. And how I had made a very clear pass at Logan, and he still turned me down. Logan, who I had slept with enthusiastically and consensually multiple times. Even knowing that I thoroughly enjoyed sex with him, he still took one look at my bloodshot eyes and decided that I wasn't sober enough to truly consent.

And...how I loved that.

Sure, I had consented with Connor, too. But after a certain

amount of time, I definitely wasn't enthusiastic with him. I just wanted it to be over. I stopped engaging, and just let him use me how he wanted to.

Connor didn't hesitate to use me.

...And honestly, what the fuck was that about?

I huffed irritation at the thought, forgetting that I was surrounded by friends and met the glance of a concerned Adam as he looked over his shoulder at me. I smiled at him to hopefully convince him that everything was okay, before staring at my feet marching on the dirt path of the little hike we were on.

Would it really have been so hard for Connor to notice that I wasn't enjoying myself? That I was biting my tongue and just wanted the whole thing to be over? Did he really care so little about how the woman that he was inside of was feeling about the situation?

Yes, I consented to be with Connor.

But also, even though I didn't vocalize it specifically, at some point, my consent was no longer enthusiastic. During the course of the night, even though I never said the words, my actions showed that I no longer truly, willingly consented.

Both could be true at the same time.

If Beck had experienced what I had, I wouldn't hesitate to explain to her that consent wasn't black and white. That it wasn't a trap you fall into by agreeing one single time. And yet, for some reason, I had been struggling to come to terms with that myself. Whenever my friends asked me if anything happened with Connor, I was quick to feel embarrassment and shame and ease their fears. Some of that, I suspected, had to do with my people-pleasing side that I was still trying to deconstruct every day. It was also probably why I didn't just give Connor the finger and leave before the night escalated.

It was also probably why I didn't just give Connor the finger every time I bumped into him since then.

Smile. Keep the peace. Don't hurt anyone's feelings.

If Logan had seen me lying there, lost in thought about something else, I knew for a fact that he would stop whatever it was he was doing. Logan was clearly a man that enjoyed enthusiasm in the bedroom. He wanted his partner to be into it just as much as him.

Which, call me crazy, shouldn't *that* be the standard of consent?

The thought of Logan caring for me back when I had my period came to mind, and I felt the smile pull on my lips before I could stop it. Nobody else noticed, except maybe Adam, who kept checking behind himself to make sure I was still there with the group.

But as we made it near the end of the trail, I was lost in thought about Logan St. James. Happier, peaceful, excited thoughts about the man filled my head. All the time we had spent together the last few months. How we had both opened up to each other and been vulnerable in order to establish trust.

How Logan and I were an item to some degree.

About how he and I were sneaking around behind our friends' backs…why were we still doing that?

It wasn't like I was interested in anyone else at this point. I loved spending time with Logan, which made my lips twitch with amusement because *oh* how things have changed with that whole situation.

I giggled along with Taylor's theatrics as we piled into Josh's SUV after the hike, and tried to engage with our friends and their conversations, but I couldn't. My heart was racing with the knowledge that Logan would meet up with us soon.

But I couldn't greet him like we normally did in private. Because everyone else was around. And we were keeping everything a secret.

The fears I had at the beginning of our physical relationship creeped up again.

What if we don't work out?

What will our friends think if we don't work out?

Would I be able to stomach hanging out with Logan if we didn't work out?

I found myself spiraling about this as I stood in the kitchen of the townhome, filling a glass of water at the sink when I heard another pair of steps enter the kitchen behind me, and I smiled at Adam as he casually approached to grab a beer for himself from the fridge.

"Can I ask you something?" I spoke up, keeping my voice a little lower to keep our conversation private. Taylor and Josh were getting more animated, playfully arguing about something, so I doubted we could be easily overheard.

"Sure," Adam replied, shutting the fridge door, and leaning back against the counter next to it. I took a moment to take him in. Adam was handsome, with dark red hair and sun-kissed skin, and freckles on his face. I had the biggest crush on him in high school, and I could remember the giddy feeling I had when we finally went out as adults. I felt like younger, adolescent me had finally "won."

And how that attitude ended up making me lose him.

I didn't want to lose him at the time, obviously. But…now I was glad that I did.

Now, I felt like that experience gave me the opportunity to find someone better for me.

"Were you ever nervous about dating Beck, and how that would work out at work and stuff?" Adam and Beck's situation wasn't the same as mine, obviously. But I felt like dating a coworker would make anyone second guess, or hesitate, before jumping into bed with them.

Adam looked towards the living room for a moment before answering, "Part of me was terrified."

I widened my eyes, "What? Why?"

Adam's lips tipped with a ghost of a smile before taking another sip of his beer, then setting the bottle down on the countertop to explain, "I only had a desire to start working at the clinic when I caught a glimpse of Beck, and learned that she was an employee there. I didn't even know her name." I widened my eyes, surprised, because I never knew that. "So I already felt like I crossed a boundary. I saw how happy and carefree she and Courtney were, and I acted like a leech. Desperate to be in their orbit, so that I could feel what they felt." Adam rubbed his neck, a haunted expression crossing his features. He had struggled with depression, something I was oblivious to at the time, which probably explained his need to feel what others were feeling. "Obviously I was attracted to Beck, but I already felt like my employment was inappropriate enough. So I never really...made my feelings known?" He tilted his head in thought. "I guess I did flirt a little bit the more we got to know each other, but it wasn't until Big Bear that I finally was open about my feelings. Even then, Beck had to kiss me first before I even felt confident initiating anything romantic."

I smiled, grateful that Adam was open with me about this. I only felt a twinge of guilt because this was the time that I was openly pursuing him to take me back. To give us another chance. Adam did us both a favor and didn't mention that aspect of this memory he was giving me, before continuing his thoughts.

"Once Beck kissed me, though," his eyes turned thoughtful, adoring, and it made my heart squeeze, "I was done for. I realized pretty quickly that it didn't matter if we were coworkers or not. It didn't matter if we ended up breaking up and having to deal with that in the workplace. I wanted her, and for some reason she wanted me. There was no reason to make us both suffer otherwise."

I quirked my lips at that. "I feel like it's easy for the man to not care about the potential fallout at work, though."

"You're not wrong," Adam shrugged. "Women tend to be more cautious about things like workplace relationships. They kind of have to be. That being said, I'm grateful Beck took the chance with me."

I sighed wistfully, loving that it had worked out for the both of them. As far as I knew, even though Beck and Adam lived together, they had no desire to get married or have children. They were perfectly happy as they were, and I was a little envious of that. To have total security in someone else, to have a partner in your corner no matter what.

I...*really* wanted that.

"How did you know it was worth it, though? The risk? Not knowing if it'll work out in the end or not." I heard myself whispering the question, exposing a bit of the fear that had made me keep everything with Logan in the dark until now.

I met Adam's gaze, and it felt knowing, so I glanced down and found myself fidgeting with my glass of water, nervous to meet his eyes. After a moment or two, I finally met his stare again, which was nothing but thoughtful and empathetic.

"At the risk of sounding like every lovesick man in every single one of Beck's books," Adam's voice was lowered a little more too, gentle, understanding, "I wanted to at least experience Beck. To kiss her whenever I wanted, hold her without hesitancy, and be with her in that way. Even if that meant that I might lose her, that we might later on discover that we weren't compatible and go our separate ways. I would much rather have her, and have to let her go, than never know what it's like to experience her love at all."

I sucked my lips in between my teeth, probably making my mouth an unattractive line on my face. But I didn't care.

Adam had a valid point.

I knew what it was like to have Logan to some degree. Our physical chemistry had always been there, I realized. But then I started to picture the two of us as a real couple. I glanced towards the living room, where Courtney was perched on Josh's lap. They both confidently and almost mindlessly reached for the other whenever they shared space. Not caring that they were displaying so much PDA in front of others.

I thought about Adam and Beck's more subtle, but still confident touches. How well Beck fit in Adam's side when they leaned into each other on the couch.

I already knew I fit well with Logan.

I tried to picture the two of us snuggling in the living room like the others, and it was very, very easy to piece the image together. Going on simple, cheesy dates with Logan. Lying in his bed while he slept after a long day at practice, while I stayed up doing homework for my ASL classes or reading a book.

Going to his hockey games and learning what was happening during them.

I thought about the group's reactions. Both to us being together, and also to us potentially breaking up.

Who cares? I thought to myself, *When has anyone here been anything but supportive?*

I released my lips from my teeth, looking back to Adam once he straightened from the countertop and retrieved his beer bottle.

"Logan's pulling up," Adam announced as he pocketed his phone that he must have pulled out while I was thinking. He tossed a friendly smile in my direction as everyone else chatted. I felt my heart racing. I wanted this. I had shared a number of special moments with Logan. I had a feeling that he was on board, too, if the way he kept reaching for me whenever we slept in the same bed together meant anything.

I recalled Adam's comment a few minutes earlier, about

how Beck had to kiss him first for the green light to go off in his brain.

I felt adrenaline start to pump in my veins when I made my way back to the living room with everyone. I stood there awkwardly for a second, before marching towards the entryway and throwing open the front door.

"Umm?" I heard Taylor ask behind me. I didn't bother closing the door. I was a woman on a mission, as I marched down the porch towards where I saw a familiar gray truck parked on the street in front of the townhome. Logan was just closing the driver's side door before he started walking towards us.

It was amazing how good a simple t-shirt and jeans could look on the man.

Logan was thumbing something on his phone before pocketing the device. His dark eyes glanced over the driveway before landing on me. A private look in his eyes.

My heart fluttered.

Was I really going to do this?

I paused halfway down the driveway while I heard the murmurings and footsteps of our friends, who clearly had followed me outside and sounded like they were lingering on the porch.

Logan halted at the end of the driveway as well, his secretive look turned to one of question. After a second or two of thick silence, due to my hesitant body language and thoughts, Taylor spoke up from behind me.

"You good, Lo?"

I bit my lip, my eyes on Logan.

His brow furrowed a bit, pink touching the edges of his ears at my direct gaze. He glanced briefly at our friends behind me, before meeting my eyes again. The question in his expression started to loosen. I was locked in on every muscle that relaxed in his jaw, his brow, his eyes. His expression slowly morphed from confusion to understanding, and then suddenly anticipation. Pink colored his tanned cheeks more, and his lips parted as he sucked in a breath as I stared at him.

"Lo?" Courtney asked. I didn't see what she was doing, I barely even registered her voice.

I took a step towards Logan, before pausing again.

What if he doesn't want this? Me?

Logan's brows raised a little bit more, and when I glanced to his sides, one of his hands was in his jeans pocket while the other was in a tight fist, the arm hanging loose at his side.

He was nervous, so when I looked back at his face again, I took another tentative step towards him before forcing my other foot to follow.

As I approached Logan in the slowest walk imaginable, I could see his chest rise and fall with anticipation. His dark eyes were locked on me, and part of my pulse fluttered with the knowledge that I was able to hold his attention so thoroughly.

A few steps away, I signed to him, *I want you.*

I was pretty sure Courtney gasped, and I thought it was Taylor who sucked in a shocked breath. Logan's chest deflated heavily at my words, visible relief coating his expression as the corners of his mouth twitched upwards before he signed back to me.

Then take me.

I smiled brightly before I practically jogged the last couple steps towards him, his arms now open and preparing for my impact. My hands went to his shoulders, and I felt his large hands secure themselves on my waist. I then slid my fingers up his neck and into his hair, just how he liked, and pulled his head down to mine.

I heard Josh squeal in excitement a second before Logan's lips descended onto mine.

I sighed my relief into his mouth, and the feel of his hand coming up to cradle my head so that he could slant his mouth over mine and immediately deepen the kiss made my heart race and my muscles relax at the same time.

"Finally," I heard Beck grumble.

I giggled at her exasperation, making Logan smile against my mouth before pressing his lips to mine again and pulling back.

He looked happy. So happy.

I was positive I had the goofiest grin on my face as well.

"Is this okay?" I asked, massaging my fingers against his scalp as I asked.

Logan nodded his head once before lowering his mouth to mine again. Our lips barely touched before gagging noises were made and we separated to see who was mocking us.

"I love this so much," Courtney smiled as she snapped her fingers at us with impatience, "But I think I know how disturbing it is to watch your siblings kiss someone now." She made a playful grimace before I rolled my eyes at her.

"Get used to it," I told Courtney, lowering my hands from

Logan's hair and wrapping my arms around his wide torso. I pressed my cheek against his chest, relaxing into this new normal for us, "I found him. I'm keeping him."

Logan's arms squeezing me against him in response made me hum with delight.

Josh stepped forward to hold his fist out to Logan, who wordlessly bumped it with his own knuckles.

That was it.

Because, men.

Taylor wiggled their eyebrows at Logan and me, before turning back towards the townhome casually. As if two members of the friend group didn't just become an item in front of everyone moments ago.

Which really just made me feel silly for building all of this up in my head.

The group adjusted so that Logan and I could sit together on the couch. Taylor sat in one of the ugly accent chairs Susan loved. Josh and Courtney shared the second, with Courtney comfortably on Josh's thighs. Beck sat on Adam's lap on one end of the couch, while Logan and I took the other. Part of me wondered if I should have felt weird that I was sitting right next to my ex-boyfriend and, well, current boyfriend. But I didn't feel weird. And based on everyone else's body language, no one else thought it was weird.

Therefore, it wasn't weird.

And I realized as we all chatted and joked around and talked about our hike that day, while I snuggled against Logan's side with his large arm casually resting behind my shoulders, that it really was that simple.

As it should be.

22

LOGAN

Even though the sight of Eloise marching down the drive-way with an expression that was somehow both determined and nervous, hyping herself up to stake her claim on me, filled me with an overwhelming amount of happiness, *this* was the highlight of my day. After we had dinner and watched a movie, Taylor left, making a comment about it feeling too coupley. Adam and Beck left after her grandmother had gone to bed. Eloise had disappeared upstairs to take a quick shower, before rushing back downstairs and gently grabbing my hand in hers, leading me up the stairs of the townhome while Courtney and Josh were whispering to each other on the couch, ignoring us sneaking off.

Eloise wrapped both of her hands around my neck as soon as her bedroom door closed, pulling me down to her level so that I could kiss her deeply. Whatever chapstick or lip gloss she wore tasted fruity and delicious, but I found myself desperate to absorb every hint of flavor that kept me from tasting her naturally full lips. The little sigh of relief she made as soon as my tongue brushed against hers made all the blood in my body rush south.

My hands wrapped themselves around her waist, and the feminine squeal she made when I lifted her up and walked us toward her bed made me grin against her lips.

"Remember when we used to hate each other?" Eloise asked with a whisper as I set her on her feet again, kissing me before I could even think about responding to that question and mumbling against my lips, "I was so stupid."

I smiled into her kisses again, one of my hands snaking up her shirt and palming her back in between her shoulder blades. After a second, I decided to be bolder and let my fingers find the clasp of her bra before pinching it and disconnecting the garment immediately.

"Naked, naked, naked," Eloise panted, fisting the hem of my t-shirt, and pulling it up for me to remove. I halted her progress by taking her bottom lip in both of mine, tracing my tongue along the plump flesh of it, and tugging.

Eloise's whimper when I did that made me want to pound my chest in male pride. I pulled away just enough for me to grab the back of my collar and tug the shirt off my body in one smooth motion.

Just like the men did in a couple of her romance novels that I read.

Eloise's bright eyes quickly lowered at the motion, and then grew heavy-lidded as her gaze scanned the entirety of my torso. I knew what I looked like. It was the result of a strict diet regimen and regular exercise. I saw her hands twitch at her sides once as I grabbed her wrists and encouraged her to press her palms flat against my chest, sliding them down just to the top of my abs before I lifted my hands to sign at her, waiting for her eyes to tear themselves away from my chest to do so.

I never hated you.

Eloise blinked, "You strongly disliked me."

I smirked and shook my head once, signing and mouthing, *I was an ass and lashed out.* Eloise smirked back at that. *I never hated you.*

Her gaze cleared a little as she processed that.

"I'm sorry, but I definitely hated you a little." Eloise frowned as she let her fingers trace the shape of my abdomen. I used my left hand to grab her chin and tilt it back up toward me before I responded.

I know, I signed with my right hand, *You were cute.*

Eloise scrunched her nose while she repeated that sign back to me in question, *cute?*

I nodded once and let my face relax into a less teasing expression before I asked, *You don't hate me now?*

"God no," Eloise breathed, releasing her grip on my abs to tuck her hands underneath her shirt, fidgeting with her loose bra on her shoulders. "I don't want to rip the clothes off of people that I hate, generally." She paused at that. "I am very intentional with the people I sleep with now."

I frowned; *We are more than sex.* It wasn't a question on my end.

Eloise pulled her shirt off, took her bra with it, and dropped the clothing to the floor, responding, "I know." I exhaled in relief, slightly distracted by her nakedness. "You really caught me by surprise, Logan." Eloise tucked her thumbs into the waistband of her shorts and quickly pulled them down, leaving her completely naked except for the lacy black thong and the inked artwork that decorated her skin.

I took my time staring at her, becoming easily distracted by the heated look in her eyes as I kept my hands to myself and admired the staggering beauty that was Eloise Bane. I was so fucking grateful to be this intimate with her, that she trusted me enough to be this vulnerable with me.

"Hey," Eloise's voice made me lose focus from the flower tattoos on her hip and thigh so that I could meet her eyes again, "I—" she cleared her throat once, a smile breaking across her face, "I want you to touch me. I'm excited for you to touch me."

I nodded. First, I wanted as much contact with her skin as possible, so I unbuttoned my jeans and shoved them down my legs at an embarrassing speed, leaving my gray compression boxers on as I stood tall and crowded her space. Her eyes widened as I started to crouch, bending just enough to get a good grip on the backs of her thighs before I stood tall and tossed her into the middle of her bed. The bounce her body made as she hit the mattress did amazing things to her breasts, and I felt my mouth watering as I quickly crawled over her and lowered my head, ready to give them the attention that they deserved.

"Oh lord," Eloise wheezed.

I always remembered how responsive she was when I did this to her the first time, my mind scrambling as I licked the hardened tip and gently bit down.

Her hands couldn't figure out where to go. They were on my neck, my chest, my arms that were caging her in as I kissed one of her breasts and teased the other with my fingers. Her hips started jerking against my stomach, and I pressed my weight into her a little bit more to tease her more.

"You're killing me," Eloise breathed.

I fully intended to. I wanted to see Eloise come undone. I was the one who could make her smile in that relaxed way she did every time she came down from the high of orgasm.

I felt my hand smooth down her side, gripping the flesh of her hip right over her tattoos there before I lowered my head and kissed the bouquet of flowers on her ribs.

Then I took her hand with the other flower tattoos and pinned it to the mattress so that I could lean over and kiss those, too. She snuck her free hand into my hair, tugging me towards her face. I quickly planted one firm kiss against her lips before I pulled against her grip to slide down her body, thoroughly kissing the artwork on her hip.

"Are you kissing my tattoos?" Eloise huffed a laugh with her question. I had no idea how to explain that I wanted to claim every inch of her skin with my mouth, because I was a mess, so I let my gaze get snagged on hers as I dragged my tongue from the outside of her thigh and inward, where I could see slickness shining on either side of her lacy thong.

"Oh, fuck me," Eloise's head fell back on the mattress, and I found myself unwilling to let go of my grip on her legs as I spread them apart, settling my shoulders in between so that I could use a finger to tug the side of her underwear out of my way.

Good god, she was already glistening for me. "I plan to…" I found myself rasping through a whisper. I wasn't confident she could hear it with how loud she was panting already.

My voice was rough and dry, and not just from the state of arousal I was in. The words burned against my damaged and unused vocal cords, but I was proud of how well my mouth and tongue remembered to form the words beyond the feeling of sandpaper scraping against the sound.

"Did you just—" Eloise didn't get to finish her question because I dove in, unable to wait a second longer to taste her. She covered her mouth to smother her squeal at the first swipe, and part of me remembered that she had roommates, but I couldn't have cared less at the moment. I was entirely focused on my actions, keeping my eyes open and on her as I explored Eloise's most intimate parts to see which licks and kisses that she responded to the most.

Within what felt like seconds, I could see a light pink flush start to coat her cheeks and chest.

It felt incredibly difficult to keep steady, and my grip on her thighs tightened with need as I forced myself to keep my pace consistent for her benefit. Eloise's hands rooted themselves into her own hair, her eyes closed and her lips parted. Soon she was squirming so much that I had to place a hand on her pelvis simply to keep her still enough for me to continue what I was doing.

When her body wasn't thrusting against me, I decided to indulge myself and pressed one of my fingers into her, watching her to make sure that it was okay. When she smiled and her hands removed themselves from her hair to grip the sheets instead, I continued to curl my finger inside of her.

"Yes. Please, please," I almost sped up the flicks my tongue was making, almost. However, I had a feeling that I needed to pin her down and keep doing what I was doing exactly as it was. Perhaps she was close and was begging me not to change a thing.

Turns out, I was right.

Eloise exploded on my tongue, her back arching almost completely off the bed as she groaned through clenched teeth. Only then did I close my eyes and let myself focus on the experience of lapping up every bit of her arousal.

Once she went limp against the mattress, I finally stopped, sitting up on my elbows and waiting for her eyes to open and look at me before I placed my finger in my mouth, licking her off of me with a satisfied groan.

"Are you *real*?" Eloise asked, face flushed and eyes hazy. I bit my lip as I smiled and started to crawl up her body again before I paused and rolled off of the bed. "Get back here!" Eloise hissed. I crouched down and grabbed my pants, digging through the pockets until I pulled out the two condoms I had tucked into my wallet before leaving my house today. I stood tall and held up the contraception, rather than explaining myself.

Eloise nodded and quickly sat up. Both of her hands gripped the waistband of my boxers, tugging them down so roughly, I almost lost my balance and tipped over, but I was able to get a grip on her shoulder to brace myself.

"Oh god," Eloise groaned when her eyes settled on my erection standing at full attention. I felt only a small flicker of self-consciousness from her ogling my cock so openly, even though it wasn't even the first time she had done so, but then she let me step fully out of my boxers while scooting herself to the edge of the bed so that she could wrap one of her delicate hands around me.

Air whooshed from my lungs at her grip.

"Damn," Eloise's lips tugged at the edges, a playful smile hinting there as she licked the palm of her other hand and wrapped that one around my shaft as well. "You might not fit. You might be too much for me." Her eyes lifted to meet mine as I stared down at her, her hands doing incredible things that made it difficult to think beyond, *Oh shit, is she serious? Have I hurt her before?*

Then I noticed the mischief in her eyes, and I felt mine narrow in response.

"It always fits, Logan," Eloise responded as she focused back on her task of giving me the most incredible hand job I had ever received in my life, "I think you'll always have to go slow with me, though. I mean you are, well, the size that you are."

A woman telling a man that they're large, or big, or whatever adjective along those lines, will always be the exact right thing to say to him anytime they're about to have sex. The primal urge in me to push her down and sink into her was almost unbearable after hearing those words fall from her lips.

I was bracing one hand on her shoulder, noticing the drop of precum on the tip of my cock a second before Eloise leaned forward and wrapped her lips around the head. I rolled my head back, spots coating my vision at the incredible feeling of her hot mouth on me.

I quickly jerked back out of her grip, silently loving the pout on her lips from my retreat.

"What's wrong?" Eloise asked. I shook my head at her and mouthed with my ASL, *I'm going to come.*

"That's literally the point." Eloise lifted an eyebrow at me, and I shook my head at her again as I huffed a laugh of my own at her. "What do you want, then?"

You, my vision wasn't as hazy anymore, and I zeroed in on her as I noticed that she still had her lacy thong on. I had never taken it off. *Well, that won't do*, I thought. I reached forward and wrapped my hands around the flimsy fabric before tugging as quickly and roughly as I could, loving the snapping sound it made in the room as I tossed the ripped material over my shoulder.

Eloise gasped, a new dark flush coating her cheeks as she stared wide-eyed at her ruined underwear on the floor. I didn't give her a chance to respond before I was on her, pushing her back on the bed and covering her lips with my own.

"Wait!" Eloise grabbed my face with her hands and pushed me back far enough to playfully glare at me, "That was my favorite pair, you Neanderthal!"

Sorry, I wasn't sorry, *I'll buy you more.*

"Just so you can feel better about ripping those off, too?"

Yes, I could only pretend to care about her shredded thong so much. She rolled her eyes at me before kissing me hard, her teeth sinking into my bottom lip *almost* too roughly.

My cock twitched between us, loving her bite, and reminding me that it needed protection.

"Fine," Eloise pushed me away, slapping her hand on the

mattress until it landed on the condoms. She picked them up only to slap them against my chest. "Cover up, then cover me." I lifted an eyebrow at her as I tore one condom open with my teeth, loving how hooded her eyes went at the sight of it.

Damn, the moves from those romance novels really did come in clutch sometimes.

As I covered my almost painful erection, I watched Eloise adjust herself on the bed until she was on her hands and knees, grabbing one of my hands and bringing it around to her breast, and making me fold on top of her back.

Jesus Christ, Eloise's ass was phenomenal like this.

"You ripped my panties," Eloise shrugged, "We're doing this how I want first."

Say less, Eloise.

It wasn't until I started teasing her nipple and kissing the back of her neck that I glanced up and realized what position she put us in. I was supporting myself on one arm and my knees as I folded over her back, when I met her eyes on me in the mirror hanging from the sliding doors of her closet.

Eloise wanted to watch us.

Eloise wanted to watch us have sex through the reflection of her mirror.

I was confident that I fell in love with her right then and there.

I grinned, loving the way her breath shuddered as I gently licked the shell of her ear and I kept my gaze on hers through the glass. Her ass pressed against my erection in the neediest way I had ever witnessed from her.

"I need you," Eloise confirmed, her gaze growing glassy as

I lowered my hand from her breast to the bundle of nerves between her legs, "Please."

I positioned myself at her center, releasing a shocked breath at how hot and wet she was still. I had one hand gripping her hips, while the other one flicked against her clit, as I slowly started to stretch her out around me.

It was insane how tight she felt.

Eloise's head fell forward as she groaned from my intrusion, and I was genuinely worried that I was going to explode before I even made it all the way inside of her. I used my index finger gripping her hip to tap her skin a few times, making her lift her head enough to meet my gaze in the mirror like this.

She wanted to watch, so she was *going* to watch.

It was probably the slowest I had ever entered a woman, but it was also the most satisfying. I could see each emotion and watch every gasp with every inch as I sunk deeper into her. Eloise looked so petite like this, my large frame bending over her as I consumed her. Just as she was consuming me.

Once I was finally seated inside her as far as I could go, I held still for her to get used to me.

Because she one hundred percent needed to get used to me.

I wasn't confident I'd ever let her go.

Her flushed cheeks and chest, the glaze over her eyes, and her heavy breathing made it incredibly difficult not to pound into her immediately.

Then, unexpectedly, Eloise released a surprised giggle.

I had no idea what was funny, and I raised an eyebrow at her in the mirror for her to explain herself. "It's just," Eloise giggled again before taking a deep breath, "I was just thinking about how convenient it is that I don't really need to be able to walk tomorrow."

Jesus Christ.

I pulled back slowly, before roughly slamming back into her again. Her gasp sounded positive, but I waited for her to nod her head at me in the mirror before I continued. She was so tight around me I could feel every subtle flutter and clench that she made. The fact that she seemed to be pushing back against me, meeting my thrusts, was making me lose my fucking mind.

But I was a prideful man, and I was determined to get one more orgasm out of her before I lost it myself.

I reached around her hips and started gently circling her clit again, and the feminine noises of approval made my already beating heart threaten to race out of my chest.

"I don't think I can..." Eloise's head fell forward again, but her words only made the competitive side of me rise. Based on how she was already occasionally fluttering around me, I had a feeling that she could.

I released her hip and used that hand to wrap around her stomach, pulling her up so that her back rested against my chest, and both of our knees were on the bed as I thrust into her. Her grip on my forearms was tight, and it only motivated me as I dropped my head and gently bit down on her shoulder.

"Oh my god," Eloise whimpered in time with a firm clench around me. I could feel her body starting to stiffen in my arms, her lips parting in shock as her eyelids almost fell completely closed.

I knew she could go again.

"…C'mon," I breathed, my lips right against her ear so that I knew she could hear my raspy, damaged voice. I ignored the burn that I would feel in my throat for a while after this because no way in hell was I using my hands to communicate when they were busy pulling Eloise apart, "…Give it to me."

Her whole body locked, her fingernails digging into my forearms as her head fell back against my shoulder and she clenched her teeth again. Her eyes were squeezed closed as she groaned and came undone in my arms. I lifted my gaze to watch us in the mirror, loving how good we looked together like this. How well we fit together, how soft, and warm she felt as she let me take what I could from her.

Only when Eloise's muscles loosened and she fell almost limp in my arms, did I let my own thrusts become erratic as I finally buried my head in her shoulder and let go. White hot pleasure raced down the base of my spine as my vision almost blacked out completely, and I had to remember to breathe when I finally spent the last of myself inside of her.

Eloise's heavy breathing, and the way she leaned most of her body weight against my chest, left me with no other choice. I used my hold around her body to simply tip us over onto the bed, loving the surprise *oof* Eloise made at the contact against the mattress.

After a few long moments embracing each other, we finally pulled apart just enough to clean each other up. Eloise had already gotten wipes so that we wouldn't have to leave the room and potentially face her roommates. Now that we were officially together, there was no need to sneak around,

302 | ANDREA ANDERSEN

but that didn't mean either of us wanted to run into Courtney minutes after mind-numbing sex, either.

The best part of the night, after we had covered ourselves under her blankets and casually chatted about the day, after I watched her slowly close her eyes for the last time that night, was knowing that I didn't have to wake up early to sneak away.

No. This time, as I fell asleep with Eloise Bane wrapped around my body, I relaxed into the fact that we would also wake up just as we dozed off.

Together.

23

ELOISE

"I should just be grateful you're here at all." My mother sniffed, once again reorganizing the flowers scattered all around her backyard dining area. This house that I had lived in with my parents for years felt alien to me. It was gaudy and flashy and reeked of the one percent lifestyle, but it also just felt...empty.

Perhaps that was why my mother was big on formal brunches and tea parties with her friends. Perhaps my mother needed to fill in the emptiness of the space, too.

"What does that mean?" I asked, taking a deep breath through my nose.

It had been about three weeks since Logan and I became official. Since he stayed the night at the townhouse, we both woke up to Courtney and Josh flipping pancakes in the kitchen. It felt a little weird to have them making breakfast for us, in a clear congratulations-to-finally-becoming-official kind of way, but not weird enough that Logan and I didn't eat every single bite of the blueberry pancakes Courtney had mastered over the years.

But then Susan asked if Logan and I were being safe, and I wanted to melt into the floor. Logan narrowed his eyes at the old woman and nodded his confirmation, and then Susan dropped it. Almost like she felt the need to check that box before continuing on with her line of questioning. She was suspicious that Logan and I had been sneaking around ever since Logan ditched the bar to cuddle with me on the couch during my period. She had even heard someone leaving my bedroom in the early hours of the morning multiple times, but didn't ask if it was Logan out of respect for my privacy.

I stared at the charcuterie board I was finishing putting together, and I realized that there was no chance in hell that my own mother would respect my privacy in such a way.

I could see her stiffen in my peripheral vision, because talking back to her or challenging her in any way was still something she was getting used to.

"It just seems like you have been too busy for me lately," she said, feigning innocence as she plucked the wilted petals off of the flower bouquet.

"That's because I have been," I replied casually. That made her straighten and stare at me, so I straightened and stared back at her. I could see the blue in her eyes, identical to mine, studying me. Trying to figure me out. I noticed when they landed on my arm tattoos, and the short cut of my hair. Two big "fuck you's" for how she had styled me growing up.

A flicker of sadness crossed her expression before her cool mask of indifference fell into place again.

"I just miss you, Eloise." My mother's voice was small,

lower, giving away the melancholy that her indifferent expression tried to hide.

I felt my heart squeeze at that.

"I miss you too, mom," I admitted, "But, that doesn't mean that I don't need to be on my own. Be my own person."

She narrowed her pale eyebrows at me, "What does *that* mean?"

I sighed, feeling my shoulders slump as I readied myself for the conversation my mother and I needed to have, something that Logan had been hyping me up for via text while he was out of town yet again for an away game. "I don't feel joy from this." I vaguely let my hand gesture to the classic and elegant random ass brunch my mother was setting up for her girlfriends, who were due to arrive within an hour. "I don't like pretending that I get along with your friends. I don't like pretending that I agree with everything you think I should be doing. And I don't like pretending that it doesn't suck that I need to tiptoe around my mom's feelings instead of prioritizing my own."

My mother stared at me; her mouth slightly parted in surprise from my words. I didn't back down, though. I fought against the urge to immediately apologize, to tell her that I was feeling tired or silly or whatever excuse I used in the past to put a band-aid on the whole situation.

"I didn't realize that I was causing you so much distress." She frowned, but I could see her pinched brow and redness starting to line her eyes as she fidgeted with the bouquet on the table she was decorating.

I wanted to roll my eyes at the manipulative language she

chose to use, but that wasn't how progress was made. "I'm glad you know now."

Boom.

She physically winced at my confirmation, clearly surprised that I didn't immediately try to coddle her or explain that she wasn't causing me distress. She was, and it was okay for her to know that. That didn't mean that I hated her. It just meant that we had some things to work on.

"Look," I sighed, walking over to her so that I could rest my hand on top of hers, "I am not angry or upset with you, though it feels like you're irritated with me." My mother opened her mouth to say something, but I ignored her and kept going, "But it's okay for me to be on my own. It's okay for me to have friends and a job and a life outside of you, to not have you be my best friend. I'm a grown woman, and I am just starting to figure out what I truly want for my life. Before, I just kept turning to you. I was more worried about doing whatever would make you and everyone in your circle happy, instead of what would truly make *me* happy. Isn't that what you're supposed to want as my parent? For your daughter to be truly happy with herself?" I blinked away the stinging in my eyes, a reaction that must be from finally, finally getting all of this off of my chest in front of my mother. "I would love to keep coming over to help you with your parties, occasionally. But that's not the focus of my life anymore. Since I moved out this last time, I learned what I need to prioritize, what I need to do to keep my peace. And sometimes that will include putting a little bit of distance between you and me, between me and the world I was brought up in."

A world I now thought of as privilege, snobbery, and shallow interests.

My mother blinked at me as she squeezed my hand, staring at me with wide eyes as if she was seeing me for the first time. As if something was clicking for her, pieces of a puzzle coming together in her brain.

She looked down at my hand, the one that had the flowers tattooed on them and lifted it up for her to look at as she squeezed my fingers again.

"I..." my mother swallowed, "I think I knew I was pushing you away." I kept quiet, trying to create a space for her to get her own words out. "I think I knew, even before I came home that day to find your room cleaned out, that I was pushing you away. I didn't want to push you away, but...I didn't know what else to do." She shrugged before biting her lip. My mother was biting her lip. A move I had never seen the elegant Mrs. Bane do.

"I don't want to keep pushing you away, mom," I took a step closer and wrapped my arms around her, resting my head on her shoulder. I felt relief blanket my chest when she rested her cheek on top of my head, her hands coming up to grip my arms that wrapped around her. "But it's okay for children to create boundaries with their parents, you know? I still want you to be part of my life, but just let me take the wheel. It's okay for you to be in the passenger seat every now and then."

My mother giggled a little, "That's a cute analogy, Eloise."

I laughed with her, "I know, I'm super clever." My mother laughed again and pulled away, wrapping her arms around me instead.

"I am so sorry," she whispered. "I love having you home, but I will try to remember that you have your own life, too."

I squeezed her back, "Thank you."

We held each other, hugging tightly as we let the words that we just exchanged float around us. With each second that passed, it was like a new foundation was being built between us. Each squeeze reminding the other that this was okay, that we were okay. That we weren't angry or bitter or upset, we were just simply adjusting to what a new normal between us would be.

Finally, we pulled away from each other and casually wiped away some stray tears from our eyes. It was a short discussion, but it was more of a heart-to-heart than we had ever had with each other.

I wanted to break the ice, while also throwing down a white flag. "I met someone."

My mother's eyes widened as an excited smile broke apart on her lips. "Do I know him?" she asked. I laughed and shook my head.

"Do you keep up with hockey at all?"

My mother's brow furrowed in confusion, like her answer should have been obvious to me. "No?"

I smiled, "I don't either, but he plays. You'd know him if you were a fan of the Ducks."

"Oh, a professional athlete?" Her eyes glowed with the realization, and I also realized it would take a while for my mother to become someone who prioritized who my partner was on the inside, instead of their occupation or income.

"The fact that he plays for the NHL is probably the least interesting thing about him," I replied. My mother's eyes softened at that, and as she studied me, I understood that she was willing to try. That she *wanted* to try. That she prioritized having a relationship with me over what she was expecting our relationship to be. I smiled as I pulled out my phone to show her pictures, and she responded by pulling out a chair at the table to sit at before we spent the next thirty minutes doing what mothers and daughters did best.

Which was ogling her daughter's boyfriend, and intently listening while I filled her in on everything that I wanted her to know. Like how Logan and I met, and how I truly hated him for a while. I delighted in her gasp as I shared with her the story of pie-maggedon, and how her daughter had the audacity to act so irrationally.

But then she grinned, like she didn't realize until that moment how proud of me she truly was. Perhaps I was just being hopeful.

"I'm glad you made him work for it," she said after some time, "He sounds special."

"He is." I sighed, staring at one picture I had pulled up intending to help my mother see what he looked like. We had also accidentally stumbled upon some marketing the Ducks had done this last summer, and my mother and I stared a little too long at one picture of Logan all oiled up and shirtless in front of his team's logo. He was clearly irritated with the whole ordeal, and his glare at the camera immediately made me laugh. My mother saw me laugh at his expression, before smiling brightly herself as she took in my response.

"You are special too, Eloise," she whispered, "You deserve somebody just as special."

I sniffed, a wobbly smile tugging at my lips, "I really like him, mom."

She grinned, her eyes glancing down at the shirtless Logan on my phone, his pants pulled dangerously low. "I can see why."

"No," I laughed, "Not that, though that doesn't suck, either." I closed out of the browser and set my phone down on the table. "I just...I'm scared, I think. I haven't seriously dated someone since Adam, and we all know how that worked out." I rested my chin on my fist, feeling emotionally exhausted and missing my boyfriend terribly. My mother sat there next to me, studying my face with a thoughtful expression of her own.

"You won't have your mother and his mother meddling in your relationship this time, though." I widened my eyes at her, because we hadn't talked about that specifically, but she still acknowledged the fact that she did, in fact, overstep.

"Are you sure?" I asked, because last I knew, Adam's mother was still kind of an asshole to Beck. Still bitter that her son picked someone she didn't pick out herself.

"Unlike Edith Hall," my mother rolled her eyes, "I know when to put aside my pride. That woman basically has no relationship with her only child now, and I do not want to make the same mistake as her." She emphasized her words with a swipe of her hand, and I giggled at the relief I felt expand in my lungs at the sight.

"Thank fucking god." I breathed. My mother gasped at my language and swatted my arm, but I just laughed and flinched out of her way.

"Please, do not use that sort of language when my guests

arrive," she squeezed my arm in reassurance, "And be patient with me if it takes some time to hear you use that language with me in private."

I rested my hand on top of hers, "Don't worry, I'll keep your secret that you're a cool mom."

She smiled again, before pressing a motherly kiss on my head and wrapping me up in her arms once more. I felt significantly more relaxed than I did an hour ago when I first arrived at her house. I pictured the worst-case scenario. I had seen how it worked out for both Beck and Adam when they stood up to their parents for their own reasons, and Beck hadn't spoken to her parents in any capacity for a couple of years now. I had only heard about this ending in catastrophe, where the parents couldn't handle their children putting up boundaries.

I was lucky because my mom and I wouldn't follow that pattern. We both wanted to make our relationship work. I was sure that we would hit snags and bumps, as any mother-daughter relationship played out. But knowing that there was a willingness to meet me halfway made me feel at ease. Like it would all work out in the end.

24

ELOISE

The flight to Denver, Colorado was uneventful, probably because I fell asleep shortly after takeoff. I had shared my idea with Courtney, Taylor, and Beck a couple days before while we were eating lunch in the breakroom at work. They originally loved my idea, but were hesitant because of the last-minute flights that would need to be booked.

Then Courtney called her fiancé, who was in Chicago recording with an artist who could not be named, and scoffed at the idea of us not going through with my surprise. Josh told me to give Logan a big fat smooch from him, and I gave him a thumbs up in response on the FaceTime call.

"Beck's really missing out," Taylor mumbled as they nudged me awake and stood to grab our carry-ons from the overhead compartment.

"We will just have to take lots of pictures of us having fun without her so she'll come next time," Courtney replied. She pushed me with her hands to hurry up, because I was still rubbing sleep out of my eyes in the middle seat, trapping her in her window seat.

Next time.

Logan and I had been officially together for just under a month, and our friends were already planning on when we would fly out to surprise him at one of his away games "next time."

The thought thrilled me more than terrified me, and I loved it.

"I'm sure if we were flying somewhere else, she would have tagged along," I replied, catching up to the conversation I was waking up to. As we grabbed our carry-ons and made our way out of DEN, I was glad we didn't bring everyone along. It was kind of fun just bringing Courtney and Taylor with me on this surprise. They were the loud and fun ones who would help me do my very best to embarrass Logan, whereas Beck and Adam were more reserved and would have happily supported me with their quiet presence.

Beck said she didn't want to waste the plane tickets on someone who still didn't understand what happened during a game of hockey, and that Denver wasn't high on her "places to visit" bucket list.

Adam later explained to me that Beck didn't feel comfortable leaving Susan all on her own, so I didn't push Beck further. Though, I was sure if we flew out of the country or somewhere warmer, Beck would have thought about tagging along on the trip a bit more—or Susan would have forced her.

"What's the car look like?" Taylor asked Courtney as they turned their cap backwards. They were already representing Logan's team with their Anaheim Ducks baseball cap, ready to stick out in a sea of...whatever colors the Colorado...some-things, wore.

I told myself that I would eventually be a better hockey partner.

Josh had his manager, Kate, schedule our hotel room and car service to take us to the game straight from the airport. As we waited outside the airport for our car, I voiced the first thing I noticed about being in this state.

"It's dry as hell here." I could already feel my hands and face starting to tighten from the lack of moisture in the air, and I was glad I always had some lotion and moisturizer in my purse as I dug it out.

"Yeah, it is," Courtney held her hand out for me to squirt some moisturizer in her palm, and Taylor followed suit.

"I'd like to go back to my southern California bubble, please," I fake whined as I slathered my hands together.

"Yeah, it must suck so hard that you got front row tickets to an NHL game, after getting free flights, with a free hotel, that you have to share with the coolest people in the world," Taylor mocked with an eye roll, as they applied the moistur-izer to their face. I noticed how they were careful not to glob any on their septum ring.

"It's cute that you think I'll be staying in your room tonight, and not Logan's," I winked at them as I capped my moisturizer and shoved the bottle back in my bag.

"I'm so glad he took Adam's advice," Taylor replied.

That made me and Courtney stop to look at them.

Taylor had just adjusted their baseball cap again, combing their short brown hair back underneath the hat with their fingers before they noticed us staring. "What?"

"What do you mean he took Adam's advice?" I asked.

"Oh, we all talked about you two months ago, back when we had the suit fitting with Josh in LA." Taylor shrugged as if this wasn't new information that I would immediately be interested in.

"Did you know about this?" I asked Courtney. She shrugged; her face masked to conceal that she clearly did know about this. "What did Adam say to Logan?"

"That Logan should ask you out. I think he said something like, 'Worst-case scenario, she says no. Best case scenario, you have a date to the wedding.'"

I blinked, thinking back to when this was. This was before Connor and Logan came to my work that one random time, before we had ever FaceTimed or admitted that we wanted to act on our mutual feelings of attraction. The fact that my ex-boyfriend was actively encouraging my current boyfriend to make a move on me made me feel a small touch of relief. Not that Adam had recently done or said anything to make me think that he still resented me for how I acted during our relationship years ago, but it was a quiet confirmation that Adam and I were good. That we had both officially moved on.

"Wow," I shifted on my feet, "That was so long ago."

"The wedding isn't until next year," Courtney added, turning to me, and wiggling her eyebrows, "And Logan wanted to lock you down as soon as possible."

I blushed from her teasing, but grinned and waved her off.

"It's amazing what texting and FaceTiming can do for couples," was all I replied.

Finally, the car pulled up, and we all climbed in. There

was a privacy screen between us and the driver, so Courtney and I changed into our fan gear. We both donned Anaheim Ducks jerseys with ST. JAMES on the back in big letters. Courtney's was way too big for her, and as we pulled out our portable mirrors to check our hair and makeup, I noticed some scribbling on the shoulder of hers.

"What the fuck, did Logan sign yours?" I asked, tugging on the sleeve of Courtney's jersey.

"Yeah, careful! Signed merch has value!" Courtney swatted my hand away, covering Logan's signature on her sleeve protectively as if I'd rip it off.

"He needs to sign mine," I grumbled, looking down at my suddenly less-than shirt.

"And my hat," Taylor added, thumbing away on their phone. They only wore the hat to the rink, deciding to stick with their white t-shirt and gray jacket instead of another jersey.

We chatted and bickered the rest of the way to the rink, me bouncing in my seat the entire drive there. Logan had no idea we were showing up to this game. I wasn't sure if he would like this surprise or not, but I also decided that it would be worth the risk. He was new to this group of friends just like I was, except it was clear that Logan hadn't had a community outside of his hockey team. He didn't have anyone to surprise him by showing up to his games.

I wanted to be his first girlfriend to surprise him at a game in a different state.

I also realized as we walked through security and made

our way to our front row, that I wanted to be Logan's *last* girlfriend.

He probably wasn't ready to have that conversation yet, but I found myself smiling at the ground as we side-stepped our way to the seats. I had just realized how I wanted this new relationship of mine to go.

The rink was filled with dark blues and reds, making it obvious even for a rookie like me to learn what the other team's colors were. I had to squint to see a smattering of white and orange in the crowd, otherwise I would have thought that the three of us were the only Anaheim fans in the entire stadium.

A couple Colorado fans started booing us from behind, and Courtney responded by immediately turning around to flip them off with both hands before Taylor grabbed her and tugged her back down in her seat.

"I don't want to be hate-crimed because of aggressive hockey fans tonight, but thanks," was Taylor's reasoning for Courtney to chill. My heart squeezed because I wouldn't have even thought about that had Taylor not mentioned it. Courtney immediately wrapped them in a tight hug in apology, before stealing their cap and rustling their hair with her hands.

"You son of a—" but Taylor didn't finish their words because the rink erupted in cheers as the hockey players skated onto the ice.

Similar to where we sat last season, our seats were right near the tunnel that led to the locker rooms, so we got an up close and personal view of every player as they made it onto the ice.

When the Ducks came out, I spotted Logan immediately. Even under all the gear I was able to recognize his form, the way he held himself as he stood taller than usual due to the skates on his feet. The ST. JAMES and number twenty-nine on the back of his jersey was a helpful afterthought.

I stood up in my seat and everything, ready to shout at him to kick ass, but he didn't see me before he skated off to run drills with his teammates before the game started. I bounced on my heels a few times before I felt fingers tug themselves through my belt loops, gently pulling me back into my seat.

"He'll see you," Courtney reassured me with a pat on my back, offering me some of her box of popcorn.

"Where did you get this?" I asked, glancing around as if it had magically appeared.

"The kid," she pointed to the other side of Taylor, where there was a teenager selling boxes of popcorn and soda. I hadn't even noticed them.

"You're much more focused on the ice now than you were last time we came to a game," Taylor commented with a wiggle of their eyebrows.

"I'm just interested in who is on the ice, actually." I tugged on the sleeves of my jersey, hiding my fingers in the fabric to try to keep my body warm in the cool rink. "If I wasn't dating Logan, I doubt that I'd care at all."

"Makes sense," Courtney shrugged after shoving a handful of popcorn in her mouth, she spoke around her bite loud enough for Taylor and me to hear her say, "I wasn't into rock music before Josh."

"But you are now?" Taylor asked with a lifted eyebrow.

"I mean," she shrugged, "I got into Josh's music first. Partly thanks to Beck, partly thanks to Josh himself. But yeah, I have definitely expanded my music taste since reconnecting with him." Courtney gave a small smile after she finally finished chewing and swallowing her bite.

The game was starting and people were suddenly cheering around us as the three of us turned to see the players zooming towards our end of the rink. Our conversation was paused as I stood up again, along with other fans around us who were pressing up against the glass to cheer on the Colorado team (the Avalanche, according to their jerseys) to get the puck from the Ducks.

I cheered as Logan successfully defended his teammates, shoving and blocking other players to clear a space for someone else on the team to take a shot.

It was a miss.

The stadium cheered, and the three of us slumped in disappointment while the Avalanche took back the puck and everyone skated to the opposite end of the rink.

"It's interesting," I mused, regaining Taylor and Courtney's attention as we settled into the hard plastic seats, "Just a couple of years ago, I would have been the woman who pretended to be into hockey in order to simply be on the arm of a professional athlete." Courtney and Taylor were silent as they let me ponder about my past life, how my old friends, Lucy and Michelle (whom I hadn't spoken to in months), would probably be excited to join me at one of Logan's games for the same silly reason I just admitted to. "But now, I feel comfortable openly admitting that I wasn't interested in the sport at all. Not until I became involved with someone that I really cared about, someone who's livelihood literally depended on it." I grinned a little bit as I watched Logan bump a gloved fist with another player, who I realized was John. I was surprised to see the two of them quickly remove one of their gloves, before tossing it to the other and quickly strapping it on before the next play started. "Even then, I'm still not really into hockey. I'm into my boyfriend, and hockey is important to him," I shrugged one shoulder, "So here I am."

Courtney's hand came down on my knee, squeezing once before she gently patted it and pulled back. "We never stop growing up and improving ourselves. It's good to acknowledge the moments that we do."

I nodded my agreement as I glanced over at my friend, grateful that she and I connected during the time that I had finally given up on reviving my past failed relationship. I was truly a better person since befriending Courtney, and Taylor, and Beck. And everyone else. Even Logan.

"Oh, they're coming back!" Taylor shot to their feet, cupping their hands over their mouth and shouting, "Get it, twenty-nine!"

"Twenty-nine!" Courtney shouted with a deep voice, mimicking her favorite character from the TV show *New Girl*.

"Go! Go! Go!" I was clapping as I cheered, the three of us on our feet and pressed against the plexiglass as a swarm of players elbowed and slapped sticks and struggled against each other. John was surrounded, but still managed to keep the puck close as he lifted his eyes, searching.

Logan was skating on the outside of the mess, and he

signed something quickly to John, with his gloved hand, before blocking someone else from getting involved in the attempt to regain the puck.

John nodded, and within a second, he snapped his stick against the puck and sent it flying in the direction of a third Ducks player that I wasn't familiar with. He captured the puck easily, because very few Avalanche players were guarding him, but as soon as they saw the puck hit his stick, everyone swarmed, leaving John and Logan at their backs.

The player, instead of going towards the net like I was expecting him to, blocked an attempt to steal the puck and snapped it back. The puck gained air, and Logan lifted his stick and caught it before it could get further out of range.

I gasped, bouncing on my heels as an opposing player, that I hadn't been keeping track of, charged Logan, who was already swinging his stick and cracking the puck into the net.

The stadium booed, but the three of us gasped and cheered.

Logan was using his momentum on the ice to skate around the net before traveling back down to the center of the rink, and I banged my fists onto the plexiglass and cheered as he did so.

He almost missed me.

I could make out his dark brown eyes, and the mouth guard he had in his lips through the mask he wore, concealing most of his face. His eyes scanned the crowd without really seeing anyone, like it was habit for him to just glance up and remember that there were fans in the room.

But right as he was about to pass, our eyes met, and I could see the recognition flare in his.

Logan finally found me.

He skidded to a stop, like a cartoon, and skated backwards a little so that we stood in front of each other through the plexiglass.

I smiled and kept slapping my palms against it, jumping and grinning and even going as far as to put my fingers in my mouth and whistle.

Logan pulled out his mouth guard under his mask to smile at me, a wide and open grin that he didn't try to cover with his hand. It wasn't until Courtney and Taylor banged their fists against the plexiglass that he let his gaze flick over to notice them, but quickly set his sights right back on me.

And my heart swelled.

He lifted a gloved hand up to press against mine through the plexiglass, then popped his mouthguard back in and threw a wink over his shoulder at me, as he skated back to the game. I pressed my palms to my cheeks to confirm that I was, in fact, blushing from his wink.

"I think he's happy about the surprise," Courtney mused as we settled back into our seats again, "I'm glad Logan isn't— oh barf."

I turned to look at Courtney, who was frowning through the plexiglass and staring at something. Taylor and I tried to follow her line of sight, but we both gave each other confused looks before Taylor asked, "What is it?"

"Daddy James," Courtney grumbled. I felt my heart sink into my gut, and the warm happy flutters I had felt from getting Logan's attention earlier were shrunken down, oppressed by the familiar feeling of anxiety my body lit up with.

Taylor and I both turned our heads to try to see where

Courtney was looking, and we both found Logan's agent at the same time.

I didn't say anything, but I heard Taylor grumble, "Yuck," at the same moment my eyes met his.

He sat a few sections away, man spread in full force as he kept his leg firmly pressed against a brunette woman who was watching the hockey game with clear interest. She was cheering and shouting at the team just like everyone else was, but Connor had settled with an arm looped on the back of her chair, his eyes on the three of us.

Logan's agent lifted a hand in greeting, a small and clearly reluctant smile on his lips accompanied with a head nod.

I didn't wave back, and neither did Courtney, but Taylor did.

It was comical, because as far as I knew Connor hadn't gone out of his way to speak to Taylor ever, but the fact that they were the only one to return his wave made his brows scrunch in confusion, and he refocused his attention on the game.

Courtney snorted, "Why did you wave back?"

Taylor smirked, fidgeting with their nose ring, "Because I knew he wasn't waving at me, and I'm a petty bitch."

Courtney and I laughed at that, easing some of the tension that had lingered in my body from the realization that Connor was here, watching the game. It was something I needed to get used to, unfortunately. Connor was Logan's agent, and I doubted that I wouldn't ever see him again. It sucked, considering Connor James was the one single hook up decision I had made in my adult life that I thoroughly regretted with my entire being.

"I consented that night with Connor," I blurted out, surprise taking over my anxiety after realizing what I was trying to talk to Courtney and Taylor about, at Logan's game no less. Out of the corner of my eye, I saw them both slowly turn their heads towards me. I cleared my throat, released a nervous smile, and faced them. I stared into Courtney's dark eyes, determined to channel just a drop of her bold demeanor as I thought about my words carefully.

"I-I consented," I said again, "But, that doesn't mean that I didn't change my mind later on." I swallowed, watching the concern etch itself into both Taylor and Courtney's facial features. "I didn't tell him I changed my mind," I added, proud of myself for how controlled my voice sounded even though my heart was thumping in my chest erratically, "And maybe I should have spoken up. Maybe I should have said something." I shrugged, and I knew Courtney was about to say something, so I spoke up again to finish my thoughts before she could interrupt me, "But, he also shouldn't assume my original verbal consent was a free pass for whatever he wanted to do." I lifted another nervous shoulder, tucking my lips between my teeth while I stared at my friends. The rock music playing in the rink was a faded, background noise to the moment I just initiated with my friends. To the vulnerability and honesty I was exposing to them.

"You're right," Courtney nodded, "He shouldn't have."

"Any moron can tell when their partner changes their mind," Taylor added, "But it sounds like he chose to ignore the signs out of selfishness."

I nodded once, inhaling a deep breath through my nose before slowly exhaling through my mouth. Just like I had seen both of them tell the toddlers that they worked with to do when they were feeling some big emotions.

"I don't want to give it too much attention," I added, "I'd like to move on. I'm never sleeping with him again, and he might be figuring that out." I nodded vaguely in the direction that he was sitting with the woman who looked like his date.

It was a real bummer that he was Logan's agent. I got a sick feeling in my stomach at the thought of running into Connor as often as we had, but that was part of adulthood. I wanted to be brave, and not be so obvious about my anxiety around him.

Plus, just because we would bump into each other from time to time, didn't mean we needed to pretend to be friends or anything. Thankfully the fact that it looked like he brought a date meant that he probably wouldn't try to corner me into talking with him. Perhaps he was finally getting the hint. Like the last time we bumped into each other at one of Logan's games.

Because I would definitely be going to more of Logan's games.

I grinned as Logan threw another wink in my direction as he fought off one of the opposing players, successfully clearing a path for his teammate on the other side of the rink. Excitement was starting to course through my veins, watching him in his element and finally being able to appreciate it all. He'd made it here, regardless of his accident and communication barriers. The guy who had no one in his corner, beyond his teammates, for years, until all of us.

Hell, Logan even managed to win *me* over. A year ago, I

would have laughed in the face of anyone who suggested that he and I would end up together. Logan, the guy who showed me the roughest parts of him first. The guy who offended me time and time again but didn't give up on trying to wave a white flag between the two of us.

The guy who took my unsolicited voice memos in stride.

I blushed, remembering that even though Logan and I had gone out on a handful of dates in between practices and hockey games and my work schedule, I hadn't ever admitted to him the total truth regarding my voice memos.

I smirked to myself as I watched my boyfriend skate past us again, earning cheers from our friends. I had a feeling that Logan would appreciate the true story now.

***

"Traitor," Taylor grumbled as we made our way down the hallway. I had just stepped out of the elevator with Logan, bidding them goodbye.

"You're just bitter that there is a one thousand percent chance that I'm getting laid tonight, and you're not," I quipped back, looping my arm through Logan's. The material of his suit was nice, and I found myself leaning into his large body more when I caught a whiff of his body wash or aftershave or whatever it was that he wore that smelled delicious on him.

Logan started tugging me away, and Courtney saluted to us as she thumbed away on her phone. The elevator doors started to close, and the last thing I could see was Taylor lifting their middle finger at me with their tongue out. I laughed, snuggling into Logan's arm that wasn't tugging my carry-on suitcase and holding his equipment bag on his shoulder.

I said I could handle my own luggage, and Logan had just ignored me.

I was on cloud nine.

We waited for the team after the game, and I practically sprinted into Logan's arms as soon as he walked through the doors. He had to catch me by placing both of his hands on my butt to support me, which I didn't think he was too upset about based on the enthusiastic squeeze he gave.

I attacked his face with kisses. It had only been a couple days since we had seen each other, but I missed him dammit.

"Get a room." Courtney had teased.

"You don't have to tell me twice," I had mumbled my reply against Logan's lips, who had grinned and returned my kisses with just as much if not more enthusiasm.

Now, though, I was bouncing on my heels as he scanned the card to his room and opened the door for us to enter.

"I was only partly kidding about getting laid tonight, by the way," I told him after he kicked the door shut. Logan had just dropped our bags and looked like he was about to advance on me, his hands clutching themselves into fists as if he was struggling to restrain himself before he tilted his head to the side and asked, *What?*

"I just mean that," I took a deep breath to keep myself from bouncing on my heels, sitting calmly on the hotel bed that was perfectly made, "If you're too tired, I'm just happy sharing space with you. You could fall asleep right now, with me wrapped around you like a koala bear, and I would be perfectly content." I grinned.

Logan's shoulders dropped, and a look of relief seemed to cross his face.

Oh, damn, he really must have been exhausted then.

"Seriously, it's no worries," I lifted my sneaker onto my knee to start untying my shoes when suddenly, Logan's hands were there swatting mine away. He knelt down and started untying my sneakers, tugging them off with my socks.

I self-consciously tried to tuck my toes away from his grip, afraid that airport traveling and jumping at his hockey game gave my feet an unpleasant smell, but he held onto my ankles and slowly started to slide his hands up my legs.

He let his large palms make it as far as the tops of my thighs, his thumbs dangerously close to an area that was immediately excited for his touch.

And then he stood up, the warmth of his hands leaving me cool.

I should rest, Logan signed, smirking at the surprised look on my face, *But I don't want to*. I grinned at that.

I'm glad, I signed back to him. I have been doing that more and more lately. I knew that he had asked Courtney to vocalize to him when they first met, and that he didn't care if people vocalized to him while he signed in return, but I wanted to learn. And he was willing to let me use my beginner's skills on him until I hopefully became as fluent in ASL as he was.

I stood up and started unbuttoning my jeans just as Logan's eyes flared and he lifted a hand for me to halt my movements.

I need to go to John's room. I furrowed my eyebrows at that.

"Why?" My fingers had just undone the button of my pants, and Logan was trying to go hangout with his buddy?

We need to swap gloves. Logan had bent down to unzip his hockey bag and pulled out the gloves he wore during the game, *it's part of a tradition after every game we win.*

"That's so gross," I wrinkled my nose, and Logan responded by waving his stinky gloves near me before I swatted him away with a giggle, "But fine. Go do that now, and then thoroughly wash your hands, because you're not leaving this room again tonight." I knew he and his teammates had silly superstitious traditions, like a lot of professional athletes did.

Logan's eyes flared with excitement, then he bent down to kiss me deeply, his tongue making a leisurely sweep in my mouth as if in promise before he rose again and left the room in a clear hurry.

"Men." I laughed to myself, glancing around the room. I sat up from the bed and made my way over to the entertainment center that had a minifridge underneath. I opened the fridge, disappointed to see it empty.

I opened the other doors and drawers, and realized nothing but empty glasses and tap water was available. I had a feeling that I would be way too thirsty in about an hour to tolerate room temperature tap water.

I decided that I would make a quick trip to the ice machine, since I had seen it near the vending machines down the hall. I grabbed the two glasses left on the bathroom countertop and decided I'd fill them before Logan and I got busy. I slipped my loose sneakers back on my feet, not bothering to tie them because I was going to be quick. I might even run into Logan on the way there or back.

But when I opened the door to the hall and didn't see anyone, I decided to send Logan a quick text that I was getting ice before I locked myself out of his room by exiting it without the key that he took.

I was humming to myself, a little skip in my step as I held a glass in each hand and wandered down the hall to where the vending machines were, just next to the elevators. There was a little opening that looked like it was missing a door, considering the size of the entry to the space, but it left the little room open to the hallway. Convenient for the late-night munchies, I guessed.

There was already a decent amount of ice made, so I simply scooped the two cups into the ice chunks and collected what I could, before turning to browse the snacks.

A shadow fell over me, blocking the hall light coming in from the doorway. In the glass of the vending machine I saw a figure come into the space and stop. I recognized that face immediately.

"Connor." I whirled, pasting on as friendly of a smile as I could.

He had a bucket in his hand, clearly intending to grab some ice as well. *Where the hell did he get a bucket?* Our room didn't have one. He must have gotten a nicer room than Logan.

But that train of thought died on my lips when I met his gaze and noticed the way his brow bunched. The way he widened his stance as he took me in, taking up the entirety of the doorway.

"Eloise."

25

ELOISE

I felt myself swallow, and something in my brain kept telling me to *run* as his gaze trailed over my body again. His eyes flicked around the room as he noticed the small space, and that he was blocking my only form of escape.

"I was just grabbing ice," I lifted both of the glasses in my hands as evidence.

"Me too," Connor lifted the bucket in his hand, but he took a step into the room as he stared at me. "But I'm actually glad I ran into you."

I felt my pulse start to spike in my veins and my polite smile drop from my face. "Oh."

"Yeah," Connor continued, oblivious to or choosing simply not to acknowledge my internal panic. "I guess I just have some questions."

I didn't say anything, I just clenched my jaw and stared at him.

I was trapped, I had to stand here and talk to him, and the expression on his face made me realize it wasn't going to be a friendly conversation. No, Connor was upset. Clearly seen, based on how his shoulders bunched and his grip on his ice bucket tightened.

"Do you have any idea what my questions might be?" Connor asked, his eyebrow raising, his voice patronizing. Like he was a disgruntled parent trying to lead a child to answer. It was gross, and terrifying.

I wanted to say, "Are you going to ask why I blocked your number?" But I just stayed silent. Every muscle in my body was pulled taut, adrenaline coursing through my veins in my panic.

At my silence, Connor stared up at the ceiling and shook his head, his jaw visibly clenching and making a muscle pop in his cheek. I took a quiet step back.

"You're such a child."

I blinked at him, my blood cooling a little in my veins at his words. "Pardon?"

"You have acted so immature. Ignoring me, pretending like nothing happened between us. It's embarrassing," Connor scolded, glaring at me from his spot in the doorway, leaning an arm against the side. It still didn't leave enough room on his other side for me to fit by if I needed to run. "But getting Logan to fire me was too far."

I felt my lips part in surprise at his tone because I wasn't aware of that at all.

"It's embarrassing for me that I slept with you, yes," I snapped, a bit of the new Eloise rising in irritation at this man's audacity to corner me like this. "Though, I would say that you should be more embarrassed that you can boldly refer to a woman you slept with as a child. That's gross."

"You didn't think I was gross that night," his tone lowered, no longer trying to hide his anger.

"That's where you're wrong," I interrupted, crossing my arms with the ice cups in my hands still. I felt my own anger rising with each word, and a small voice in my head told me to drop it and play nice for the sake of getting out of here safely, but I couldn't quite listen to it yet. "I didn't enjoy it. I thought I made that very clear when I blocked your number after you didn't get the hint and kept calling me."

I swore I could hear Connor's teeth grind at my words, his nostrils flaring when I made a blatant hit to his pride.

"You didn't—"

"Why are we even talking about this?" I interrupted him again, feeling exasperated with it all. "Don't you have someone waiting for you? I'm sure she's wondering where you are."

Connor snapped his arm back and hurled his ice bucket at the wall to the side of us. I gasped and folded my arms over my head as it bounced against the vending machines and clanged on the floor.

I didn't think, didn't hesitate, as I used my cups of ice and tossed them both at him as soon as he took a step towards me.

He blinked as he swatted the ice off of his face, staring at all the melting cubes on the ground before looking at me like I was insane. As if *I* was the one being ridiculous in this situation.

In the back of my mind, I barely acknowledge the sound of a door opening down the hall, followed by a guy's voice and chuckle.

"Don't come any closer," I warned, my voice low. I still had glasses in my hands. I was shaking from the sudden tantrum this grown man was throwing in front of me, but I was sure I could do something with the cups to defend myself if needed.

I then heard heavy footsteps thudding down the hallway the same moment Connor shook his head, and I saw the resolve click in his expression as he took another step and reached out for me. "You little—"

But he was cut off. He was suddenly being ripped backwards, making him stagger against the wall before a large hand wrapped itself around his shoulder and shoved him to the ground in the hallway.

John's large body loomed over his agent, who tried to grab at the athlete before John caught his wrist and twisted it. Connor cried out in pain as John growled, "Cut the shit."

Then Logan shoved John out of the way, and suddenly he was in the room with me, his dark eyes scanning my body before noticing the cups I was gripping in my hands, the ice on the floor, the discarded bucket randomly on the ground.

"I'm fine," I immediately spoke up, but my trembling gave me away. Logan stepped into my space, lifting his hands with a question on his face. "Please hold me," I whispered. He didn't need to be told twice. He pulled the glasses from my hands, setting them somewhere, before his large arms wrapped themselves around me.

"I'm calling the police," John announced from the hallway, still towering over a glowering Connor.

"That's not necessary," Connor argued, "You're over-reacting!"

"Shut the fuck up." John flinched towards Connor, who flinched back as he stared up at the large Thor-looking man.

"Thank you," I whispered, squeezing against Logan's chest, "Thank you."

Logan shook his head, a movement I could only feel on the top of my head where his chin rested, and we didn't need to say any more. I stayed there, trembling in Logan's arms while John ensured that his agent stayed on the ground until the police came.

Logan walked me out into the hallway, carefully placing his body between me and Connor so I didn't have to look at him. He had pulled out his phone with one hand, reassuring his grip on me with a comforting squeeze with his other, and typed out a message. A few minutes later, I heard the elevator ding and suddenly, Courtney and Taylor were both running into the hallway towards where Logan and I had slumped onto the ground, my trembling and heart rate felt out of control.

"Are you okay?" Taylor asked before shaking their head. "Stupid question, how can I help?"

"Do you need anything?" Courtney asked. They both had fallen to their knees on either side of Logan and me, and a relieved sob broke from my lips as tears started to slowly fall from my cheeks.

"I'm okay," I shook my head, "I mean, I'm not. But I'm okay."

Courtney's expression turned thunderous as she sat taller on her knees to look around Logan and John, probably making eye contact with the worst mistake of my life before declaring in a calm but furious tone, "I am so relieved that you lost the custody battle." I hadn't known that had happened, but I felt a weird amount of relief expand in my chest as well, knowing that Connor's ex-wife had the good sense to both leave him and fight for their child.

"Fucking bitch," Connor spat back, making me wince.

"I'd stop talking until you have a lawyer present, asshole," John threatened. A couple doors opened down the hall and the faces of Logan's teammates were starting to poke their heads out to see what the commotion was.

I faded in and out of what was happening around me then, the shock of the situation starting to kick in as it kept me from processing my surroundings fully. I didn't even remember the police showing up, they were just suddenly there, shooing the rest of Logan's team back into their rooms unless they had useful statements to give them regarding what happened.

I did catch a few details though, like how Logan had fired Connor as his agent weeks ago. How Connor clearly thought that I had pressured or convinced Logan to do so because of our history. How John, who had no idea what was going on between his agent and I, was more than happy to fire Connor as well.

I didn't convince those men to do anything, but I had slumped against Logan even more knowing that I wouldn't have to face him anymore.

I did hear the police mention video footage in the vending machine area, and I hid my face against his button-up shirt. His large hands made soothing passes down my back, my arms, my legs, my neck, whatever part of me he could touch.

As if he was both trying to reassure me and himself that I was okay. That I was here, and that he had me.

After giving my statement to the police, I didn't want to stick around to wait for John and Connor to give their official statements. The police did ask if Logan would stick around to give his, and Courtney volunteered to interpret for him.

With that, Taylor pulled me to my feet and led me back to Logan's room.

"I'm so sorry, Lo," Taylor helped me dress down into just the jersey I was still wearing, pulling the covers on the bed back and tucking me in nice and tight, before sitting on the other side of the bed above the covers and reaching for the TV remote.

"Courtney and I couldn't find much on the TV in our room," they shrugged, snuggling in so that even though they sat above the covers, they pressed the entirety of their body against my side. I didn't realize that I would appreciate that contact after an event like this, but I rested my head on their arm that held the remote as they flipped through the channels.

"Thanks." My voice was small, but my trembling was slowly being replaced with what felt like pure exhaustion.

"Don't mention it," they replied, "I'm just glad Logan found you."

We sat in silence as Taylor flipped through channels, adrenaline leaving my body with each channel that they snubbed without explanation. My eyes were staring at the TV, but I wasn't seeing what was on it. I wasn't even thinking about what had just happened to me moments before this.

Instead, I was thinking about Logan. How he held me

tight just now, and almost every other moment I shared with him.

How he tried to talk to me at the townhouse the second time we met, clearly trying to be less of a socially repressed asshole even though I was too stubborn to see it. How Logan was ready to tease me and act like the rest of our friends, and I responded by attacking him with pie. How he checked in with me after showing up at my workplace, how he showed up outside my bedroom window when he realized he hurt my feelings again and didn't want me to go to bed before he could apologize.

How he slammed up against the plexiglass at the first hockey game of his I attended.

How he rested his hand against the plexiglass earlier to-night, as if he would take what he could in that moment.

It was wild, how a relationship with a person could change so dramatically over time. How even though Taylor's presence was nothing but comfort right now, I still longed for the man outside talking to the police with Courtney. How I wanted him beside me. How I wanted to feel his arms wrap around me as I fell asleep, like so many nights before this one. Before we even decided to claim each other from anyone else. How even just his physical presence was soothing to me.

I grinned a little, snuggling under the covers some more before releasing a heavy breath in exhaustion. "I'm glad that Logan and I found each other," I said in response to Taylor's earlier statement.

They paused their channel surfing to look at me for a solid moment before saying, "Well, that was cheesy as hell."

I shoved them away from me, and they laughed before settling back in while we waited for our friends.

26

ELOISE

"I have something to tell you and I am super nervous about it because I have definitely waited too long to do so," I spat the words out in a rush, sinking back into my seat as the airplane finally reached its altitude and flight attendants started serving snacks and drinks.

Logan just turned to look at me, his grip on my thigh tightening a little as he visibly tried not to look too concerned from my sudden build up to a confession he clearly wasn't anticipating.

The rest of the team flew back to Orange County early this morning, but Logan and I slept in and took a later flight out. I didn't want to rush getting up and packing for the airport, and neither did he. Thankfully, neither did Taylor or Courtney, who sat in the two seats in front of us.

"Are you ready to hear it?" I asked, sucking in a breath, and tucking my lips in between my teeth in clear nervous anticipation. His brows scrunched at my expression, and he shifted in his seat to face me as he kept one hand on my thigh, almost like it comforted him more than me.

I inhaled a deep, dramatic breath before holding it for a few moments. The way Logan leaned into me was almost comical, his eyes were wide and he was clearly struggling to keep calm about this. I just needed to get it out.

"The voice memos I sent all those months ago weren't about you."

Logan was frozen, except for one slow blink as he stared at me.

I sat there in silence, waiting for him to say something.

After a few very painful seconds, he finally lifted his hands, *What do you mean?*

"I mean the voice memos that I sent you in the middle of the night," I inhaled another nervous breath, but I was also smiling because the whole thing was just so ridiculous to me now, "The ones where I was clearly tipsy and rambling about attractive men."

Logan nodded, *I asked you if you meant what you said,* he even shifted his hip to pull his phone out to set on his thigh, like he was getting ready to show me the text messages as proof, *and you said yes.*

"Um, no," I giggled, giving his leg an encouraging squeeze, "You asked me if I meant what I said in the voice messages, and I said that I didn't mean to send those to you. But that I *did* want you. I never specifically said those messages were referring to you at all."

Logan was staring at my face, seeing the smile there and noticing the intimate touches I was giving him on his arm and leg, a little bit of relief touching his features when he realized that I was still very much into him. *If they weren't about me...who were they about?*

"I was reading some pretty explicit alien erotica that Josh and Beck had told me about during your game." Logan's eyes widened a little, and he huffed a laugh before he reached a hand up and rubbed the side of his neck that had the scars. He sat back in his seat a little bit as he thought about my words, the face of a man who was probably reevaluating every conversation we had about the whole ordeal. This was proven when he sat straight again and turned to me to sign his next question.

*At the gym, when you said you read alien erotica...*Logan let his sentence trail off as I laughed.

"I almost told you then, but the thought of you making fun of me for what I chose to read for fun didn't seem worth it. I was still a little sensitive and bitter about your teasing then." I shrugged, pulling his arm closer to me so that I could snuggle into his side some more, "But I'm not so easily offended now."

Something flickered across Logan's expression, before a small pinch formed in his eyebrows as he stared at me intently.

"What?" I asked, lifting my head up from his shoulder to look at him. That was the face of guilt. I hadn't seen Logan looking guilty before, so this was both new and mildly concerning. Sure, I kept a secret for a while, but it wasn't a harmful one. It was mostly nonsense at this point.

I... Logan paused, before lifting his phone from his lap

and thumbing through it. I expected to find another message from him on his note app, but when he handed his phone to me, I was looking at something else.

It was his ereader library, which was unexpected.

Mostly because it was filled with romance novels.

I knew that they were romance novels, because I had personally read every single one.

"What am I looking at right now?" I asked him as I scrolled. He had dozens of e-books downloaded. And I could see that he had either read some of the books entirely, or he was at least eighty percent of the way through the others.

I pulled back from my grip on his arm so that Logan could sign to me, *I took the book.*

I stared at him before finally signing back, *What book?*

Courtney's book, Logan explained, his eyes flicking to the seats in front of us where she sat, *The one you bought at the bookstore with Beck. I have it.*

I widened my eyes at him, "You stole her romance novel?"

I thought it was yours. Logan shrugged as if that explained everything.

"Wh-what?" I shook my head once, setting his phone down to sign clearly, *When did you take the book?*

A small secretive smile touched Logan's lips, his handsome face making my heart flutter before he replied, *Our first night together. You fell asleep, and I saw it on the floor. I took it.*

My mouth was parted, still just flabbergasted as I stared down at his phone in my lap, all those romance novels on there, while processing the knowledge that he stole a paperback of a romance novel as well.

Because he thought it was mine.

"But…" I shook my head and signed the rest of my question, *Why?*

Logan gently cupped my chin with his hand and tilted my face up towards his. He brushed his lips over mine, once, twice, before pulling back and lifting his hands, *I wanted to get to know you. What you like.* He pressed his lips to mine again, his tongue gently tracing my bottom one before pulling back enough to continue signing, *I was scared I would do something to make you hate me again, and I thought maybe reading your favorite books would help me…out.*

I felt my lip trembling from the vulnerability Logan was sharing with me on this flight. I remembered feeling similarly sentimental the night he came over from the bar to rub my legs and cuddle with me on the couch because my period was so bad that day. He had been just as supportive and soothing every cycle I had after that moment.

This man read romance novels because he knew I liked them.

Because he didn't want us to go back to that place that I put us in when we first met.

"You don't have to worry about that anymore, I think." I smiled up at him, swiping away a sentimental tear that escaped my eye and rushed down my cheek. Logan leaned forward to kiss my forehead gently, and I pulled back to continue my thoughts.

"I love you."

Logan froze, one of his hands on my jaw, as his dark eyes locked onto mine.

"You don't have to say it back," I added, smiling, "But that's where I'm at. I just...thought you should know." I bit my bottom lip a little, before releasing it and smiling up at him instead.

Logan looked wrecked.

I couldn't tell if it was a good wrecked or a bad one, but his face had gone slack and it looked like he was trying to control his breathing to make it stay even.

"...Seriously, you don't have to—" I was cut off with his tongue immediately entering my mouth. I giggled against his sudden kiss, thinking that this was a funny way to move past the awkward, "I said I love you but you aren't ready to say it back" moment. I didn't want him to feel guilty or embarrassed or nervous about my declaration. I wouldn't hold it against him because I realized how fast I had developed these feelings. That we had only been officially dating each other a month or so. I wasn't worried about it. I knew Logan had no interest in anyone else. A man didn't read dozens of romance novels because the woman he was dating likes them, if he was only casually interested in her.

After kissing me way more aggressively than was appropriate on a very public flight (thank god no one had the aisle seat on the other side of Logan), he separated our faces and I could feel just how ridiculously swollen and plump my lips were from his.

I blinked a few times, trying to compose myself as I remembered where we were, and pulled back to smile brightly at him.

It's okay, I signed.

I love you, Eloise, Logan signed back, a smile pulling on his own lips as he cupped my face with both of his hands, pressing another smacking kiss on my mouth, then lowering his lips to my ear to whisper in his low, scratchy voice, "I love you."

I clapped a hand over my mouth to keep myself from sobbing, or whining, or releasing whatever noise was about to come out of my throat from the sound of Logan's voice whispering those three words.

I pulled away enough for me to sign back to him, *I love you.*

I love you, He immediately signed again, grinning as if he was a person who had just discovered the words.

"It's not like, a get-the-last-word-in thing." I laughed, "You don't always have to say it when I do."

I love you, Logan signed anyway, touching the tip of my nose with his index finger before I grabbed it and kissed it.

I love you! I signed more enthusiastically, as if *I* was trying to get the last word in.

Logan grabbed my hands to kiss them on the knuckles, and I was immediately brought back to the memory of us at Josh and Courtney's engagement party. Where Logan once again tried to call a truce between our childish bickering, and I was too stubborn and prideful to take him seriously. I had tried to storm off, and Logan had grabbed my hands to press a quick kiss on my knuckles.

Based on the look Logan was giving me as he kept his lips on my hands, I knew he was remembering the same moment.

"When you did this at the engagement party," I whispered, "I thought it was the hottest thing a man had ever done."

Logan's smirk pulled on the scars marring his cheek, his eyes lit up with mischievousness as he lowered my hands so he could sign, *I know you like my lips better when they—*

I gasped and slapped his hands down, making him huff his laughter as he pulled me against him to kiss me once again.

"Are you two just going to make out this whole flight?" I heard Courtney ask from her seat in front of us. She was peeking between the seats and wiggling her eyebrows when Logan lifted his middle finger at her and kissed me harder, messing up my hair as he pushed my head back against my seat.

When he pulled back, I was positive I had a dopey lovesick expression on my face, like in the cartoons I used to watch on Saturday mornings as a kid.

"Courtney?"

"Yeah?"

"Shush."

27

LOGAN

It was comical that I was so nervous about this day, but the small hand that squeezed mine as we strolled through grass made me relax my shoulders a little bit more. Another small hand came up to grab onto my forearm, as if knowing that I would need all the contact right now.

I glanced down at Eloise, admiring her features as the morning sunlight started to shine through the various trees and gravestones.

"Is it silly that I'm nervous?" Eloise asked.

I squeezed her hand back in mine, leaning down to kiss her head as I tugged her along the path that I had only made a handful of times since laying Anna here to rest years ago. I could see Eloise glancing at all the names on the gravestones that we passed, curious interest lighting up those eyes that I would never, ever get tired of seeing.

It had been a month since Colorado. Since John fired our former agent and Eloise's parents had met us at the airport at LAX. It was a weird weekend. Within twenty-four hours we had gone from John and I sprinting down the hotel hallway after hearing Eloise's voice warning Connor to not come any closer, to Eloise telling me that she loved me on the plane home the next morning, to meeting her parents a couple of hours later when we landed.

A whirlwind of a weekend, but I didn't mind. Not in the grand scheme of things.

That didn't mean I wasn't nervous to meet her parents, considering I never had before. I didn't think I would be the kind of guy who needed the approval of my girlfriend's parents, and yet, when Eloise and I stepped out of LAX and she waved at a cream-colored Rolls Royce waiting to pick us up, I felt my palms start to sweat.

Immediately, a woman who had the same hair and eye color as Eloise stepped out of the passenger seat. The woman even had a petite build like my girlfriend, so I knew it was her. I was swallowing my fear, getting ready to hold a hand up to introduce myself to Eloise's mother, when I was caught completely off guard by the woman.

The woman, who was dressed in a white blouse, khaki knee-length skirt, and heels to pick up her daughter from the airport, had left the passenger side door open and ran to meet the two of us.

And then she wrapped both her daughter and me in a hug, my hand left awkwardly out to the side of us. I heard Eloise giggle and returned the embrace her mother was giving the two of us. Each of her arms around the shoulders of Eloise and me.

Mrs. Bane leaned back, settling on her heels, and took her daughter's face in her hands immediately. The look of a concerned mother scanning her daughter's face made something stir in my chest, realizing how much Eloise's mother truly loved her daughter.

"Are you sure you're okay?" Mrs. Bane asked.

"I'm okay, mom." Eloise's eyes watered a little, reaching up to squeeze her mother's hands in reassurance before Mrs. Bane turned to me and immediately grabbed my face. She pulled me down to her level so that she could wrap her arms around my shoulders again, and I gave Eloise a wide-eyed look at being aggressively hugged twice by her mother within the span of seconds.

"Thank you," Mrs. Bane whispered to me. "Thank you for being there for my daughter." I gulped nervously while awkwardly returning her hug once more and nodding my head when she pulled back.

"Let them breathe, Lydia." Mr. Bane was stepping out of the driver's seat, leaving his car running as he approached his family and me. He bent down to embrace Eloise in a one-arm hug, while also grabbing her bag and dragging it towards the trunk of his car.

Mrs. Bane looped her arms through both mine and Eloise's and dragged us to the Rolls Royce as well.

"I'm going to kill him." Eloise's mother and I immediately had something in common.

"Mom," Eloise sighed.

"Your father is already getting the paperwork for a restraining order set up—"

"I don't want to talk about that right now," Eloise interrupted, giving her mom a stern look. I knew Eloise had struggled to stand up to her parents before, and even though

I desperately wanted to talk to her parents to see what all they were doing to ensure that my former agent never, ever caught a glimpse of Eloise again, I set my hand on the small of her back in support.

We had time to discuss these things later.

"That's alright," Mr. Bane agreed after shutting the trunk, and walking over to where we stood. Eloise and her mother were helping themselves to their seats in the car, Mrs. Bane taking the passenger seat and Eloise sliding across the back to make room for me to follow, but Mr. Bane halted my progress with a firm grip on my shoulder. I was taller than this man, but even though I was looking down at him, I knew how important he was to Eloise. And how I desperately wanted to make her happy.

He gave me a once over as he held me still with his grip on my shoulder, before taking a very distinct look at the scarring that everyone who first met me noticed, and met my eyes again.

"Thank you," Mr. Bane said with a firm nod. "Until Eloise says otherwise, you always have a place in our family."

I blinked in surprise at his words, before managing a very stiff nod in acknowledgement. That was that. Mr. Bane released my shoulder and made his way to the driver's seat as I folded myself into the backseat next to my girlfriend.

My girlfriend.

Eloise Bane was my girlfriend. And we loved each other.

A few days later, while lying in Eloise's bed and changing my phone's wallpaper image to one of the two of us, Eloise mentioned visiting my sister.

I shrugged, informing her that Anna's birthday was coming up.

Eloise didn't need to be told anything else. She then announced to me that since she was occupying mine and my phone's attention, that the least we could do was visit Anna on her birthday.

I had a feeling that she meant it as the start of a new tradition, and I didn't hate the fact that my girlfriend was so considerate of my family. The family that I cared about, that is.

Which is how we ended up at Anaheim Cemetery, walking through the graves and finally, finally approaching the two that stirred unresolved feelings of grief in my chest.

The two gravestones weren't large, or gaudy. The fact that my father scraped enough money together to find these two slabs of stone was a miracle. They were the ones that laid flat on the ground, and the groundskeeper needed to constantly trim the grass around, so that they didn't accidentally become obscured by landscaping.

On the left was my mother, her name in bold lettering:

FRANCESCA ST. JAMES

On the right was my sister:

ANNA MARIA ST. JAMES

Their lifespans are underneath. No unique imagery, no sentences saying who they were to anyone, or who would miss them.

My father was a real piece of shit, wherever he was.

Without a word, Eloise released her grip on my hand to reach out for the two bouquets I was supporting with my other, placing each beside my mother and sister. She then tugged my hand down as she started to sit, crisscrossing her legs in front of the stones, and I followed suit.

I had visited their graves before, mostly standing awkwardly and staring at them and feeling a mixture of emotions like rage and sadness at the circumstances. But I hadn't ever sat down, as if I was settling in for a friendly visit.

"Was your mother Italian?" Eloise asked after we settled on the grass, nodding towards my mother's name.

I nodded.

"But your last name is your father's I'm assuming?" I nodded at her words again. "Do you take after your mother?"

I smiled, *Yes*. My father was the epitome of Irish, with blonde hair and blue eyes. It was where Anna got her blonde hair from. I, however, inherited my mother's dark curly hair and brown eyes. Something I was grateful for every day.

"Your son is like a steel vault of information, Francesca," Eloise had turned and rested a reverent hand on my mother's grave, immediately making an annoying burning start in my eyes as my vision suddenly became blurry, "It's truly a miracle we were able to form a relationship at all." Eloise smiled, tracing her finger over my mother's name before pulling her hand back to wrap mine in hers, still chatting with my mother's grave as if my heart wasn't being beaten open with a hammer at the sight, "...But he's worth it. Oh, and happy birthday, Anna."

I didn't bother to wipe away the tears that leaked from my traitorous eyes, I just allowed myself to sit in this moment. Something my therapist had prepared me for the last session we had, after filling them in on my girlfriend and this trip we had planned. I knew it would make me feel things I didn't want to, things that are inescapable when it comes to grief.

But I wasn't expecting just how shattered I would feel, how raw and exposed I would be, sitting here silently crying while Eloise acquainted herself with my mother. My sister. And how it was okay that I was feeling this way. I was safe here with Eloise, feeling practically cut open by sharing this first with her. Chatting with them as if they were sitting here with us. Taking time to stay and honor their lives with our presence, instead of the quick and thoughtless visits I had made in the past.

I knew what I had with Eloise was real. I had known in the past, of course, but I was being blatantly reminded of that fact as we filled my family in on our lives. Telling them about our friends, our jokes. Nothing got left out, not even how Eloise and I chased each other through the townhome and I successfully coated her hair with chocolate syrup.

I knew my sister would have appreciated that story.

We stayed there for most of the morning until the sun rose high enough to start to be too warm. Eloise wasn't wearing anything but a t-shirt and shorts, and I didn't want her to get burned. That was the only reason we eventually said our goodbyes, promising to visit more often, and walked back to my truck hand in hand.

Once we were settled in the car, buckling ourselves in,

I felt Eloise's hand squeeze my leg before I turned to look at her.

Thank you for sharing that with me, Eloise signed, something she was improving her skills with rapidly, *I love you.*

I grabbed her hand in mine, kissing the knuckles of her fingers before settling her hand back on my thigh and pressing, telling her to leave it there before replying with, *Thank you. I love you.*

It was pure, stupid luck that I had managed to convince a woman like Eloise to give me the time of day. To give me a chance, and to love me like she openly did. I wasn't going to be careless with the gift that Eloise Bane was. She was mine, and I was hers. And I would spend as much time as Eloise gave me to show her how much that mattered to me.

28

"This cake sucks," Taylor had shouted to us across the table, loud enough to be heard over the DJ. "They should have gone with something better, like pie or cheesecake. Maybe ice cream."

"Good thing this isn't your wedding," Beck rolled her eyes at our friend. "You don't have to eat it."

Taylor narrowed their eyes at her as they deliberately forked another massive bite of the cake that they had a beef with into their mouth. I snorted, laughing at our friends as I rested my elbows on the table.

It took a ton of planning, lots of phone calls, and demanding that catering services took me seriously despite the way my face looked, but we all finally made it here. Courtney and Josh were married, and the two lovebirds were busy twerking and grinding and dancing on the makeshift dance floor in the most inappropriate way possible, while their friends and family laughed and cringed at their antics.

Courtney and Josh decided to tie the knot in the state that originally brought them together. In a small venue on the Oregon Coast, surrounded by pine trees and ivy and grass, with the taste of the ocean breeze in the air. The venue was partially indoors, and partially outdoors on the off chance it wouldn't rain. Thankfully, the outdoor bar had a covering that allowed guests to enjoy the air and scenery, without getting wet. Strings of lights were hung all over the venue, lighting the party up in a tasteful and elegant manner without taking away the beauty of the modern lodge the reception was hosted at.

Josh had already ditched his tie, unbuttoning his dress shirt to show off all the tattoos on his neck and chest and un-tucking it from his pants as he danced with his wife, stars in his eyes.

Courtney had her dress altered so that she could pin her skirt up high enough so that she could move around as she liked. She had left her heels next to me at the table, while dancing barefoot with her husband.

"When you plan your wedding, I'll make sure there isn't a single slice of offensive cake," I winked at Taylor. Their eyes widened as they swallowed their piece and shook their head.

"I'm never getting married," they emphasized their words with a slice of their hand, "That's gonna be a no from me, dog."

Beck smiled and reached a hand up for Taylor to high-five, which they met enthusiastically. Beck had confirmed my previous suspicions earlier, on the flight here. Due to her extra fun layer of religious trauma she endured from her childhood, she couldn't wrap her head around doing something so traditional and archaic as getting married. Adam, apparently, could go either way. But if his girlfriend had no interest in getting married, neither did he. The two of them were perfectly content to continue "living in sin" as Beck described it.

I...was pretty sure I wanted to do something traditional. I mean, if big raging feminist Courtney Henderson could formalize her partnership, why couldn't I?

Honestly, any excuse to throw a fun party.

I glanced around the room, looking for my date to my friend's wedding. My date, who locked us down for this event just over a year ago.

"I saw him and Adam heading towards the bar a moment ago," Beck informed me with a finger past my shoulder. I turned my head around, looking out towards the open-air space where the bar was located.

I nodded my confirmation at her and settled back in my seat.

Taylor continued to list off the reasons why cake was a poor choice for dessert, when Beck's eyes perked up at something behind me again. I turned around, a massive grin pulling at my lips.

Adam and Logan were returning from the open bar, two cocktails in Adam's hands while he tried to make his way through the tables, and also hold a conversation he was having with Beck's grandmother, Susan.

Susan was being pushed in her wheelchair by Logan, who smiled and shook his head at me. Susan probably just said something ridiculous to him, and I couldn't wait for him to tell me what it was.

"I was worried you got lost," Beck smiled as she lifted her

head for Adam to press his lips to hers. Logan settled Susan's wheelchair right between Beck and me, and Adam set both of the cocktails down on the table in front of her.

"You couldn't decide between the two?" I asked Susan with a lifted eyebrow.

"I didn't even bother trying. It's an open bar. YOLO and stuff." Susan winked at me before taking one of the cocktails and slurping loud enough for Courtney to shout from her spot on the dancefloor to, "Knock it off, Susan!"

I laughed as Logan took his seat next to me, leaning in to press his lips firmly against my neck, and inhaling deeply. I blushed under the intense PDA, but our friends were used to it at this point. While Adam and Beck were more reserved about their PDA, and Courtney and Josh didn't hold back theirs in any way, Logan and I were a comical mix between the two.

Logan was always the first to reach for me. To reassure himself with my presence by touching or kissing me, regardless of the company we kept. The only time he truly held himself back was if we were having dinner with my parents, and even then, he kept one of his large hands either on my leg or my hand under the table.

I wasn't as bold as Logan. I didn't initiate physical contact between us nearly as much, but I never shooed him off of me when he did.

I never wanted to push Logan away. I found myself growing more and more comfortable with his displays of physical affection this past year. I think a part of me would always feel guilty for how stubborn I was at the beginning of our friendship, and then romantic relationship. I knew I didn't need to carry the guilt of my behavior forever, but I also loved making it up to Logan in this way.

It was one of those rare times that the former people-pleasing Eloise perked up, happy to be her boyfriend's reassurance when he needed me to be.

The conversation around the table started, but Logan's fingers tapped my arm so that he could get my attention.

Want to know what Susan just told me at the bar? Logan asked, his eyes glowing with mischief.

Obviously. I signed back. Logan smirked.

She asked if you and I were next.

I rolled my eyes, before giggling and signing back to him, *What did you say?*

Logan shrugged; *I wasn't the one she needed to ask.*

I frowned at him; *You made it sound like I am the one holding us back.*

Logan shrugged again. I pinched his thigh, and he huffed his laugh before letting his gaze wander over to Courtney and Josh, who were now slow dancing like mature adults to a slower song the DJ was playing for them.

I followed his gaze, taking in our friends' expressions. How they looked at each other as if there wasn't another single body in the room with them, and I felt deep in my bones that they were designed specifically for each other.

Similar to how I felt about Logan.

There wasn't anyone else I had met in my life who understood me the way he did. That was as perfect for me as he was. Who let me have my emotional freak outs, who rubbed my feet when my period felt unbearable. Who challenged me to a food fight in the kitchen when I started one.

Who loved me unconditionally, as I did him.

That wasn't to say there weren't moments when he and I didn't act like complete dumbasses around each other. We did. There were times when one of us would be tired and cranky, either from his hockey schedule, or my work schedule, or my mother's excessive and demanding rich-lady parties. But every time, we took a breath, and did what our friends taught us to do when things got heated.

We talked it out.

Sometimes, we even gave the other space to feel their feelings. Unjudged.

Which was significantly easier for us to do now since my signing had improved so much this past year.

It really helped that I was sleeping with my ASL tutor, not gonna lie.

I got up from my chair at the table and pushed Logan's shoulder back for him to scoot his chair out. His lap was available now, and I plopped myself right on his thighs and looped my arms around his shoulders.

I leaned in to brush my lips against his, nothing aggressive or sexual, just simple passes, before pulling back to sign my thoughts, *I'll let you know when I'm ready for something like that.*

Logan's eyebrows raised as my favorite smirk of his made another appearance.

I'll be waiting, he replied.

I nodded and leaned into him, resting our heads together as we watched our friends joke around at the table because it was just that simple. We both wanted the same thing, and we would patiently wait until the other was ready to catch up. Safety and comfort, like what our friends had with their partners.

29

Epilogue

LOGAN
YEARS LATER

I was used to cemeteries at this point in my life, thanks to Eloise.

That thought came off a lot darker than intended, but it was true. It was habitual at this point, how often we made visits to my mother and sister. Though, I was more familiar with the Anaheim cemetery because of those visits.

This was the first time I had visited a grave at the Laguna Hills cemetery, though.

"Whenever you're ready, Beck," Adam held his girlfriend against his side, his low words making her nod as she inhaled a shaky breath.

Eloise stepped into my side, and I could hear her sniffling as well. I stood tall, letting my fiancée use me for physical support as our group all stood around the freshly marked grave. The rest of Susan Scott's friends and family had already paid their respects and left, including Beck's parents. Their attendance had been a surprise to everyone here, and they had even managed to paste friendly smiles on their faces as they nodded at Beck and Adam.

Beck's mother had tentatively wandered over to where we stood as Susan's casket was being lowered into the ground. I wasn't sure what her mother said to her, but Beck had only squeezed her mother's hand and nodded before her parents excused themselves.

The seven of us had all lingered, though, just like Susan asked of us.

I had originally planned to wear black because that was how I remembered funerals looking in the past. However, Beck had informed all of us that Susan demanded we not make her funeral a drag. She insisted only bright and happy colors, or colors that brought us all joy, as we said our goodbyes.

Taylor had done their best by wearing a blazer that reminded me of sherbet ice cream, with peaches, pinks, and yellows blended together like a watercolor painting. Their solid orange slacks balanced the look.

Josh and Courtney both wore matching t-shirts with Susan's face on them. Her face was cross eyed and grinning, her gray hair in a knot, haphazardly tied on top of the old woman's head. They paired their shirts with casual jeans, and dress shoes.

Their daughter, Susie, wore her favorite t-shirt, one that Beck's grandmother had gifted her that showed a sparkly unicorn with a rainbow horn on its head. The toddler had her blonde hair in pig-tails and wore a bright pink tutu with white converse sneakers. Her arms were covered in temporary stick-on tattoos of flowers and butterflies and dinosaurs because she decided recently that she wanted art on her body, just like her dad.

Beck wore a simple bright blue blouse, with a black skirt. Adam wore a lime-green button-up with black slacks.

Eloise wore bright pink with a cream-colored skirt, and I wore a mustard button-up shirt with gray slacks, because that was the only colorful dressed-up clothing I had.

"I'm ready," Beck sighed as she reached into her pocket and pulled out one of two envelopes. We all followed suit and pulled out our own personalized envelopes. Susan knew her time was coming to a natural end and took the time while she was stuck in her hospice bed to write us all personal letters. She instructed Beck that we were not to open these letters until she was settled in the earth, and to start with the first letter addressed to all of us, before we all took turns reading our own out loud.

Beck had opened the first envelope addressed to all of us, and unfolded the paper before she took another breath and started reading, "*You all are the most codependent group of adults I had ever met.*" Beck paused, before uncontrolled laughter bubbled out of her at the first words Susan had wanted us to read after her passing. We all laughed, though Courtney and Beck laughed the loudest. Even little Susie smiled up at her parents, tugging on her dad's pants and lifting her hands up, asking to be held. Josh bent down and settled his daughter on his hip, wiping a tear from his eye as he kissed her blonde head in reassurance, before Beck continued.

"I know you all are desperate to hear some words of wisdom from me, even though I'm literally *dead, because heaven forbid you let me rest in peace, so I decided to write each of you a letter. Because I'm the best there ever was."* Beck had to pause to laugh again, happy tears streaming down her face as even her boyfriend laughed with his head tilted back, one of his hands covering his mouth in an attempt to control himself. *"You can read your letters out loud, or read them to yourself. I don't give a shit. Just know that I loved each of you as if you were my own, and that even though I'm physically gone, and you'll miss me shuffling through the townhome, I'll still be haunting your asses as soon as I figure out how to do that."*

With that, Beck folded that letter up and returned it to its envelope, before opening her own letter and scanning the page with her eyes. We all knew Beck would go first, and we all stood in respectable silence while Beck read her letter silently to herself, letting Adam squeeze her shoulder as he kept his gaze on the ground. Her eyes teared up again, and she wiped at them a few times while a giggle and smile tugged at her mouth.

Adam followed suit, reading his letter to himself but letting Beck read over his shoulder. He chuckled a little bit, before nodding and folding his back up and putting both of their letters in his pocket.

Taylor spoke up after them, "Well, as much as I love standing over Susan's grave in silence, I'm reading mine out loud." They cleared their throat as they opened their letter and formally shook it out, as if they were about to announce a royal decree of some kind, "*Taylor. There is a hidden suitcase of gold blocks underneath the floorboards of my bedroom.*" Taylor laughed as they continued on, "*Just kidding, but you considered ripping up my floorboards for a second there, didn't you? You greedy sonofabitch.*"

"Sonofabitch," Little Susie promptly repeated.

"Fuck." Josh sighed as he pinched the bridge of his nose.

"Fuck!" Susie repeated with a grin that reminded me way too much of Courtney. It wouldn't put it past me if their two-year-old knew she was messing with her dad and simply leaned into it for the comedy of the moment.

"Keep going, T," Courtney laughed as she held Josh's hand that wasn't holding their daughter.

"*Thank you for blessing our home with your humor, your kindness, and your badassery. You are my hero,*" Taylor's eyes rimmed red as they took a deep breath to control themselves, "*Please keep the rest of these hooligans in check for me while I am gone. And don't be afraid to knock their heads together now and then.*" Taylor's eyes skimmed the rest of their letter as they decided to read the rest of Susan's words to themselves, before smiling and folding their letter back up and putting it into the pocket of their blazer.

Courtney opened her letter next, "*Court. Thank you for baking blueberry pancakes as often as possible, even though the sugar in those is probably what ended up stopping my heart*—Oh my god, Susan!" Laughter erupted from the group again, and

Eloise covered her face with her hands, turning her body into my chest, desperately trying to keep her composure together even though Susan seemed to bend over backwards to get us all to laugh together on this day. *"You brought my granddaughter out of her shell, and helped her become more confident in herself. Your friendship with Beck is what caused the ripple effect for this group to expand and allow others in. I am so grateful to you because now my granddaughter has the world's best support system ready to go while I am gone."*

Courtney sniffed while she opened Josh's letter for him, since his hands were full with little Susie, *"Joshua. I am so grateful that I am finally able to share this with you because I have been holding this close to my chest for years now. But your music is ass."*

Eloise and Taylor both snorted their laughter, and even Josh cackled at Susan's parting burn, *"What even is it? I love your acoustic stuff, your voice is beautiful. But then you scream and Kyle randomly bangs his drums, and it ruins the whole vibe. But I guess others like it enough because you're famous or something. But even with all your fame and celebrity money, I hope my gift to you and your family doesn't seem as underwhelming as it feels, because the townhome is yours ."*

Beck smiled big, as if she and Adam were both waiting for this reveal. To see Courtney's eyes widen and her jaw drop as she swung her head to look at her best friend. Beck and Adam both nodded, confirming Susan's letter. Courtney and Josh had moved out just before Courtney gave birth to Susie, and Courtney had been complaining the last couple of years how their condo in Costa Mesa just hadn't felt right. Josh had been incredibly patient, even going as far as to encourage Courtney and Susie to stay with Beck's grandmother when he had to go out of town for his music career.

Eloise and I had been living together ever since Courtney and Josh got married. At first, Susan was bitter about everyone "growing up" and "leaving her in the dust" but Taylor and Beck had gone out of their way to visit the elderly woman multiple times a week, sometimes every day. We also had family dinners at the townhome weekly to keep her included and updated in our lives.

"Are you sure?" Courtney asked Beck.

"Absolutely," Beck replied with a wink.

Courtney laughed in disbelief as Josh shook his head and pocketed his letter, snuggling their daughter as Susie stared at everyone and then at the grave we stood before.

Eloise pulled out her letter.

"*Eloise,*" my fiancée started to read, "*You are the sweetest woman alive, but also someone I consider to be the strongest.*" Eloise inhaled a breath before she continued, "*Only you could seduce someone as grumpy and introverted as Logan. I am so glad you did because you two are perfect for each other. You both bring out the best in the other, as every successful relationship should.*" Eloise smiled up at me, her bright blue eyes shining before she continued, "*I expect you to come say hello and fill me in on what you are up to as often as you visit Logan's family. Make sure to bring flowers, because if you don't, I'll haunt you even harder than the others. Once I figure out how to do that, of course.*"

At last, it was my turn.

I unfolded my letter, obviously deciding to read to myself as everyone waited for some sort of reaction. *Logan. I love you. Thank you for trusting all of us to love you. Thank you for being the best partner for my girl Eloise. I am a little bitter that you couldn't get Eloise to tie the knot with you before I passed because I would have loved to get drunk at a party on someone else's dollar one last time, but I have decided to be the bigger person and not to haunt you over that. To make it up to me, if you and Lo do decide to have children one day, I fully expect you to also name them after me in some way, just like Courtney and Josh have. Until then, keep doing what you're doing, because you and Eloise are disgustingly happy, which means you both must be doing something right.*

I smiled, before pocketing my letter.

"Can I read it later?" Eloise asked me. I nodded at her before we all stared at each other. Eyes red, tears sneaking down our cheeks, and peace settling on all of us.

Susie decided to pat her dad's chest to get his attention, before signing clearly, *I'm hungry.*

"We'll get some lunch soon," Josh reassured his daughter.

"Would you like some time alone with her, Beck?" Eloise asked. Beck stared at the grave with a small smile on her face, before lifting a shoulder and nodding her head.

"Thank you all for being here," Beck spoke up, leaning into Adam's embrace, "I'm so glad we're all friends. And that Gram got to meet and know each one of you."

I pressed a kiss to Eloise's head, who squeezed my hand in return.

The rest of us all started to make our way back to the building where the rest of Susan's friends and family were gathered, little Susie wiggling excitedly in her father's arms when the smell of food started to touch the air.

I stared down at Eloise at my side, who was busy wiggling her fingers and making silly faces at Courtney and Josh's daughter. Susie squealed in delight, and I took a moment to appreciate my world.

The first time I met Eloise Bane would always haunt me in some way (just like Susan had promised to haunt us in some capacity) because of the pure embarrassment I felt at the memory. But, as time passed, I cared less and less about *how* she and I got here and more about what lay ahead for us. How we still had our entire lives to live. Perhaps that was what Susan's point was by keeping her goodbye letters short, light, and to the point.

It didn't matter what lay ahead for any of us, only that all of us would be there for the other, supportive in any way we could offer.

As long as Eloise was by my side, I couldn't find any reason to worry about what came next.

THE END

Acknowledgements

This one is for the romance lovers.
My family supported me to write.
My friends encouraged me to write
But you readers were *excited* for me to write.
Leaving comments like, "frothing at the mouth for this
story" really boosts a writer's ego, in the best possible way.
Thank you, romance readers.
Without you, I have no audience.
You are everything to me.
Thank you for being you.
I love you all.

Andrea Andersen is an author living with her little family in Southern California. Using her maladaptive daydreaming to her advantage, she likes to write love stories filled with kisses, laughter, and happily ever afters. When she isn't writing, she can be found rewatching her favorite TV shows or taking too many naps.

Other books by this author:
WHAT IT MEANS TO BE WHOLE
WHAT IT MEANS TO BE BRAVE

Socials:
TikTok: @andreaandersenauthor
Instagram: @andreaandersenauthor
Website: www.andreaandersen.com

9 798987 395042